Imperfect Burials

For Cheryl,
With great affection

Imperfect Burials

Tom Pope

THOMAS HENRY POPE

Vermont, Summer 2021

SHIRES PRESS
Manchester Center, VT 05255
www.northshire.com

IMPERFECT BURIALS

This is a work of fiction. All of the characters, organizations, and events portrayed herein are either products of the author's imagination or are used fictitiously. Readers will note it is true that 21,857 Polish Army officers and members of Poland's professional class were massacred at Katyn in 1940; that the Polish trade labor union Solidarity did exist in the time depicted; that Hungarians staged a revolution against Soviet oppression in 1956: and that East Germans escaped from Hungary through Sapron village in 1989 leading to the collapse of the Berlin Wall and the Soviet Union.

Library of Congress Publication Cataloguing-in-Publication Date
Name: Pope, Thomas Henry
Title: Imperfect Burials : a novel / Thomas Henry Pope
Description: First Edition | Shires Press 2021
Identifiers: LCCN 2021908908
ISBN: 978-1-60571-577-3 (Hardcover) |
ISBN: 978-1-60571-576-6 (Paperback) |
ISBN: 978-1-60571-578-6 (Ebook)

Cover by Dissect Designs

Printed in the United States of America

For Claire,
wherever she may be

To the living, one owes consideration; to the dead, only the truth.

—VOLTAIRE (LETTRES SUR OEDIPE)

Truth will come to light; murder will not be hid long.

—THE MERCHANT OF VENICE by WILLIAM SHAKESPEARE

Acknowledgements

Stories are among humanity's most valuable creations. And like most, ***Imperfect Burials*** was forged in great struggle. Without the support and expertise of teachers, fellow authors, editors, and readers this story would not have been finished. I cannot thank you enough: David Corbett, Vaughn Roycroft, Valerie Smith, Thom Elkjer, John Hadden, Dave King, Bernadette Phipps-Lincke, Jan Wax, and Zoe Quinton. For help into minds sorting through PTSD, I am grateful to Maggie Bernstein PhD. I bow to Mimi Rich for her careful proofreading and to Monika Fuchs, who polished my German dialogue. Thanks also to Amanda Van Tuijl for finding the matryoshka doll featured on the cover.

Author's Notes

Belarus and its adjective Belarusian supplanted many variant spellings in use at the timeframe of this narrative. For clarity for today's readers, the editorial choice was made to go with these modern forms.

The Э in the title IMPERFЭCT is the 31st letter in the Russian alphabet and makes the same sound as the "e" in the English word "get." Therefore the pronunciation of IMPERFЭCT is unchanged. In Russian, the vowel's name is э оборотное, which translates as *E reversed* and it came to the Cyrillic alphabet as a result of Peter the Great's efforts to bring Russia more in line with European culture.

For signed copies, other links, essays, helpful hints, and discussion
please visit:
https://thomashenrypope.com

Denmark
Copenhagen
Hamburg
Berlin
Poland
Warsaw
Germany
Prague
Czechia
Munich
Vienna
Slovakia
Austria
Budapest
Hungary
Slovenia
Zagreb

Riga
Latvia
Moscow
Москва
uania
Katyn
Mosalsk
Vilnius
Minsk
Мінск
Dyedna
Belarus
Kyiv
Київ
Kharkiv
Харків
Ukraine
Moldova
Chişinău
Odesa
Одеса

Book One

Warsaw, 1989

One

THE NOTE LOOKED INNOCENT. Simple card stock folded once with care. The sassy, narrow-waisted photographer from Naples Finn had brought up with him from the foreigners' lounge scooped it off the floor as they entered his hotel room. Laughing, she held it behind her for the ransom of a kiss. And he paid her price. Three times.

But what he read stunned him, and he lingered on it until he heard the click of her heel. She had taken a step back and folded her arms. Her dark eyes had narrowed to slits. "It's true of you, how they are talking," she said. "You love work more than people."

Moments later, with her bitter stream of Italian fading behind him, he trotted down the worn marble staircase, crossed the lobby, and headed into Warsaw's unlit streets. Rain fell on grimy snow and except for soldiers huddling miserable in doorways, the city prepared for sleep. His throat burned from the smoke of coal stoves that wives had lit to warm husbands returning from the day's demonstrations, and curtains drawn to hold the heat made the night seem thick with secrets. Underfoot, slush masked ice.

Finn didn't see the pair of soldiers until they had flattened him against the door of a bank. They were surly, not young, and when his ace in the hole—his American passport and press ID—failed to appease them, he grabbed the first thing that came to mind. "I'm on my way to the cathedral to pray for your countrymen." His perfect Polish caught them off guard. Not pausing to consider the cathedral was behind him, they released him with smiles and thumbs up.

Further on, as he turned up his collar to ward off the rain, his feet slid in different directions on a patch of ice. He didn't fall—he'd grown up in snow country—but he took a moment under an awning to gather himself and to check the address. The note was written in a confident hand: *Strategy meeting. Come on foot and alone to the fourth floor. No recorders, no pen or paper.* It was signed with a red ink stamp. *Solidarnosc.* Solidarity, Poland's trade union, which had become, in effect, the sole representative of the Polish people. Finn understood the caution. Any leak from a meeting of union leaders could hand advantage to their opposition at the Round Table Talks, Jaruzelski's Communist government. Still, he felt naked without the tools of his trade.

Behind the old school at Kowalski 137, he found a matchbook inserted between the doorjamb and the strike to keep the heavy wooden door unlocked. Once inside, he headed up the darkened stairway onto which the door opened, lighting a match at each landing. His footsteps echoed. Through his shoes, he felt the swales that countless feet had worn into the stone treads.

Had he been using all his senses, he might have smelled the man who grabbed his arm on the third-floor landing. Russian tobacco left a bitter odor on the breath.

"Kill the light if you want to live."

Finn's hand jerked. The flame died.

"What are you doing here?" The voice was thick with phlegm. The accent wasn't local. Finn put the man in his sixties.

"I'm here for a meeting of . . . some old friends."

"It's late for a meeting, isn't it?" There was wariness in the voice, with a splash of amusement, as if the man held a strong hand of cards.

Finn wondered which card might get his attention. "Some soldiers kept me standing in the rain, so I'm later than the note specified."

"The note?"

"The one slipped under my door this evening. Sometime before ten-thirty."

The man's chuckle rumbled in the stairwell. Or perhaps he was clearing his throat. He flicked on a flashlight. It cast a weary glow on heavy wool pant cuffs gathered on street shoes. "Go to the next landing. If you're the right man, we may meet again."

Finn climbed another flight and felt for the knob. The door scraped on the concrete. Dim overhead bulbs lit a long hallway. A sturdy fellow leaned against the wall, hands in jacket pockets, his breath steaming in the air.

"Name?"

"Finn Waters."

"The hot-shit journalist who speaks Russian." He was in his late thirties, heavy browed. A thick mustache conveyed virility. The hand he extended was missing the index finger.

Finn shook it, wondering how he managed a pencil. "Yes, I speak some."

The man inspected him up and down. "And your Polish is good."

"My mother was born in Poznań."

"You have no recorder, correct?"

Finn shook his head, trying to imagine why his knowing Russian was important. Most Poles spoke some or could get by because it was a sister language. Perhaps Solidarity had caught a spy or someone had defected to their cause. A Western journalist's wet dream. Definitely a prize for his paper, the *New York Times*.

His wife would argue otherwise. The day he'd left for this posting, Clarissa made him promise to quit rushing into dangerous places. "The Soviet Union is a coiled snake right now," she'd said. "Be smart."

"Arms out," the man said. "Spread your legs."

Finn's credentials usually spared him being frisked. Excited that perhaps Wałęsa, the head of Solidarity, had asked to see him, he raised his arms. Hard strokes on his torso and legs threatened his balance.

The man poked his chin down the hall. "Follow me." In a distant room, voices rose in bursts, overlapping each other like waves on a beach. The cadence of fierce debate.

Finn's escort rapped and silence fell. The door opened, revealing a barren classroom. No desks. Jaundice-yellow paint, peeling. For a moment, cigarette smoke obscured the faces. Finn had never been allowed into the big room when the Round Table Talks were taking place, but the wide-necked man in the worn wool vest whose chair faced the door often spoke to the press during the breaks. Mateusz Dabrowski, an organizer from shipyards in the north, wore a stevedore hat even during the sessions. The word was that he would take over if anything happened to Wałęsa.

Dabrowski smiled broadly. "You," he said, beckoning with a hand the size of a baseball glove. "You came on short notice. You obviously weren't with a girl. Don't you like Polish girls?"

Laughter rolled around the room. Finn met it with brightened eyes. He did like Polish girls, dammit, in particular, the ones who served food and coffee to the press corps. After they cleared the plates and hung their aprons, they poured forth passion and intelligence such as he only heard in places like Rotterdam. And there was one among them he had slept with not ten days ago, though, like him, she was married. That night at least, sex had seemed the only cure for the ache she was carrying for her people. In return, she had eased his loneliness now that Clarissa's depression had become so intractable.

"A chair for our American guest," Dabrowski commanded.

"And vodka, too?" The speaker wore ratty boots, unlaced.

"No, though after, he may beg to drink to keep from pissing in his pants."

A chair was set facing Dabrowski. Finn feigned calm. The slight-shouldered fellow with wire-rimmed glasses on Dabrowski's left was one of the Solidarity assistants who stayed in their own room down the hall from where the press corps waited for announcements. Sitting on Dabrowski's right, taking notes was Viktor, wearing his signature bolo necktie. He often drove Wałęsa to the talks. The rough clothes and manner of the other seven men cut a sharp contrast to the cardboard formality of the generals and government party officials. To remember them for any article he would write, Finn linked their faces to friends from high school.

Dabrowski scanned him as if assessing his character, then spoke in perfect Russian. "We have been watching you." He placed his palm on his chest. "I became a fan, reading your coverage from Berlin."

Whatever this gathering was for, Finn hadn't seen the like in his time abroad. He bowed his head. "Spasseba bolshoya."

"And do you like me?" Dabrowski asked.

Finn considered his answer, looking also for the right words in Russian. "I don't know you well enough to say, but when you speak to the press, I find complicated ideas making sense." He paused. "I steal things from you."

It seemed the room took a collective breath. Several men slapped each other's shoulders in delight. "He speaks like a Russian."

"And I intend to sue you," Dabrowski said with a laugh, "as soon as we have courts that respond to more than money and bullets." He switched to Polish. "So you're safe for now. Safe to talk about opinions. Your newspaper proudly says it doesn't peddle opinion. Is this true?"

Finn realized why Dabrowski could sit at the table and fight with generals who had the power to have him shot. "I try to adhere to facts." He looked around the room at men whose press had lied to them at every turn and hoped he wasn't ruining whatever goodwill they had. "But a man who has no opinion probably writes . . ." and he hesitated, thinking again of Clarissa, back in their early days, when she'd taught him to speak directly as things arose in his mind. "Probably writes shit."

Glasses of clear liquid appeared in the hands of several of the men. After exultations, they finished them off with the confidence of butchers strangling chickens.

Dabrowski raised his hand for quiet. "Good. So how do you deal with opinions?"

Finn hated not being in control of the questions. "If they get too loud when I'm writing, I shove my pen down their throats."

Dabrowski stood on massive legs, walked outside the circle, and ran a finger across the old slate blackboard. When he came to the youngest fellow in the room, he placed his hands on the man's shoulders. "And if you could find the truth to an old secret, could you be trusted to tell it and not expose the people who brought you to it? Do you have opinions about that?"

Ah, this was a test. "What does a secret have to do with opinion?"

Dabrowski sucked his lips. "Opinion is the juice that makes a man care. Being true to the facts shows that he does."

In salute, Finn lifted a glass he didn't hold.

Acknowledging the gesture with a nod, Dabrowski continued. "And protecting his sources shows his humanity." He turned to address the wall behind him. "And the Soviets? What is your opinion of their treatment of the Eastern Bloc?"

"My opinion?" Two nights before in the hotel lounge, Finn had argued this very issue with two right-wing journalists from Belgium. "Some worthy ideas poisoned to garner power. Though in that regard, capitalism comes in a close second."

Dabrowski turned back to face his men. He seemed pleased. "Frankly, I've never been able to understand why you Americans don't all kill each other." He resumed his pacing. "But here's what I want for Poland, and it's something I can't give my country. Time. More than anything, she needs time. Time to negotiate an end to this oppression." He speared his index finger into his palm. "These talks are the only ones we'll get in my lifetime."

Heads all around nodded. "And though Gorbachev may mean what he says about keeping his hands off—God knows he's ass deep in his own problems—our informers tell us his generals are pushing for riots here to make him send in the troops sitting on our border." He placed his palms together like a priest. "Jaruzelski—our beloved president—will gladly crush Solidarity to keep his government in power. For now, he still has to go through Gorbachev, but if two generals act on their own . . ." Dabrowski drew the fingers of his left hand across his neck, "all will be lost on our side in a matter of days."

As if sensing Finn's impatience to know where this was leading, Dabrowski continued. "As you wrote so eloquently last month, the Soviet empire is stumbling like a drunk. We need someone to trip them, so they won't be able to invade us. It can't be a Pole. It can't be anyone in the Communist sphere." He spat. "Pack of thieves and bullies. We need the truth to get out to the West."

"The truth about what?"

"The biggest lie ever told, at least if you're Polish." His face suggested he was going to be specific, but all he said was, "Will you help us?"

The contest for the biggest lie ever told was crowded with entries. New ones cropped up every year.

"My mother was Polish," Finn said. "Russians kidnapped her father. She saw her grandparents skewered on German bayonets." Unsure of where this tack was taking him, he stopped, but he knew from the quiet of ten half-wild men that he was in the presence of history. He longed to join it. "What do you need?"

"Go to Belarus. We'll help you get there. Talk to a man and bring his story to the West. Get your paper to print it."

The Round Table Talks had been fraught with struggles over minutiae and had been stalled for the last four days, but if Finn was absent when they resumed, the Times would fire him. Something Clarissa would cheer, no doubt. "How long will it take? And the risks?"

"A couple days," Dabrowski said. "And since you ask, you could create an international incident. Or simply disappear." He backhanded the air with such disregard it took Finn several seconds to realize it was his life Dabrowski was dismissing.

As Finn's heart slammed once, Viktor flicked his hand to get Dabrowski's attention. "Tell him we know what happened to his father." His voice was not unkind.

Finn snapped his head to look at Viktor. "You know?" His mind leapt to the noir eight-by-ten photograph of the journalist Jordan Waters from the shoulders up. He was standing in the light of a street lamp. A fresh cigarette in his hand hovered near his mouth. The smoke of it still in him. His square jaw so much like Finn's. Head cocked with a glint in his eye as if just called by the photographer. The rooflines behind hinted at some European city.

Lately, Finn had seen that confidence in the mirror staring back from his own dark eyes. Though the lines around Finn's carried grief his father didn't seem to have.

The day after his mother had howled that his father wouldn't be coming home, Finn, then six years old, found the pieces of that photograph in the trash. In the early years when she slept, he would fit his father back together on his desk. Even now, the meticulously repaired image traveled with him in a laminated cover.

Dabrowski pulled him back. "Viktor's wrong. We don't know what happened to your father. We know he was a casualty of . . ." and he made small loops with his hand to signify everything that could go wrong, "the troubles inside the Curtain."

There it was. The troubles inside the Curtain: a simple way to evoke Soviet tyranny grinding forty distinct nationalities into one ruined tribe. Jordan Waters vanished on assignment in 1956 during the twenty-four hellish days of the Hungarian Revolution. From all Finn had been able to determine, the United States government absorbed the loss of its citizen without protest or homage.

Dabrowski clapped his hands to keep himself on track. "We're sending you to finish fifty years of mourning and to help us create a new era. In return, we'll do this for you: If you're not back in seventy-two hours, we'll delay the talks another day, even if Jaruzelski begs to give us everything. And we'll do all we can to get you out." He looked each of his men in the eye. "If you succeed, Poland will become free in the present and free from the past." He gazed wistfully at the map of his country that hung crooked on the bare wall to his left. "Her remaining free in the future depends on whether we Poles are idiots or if we are truly tired of being ruled by them."

Finn had cut his journalistic teeth covering the fall of Saigon. He'd visited Jonestown right after the communal suicide. He'd spent two years reporting on Lebanon's civil war. Since covering the Chernobyl nuclear accident, he'd been assigned almost exclusively behind the Iron Curtain. But unlike his father, he had never broken "the great story."

His heart was thundering in his chest. “Promise me, this is news and not spying.”

“Some don’t believe there’s much of a difference.” Dabrowski pointed his finger as a warning. “No one ever needs to know how you get this story. That’s your protection.”

“Where am I going?”

Dabrowski leaned forward and spoke in a stage whisper. “I presume your mother told you about the massacre at Katyn.”

Two

YES, FINN KNEW about Katyn, the lonely Russian forest where thousands of Polish officers were executed and buried in trenches. Each cadaver, still in uniform, was exhumed, carrying identification linking his living self to the battalions the Russian army captured in 1939.

"Katyn," Finn said to Dabrowski. "I thought there were no survivors."

Dabrowski walked again, his right fist tapping his jaw. "Correct. No survivors."

German forces marching on Moscow in 1943 discovered the site. Realizing the news could split the Western Alliance, Field Marshall Göring invited representatives of Russia's allies to witness the exhumation.

Stalin counterpunched. Nazis were famous for such massacres, he said. And he swore he'd sent the Poles home on foot as his forces retreated before the German advance.

"No survivors," Dabrowski repeated. "And to keep it secret, we suspect Stalin also executed the shooters."

Finn's Stanford professor had taught Katyn as a war crime that stood out in a war replete with them. The stakes had driven Russian and German forensic investigators to produce evidence proving the other side's guilt. But after the war that killed sixty million people, no one thought twenty thousand dead Polish officers deserved special attention. No one except the Poles.

"Mateusz," Finn said, "no survivors means no story."

Dabrowski half-smiled. "We believe they missed one man. With the talks stuck, Waters, we have a few days to get you there and back."

Finn reflected on all he had to lose. "Why me?"

Heads turned back to Dabrowski, who shoved his hands in his pockets. He clamped his mouth shut.

"Look at you," Viktor said. "You have Slavic blood. You speak Polish. You speak Russian better than most of us. You write. You care." He uncrossed his feet from where they had rested on the low table in the center of the room and slapped them on the floor. "The Soviets can't touch the *New York Times*. The truth coming out now will throw their government into chaos and give us the time we need."

They had thought this all through. When Finn smiled his assent, the room burst into life. Eleven double-shot glasses were filled with vodka. Dabrowski handed one to Finn and raised his. "Drink with us. Seal your purpose."

Finn stared into the liquid. Lately, Clarissa had been drinking too much. He'd been planning to quit when he went home to help her do the same.

Viktor nudged his arm. "Where you're going, drinking with conviction might save your life."

Finn poured it down his throat. He didn't flinch with the burn.

"Not bad," Dabrowski said. "Next time, smile. Take it fast and hard. Think of it as the kiss of a woman you can't resist."

Among the men were a tailor and a photographer. In less than a minute, the tailor measured Finn for a suit. The photographer hung a sheet over the map of Poland and took Finn's picture.

Several men helped Finn back into his coat. "A taxi will pick you up at your hotel at 8 a.m.," Viktor said. "It will take you to a butcher shop in the eastern part of the city. Go in and ask for American-style piroshky."

Dabrowski embraced him like a family member. "Do you know how to draw, Waters?"

"A little. Why?"

"That will have to do. Don't bring any supplies of your own. We'll take care of that."

"What about my camera?"

"Sure. A professor would have a camera."

FINN RETURNED TO his hotel and dashed off shorthand notes—who said what, and two possible ledes for the story. Then he went to the phone bank next to the lobby. He suppressed a smile at the fluff text other correspondents were reading over the lines. He dialed his editor, Sam Rich, in New York at the hour he would be returning from dinner. Sam answered with his usual take-no-prisoners bluster. It was 2:15 a.m. Warsaw time.

"It must be important, calling me instead of Diana." Diana was Chief of the Foreign Desk. "What have you got?"

Because it was well known that every phone had more than one listener, Finn had thought his language through. "I'm not feeling great. I need your permission to lie low for a couple days. I'll work from bed on a new idea."

He could hear Sam slapping his clustered key chain on his thigh. "What kind of symptoms?"

"A local flu, I think. If my temperature climbs any more, I'll go to the hospital. See if I can pick up something worse. Then Blue Cross can put up or shut up about being an international company."

"That's my man," Sam said. "Always creative. If there's a good time to be ill, you've picked it. Any word on the talks resuming?"

"Both sides say they want to reconvene," Finn said, "but they're bickering about the procedure of vetoing the other's points."

Sam made the sound of a man choking. "The world limps forward."

"We should send them all to Washington," Finn said, "to show them how kielbasa is really made."

Sam gave his steam-whistle laugh. "The Soviets would love that. Clear the city for a few days so they could march in."

"I'll let you know when I'm feeling better. In the meantime, I think you'll like what I'm working on."

"If I don't hear from you by Friday, I'll send flowers."

Flawless. The word *flowers* meant Sam had heard all the clues. But if Finn wasn't back by Friday, sending a coffin might be more appropriate.

AFTER FIVE HOURS of tumbled sleep, Finn wrapped a scarf around his neck. He noted his wool coat didn't cover his pajamas and bathrobe. He shuffled to the taxi as if hammered by fever. His cabbie had no words for him and took him to a butcher's shop in a part of town Finn didn't know.

"No fare today," the cabbie said, when he reached back to Finn's extended cash. Like a magician, he produced a bill of his own and made a show of taking it back. "Never can tell who's watching. I hope things go well for you and that we *all* feel better soon."

The shop smelled of meat and spices. Most of the light came from fluorescents in the butcher case along the back wall. Standing in line, fingering his camera in the pocket of his bathrobe, Finn felt a folded piece of paper underneath it. Dammit. Clarissa's letter. He'd parked it there several nights before after reading only one paragraph. He was contemplating reading it by the light of the case when the butcher signaled it was his turn.

"Do you have American-style piroshky?"

A middle-aged woman sitting in a darkened corner popped to her feet. "Yes, they're in the back. Come with me."

In the living quarters behind the door, he found the tailor from the previous night pulling threads off a wool suit—rusty brown—the coat cut with the wide lapels the Polish favored. "Good day, Mr. Sobczak. Your passport is in the breast pocket. It looks very nice." After watching Finn dress, the tailor yanked the fabric to set the shoulders. "You're big across," he said. He seemed particularly pleased with the fit of the pants but apologized for having forgotten to get Finn's shoe size. When Finn's feet proved too big for the shoes he'd brought, the tailor removed his own boots. "Take these. Losing them is a small price to pay for what you're attempting to do."

Finn transferred Clarissa's letter into a breast pocket, unsettled by the tailor's choice of the word *attempting*. "What's my first name?"

"Karol." The *R* rolled on the tailor's tongue. "Karol Sobczak. Pleased to meet you." The tailor draped a heavy three-quarter-length overcoat on Finn's shoulders and shook his hand. "There's a hat in the car outside."

The sedan he referred to was an old Moskvich, not a taxi, though while in the city limits the old man at the wheel had him sit in back. He gave no other orders until they were puttering through the farmland east of Warsaw. Now in the front, Finn asked if they were going to Katyn.

"There's nothing there to see." Wiry hair, unruly, as if he cut it himself without looking. No hat, a strong neck. Imposing eyebrows. He hadn't been at the meeting. He was at least seventy, as if chiseled from granite. Why had they given him such an old man?

When he coughed, Finn realized where they'd met. "That was you last night in the stairs."

"You passed the test." The old man looked at the sky. "I hope we don't run into snow. The tires are bald and the heater is temperamental. It's not my car. We did our best to find a clunker."

In the land they were heading toward, the winters of 1812 and 1943 had destroyed two huge armies hoping to take Moscow. Finn consoled himself that it was March. "Isn't it stupid to go out of the country in it?"

"Poles didn't murder their own people," the man replied, as if engaged in a different discussion.

"You have an accent I don't recognize."

"Belarusian." He pointed east to Poland's neighbor. "Old cars attract less attention."

"So you speak Russian?"

The man's sad cast brightened, then faded. "My parents were Polish who spoke Belarusian at home. Our neighbors were Lithuanians and Jews. I speak all their languages, but I had to study Russian in school."

"You were ambitious."

The man shifted his shoulders. "You should learn your history. Empires have always surrounded the land where I was born. Our greatest import is foreign armies. They come, they conquer us, impregnate our women, and tell us what language we must now speak." He belched something that smelled like a brown cloud. "After we learn it, they flee when the next invaders come, and we start all over again."

They drove on, grabbed lunch at a bus station west of Siedlce, where Finn learned his driver's name. Mikolai. When signs announced Biala Podlaska, a small industrial city near the border, they turned north onto dirt roads cutting through farmland. Rain turned the roads to mud. Their progress slowed. Water leaked through the dashboard. "Are you cold?" Mikolai asked.

"A little."

"That's too bad. Let's get our story straight, Karol. You're a professor of ornithology. I'm your guide."

"Birds? They should have given me a subject I know something about."

"No matter. If you get questions, make things up. Act arrogant. People don't know birds."

"But there are no birds here this time of year."

"They're coming earlier these days, and you are researching signs of their arrival." Mikolai tapped a good quality sketchbook on the seat between them. "Open it."

Inside, Finn found original pencil drawings of a variety of birds—a couple of hawks and owls, an array of meadow birds.

"You drew them," Mikolai said, with a guttural laugh. "You're pretty good."

Finn faked amusement. "My mother will be surprised. What is my university?"

"How about the University of Silesia? Very small. You've just been hired, and you want to publish to prove yourself."

"And what birds are we looking for?"

"Study the book. When we cross into Belarus, you'll be in back. Leave your passport with me."

"Who are you, really?"

"Seeking justice has required me to work with many sides. Today I work for Poland."

Finn leaned against his door and studied Mikolai for any sign that his loyalty was still for sale. He had the eyes of old fishermen in Gloucester, slow moving but observant. In complete command, he weaved the car through the ruts. As they went, Finn composed phrases that captured things Mikolai said and details about towns they drove through.

Then, in case things went very wrong and he had to abandon all his notes, he clustered them into verses to fit nursery rhymes to unpack later. The last thing he heard Mikolai say was they wouldn't get to the border until late afternoon.

THE CAR COMING to a stop woke Finn. His skull was cold from resting against the window. Daylight was fleeing. Mikolai had parked by a bridge. He got out to piss in the snow bank. Finn did as well.

"Get in back," Mikolai said, "and put your ring on your right hand like we Slavs do."

At the place Mikolai had chosen to cross into Belarus, a sentry rail blocked the road. The guard was eating an evening meal in his wooden gatehouse. He must have had a radio on because he didn't respond until Mikolai honked the horn.

"This is the border to Belarus," the guard said. "Do you know where you're going?"

"I was born up the road, son. My daughter still lives in the old house."

"And who is this man?"

"A professor." Mikolai handed over both passports. The guard bent to peer at Finn. He tempered his laughter with a sneer while rubbing his thumb against his index finger. "Nice clothes."

"He's doing well in spite of what's going on back there." Mikolai jutted his thumb toward Poland. His laugh matched the guard's. "He studies birds. Can you believe it? A man can get paid for almost anything nowadays."

"I shoot birds and eat them," said the guard. "Tell him that."

"He's not deaf. You tell him."

"I shoot birds, too." Finn said. It was true, or had been when he was a boy. "What kind of a gun do you use?"

"A nice one." The guard held two fingers to show a double-barreled muzzle. "But the company name was filed off before my father stole it."

"Can we go?" Mikolai asked.

"If you promise to bring me some game when you return."

"We won't be back," Mikolai said. "We're going to Moscow to steal the Kremlin. Apparently it's of no use to them anymore."

The guard thumped permission to pass on the roof of the car. Mikolai pushed the shifter forward and drove off.

"That was the hard checkpoint. I have a pistol under the seat. I didn't want to have to use it. I liked him."

Mikolai's demeanor improved dramatically. When they passed two columns of Red Army personnel carriers at dusk, he waved. "We're in the USSR now. You can tell because the soldiers aren't quite so skinny."

In contrast, Finn's mood sank. They were in an old car, riding on dirt roads, pursuing a story that could impact the Cold War. His driver was maybe a triple agent who seemed to have no compunction about killing, even blowing away a border guard in the midst of Russian troops. He was crazy and brilliant, qualities Finn's colleagues had accused him of having.

The facts: Finn could never report this part of his adventure. His press credentials gave him no immunity from organs of state terror. If Mikolai had a heart attack, Finn wouldn't have an alibi for being in the country. He acknowledged Clarissa was right about him.

In any case, there was no turning back. He reflected on how one well-placed article could help a whole generation of Poles. Maybe win him a writing award. Upon reflection, this last thought disgusted him. Mikolai was the hero here. The man had nothing to gain.

Disappointed in himself, Finn used the last of the light to study the names of birds.

Three

MIKOLAI HAD LIED about his daughter living up the road. He didn't have one that he knew of. But he did know of a defunct railroad underpass, and he parked there for much of the night, running the engine on occasion to heat the car.

When Finn woke at dawn, they were already traveling.

Mikolai didn't look over. "For a journalist, you don't ask many questions."

Finn felt the ground under him fall away. "Am I supposed to be interviewing you?"

Mikolai gave him an incredulous look.

"But you know where we're going?"

"I have a town and a name."

"Man or woman?"

"Man. Janis Semyonovich."

"And he's at Katyn."

"Was." He smiled ruefully. "Only dead people live at Katyn."

Finn did a quick calculation. Janis had to be at least in his seventies. "How far from here?"

Mikolai held four fingers, then five. "Hours," he said.

The land in Belarus was even flatter than eastern Poland, and they passed through a number of small villages where farmers drove ox carts and spread manure by hand. Filling the gas tank in Slonim, Mikolai smiled while speaking his mother tongue. Seeing the context of conversation, Finn found he could understand a good part of what was said.

In spite of his cough and his age, Mikolai still cut a powerful swath. But in case his time was near and Finn had to return alone, Finn made a mnemonic out of the first letters of villages they passed through. In tiny script, he wrote the letters in his bird book, burying them in the wing feather of a pallid harrier. They wended their way north and east, avoiding Minsk and larger roads. Haradzisca, Haradziela, Uzda, Klinok, and on and on. The names dizzied him. East of Mahilyow, they inquired about a little berg named Dyedna. From then on, there were no stores or villages of any kind. Mikolai picked his way east, comparing landmarks to notes he carried in his head.

Finally, a cluster of rusting silos standing lonely in a vast landscape caused him to point. "An old collective. I grew up on one of those." He stuck out his tongue. The buildings were grey, missing windows and doors. "Like the works of Ozymandius. Do you know Shelley?"

Finn would never have guessed Mikolai was the literary type. "I do. Tell me what it was like, the collective."

Mikolai snorted. "Not much worth telling. Humans resent being trotted around like animals. When they resent enough and come to agree on a better way, they are taken out and shot."

The land beyond was a mixture of farmland and forest. It would have been more beautiful with a little contour. The color palette was heavy on grey, white, and brown.

At last, they stopped across the road from a small brick house with a plank-walled addition. A chicken coop in back bore fresh yellow paint. "A distant cousin of mine from Krakow married his grandson."

Behind the house, a small fenced garden gave way to a large field. With the collective system collapsed, Finn wondered who worked all this land. "This is where the secret of Katyn lies?"

"I've never met the man. But apparently he was there."

In the desolation of that place, their car called attention to itself. Wondering if the Polish plates were a danger, Finn scanned the fields for signs of life. "Are we going on more than hearsay?"

"All I know is the signal was new paint." Mikolai laughed. "I bet he had trouble keeping his brush from freezing."

The door to the coop opened. An old man appeared, carrying a wooden bucket. He wore no gloves. He was tall, boney. His gait showed an unsinkable fortitude.

"Does he even know we're coming?"

As the man came close enough for them to see patches on his wool clothing, his right hand reached into the bucket. It returned with a small hatchet.

With the craft of a snake Mikolai slid his hand under his seat where the pistol was. "He wants to tell his story. We told him we'd help him. That makes him a brave fellow. Be respectful."

Finn wondered how killing him would fit with respect.

The man leaned down to peer through Mikolai's window. Square shoulders, big ears. His face a web of wrinkles, eyes blue as the Baltic. Finn flashed on him as young and dashing in Polish officer epaulettes. Images for an opening paragraph came to him. A meeting in a lost field. A convergence of history, lies, and ambition.

The man tapped the glass with the hatchet handle. Mikolai rolled the window down.

"If you want eggs, I don't have any." A voice softened by years.

Mikolai shook his head. "We're lost. Do you know the way to Katyn?"

The man responded by dropping the hatchet into his bucket. He put a hand on the doorframe and gave Finn an intense look. "You've made it. Is he the one?"

Finn dialed up his best Russian. "I'm a journalist for the *New York Times*. Are you Janis Semyonovich?"

The man's eyes widened. He didn't answer the question. At length he straightened up, massaged his lower back. He turned to look down the road, not with worry, just with unending interest. "Maybe I do have eggs after all. Come, let's take a look."

Before Mikolai was out the door, he began speaking yet another Slavic dialect, maybe Latvian. The man said his name—Janis—and words that sounded like *wife* and *food*. They were close to the same age, Mikolai shorter, sturdier, his head perched forward as if to plow his way through events. Janis had square hands. Finn wondered what he had done with them to survive this long. Excited, he grabbed the note-book and tromped through the snow.

Switching to Russian, Mikolai said, "This is Karol. He's one of us."

It was a flattering way to be introduced. "Actually, my name is Finn Waters. Karol is for the trip."

When the three of them gathered on the far side of the road, Finn noticed Janis's left cheek and his lips hung slack. He saw Finn looking and pointed to it. "A stroke. My second one."

At that, Finn held the old man's hand a little longer. In spite of the temperature, it was warm, still strong, though the skin felt thin like phyllo dough.

Mikolai turned toward the car. "He can help you with what you need to do. I'll wait in the car and drive away if somebody comes."

Janis pointed to the road. "This time of year, the only people on it are lost." There was no vehicle on Janis's lot. No place cleared for one. He touched Mikolai's elbow. "You go in. Old men like you need to be warm." The healthy corner of his mouth grinned. "Her name is Isabel. She's younger. If you want to show off, carry in some wood."

Mikolai showed Finn his crossed fingers. "If you have worth, now's the time to use it." He strode in the direction of the woodshed.

Janis walked toward the chicken coop. "Don't talk here. She has ears like an owl. It's gotten me into trouble many times." Behind the coop the trail split. Carrying the hatchet with him, Janis took the one heading into the woods beyond the field. A hundred yards into the trees, a small fire blazed. Tools for sawing and splitting leaned against a pile of firewood.

Janis slammed the rails of a weathered chair into its stiles and settled himself gingerly in it. He offered Finn his splitting block as a seat, then motioned toward the house. "I told her we might have company today or tomorrow. She probably thinks I'm a fortune-teller."

"I hope you are," Finn said.

"She doesn't know why anyone would be here, and I expect you to keep it that way." He nudged the coals with the cracked toe of his boot. "They can't do anything to me that time isn't already doing better. But she's still young. She'll need my pension."

A man readying himself to die.

Janis leaned and renewed the fire with kindling, then added two birch billets. "I thought you were American. You look like a party member."

Finn tugged the lapel on his jacket. "They made this for me in case we were stopped."

"Things haven't changed. Not in my whole life."

"Thank you for letting me come. I hear you survived Katyn."

Janis grumbled. "You don't know *anything*, do you?"

For once, Finn regretted escaping service in Viet Nam. "I guess not."

"Then why are you here?"

"I know about lies." That got Janis's attention. "And I live to untangle them." The myth Finn carried about his father was that he had perished in that same pursuit. How much of that was a lie Finn had invented?

"Katyn was a lie even before it happened." Janis palpated his limp cheek. "Why do you care?"

"Truth keeps men from becoming wolves."

Janis measured a half-inch between his thumb and forefinger. "We're never farther than this from lies." He snapped his fingers. "This far from insanity." He was settled and deep in the way Finn hoped to be someday. He bent forward and warmed his hands by the flames. "Let's get one thing straight. There were no survivors at Katyn. None whatsoever."

"So you aren't Polish?"

Janis shook his head. "Lithuanian. Five years after the war, they forced me here. To a collective."

"But you've heard what's going on in Poland? Is that why you want to talk now?"

"Our papers only talk about our patriotic army pacifying all of Afghanistan, and of course, corruption in America." He spat in disgust. "But soldiers coming back, they talk. They have brothers serving in Poland. So yes, we know. The Poles are trying to wriggle out of the noose." The way he added, "Good for them," gave the Poles no hope.

He pulled off his boots and laid them flat near the fire. He rested his feet on them. He wore no socks. His skin was a mottled purple.

Finn opened his notebook. Under the drawing of a starling, using shorthand to baffle border guards, he wrote Janis's initials and the start of a paragraph any scientist might jot as notes. "How do you know about Katyn?"

Janis lifted his wool cap, stroked his scalp, then reset it. "I need your promise my name won't be used. Not until she's dead."

Finn promised and waited while Janis gathered himself. "When the NKVD burned my village in the pogroms, I was caught trying to escape. Twice the lieutenant put his gun to my head. Twice it misfired. He laughed and yanked me by the hair. 'You're a powerful spirit,' he said. 'Join us or I'll get another gun.' "

"So you joined the NKVD."

"October '39. I was seventeen. The lieutenant took me to Kozielsk, where he just had been appointed commandant of a new camp. It housed Polish officers the Red Army had captured the month before when they took Eastern Poland." Janis's eyes wandered with memories. Already the talk seemed to exhaust him. "It's hard to hate someone who spares your life. All winter I cleaned his toilet. I made his bed. When the decision was made to move the prisoners, the commandant promoted me. He told me the mission would set me up for life. I didn't know what was coming.

"In early April, Black Marias arrived—you know, the Soviet military bus with the little windows. Their gears made a special grinding noise. You could hear them coming two kilometers away.

"The prisoners had been told they were going home and they cheered the buses. Our caravan lumbered through the night. The prisoners sang Polish songs like their hearts would break. Some sang beautifully. We arrived at a forest outside of Smolensk. The buses parked sixty feet apart back from a long bulldozed trench. The soil was soft. It would have made great farmland. The busses and bulldozers kept their motors revved to light the place up and cover the sound of gunfire.

"Each bus had three NKVD men: One pulled the prisoner out and held him; the second tied his hands behind his back; the shooter walked him to the edge of the pit. Because the kick from Soviet pistols would practically take your hand off, we used early issue Walther P38s. The Germans made the best pistols in the world."

This joggled Finn's memory. Though most forensic evidence pinned the massacre on the Soviets, Stalin touted the fact that investigators pried German bullets from the cadavers' skulls. "How," Finn asked, "did the NKVD get the Walthers?"

"In 1939," Janis said, feigning wartime pride, "Stalin and Hitler pledged to be lifelong allies." The cheer fell from his face. "Within two months, Hitler showed he never intended to send us anything. What I heard was . . ." he cocked his eye at Finn, "American businesses helping the Germans build their war machine finagled eighty cases of them for us."

"Americans?" It rang a bell. After the war, Congress held hearings about American businesses collaborating with the Nazis. But the rising Red Scare had crushed the investigation.

Janis looked disgusted. "Don't be naïve. You Americans played both sides." His sigh grieved for all mankind. "Anyway, after shooting a couple magazines, even Walthers would get too hot to hold, so the second guard's other job was to keep a cool one loaded."

His look shot skyward, remembering something. "The commandant ordered me to shoot the first prisoner. I guess he wanted to see if I'd been worth his time. When I hesitated, he walked up and fired a bullet into the back of the man's head. The body fell like a bag of potatoes. He ordered me to stand on the edge. He put his gun to my head. 'I assure you my Walther won't misfire,' he said. 'These are enemies of the Soviet Union. Treat them as dead.'

"Then he yelled over the engines for everyone to hear. 'That's how it's done. Do your jobs. If you fail—' he pointed to the trees behind the buses—'you'll be staying here.' That's when I saw there was a machine gunner for each bus."

Janis smiled an odd smile, contrite and something else. Finn wanted the images in that old head. "The air became full of pistol fire. I saw bodies falling down the line. My first man was a lieutenant, handsome. He was crying. I pulled the trigger but didn't watch him fall. It was easier that way. Some prisoners fought and had to be dragged, but most of them bleated like sheep. They had soiled themselves. You could smell their shit over the diesel fumes.

"Once we learned our routine, we didn't talk. All you could hear was motors roaring and pistols popping every ten seconds."

He produced a tin of tobacco from a coat pocket and rolled himself a cigarette. Finn waited while he smoked half of it in deep reflection. Finally, he began again. "At one point the shooter in the bus next to mine started screaming and threw his pistol down. I turned to look. The commandant bobbed his head one time. The machine gunner shot him. A replacement was brought onto the line. We all went back to work."

"Janis, how many buses were there?"

"They kept coming. We worked all through the night. I've tried to estimate how many I killed. About one every minute. My hand began to ache and my ears rang." He cupped his hands over his ears as if the sound was still inside. "All the while an NKVD guy we all hated walked in the pit. A stupid fuck, the kind who would enjoy violating his sister with a stick. He bayoneted the bodies to make sure they were dead.

"You may ask why I didn't kill myself." He ran his tongue along his upper teeth, then turned sharply as if someone sitting to his left was trying to shout him down. When he turned back, his nostrils were flared. "I had fifty chances to kill the commandant, maybe take one or two of the NKVD down with me." He wagged his finger. "Here's why: Early on I began to feel a kinship with the prisoners. I was one of them, a disposable thing, just a Lithuanian in an NKVD uniform. Stalin had cleared entire villages of my people. When you live through that, you expect it to happen again."

He snubbed out his cigarette and emptied the remaining tobacco back into the tin. "After I had killed about twenty or so—I was on my third pistol, I think—one man, very high rank, managed to catch my eye as I walked him to the pit. I didn't have to pull him. He walked dignified, like a real soldier. Without turning his head, he whispered, 'Don't do this. You don't have to do this.' And while I hesitated, he looked down. Then I looked. I couldn't believe the bodies piling up. I heard myself say, 'I'm sorry.' He did a surprising thing then. He said, 'I forgive you,' and leaned back into the pistol.

"From then on, I whispered 'I'm sorry' to each prisoner. I whispered in Polish so they could feel something of their homeland. The strange thing was, when I placed my pistol on the back of their heads, many of them relaxed."

Janis spat into the fire and put his elbows on his knees. His decades of preparation for this meeting rendered asking questions unnecessary. At that moment, Finn realized what he was hearing carried no elements of proof. It was just a story. An authentic-sounding narrative, certainly. But nothing to prove which side was lying in a fifty-year-old argument. Taking Janis's picture would prove nothing and would sign his death warrant. And his wife's. Perhaps his whole family's. What had Dabrowski been thinking? Without linking the massacre to the Kremlin, Janis's story was just another in the mountain of charges. Finn pressed on. "Was it just that one night? How many men do you think died in those trenches?"

Janis returned from his thoughts. "No, many nights. We slept all day. It began again after dusk. The corpses began to stink. I'd rather go to hell than smell that again. I didn't pay close attention, but I read one account smuggled in from Hungary. The bodies were piled ten deep before the bulldozers covered the pit. Then we started on another one."

He looked toward his house. Finn visualized Mikolai enthralling Isabel with stories.

"She knows nothing of this," he said. "If she did, she wouldn't want to be with me. If women knew what war was, they would all leave us." He jammed his thumb over his shoulder. "Humanity would cease. Keeping women in the dark is part of the crime, part of the secret, part of the power." He sucked in the good corner of his mouth. His eyes swelled. His breathing came fast and shallow. Worried he was suffering a heart attack, Finn rose. But Janis waved him off. "Promise me again she will not have to know."

A cool gust blowing in from the field heightened Finn's sense of loss that the story everyone wanted would go untold. He shoved his hands into the coat sleeve of the other. "I promise." He looked at his feet. "Do you have anything that can prove your story? A picture, maybe, of who was there? Do you still have your pistol?"

Janis worked his jaw. He stared at the end of his nose. "After the war, they took our Walthers. And being Lithuanian, for good measure, they sent me to prison camp. Four years." He ran his finger over one of the patches on his pants. "I've waited too long to tell this, haven't I?"

"Your story is good, very good. The way you tell it, the pictures it carries—it must be heard. But words by themselves—the Kremlin will say you did it for money or fame. They'll say you're old or psychotic. That you made it up. Or that I did."

Janis seemed to shrink. "You haven't been in war, I can tell. To survive, you abandon the part of yourself that protests. What good is a campaign buckle or a piece of paper?" He put his boots back on. His voice became childlike. "I had hoped telling you would free me a little, maybe even give something to the Poles."

"Maybe it can, Janis. Who else knows this? Can you think of anyone?"

"Anyone who would want to tell? No." He raised his brows and pointed east. "I hear the commandant is still alive. His son married a woman near here. He told me where the bastard lives. Toward Moscow, in Kaluzhskaya Oblast, a village called Mosalsk. He's had several names, goes by Andrei Kurishenko now. It's hard work staying disappeared. He made money as a surveyor, so I bet he's got a good pension. Nothing would make him jeopardize that."

"Have you talked to him?"

"If I could, I'd finish him off with a shovel."

Finn thought of Mikolai's pistol.

MIKOLAI WAS DISAPPOINTED to learn Janis had only words to offer. But as they stood in Janis's yard, Finn asked, "Would a picture of the commandant hiding under an assumed name stir things up enough to meet Poland's current needs?"

Mikolai brightened. "Let's go to Mosalsk. If we leave now, we'll have time to see if he likes birds."

Four

THE ROADS EAST were two-lane and poorly marked. With the help of five crisp US twenty dollar notes, they crossed at night through the checkpoint into Russia. They put Smolensk Oblast behind them and arrived in Mosalsk before dawn. For breakfast they bought sugar rolls and cheese. They drank strong coffee to get them through the day. Given Kurishenko's history with Poles, they changed Finn's bloodline to Ukrainian and his name to Karol Mertov. Unspooling their ruse, they asked farmers for permission to check wooded parcels and meadows for bird activity. When the farmer seemed willing, they conversed. Gradually, they teased out where the commandant lived.

Toward evening, Mikolai stopped nearby and lifted the hood of the Moskvich. He pulled a wire off a spark plug and drove to the Kurishenko house, which was set back at the base of a wooded hillside far from any neighbors. Nothing grand, twenty-two feet on a side, needing paint and some shingles. A few outbuildings. Signs of a small tractor having done tasks. A simple place to die.

Though Mikolai left the car coughing and backfiring in the yard, the dumpling-shaped old woman who answered their knock seemed wary of their story of engine trouble. She closed the door. Mikolai knocked again. He called out for permission to spend the night on her porch. This time, she relented and let them in.

The smell of boiled potatoes and mint stirred Finn's appetite. She must have sensed it. "My husband and I have already supped." She pointed to a large man with a great shock of white hair asleep in the stuffed chair. Mikolai explained they had eaten a great dinner in the early afternoon at a roadhouse that they had actually passed before sunrise. "We can't possibly eat another mouthful," he said. "But we'd be happy to share our unopened bottle of vodka if, by chance, your husband wakes up."

Like a dog alerted by the sound of food in his bowl, the man raised his head and stretched. The large volume that lay flopped open upon his barreled midriff tumbled to the floor.

"Up, up, Andrei. We have company," Mrs. Kurishenko barked in a high voice. "Help me clear places for them on the divan." For Finn and Mikolai's benefit, she whispered, "He never used to sleep this early. And I guess the day got ahead of my housecleaning."

Andrei watched from his place as his wife fulfilled her own commands.

The alcohol hitting Finn's empty stomach inspired him to share everything he'd learned about birds since leaving Warsaw. He mentioned teaching at the University of Silesia. Their hostess, Irina, stiffened. "You said you were from Ukraine."

Mikolai laughed. "I apologize for confusing you. I was born in Belarus. The professor is *from* Ukraine. Tell us about your hometown, Karol. And how you came to work in Poland. I would like to know something about you before you win the Commissar's Red Star for measuring bird poop. But first, drink some more to enrich the memories." Mikolai topped off three glasses. Irina covered hers. With an unsubtle eyebrow she admonished her husband to use moderation.

Andrei snapped. "I haven't coughed up any blood today."

Mrs. Kurishenko made no effort to hide the face that said she knew he was lying.

Finn winked at Andrei and stood. "To my dear mother." He imagined the vodka as the lips of Chantelle Mugatando, the ebony-skinned correspondent from Le Monde, who enlivened the lounge in his Warsaw hotel. Clarissa appeared in the bottom of his glass, standing beside the statue in Vienna's Josefplatz.

For his narrative, Finn commandeered his mother's childhood stories, changing place names and inventing people. Stories of fishing in the brook running through town. Stories of Red Star marches and of kissing a girl behind the commune's machine shop. Andrei's dour look lightened. He told stories of his boyhood outside of Petrograd.

"You mean Leningrad," Mikolai said.

Andrei fired back, "Stalingrad."

"Soon to be Gorbachevgrad," Finn said.

"Not if *I* live," Andrei said. He straightened his pinky in his groin. "That little prick." He drank his glass and refilled it without it touching the low table between them.

Mikolai interspersed his exploits of helping the Soviets beat the Germans with digs at Finn for being born too late for any meaningful service for the Motherland.

After Irina retired to the bedroom, Andrei began his stories of the war without mentioning Soviet nationalities his unit killed.

"When I was thirty," he said, "they made me commandant at the camp in Kozielsk."

"That's tragic," Mikolai said. "You ended up checking lists and ordering barbed wire and noodles."

Andrei bristled. He looked from his drink to his company. "Maybe *you* would see it that way." He slammed his palm against his sternum. "*I* traveled to Moscow once to meet with Beria. Not many can say that. In fact, *Beria* summoned *me*."

"The big dog, eh? You know him, don't you, Karol?" Mikolai kicked Finn's foot theatrically. "Head of the NKVD. A noble man. Some say a scary man." He swirled the liquid in his glass. "Which side were you on, Andrei," he paused and lowered his voice, "when they executed him? I hear he squealed like a baby when they dragged him off."

"Taking sides in Moscow's squabbles," Andrei said, rolling with the punch, "has never proven good for one's health." He laughed. It was his first of the evening, deep-throated and cynical. "From the years on you, you look like you must have learned that, too."

"Actually, Andrei, what my sixty-nine years have taught me is to take every side I can." Crumbs of truth allowed Mikolai to tell any lie at will.

Aware that alcohol was dulling his memory, Finn linked chunks of the dialogue to objects in the room. The lampshade became Poland. The closet doorknob, Moscow. The edge of the carpet, a timeline of events. "So what *about* Beria?" he asked. "You went to Moscow."

For a long minute, Andrei took interest in the gloom of a far corner. "I shouldn't have brought it up. It was a secret meeting."

"A meeting?" Mikolai said. "You think a meeting miles from the front tops my sneaking into Nazi headquarters disguised as an SS major and stealing documents of troop movements right under their watchful eyes?" He laughed while pouring them all another drink. "Do you know how many men died as a result of my little dance that one afternoon?" He may as well have slapped Andrei with his glove and thrown it at his feet.

Andrei tried and failed to cross his legs. "You underrate discipline, which shows you were low-level. But I can at least say it was exciting to be in the capital. It was a jewel then. The river and the bridges. Before the Luftwaffe attacks." He swilled the rest of his vodka. "The tsars had an eye for architecture."

"That's about all they did right," Finn said. "But surely you don't find fault with everything in Gorbachev's Russia."

Andrei pounced. "We Russians are gutting ourselves while the whole world watches. I'm glad I won't be around to see when dogs lick our entrails. Glasnost is treachery. The Motherland has no future." His cough snowballed until he lifted a bowl that was on the floor by his chair. Even in the low light, his spittle showed red.

"Maybe." Mikolai waited and waited. "Then again, it might mean your meeting doesn't have to be secret any more."

A centripetal force was enlarging Finn's skull, sweeping away the last of his caution. He locked eyes with Andrei. "Secrecy is noble. But when we've saved lives, we deserve honor. What do you say, Mikolai? Is honor half as good if it comes to us after we die, or only a quarter?"

With a growl, Andrei rose, a bear of a man, his age and infirmity showing more now that he was standing. By the math, he was eighty. Perhaps vodka *was* the water of life.

Andrei placed a stool in his closet. From a bag on the top shelf he pulled an NKVD commandant cap and a sidearm holster on a wide belt. He laid the latter reverently on the table between them. With a shirt-sleeve he buffed the visor of the cap and its star. He put it on with practiced authority and sat again in his chair, this time, bolt upright.

"Your diddling young scientist friend here will live to see the cancer caused by Perestroika. If we continue allowing criticism and making peace with our enemies at the first sight of blood, there will be more birds for him to . . ." he mimicked an aristocrat parading with his nose in the air, "s*tudy*. Cannons kill more birds than people, you know. And there'll be more dancing in the streets. Have you noticed that every year we're losing more heart for military parades?" He soured his lips. "So because you push me to it, here's my contribution to *openness*, before all honor is forgotten, and we real heroes die off. This, my Belarus comrade, is the secret I've had to keep all these years."

Finn contemplated the lump under the holster's flap and recalled Janis's description of Andrei executing the first victim of Katyn.

"Because Poland has always been our enemy," Andrei said, "there's nothing I'm about to say any Russian should be ashamed of. Which includes you folks, since we dragged both your whining peoples from the Middle Ages."

Mikolai shielded his clenched teeth with his glass. "All the people of Belarus thank Russia for that." He tipped it and drank.

Andrei drank too. "I'm glad we agree on that much. Listen now. It will always be that Poles kill us and we kill them." And he explained how, following orders from Stalin, he designed the execution of 4,400 Polish officers that he held as prisoners in his Kozielsk camp, beginning with selecting the remote site of Katyn, procuring the bulldozers, and training his guards in handling prisoners. The schedule and transport routes were *his* work. "And I pushed my men to interview the prisoners one last time in case there was someone we could use during the war and after." He volunteered that Beria arranged for the Walther P38 pistols. Kozielsk got sixty of them. Brand new. He even mentioned bayoneting the corpses. There would be no survivors.

The details sharpened Finn's retention.

"There were four other camps doing the same," Andrei said. "I don't know the exact number of the dead. Kozielsk was one of the biggest. We had a lot of generals." He nodded toward the Western Front. "We haven't heard from the Poles since, though at the moment a few of them think they're big shots. I'd like to get them in the open field one more time to watch them run."

The floor seemed to vibrate with voices freed from the constraints of time, the droning grief of 22,000 Polish families. Finn thought of his broken-winged mother and wondered where her physician father had been dispatched. And of her cousins' families that had scattered into the countryside, forced to live on dogs and tree bark. And of the mountains of ash of Jewish bodies incinerated in the camps. And of the never-to-be slaked thirst for retribution bequeathed to the survivors in Israel and beyond.

But Mikolai laughed so hard Finn thought he would wake Mrs. Kurishenko. "Rumors. I'll say this, my generous Russian host: Many people in the safety of the most powerful nation on earth and with vodka in their blood might try to take credit for such patriotic duty. My bet is you've made up a story from rumors floating in Slavic winds. Even *Stalin* blamed the Germans for Katyn, remember?" He refilled Andrei's glass. "Me, I am unbowed by your tale. Real heroes don't need to talk. They have proof." He drained his glass and placed it on the table with loud click. Then he softened. "I don't want to appear ungrateful in the face of your hospitality. Your story is entertaining, and sleeping on the porch would be cold. So the bottle is yours, in any case."

Andrei froze like a swayback mare on a slaughterhouse conveyor.

In the silence, the pistol called to Finn like Bilbo Baggins's ring. He wouldn't know a Walther if he tripped over it. The odds were miserable that Andrei had carried this one during that part of the war. But ballistics tests might match it with bullets plucked from Katyn cadavers. He placed his hand on the holster and pulled the flap back. "That's a Walther, isn't it? I'd love to see it. Is it one of the guns Beria sent?"

Andrei lunged forward, but his belly prevented him from topping Finn's hand. "No one touches that."

Finn was not intimidated. Still, he bowed slightly. Journalism 101 taught that when the upset subject fields the oddball question, he tends to spill random information. "Something smells here," he said. "Hitler had already declared war on us, right? So how could Beria have gotten his hands on German guns?"

Andrei wormed his hips forward in the chair and dragged the holster onto his lap. Having it there roused him. "Guns are like money. They go where they're needed." He unsheathed the pistol and admired it by turning it in his hand. "This gun is German-made, but it came courtesy of the Americans." He aimed it at Finn's forehead. The acid in his snicker revealed the part that could murder without regret. "Walthers were the best." He mocked firing the pistol and with a theatrical smirk he slid it back into the holster.

Having poured the last of the vodka into his glass, he waved the bottle at Mikolai. "When I've downed this, I'll show you proof." He leaned forward heavily, elbows on his knees. "Then you'll apologize." He lingered on the point. "If you do it so I feel something here . . ." he placed his hand on his heart, "I won't kill you and your little bird friend." Finn saw the bottle flying toward him and managed to jerk out of its path. It bounced off the divan and clunked on the floor. Andrei laughed for the second time.

Mikolai sat still as a fisherman on a riverbank.

Andrei's breathing rumbled with privilege. He hammered his pointer finger on the table. "This house holds a great Soviet legacy. One no one knows about." He seemed to be debating himself and patted the holster. "Mind you, if you tell anyone, I'll hunt you down and kill you." He waited for his words to affect his guests. Seeing they didn't, he continued. "I saved Stalin's orders, signed by him and the other three."

Finn fought the urge to look at Mikolai. If Andrei had the orders, history and the present were about to merge.

Andrei raised his glass, flipped *Fuck You* with his free hand in the direction of Moscow, and crying, "To Glasnost," he sucked the full glass empty and slammed it down. He worked his elbows like ski poles into the stuffed arms of the chair, but they kept slipping off. "Come on, you old dog," he yelled at himself. He puffed until his face turned dark. Finally, one arm made its way around his back. He was strapping on the pistol belt. With shaky hands he threaded the free end through the buckle. He drew it tight just below his breasts.

Forgetting the stakes, Finn laughed. At first Andrei's glance portended evil, but finding the holster in his armpit and the gun inaccessible, he shrugged at the absurdity. Instead, he leaned for the flashlight beside his chair. "Help me up. Let's go see Stalin's orders."

After three steps with Finn and Mikolai each on an arm, he started gasping. Realizing the belt was restricting his lungs, he yanked the buckle free and the whole assembly tumbled to the floor. The three of them moved as one, sideways through the front door. They crossed the yard to the tool shed. Andrei pulled a key from his pocket and opened the padlock.

Once inside, he said, "You can't be too careful with history." With that, he drew a workbench drawer all the way out. He fished a tin box from deep inside the space. He fumbled with the lid. The only item inside was a folded document with typing on both sides. "You have to go outside now," he told Finn. "This honor is reserved for veterans."

Finn wiped sweat from his temple. "That's crazy. Seeing this will help my generation know what you sacrificed."

Andrei's posture improved, while Mikolai hung his head. "This is embarrassing. Schools in Belarus weren't like Russian schools. I'm good in the woods. I can impersonate Nazis. But I . . . can't read."

Andrei fingered the document. "An odd couple, you are. A professor and a cretin. How about if the scientist reads it for you? He's not good for much else." He roared a laugh and was so clumsy unfolding the paper, it was all Finn could do to resist tearing it from his hands. At last, Andrei gave the workbench a ceremonial wipe with his sleeve and laid the yellowed document down. Seeing the text drop in and out of focus, Finn blinked hard.

Under the seal of the USSR were the official name of the NKVD—the People's Commissariat for Internal Affairs—and the words *Top Secret*. Under that was the date that freed the Nazis from guilt for that one abysmal act: March 5, 1940. Below that lay the text that ordered the NKVD to liquidate Polish army officers and members of the professional class who were being held in camps since their capture in Eastern Poland. Above the signatures of his three brutal Politburo henchmen, Stalin had signed his name in red ink, huge across the text.

"Read it aloud, you idiot," Mikolai said. "And if you don't mind, I'm a little tipsy, so read it slowly. I don't want to miss this."

While Finn read, Andrei perched by him, mouthing the text like a priest overseeing a child reciting catechism. When Finn had finished, Andrei folded the page, kissed it, and returned it to the box. He paused with his hands on the lid, not out of reverence, but to steady himself. "I must lie down. I'll put it away in the morning. But you see my point. That's the courage that wins wars."

The three of them helped each other out the door and, dizzy with success, Finn leaned back against the shed's outside wall. An arm of the Milky Way wheeled through a hole in the clouds.

Mikolai took responsibility for clinching the lock over the hasp. "Your secret is safe again," he said. "And you win. Absolutely. Now, let's see who can pee the longest." And like the old Gloucester fishermen used to do, hanging off the pilings of the bait pier, the three of them unzipped their flies and watered the earth. No one remembered to declare the winner.

They ushered Andrei to his bedroom. They heard him collapse on the bed like a doomed dirigible. But Finn couldn't get his mind to strategize next steps. He felt blissful. The cushions of the divan embraced his back like a lover. His feet dangling over the arm made him giggle.

Perhaps he slept, but he wasn't dreaming when Mikolai's powerful hands dragged him up and out the door. He found himself bent over the porch railing. The cold air stung. His feet were numb. “Stick your fingers down your throat, Professor. Get it all out.”

Vomiting brought some clarity. The sky was clear with no moon. “What time is it?”

“Time to go.”

“Are we done here?”

Mikolai’s teeth shone in the starlight. “What did Dabrowski ask you to do?”

Finn shook his head to clear it. “He’ll want that document. We should have clubbed the old bastard and locked him in there.” He looked at the tool shed. It seemed far away. “Does the car have a tire iron to rip the hasp off?” Mikolai hauled him across the yard. The padlock was hanging open. “You’re a magician, Mikolai.”

“People see what they want to see.”

Inside, Finn worked the top off the box. As on the night they met, Mikolai held the flashlight. How many days ago was that? Mikolai helped him lay out the document. “Take your pictures.”

Finn had forgotten about the camera, but there it was in his coat pocket. “What if they don’t come out?”

“Two things,” Mikolai said. “If he finds the orders missing tomorrow and still has connections, they’ll close the borders. We’ve admitted we’re from Poland.”

“But if we put the box and drawer back,” Finn countered, “he might think he took care of it and not check. Maybe he’s so drunk he won’t even remember showing them to us.”

“Is that how you read his character?”

That wasn’t how Finn read his character. “What’s the second thing?”

“NKVD officers were supposed to destroy their orders. He might not want to explain to the KGB why he kept them.”

Adrenaline coursed through Finn’s body. “We’ll put the box back and I’ll leave a note in it that makes that clear. Maybe he won’t check it for a day or so.”

Mikolai cocked his eyebrow. "It's your decision. You have more to lose. I'm an old bastard on his last caper."

"But you're the pro."

Mikolai picked at his cheek. "At night, even good drivers hit deer."

There was no telling how bringing in the document would ignite Finn's career. Books. A speaking tour. A movie, maybe. Historians would pore over his writings. "Give me the odds."

"Hard to say," Mikolai said. "But consider this. If Poland weasels out of the net, other countries will follow."

Finn felt Clarissa scowling. "They'd kill us, wouldn't they?"

For the first time, the old warrior seemed vulnerable. "The land between here and Warsaw is thick with unmarked graves. Another will go unnoticed."

Finn was touched that on his last adventure, Mikolai was placing his fate in his hands. Besides, stealing documents wasn't journalism. "Pictures will have to do," Finn said, attaching the flash to his camera. He framed it with his ring finger for reference and shot both sides of Stalin's orders.

Folding the page, he felt again how easy it would be to steal it. Film could be doctored. Forensics could prove the paper's veracity. A great wrong would be corrected. A slew of countries could go free. The world could become a different place. He could make a difference. He imagined his father cheering. "History trumps news," he said. "It trumps the risk. I'm going to take it."

Mikolai sucked his tongue but didn't protest. Finn slipped the orders into the breast pocket of his suit. He told Mikolai to get ready to go. On the porch he pressed his ear to the door. The house was still. No one stirred when the hinges squeaked. He tore a page from his portfolio. On it he wrote a note identifying himself as KGB. "I am taking the orders to protect them forever. But because of your kind hospitality, I won't report you for holding a piece of history. Commandant, live out your years proud of your service."

Returning the flashlight to the floor by Andrei's chair, he came upon the holster. He slid back the flap and palmed the gun. It was cold and clean, the hardest steel, the religious object of a mass murderer. It had no manufacturer's imprint, just the letters JP and a number 106 embossed on the casing.

A voice nagged in his ear. The Soviets would denounce the orders as a hoax, particularly if the story came from the US. But the gun. The gun just might settle the issue. Perhaps he could get it into Poland hidden in a door panel of the Moskvich. The US embassy could ship it out by diplomatic pouch. How, though, could he ever get his hands on a matching bullet from Katyn? Could he steal one from a museum? Maybe Hitler had demanded some for his files. What were the chances the West Germans still had them?

In the end, though, he thought traveling with the gun would be tempting fate. He slid it into its holster and returned it to the closet shelf, a tactic he saw as possibly delaying Andrei's checking for the orders until he and Mikolai were back in Poland.

In the workshop, he put his note in Andrei's tin box and slid the shelf home. As he clicked the shed's lock in the hasp, Mikolai gently lowered the hood of the Moskvich. With a silent cheer Finn trotted toward the car. A minute later they motored into the night.

Five

FINN'S EXHILARATION WORE off with his intoxication. Crossing the first border could trigger consequences that would follow him forever. They could cause the "international incident" Dabrowski had blithely referred to. They could get him buried without a marker. The Moskvich's cigarette lighter could set fire to the evidence. But if Kurishenko woke with perfect recall of the night's events, that might not matter.

Finn considered his father's disappearance in Hungary in 1956, and the question his counselor at Stanford had posed bloomed in the night: *Do you suppose, Waters, you're drawn to journalism because you don't know what happened to him?*

Breaking from his own thoughts, Mikolai summed up the black disc of land they were traveling through. "There's something about this part of the world that inspires men to go berserk." He laid his sternum on the steering wheel and looked at the sky. "On a clear day, hedgerows and woodlands allow you to only see a few miles. You're left with the agony of knowing the land stretches flat like this forever."

Somehow he remembered the unmarked turns he'd made the night before. Finn checked his watch; in eight hours, they would have been gone three days. Mikolai read his mind. "Dabrowski told me he'd cover for us an extra day."

FINN WOKE TO Mikolai clanging the petrol nozzle into the fill hole. It was dawn. He got out, stretched his legs. He washed his face in water from a hose. "I'll drive when you can't."

Mikolai jerked his chin to show he'd heard. When they were underway again, he said, "I'll have plenty of time to rest in the coming years." He exhaled. "We'll be crossing into Belarus soon. Pull the radio out. I taped three US twenties to the back."

At the border, Mikolai handed over the passports with the bills showing. The guard turned his back to his office, folded the money into his palm, and waved them through.

"Do you have a place in mind to go 'rest'?" Finn asked.

Mikolai pointed north. "My nephew's. He's a teacher. She's a baker. They have a son I've never met. Eight years old. He needs a grandfather."

Finn had difficulty seeing such simplicity satisfying him.

"I trained to be an editor, Karol. Events didn't give me the chance. I want to settle down with some books. Belarusians have written a lot of good poetry, you know." With a grunt he scraped up and swallowed a wad of phlegm. "But Nikita Sergeyevich banned them." He patted Finn's pocket that held the orders. "You'll need to hide these. To get into Poland, we're going through the main checkpoint."

"Why not the way we came in?"

"Guards at little posts know that if you're leaving the USSR, you're smuggling something. Old orders from the Kremlin qualify. They'll rip through every inch of the car looking for whatever you have. It's safer to hide in numbers."

"Where don't they look?"

Mikolai raised his index finger, to remind them both. "And the film, too. I've heard some people get held for two days waiting for prints to be made."

Finn being gone two more days would alarm his paper. And he had never let five days pass without phoning Clarissa. The good news was if they were seized at the Polish order, her father might be able to help. As the retired ambassador to Austria, he still had many contacts.

Mikolai pulled a glass vial from under his seat. "Your film canister should fit in this. I'll wire it inside the top of the rocker arm cover. They've never looked there."

"Oil won't get into it? What about the heat ruining it?"

Mikolai smiled. "It'll survive a few kilometers. I'll 'check the oil' at the last petrol station in Belarus. I've got the operation down to about two minutes."

Finn flipped down the visor and poked the fabric overhead. "You have a slot up here for the orders?"

"That's the first place they look."

"Where then?"

Mikolai tapped the bird book. "Put it where they will find it."

"Not seeing what they expect?"

"You're learning. Gradually."

"That scares me to death." He saw himself in the bowels of a Soviet prison.

"When guards catch you trying to outsmart them, they get very smart." He modeled beating someone with his fist.

Finn pulled out the orders and opened the book.

"Just past the middle. That's where the pages are tightest. Put it so the lettering is upside down and shove it into the binding."

LONG COLUMNS OF Red Army troop carriers headed west on the highway that connected Minsk with the Polish border city of Brest. Finn made a point of waving to soldiers they passed, and he practiced his narrative about his mission—birds he'd seen and those he hadn't.

The warmth of the soup they bought made Finn drowsy. He awoke to the motor not running. The car was squeezed between mud walls so close that neither door could open. From rafters overhead, rotted sheaves of thatch sagged like Dali clocks. An abandoned barn. Mikolai was slumped over the wheel as if someone in the back seat had assassinated him. But he was snoring.

Finn checked his breast pocket for the orders and finding them gone, dug deeper. His hand drew out Clarissa's letter. Border guards finding a letter in English would blow his identity. He pushed the cigarette lighter in, recalling how the mewling tone of her first lines had made him quit reading it. He cranked the window down in preparation of setting it on fire but decided he should at least read it.

My Darling,

I should know better than to write when I'm in this frame of mind. I know you don't like it. But writing seems like the best way to make sense of myself. God, I hate being so constipated.

I know I wasn't this needy when you married me. So long ago now. Fuzzy like a dream. I know it affects you. And I sense you're not telling me everything, the way we promised to do in our vows.

I used to be so confident, didn't I? What the hell happened? Thirty-eight feels so old. I'm like a house with termites in the walls. I need a carpenter, Finn. Come home and renovate me. Get me started. I'll take care of the rest.

With you gone, I have no voice. My father should be grieving, but he's keeping mother alive by having me do everything she used to do. Cancer is the worst fate.

With reminders of death all around, it seems impossible to follow your advice. When we get back to Rotterdam, I'll get myself back on track, if I can remember which end of the train the engine is on.

Sorry. I've broken my promise to not write this drivel. Still, I feel better, connected to you somehow. You have enough to worry about, though I like to think I've earned the right.

You've come a long way,

Clarissa

In another pen she wrote:

> *P.S. It's morning now and I see I shouldn't try to make sense when it's late, but I'm going to send this anyway, so when I'm out of these doldrums, we can look back and laugh.*

For the last six months, his loneliest days had been in her company. She had lost a whole dimension. The cigarette lighter popped out. He lit a corner of the paper and held it out the window, wishing her misery would burn with it. He threw the last of it into the air.

Mikolai shook bolt upright. He leaned back. "Does your wife know what you do?"

Finn wondered if Mikolai was psychic. "I've never stolen anything before, if that's what you mean."

Mikolai blew his nose into his hand and wiped it on the steering column. "If she finds out about the trip, tell her the truth: You've been gathering news."

"From now on," Finn said, "I'll stick to interviews and press conferences."

Mikolai gave the same laugh he had in the stairwell of the school at Kowalski 137. "Once tiger cubs taste meat, they give up mother's milk."

"No, this is a one-time thing."

Mikolai snorted disagreement. He reached under the seat and withdrew the pistol.

"What are you doing?"

"I hate having to do this." Mikolai laid the pistol in his lap; his finger hooked the trigger. He looked sad, almost regretful.

Finn's limbs went numb. His thoughts went into overdrive, realizing there was no escaping the car. Mikolai had planned it all from the beginning, right down to taking a snooze before killing him. He'd followed Mikolai's every command. Oh, how the old man would laugh at the telling.

"What good are the orders to you?"

Mikolai shrugged off the question, seemed beyond caring. He sighed and lifted the gun, examined it as if making communion with his actions. He kissed it. Then he rolled down his window and tossed the weapon forward so that it cleared the car's hood. It landed with a thud onto the barn's earthen floor. He started the car and backed out. "You're fooling yourself if you think you won't do this again," he said. "If Poland gets free with your help, I guarantee you'll be *reporting* in other places." He glanced over. "Relax. I never take guns going west. Too risky."

IT WAS NEAR DUSK on their extra day. Finn was sitting in back when they joined the parade of taillights inching toward the Polish border. The whistle and blow of air brakes. Diesel fumes. He saw a story in the Russian troops and acres of field armaments parked in that last mile. This trip had elevated his appreciation of Poland. To get there, he'd have to bluff his way through guards who had a dog's sense about people hiding things. He practiced his nonchalance.

At the checkpoint, Polish soldiers were relegated to watching their Russian counterparts—still in their heavy winter uniforms—handle each vehicle. When it was Finn and Mikolai's turn, a weather-beaten soldier shined his light in Mikolai's window. "Get out, Grandpa."

As if this were his cue, Mikolai became struck with the frailty of old age. He grunted and hummed in the exertion of swinging and lifting his thighs out the door. He groped the car roof to steady himself. A newfound palsy in his hand made him fumble for his papers. He complained that the engines idling all around made the soldier's questions hard to hear.

For his part, Finn now didn't speak any Russian. A sergeant had to be dragged over to translate. Professor, yes. University of Silesia. Birds. Migration patterns and their messages. You mean like canaries in coal mines? No, evolution. Anything to declare? No. I don't believe you. Get out.

He slammed Finn's arms onto the trunk of the car. "You Poles always take something home to sell." He frisked Finn's groin hard enough to make him jump. "Give me your camera and I'll spare you the strip search." He didn't wait for Finn's answer.

Mikolai limped to the trunk and laid his arms next to Finn's. "Frisk me, too. We don't have anything, but go ahead and look."

A double-chinned dog handler with a German shepherd appeared in the floodlights. As soon as he opened the driver's side door, the dog shoved his snout under the seat. It barked and whined. Guards rushed over. With wrecking tools, they bent the seat springs and broke the underside of the dashboard. They pried off the inside door covers and the rocker panels. Rummaging in the backseat, the sergeant came out with the bird book and flipped through the first drawings. "Did you draw these?" he asked Finn over roof of the car.

"Yes.

"My daughter loves birds. I'll pin the pages to her wall."

"That'll be great," Mikolai said. "But you should have him sign the pages." He craned his neck toward the guard. "He's going to be famous someday, you know."

Being the Soviet Alger Hiss wasn't the fame Finn sought.

Laughing, the sergeant raised the book over his head to catch the light and fanned the pages. "I've changed my mind," he said. "I need money. How about you buy this back for a reasonable sum?"

"Money?" Mikolai said. "I'll get you money." And he hobbled off toward a cluster of Russian soldiers standing with their palms on the stocks of their rifles. He held out his hand to them. He struck the proper pose of offense and confusion when they laughed at him. Coming back, he dug in his pockets for a few crumpled bills. He disappeared for a second as if picking up one he'd dropped, then handed them to the guard.

The sergeant counted the money. "Nice try. It's not enough. The book is mine. Take your faggot professor back to Poland. And come again to the Motherland."

Tossing the car parts into the backseat, Finn stuffed his pique at losing Stalin's orders and all his notes. Without speaking, they drove a mile to a streetlight. Mikolai got out and popped the hood. Finn had forgotten about the vial of film he'd hidden.

"It's that easy," Mikolai said. "Totalitarianism is so paranoid about danger, it overlooks the worms that devour it from within."

Finn clutched the vial as if it were lifesaving medicine. "I guess all's not lost."

"Lost?" Mikolai reached into his coat pocket and pulled out the orders Finn had risked their lives to steal and ceremoniously laid them in Finn's lap. "They fell out when the guard was taunting you. Sorry about the dog stepping on them, but I think they'll still do the job."

"You're a master, Mikolai."

Mikolai shoved the car into gear.

Arriving in Warsaw after midnight, Finn was sorry to find himself standing by the car's passenger-side door across the street from his hotel. He wished Mikolai well with his nephew.

"I like to think," Mikolai said, "I've caused as much trouble for Russia as Andrei did to Poland." He waved and drove away.

FINDING NO ONE at the hotel desk—unusual, even at that time of night—Finn slipped behind the brass-edged counter and pulled his mail from the bank of slots for hotel guests. Clarissa had left multiple messages, asking where he was and demanding he call. Damn, she knew better. It was like waving a flag to apparatchik-minded Poles that something wasn't right.

He hoped his story to Sam Rich had covered his ass. There were several pieces of mail from the US, all steamed opened and resealed with no attempt to hide the violation. They were all dummies, sent by the *Times* from various locations, part of the cost of doing business in the Eastern Bloc.

His tossed-off bed covers hadn't been touched. He showered in tepid water, dressed, and went to the correspondents' phone bank. Sam Rich was working late.

"I'm much better, thank you," he replied to Sam's question. "How are things in New York?"

"With your talks being stuck, we're chasing fire trucks to find news."

"I doubt that, Sam. But listen, while I've been lying in bed these last days, I've come up with a draft placing these talks in context of the last fifty years—make that the last five centuries." He took a breath; he hated to deceive his boss, if only for a day. "I want to bring the draft in myself. There is someone at NYU I need to consult on the history. I'll make it a quick trip. I have a sense things are going to break here soon."

"Are the Russians going to come in? The *Tribune*'s editor is speculating they will."

"No one knows. Is there money for me to come over?"

Sam hemmed and hawed, then said, "You haven't been here for six months, is it? Get on a plane. I'll send someone to meet you."

"You won't regret it, Sam. I'll call you from Berlin when I know which flight."

Six

FINN KNEW THE PRICE for not calling Clarissa first thing in the morning. He resolved to pay it when seeing her face-to-face. After four hours sleep, he scribbled three pages of notes on his trip and checked out of the hotel. He took a taxi to the American Embassy, where in a short meeting with the first secretary, he prepared the Katyn film and his pages to go direct to New York under diplomatic pouch. It was to be delivered unopened to Sam Rich at the New York Times. Because the embassy phones were also bugged, he would wait until he got to Vienna to call Sam about the change in his itinerary.

A taxi dropped him at the central train station. He mingled in the ticket lines, made a show of needing a paper, and used it to ward off the light rain when he walked out another entrance. He had a cab drop him two blocks east of Solidarity's headquarters and walked cheerfully without looking back. Upon arriving in Warsaw, he had toured that building. Today he found renovations there in full swing. The front desk was operating inside a cubicle of plastic sheeting. He asked to see Mateusz Dabrowski.

Dabrowski came down and crunched Finn's shoulders in a bear hug. On the way back to his office, he dragged Finn into Wałęsa's suite for a quick meet-and-greet, everything off the record. Nothing was said of his trip into Russia—the expectation was any room in Poland could be bugged—but Wałęsa's expression of gratitude made it clear he had been informed. Up close, Wałęsa was under-proportioned for the damage he was doing to Communism.

"Are you carrying any Soviet souvenirs?" Wałęsa asked.

Finn inhaled to say *yes*, then stopped himself. "Nothing that should stay here."

Wałęsa shrugged like a boxer determined to go the distance. "Souvenirs don't last here very long. But I'd be happy to see what you have."

Finn slid Stalin's orders from his bag onto Wałęsa's desk. He and Dabrowski hovered over it. They wept as they read.

In Dabrowski's office, Finn laid Karol Sobczak's passport on the desk. "Is Mikolai here?"

Dabrowski hid his mouth with his hand. "Come and gone."

That was as Finn expected. "He hardly slept the whole time."

"I doubt he ever will. A number of people have always been interested in his whereabouts. By the way, he says you have promise as an actor."

"He's a good teacher," Finn said, "but I'm just a writer. He says he's headed to be a grandfather and read books."

Doubt crenulated Dabrowski's chin. "He slips out of his skins like a lizard."

"All the same," Finn said, "I want to send him something."

"I'll see that he gets it. In the meantime, we'll all await your article." Dabrowski wrote on a scrap of paper: *May it splatter on the Kremlin walls, like the blood of my countrymen. Russians are so fond of red!!!* After Finn read it, Dabrowski shredded it.

AT OKECIE AIRPORT, Finn booked a direct flight to Vienna. As he read a Polish journal in the lounge, a babushka plopped herself into the seat next to his. She pulled her several bags around her. She had runs in her thick hose and smelled of cabbage and sweat. She took ownership of the armrest between them. Finn felt her eyes. The question was coming.

"Where did you get those clothes?"

He focused on blackheads on her nose. "New York."

"You're a party big shot?"

Finn gave a practiced laugh. "An American journalist."

Her mouth made an impressed *O*. She looked around the room as if to see who might be watching. "Where'd you learn to speak Polish like that?"

"At home like you did. Where are you going?"

From the belt of her coat, she pulled a kerchief the size of a small tent. She waved its germs to the room and blew her nose. "Vienna, like you."

Unnerved, he returned to reading his journal.

"I'd think you would want to go to New York," she said. "The best city in the world. I've always wanted to go."

Defend, deny, distract, he thought. "Too many murders. What takes you to Vienna?"

She fingered food out of a crevice in a back molar. "I buy fabric for a dress factory."

Most Poles could only afford black cotton goods like she was wearing.

"We ship everything to Moscow for all the beauties there."

Was her laugh forced? She clicked her tongue with derision at her lot in life.

"I'd love to work in Moscow," he said. "But it's hard getting posted there." He lifted his bag onto his lap. "Change makes people nervous, don't you think?"

"Change," she said, "is rehearsal for death."

He stood and pointed to a stall in the distance. "I need another paper."

"But what's in Vienna?" She grabbed for his jacket, but he was off.

Down the concourse he ducked into the bathroom. Coming out, he scanned where he'd been sitting. The old woman was gone. Probably secret police. Hopefully just one of the battalion of scanners assigned to snare illegal émigrés and other enemies of the state. He would include this in a story soon. He traced his day backwards to see if he'd been sloppy. Poles monitoring the tapped hotel phone lines would have heard him tell Sam he would call from Berlin. Had she guessed Vienna was his destination? Faking a phone call in a booth, he slid Stalin's orders upside-down into the middle of his journal.

Waiting in line to board, he half-expected to be pulled out. He prepped a story about Clarissa not being well. That was true enough. With his foot he nudged his bag toward the checkpoint, while pretending to read his journal. The boarding guard copied his name from the passport onto a manifest and let him through. The old woman wasn't on the plane.

Lifting out of the grey air that had enveloped Warsaw since he'd arrived in early February, Finn felt as light as he had the night he met Dabrowski and for all the same reasons. This might be the last flight where he went unrecognized. When the story came out, his colleagues would both cheer and be depressed. He knew that ambivalence very well, having seen other journalists land great stories. He wondered if his mother would celebrate. She'd warned him not to follow in his father's footsteps. Now he understood more the warp and weft of her dread. But Clarissa's father, Albert Fortier—Fortie to his friends—would celebrate the news. Clarissa's response? He didn't know.

As soon as the plane reached cruising altitude, it began its descent. Out the starboard windows, Finn saw the tops of Vienna's buildings catching late afternoon rays of sun. He disembarked into the new concourse, a place not far from Warsaw, but another world. Voices rang with frivolity. Even people who hurried toward customs did so with a sense of delight. Dressed in darker clothes and dragging the burden of oppression, Poles pouring from his gate reminded him of a muddy tributary joining the clearer waters of the Danube as seen from the air. Once out of customs, he changed złoty to schillings and dialed the Fortier home. He had his apology ready.

Clarissa answered. Hearing his voice, she inhaled in chunks. "Your excuse better be good. I thought you were dead."

"It is."

"But not something to share with the Secret Police?"

"It's complicated. Have you eaten?"

"I'm here alone. Fortie's out with colleagues. Lately, he's starting to act like his old self."

"How about I pick up something on the way?"

"No." Her voice was feistier than he'd heard in a long while. It echoed in the stairway hall where the main phone sat. "Meet me at Figlmueller. I'll get a table overlooking the river. I have news, too."

"I've got to call Sam, but I'll make it short."

As the phone rang in New York, he breathed relief. For the first time in weeks they could speak freely.

"You're in Berlin?"

"No, Vienna. I had to bluff, but the important thing *is* coming to you. The State Department will call about a diplomatic pouch. Don't let it sit. There are pictures in there that will strip the Kremlin's gears."

"Kremlin? That will make the publishers happy. What's coming?"

"A roll of film. Have Stevens develop it. He's the best. Then hire a Russian translator, one who knows what *confidential* means."

"Hints?"

"Stalin with his pants down."

"Stalin's a dinosaur. Extinct."

"*And* twenty thousand bodies in the mud that nobody wants to take credit for."

"You have the pictures? Holy God!"

"Better. I have the orders, Sam. He's busted. Fifty years of denial is about to come unraveled. I'll be writing the story in the next few days."

"That's not front-page stuff. Who's going to care at this late date?"

"Who? The Russians. Germans on both sides of the Wall. The Poles, who, as we speak, have everything to gain." When Sam was silent, he said, "You'll see."

"And printing this won't ruin the talks?"

"It'll save them. You've got a page of history coming. You should have the pictures possibly as early as tonight. I'll call in the morning. Don't tell anybody until we talk this through."

WHILE THE MAÎTRE D' checked Finn's suitcase, Finn eyed Clarissa taking in the Danube at dusk. Her hair was down. She was wearing a black silk dress with a plunging back. Treading softer than the house music, he checked again the fit of his happy husband mask, one who hadn't slept with another woman since last seeing his wife. He reviewed his answers to the first five questions she would ask. After that, he could engage her in real time. He set his shoulder bag behind her chair. At the touch of his hands on her shoulders, she stiffened. Then just as quickly, reaching behind her one-handed, she gripped a fistful of his hair, pulled his head over her shoulder and rolled her mouth to meet his. She gave him the deepest kiss he could remember.

When she released him, her mouth hung huge and red.

"I'm sorry," he said.

"Don't be. Kissing's like riding a bicycle. You'll get it back. "

"I mean for not calling you." He tipped his head. "Was my kiss that bad?"

She turned his chair out with her foot. "You'll have a chance to make it up. Wine?"

"Anything but vodka."

"Tired of Poland, huh?"

"Tired of work. Half the time I have to drink for stories."

"Urchins sing for supper," she said. "Journalists drink for ledes."

She summoned the wine steward and tapped an entry on the wine list. "A bottle."

"Excellent choice, Madame."

While waiting for him to be gone, Finn wondered what would be the best way to get her to stop drinking. "That's an expensive one."

She jabbed her finger at the air between them. "My mother just went through hell to teach us all that life is short."

"How's Fortie doing? Really?"

"You don't want to know how I'm doing?"

"I can see how you're doing. I almost don't recognize you."

"That's good, isn't it?"

"You're hard to improve upon."

"Bull! We both know I haven't been myself. Not for a long while."

"Because you loved your mother, and there was nothing you could do."

She nodded. "My father's started taking care of her orchids."

"That's kind of a steep climb to begin with, isn't it?"

"He's a high achiever."

"Like father, like Clarissa."

"Would you like me better if that weren't true?"

None of the questions she was asking were on his list. He knew he couldn't reveal where he'd been, but her self-possession toyed with his desperation to tell somebody.

"You don't have to answer that," she said.

The waiter took their orders. Fresh salads landed without a sound. Clarissa ate as if the leaves guaranteed eternal life.

He poised his fork above his plate. "I like you just fine."

"Good," she said, her mouth full. "We're married."

"I've missed you."

"Just lately? You've seemed distant since we came to Vienna."

"It's been hard, watching her go."

She shook her head to change the subject. "I may want to stay here for a while."

"You don't want to go back to Rotterdam?"

"It's just a thought. My mother's buried in St. Stephen's. My father's clear he's not moving. And I was raised here. If I have healing to do, this is a great place. A great time."

Finn gulped his wine, hoping for the rush of vodka.

"Sam has wised up that you belong in Eastern Europe. And Vienna is an air hub." She slid the fingers of her right hand down the "V" of her front and his eyes burrowed for the curve of her breast. "Every city has flights to every other one."

He had to slow her down somehow. "So how *are* you?"

"I think I'm over my—all that dashing around in Holland. It's like I had the flu."

Finn thought of her languishing thesis and the nights of frustrated tears. She'd been right. Who, really, would care about how Ottoman trading routes affected the High Period of Byzantine Art?

He saw the letters from her advisor at Rotterdam's University piling up unopened, saw her coming home exhausted from volunteering for disadvantaged youth in the schools, saw her at the sink scrubbing paint off her hands from her stint apprenticing for a madcap silkscreen artist south of Amsterdam, remembered the pans of spices burned beyond service when she was studying Iranian cooking.

"I'm doing all the talking. Do you have any news?"

"I write news."

Her mouth tightened in chagrin. "I set myelf up for that one."

He let go a breath he didn't know he held. "That was uncalled for. I'm sorry."

She paused, then eyed him sweetly. "How am I? I'm ready to settle down."

They sipped their wine. Boats moved on the Danube. Silverware clicked on plates. Vienna's well-to-do spoke in hushed tones. The aromas of heavy German food.

"What day is it?" he asked.

"You're kidding, right? You know when editions are coming out around the world, and you want to know the day of the week? It's Tuesday, and I want you to remember the day and the date."

He fumbled in his coat for his boarding pass and made a shtick of being an old man trying to read it. He thought of Mikolai at the Polish border. "March fifteenth."

"Beware the Ides of March, Waters. The doctor says my numbers are up."

"Your blood count?"

"Well, yes, that, too. But I mean my hormone levels are back to normal. She says there's no reason that . . ." He wondered later why she hadn't just come out with it.

"You want to try again?"

Her nod made him think of a happy crocodile. "It will be good for my father, too," she said. "He especially needs to know that life goes on. We all do."

They hadn't talked about this for more than two years. Though she hadn't said so, he suspected that her clock running out had been contributing to her despondency. "Have you told anyone? Fortie?"

"No need to jinx it. I don't want him to get his hopes up unnecessarily. But I have plans for you tonight." She bobbed her brows.

He pointed at her uterus and questioned her with his eyes.

"Yes," she said. "I'm back on schedule."

Book Two

Vienna

Seven

Clarissa woke to wind in gusts and to rain strafing the casement window in the bedroom in which she'd spent her childhood. She woke to a wad of failure lodged over her heart. Seeking Finn's heat, and with it, another chance to have the night just past turn out differently, her hand probed the sheets. Finding them cold, she lurched onto an elbow and patted the bed. He was gone.

The pounding in her temples rolled her back down. Resting her wrist on her eyes, she relived their wild kissing on the taxi ride home. Every lick and suck confirmed they were going to make love. But after the taxi drove off with Finn's briefcase and he'd sprinted to catch it, his mood changed. In the room, he fussed forever with something in there —putting it away properly, he'd said.

The kicker was his blasé attitude at not getting hard and then cooing that everything would be all right, as if she was to blame. The last thing she remembered was cursing him under her breath. While wishing the bed to stop reeling, she stumbled across the jagged realization that turnabout was fair play. She'd refused him many times over the months when cancer was eating her mother in the room down the hall.

In a quiet spell of the wind, bursts of scratching, like a dragonfly trying to free itself from a spider web. She rolled toward the sound and cracked an eye, felt clobbered by the light. Finn was writing at her makeup table, pants on but no shirt or socks, bent over his yellow pad. Miles away, as if his plane flight yesterday had been her illusion, and she was dreaming of him working in Warsaw. That passion he had for things, she used to have it, too.

She thought back to their dinner. Yes, she'd been clear about wanting a baby again and about being in her fertile days. She might have prepared him a little better, but it wasn't like the subject was coming out of left field. They'd worked that out in therapy in Rotterdam. Just when he'd gotten over his hesitations, her mother had called with her diagnosis. All the cards had flown out of their hands. Two years ago. Now time was fleeing.

Hearing Finn's pen on a furious sprint, she allowed a glance. Gray light highlighted his musculature, flesh still taut from the bravado of youth. Yearning for him, she reached down and stroked herself where he had not. When a groan of sad relief escaped her, she froze, listening to see if he'd heard. If so, he didn't show it. That disappointed her more. He could hide like that behind the excuse of informing the world, and she'd never found a way to call him on it that didn't sound petty. Like her mother, she'd learned to take her husband's side to keep things civil. But the humiliation wouldn't leave her. Deep down she suffered a wracking feeling, like the joints in her skeleton were about to fail. As if to make room for a baby in her abdomen, she fisted her self-loving hand and pressed in hard.

"You're awake." Finn had spoken without looking over.

"I'm in Vienna," she said. "Are you here?"

Finn's writing hand flattened on the paper. His upper body rose up, but his eyes stayed on the page. "Not exactly."

"You look like you're writing to a lover." Hard, her tongue clicked in self-chastisement.

Finn sighed to the page. The seconds he made her wait smacked of cruelty. "That's how writing is."

The weight of the wine crushed her ability to come up with a rejoinder.

"Love letters to a future free of suffering," he said. He turned to her.

There he was, his own bold version of himself. He must have been awake for hours to dredge up something that poetic. The wave of what she loved about him beyond his body and his voice rolled over her. He was grand, a manifestation almost opposite to her father. Albert Fortier and his kind were the barges that steamed up and down the river of ambition. Finn and his journalist colleagues were the locks on that waterway. At times, these two men in her life needed each other. At others, mistrust took oxygen from the room. Though lately, death had taken some of the fight out of her father.

She swallowed. Her mouth tasted like metal. "How can you manage to be cogent with a hangover?" Anything to keep him talking and her mood from ruining the moment.

"Discipline." Rain on the sash distracted him a moment. He turned back to her. "But ask me after I've sobered up whether this is any good."

"You said you were going to cut back on drinking."

His cheek balled in amusement. "Alcohol is ante to being in the game."

If he was going to be in his head, the bed wasn't a safe place to linger. She rose and with an angry flourish made a toga for herself out of the top sheet, then winced as the bedside lamp crashed to the floor. Stepping over pieces, the weightlessness of death came again. Sometimes the bliss of permanent nonexistence called to her.

Though the tipping of the room demanded most of her attention on the way to the shower, she saw the sheaf of pages he had filled. The latch clicked behind her. And she breathed. On the sill outside the high window, a pigeon huddled from the storm. She identified with its plight.

Her eyes disobeyed her command to avoid her reflection in the mirror. How self-doubt ruined the promise she'd seen there just twelve hours ago. Without it, age was upon her. Time had tricked her. Daughter of an ambassador, educated in Swiss boarding schools, an academic scholarship to Stanford. Marrying the son of Jordan Waters, *the* Jordan Waters of the *Boston Globe* and the *Christian Science Monitor*.

Having closed the train of the sheet in the door, it stayed behind as she turned from the sink. A glimpse of her naked self, still not enriched by childbirth. Waiting for the water to warm, she prayed the disappointments that enveloped her life would wash off.

The hot water did her good. She finished with a blast of cold that brought back some of her thirst for life. As she toweled off, she considered Finn was only home for three or four days. Maybe last night, his failure *had* been the alcohol. Or fatigue. He'd said he hadn't been sleeping much. She cinched herself into the towel and stooped for the sheet. It was gone. She found Finn making the bed, and managing a smile, finished the ritual with him. He had already straightened up the makeup table, his pages tidy and his pad on top, to hide the work. That's how he was until pieces were finished.

"You've been up a long time."

"The light woke me," he said. "I'm pushing to get a piece out."

"Is Poland getting free?"

He shook a shirt from his bag to life, put it on, and concentrated on the buttons. "Don't know," he said. "But I took an interesting side trip."

"Is that why you didn't call?" She stepped into a pair of silk panties, worked her breasts into a bra.

"I was out of the city." He caught her tracking his movements. "It's politics."

"Everything you report on is politics."

He shrugged—meaning, he agreed. "But this is different. You'll see."

As they got ready to leave the room, he held her, though not long enough to dispel the sense of loss from the night. How had she let him get away?

"Are we ready to handle your father?"

"He's been a lamb the last few days."

Finn grunted. "The wolf who wore fleece the whole time we were engaged?"

At the upper landing he put a finger to his lips. The voices of old men downstairs.

"He'd said he was determined to have company this morning," she whispered. "I'm glad he followed through."

The resonant voice of Herr Schneider rumbled up the stairwell. “But there’s a chance, Fortie. And if they do, the Stasi will be scrambling like rats from a burning ship.”

A voice Clarissa couldn’t name. “That’ll be a god-awful mess. If Jews examine every painting, the price of art worldwide will be tossed into the wind.”

She squeezed Finn’s hand at her father’s laugh. “Gentlemen, don’t forget. Every disaster presents an opportunity. Art forgers will be working around the clock.”

From the laughter that followed, it seemed there were at least six people down there. A wavering voice broke through. “Why forgers, Fortie? And why is that a good thing?”

“Good, bad. Who’s to say?” Her father sounded close to his old stride. “But I tell you this: Men with prized art collections won’t want to explain to their wives why some of their favorite paintings have suddenly disappeared.” Another round of laughter. “I assure you, the most unpleasant appraisal for an international art collector is . . .” he had the timing of a standup comic sometimes. “*Guilty*.”

Coughing and a few handclaps.

“Imagine if the World Court gets involved.” The voice of the old entrepreneur Herr Meissner. “Germany’s coffers can‘t handle those reparations.”

Finn dropped his chin to his chest a moment, then tugged her hand to head down. They hadn’t gone five steps before being discovered. As the stairwell header revealed the legs of men sitting in the parlor, a fellow with a cane budged himself forward in his chair. “Fortie,” he said, “it appears you have company.”

Her father was first into the main hall. She liked that he extended his drink hand to her and Finn and the other toward his company, the mediator bringing parties together. A blue blazer and tie. The stars and stripes pin on his lapel riding atop his ambassador pin. A chorus of good-natured groaning, feet scuffing the floor and bodies tottering upright.

"Look at the gorgeous guy I found last night," she said. "He was looking for a meal."

Her father looked at Finn. "I had no idea you were—"

"Papa, I left you a note on the kitchen counter."

Her father searched for words. "I haven't been—Gentlemen, you all know my son-in-law, Finn Waters."

Too late, Finn gestured like a traffic cop. "Please, stay where you are."

"Mostly by reputation, Albert," said Commandant Wolff. "The wunderkind correspondent from the *New York Times*." Though retired, Wolff was sporting his full police regalia—ribbons and medals. As if ready for a photo op, his hat was tucked under his arm.

Herr Schneider's eyebrows perched on his forehead like little grey ducks. "Yes, that objectionable little rag intelligent readers open to learn what tomorrow's rumors will be."

Clarissa sensed Finn's chuckle didn't cover his irritation.

"I'd love to catch whoever thought liberals should be trusted with public discourse," Fortie said.

"Papa, he's just arrived."

"Yes, darling, which is the best time to see what he's made of."

A potbellied man with a gleaming brown toupee pooh-poohed that notion. "I, for one, haven't had the pleasure of meeting him. Good to see you, young man. Charles Goodwin. I'm not quite like these fellows. I'm from Iowa."

"Which explains everything about him," said Herr Mosheim.

The men she knew kissed her on the cheek. She introduced them to Finn.

"We're sorry to interrupt," Finn said.

"Yes, Papa, please continue with your . . ." her cheeks got hot, "whatever." Finn shook her father's hand last. He slapped Finn's shoulder. All seemed well.

"You've heard," her father said, "the new ambassador has arrived?"

"Really? How do you feel about that?"

"Britcher, Edmund Britcher. I introduced him to President Waldheim at my retirement dinner. He's quite fluent, which always goes a long way. But you know that."

"Your German's fine, Papa."

"Then tell me why are we all speaking English here?"

"Stop," she said. "Waldheim's always loved you."

"As well he should," said Wolff. At this point they had all drifted back through the archway into the parlor. Finn turned as if to get free.

"Waters," said Herr Meissner, "what's the latest from Warsaw? You don't think they'll give Solidarity the time of day, do you?"

Her father crossed the room and took a position by the big fireplace on the parlor's far wall. "Willem, let's let the young people go."

"No, Fortie. That's really all we're talking about here. And he's been there. *New York Times* or not, he's closer than we are."

Finn scrunched his lips in thought. Clarissa anticipated how her husband might plow the ground under the feet of this older generation. "If I knew the future," he said, "I'd quit my job. But so far, the government's dusting off its old tricks, hoping people will cower, and everyone will go back to being agreeably depressed."

The room grew quiet. Clarissa found her hand on Finn's back, felt the cable of muscle along his spine. In her gesture, she saw her mother and remembered her voice resonating against the wood of this same hall. Being there for her father, never complaining. A noble sentinel. The cancer had seemed a rebuke to all that. She had never followed through on her own desires. Clarissa had to think about what they even were. Art, she'd just dabbled. And tennis, she'd played doubles when her father entertained diplomats who brought their wives. Cooking. Mothering.

"But what's different now," Finn said, "is the government has nothing to fall back on. The country is broke."

Meissner took a small step forward. "But Gorbachev will send—"

"No, sir. That would be a disaster on so many levels. The Russians are broke, too."

"But their troops are there. So what's the problem with sending them west? I guess my point really is that the Poles are skilled at losing."

Finn's jaw rocked to the side. He tongued an eyetooth. She patted his back and was pleased when he took an easy breath.

"Yes, sir. The troops may come. And if they do, Poland will fold. They have nothing to fight with. But I should remind you it wasn't long ago that in a similar situation Austria resisted the Führer for about an hour and half. So how is that different?"

Throats cleared, portending rebuttal, but none came.

Clarissa stepped forward, forcing a smile. "Of course, my husband's just a journalist. And you all have your crystal balls. We'll have to wait to see who's right. I just hope the people don't suffer too much."

To break the silence, Fortie called across the room, "It's good to have you home, son. We'll catch up later."

Eight

IN THE KITCHEN Clarissa slipped out of her shoes. She sat on a stool by the island and tucked one foot under her. Finn was opening cupboards, grumbling, looking like he wanted to kick something. At last he found the skillet.

"Eggs for you?" he asked, looking into the refrigerator.

"I'll eat the fish leftover from lunch yesterday. On the middle shelf. I took him to Strüebers. Like I said, he's been undone."

"I sure as hell couldn't tell."

"Being with friends puts him back in the groove. It's good to see."

"The only one *I'd* care to chat with was the old guy with the cane."

"The one that didn't say much?"

"Yes. Fewer stupid statements."

"Don't be so hard on them. Austrians still have their tails between their legs."

"It's been fifty years. Fifty years *without* an apology." He gathered a mixing bowl and a whisk. "So do you want to talk about last night?"

She slithered from her stool, poured orange juice into a crystal wine goblet, replaced the carton in the refrigerator, and took a long drink. "The food was good, don't you think?"

One corner of his mouth reflected the irony she was trying to avoid; the other showed exasperation. "I guess neither of us does," he said.

"When are you flying out?"

"Sam wants me there Thursday."

"Just two more nights?" She heard her own pique.

"I told you that."

"No, you didn't."

"I did. You've just forgotten."

"Was it before I kissed you at the table?" she asked. "Because after that, you weren't thinking clearly."

He cracked an egg on the bowl edge, thinking. Then he said, "It was a good kiss."

She dropped her chin and looked at him through her brows. "Just *good*?"

He locked eyes with her and deftly parted the shell. The egg took its place on the counter beside the bowl, staring at the ceiling like a bright yellow breast.

"Actually," he said, "it was inspired."

"On the other hand," she said, "your egg technique could use a brush up."

Seeing his mistake, he barked "Christ," louder than he needed and cast about for a scooper. He settled on a butcher's knife and cut underneath the egg, driving it into the fleshy part of his free palm. Clarissa drank again, watching him around the rim of her glass. When he raised his hands toward the bowl, she saw he'd cut through the yolk and it was leaking all over. She waited while he hovered.

"I need your help, Clarissa." His young-boy voice.

How quickly life gave her another chance. "Okay, if you'll agree to talk about us."

"Deal. I need a sponge."

Her father backed through the swinging door with glasses on a tray and sized up the situation. "Looks like you botched that transaction, Finn." He slid the *Washington Post* under his arm, his jaw contorted as when an opponent double faults to lose the set. She couldn't tell if Finn caught that look, but she was happy to see it again. She padded to the sink, returned with a dishrag, wrapped his hands, the knife, and the egg and ushered him to the sink. "Do your friends need anything?" she asked.

"They've left. I'm on my way to the embassy club with Meissner and Mueller. We're going to attempt squash."

"Squash? It's been a while, Papa."

"September, I think. The day your mother vomited blood for the first time."

For a moment she regretted that assaulting a parent was a crime. "Go easy, then," she said.

He gave her a thoughtful look. "Mmm. Sometimes you sound just like her."

She wondered what Finn thought of that. He was at the sink, his back to her.

"What are your plans today, you two?"

She saw the brass ring, reached for it. "Finn and I were just discussing moving to Vienna . . . permanently."

AS SOON AS the Rolls started in the garage, Finn lit into her. "When were we going to discuss this?"

She wiped the counter down and rinsed the rag. "We talked about it last night. Right after you made love to me. I was in your arms in the afterglow and I told you I wanted to put money on an apartment."

"We didn't—"

His torn look gave her great satisfaction. She stared him down, balling the rag in both hands. "I know you, Waters. You weren't so drunk that you couldn't get it up."

Finn inhaled and set his shoulders. "I'm writing the greatest story ever."

"And I'm next in line to the throne in Monaco. Is your article too goddamn great to give me fifteen minutes of your hormonal best?"

When his eyes went to Warsaw—or somewhere—she caught him square in the face with the rag. He didn't flinch. After a few seconds his mouth flattened as when getting a joke. He glanced at her sideways, skin flushed, and not with anger. "Batter, take your base," he said.

"You've been gone a month, and you're here for only two more days." She picked up the butcher knife and waved the point at him. "We moved to Rotterdam for you. Though my father can be a ball-breaking, pinch-eyed Republican, he's held down this corner of the empire for going on forty years. The sad truth is his kitchen skills make yours look cordon bleu, so he needs me here. Now for once we're going to do what *I* want."

They communicated across the kitchen island with breath alone—she, as if she'd just crossed a finish line. Finn, slow, restrained.

"You're hardly home, anyway. What difference does it make? Your friends—such as you let anybody close—are in rooms down the hall in whatever hotel you happen to be. But I still have friends here from school."

Seeing him not cranking out counterarguments, she leaned her forearms on the island and clasped her hands, took a few breaths to calm down. "I've loved you since your father held me in his lap and told me he had a beautiful little boy at home. My father loving him just made me love you more. If we're going to make it, it's time for us to figure out what we're about."

Finn was nodding, his eyes not there. She hoped he was reviewing all the turns in the road that had sealed their fates.

"If you have a great story, fine!" She rolled her palms to the ceiling and shrugged. "But I'm at a point where I've got to start putting things back together for myself. We both know this thing that's been eating me preceded my mother's illness." She laid her hands on the island like a pianist preparing for a solo. Her voice dropped to a whisper. "I don't know what it is. Maybe it's your success."

She liked that he huffed in self-derision. At least he was paying attention.

"I'm a thoroughbred, Finn, but I've got shin splints. If I'm going to be worth anything, I need care." Finn was looking at her, his every cell listening. "I chose you and . . . you chose me."

His gaze slipped to the right, miles away.

"Now we've both lost a parent. I'm getting an idea of what you live with. Maybe we can come together over this."

He was up, moving. Yes, coming toward her. What had taken him so long? No matter. He came to her humble, looking for forgiveness. Her arguments fled like vapors. She rose and turned square to him like a plant to the sun. His hands hooking her waist, hers resting on his chest, soft but ready to push him away if he screwed up.

Sometimes his lips on her forehead meant he was dismissing her argument. This time they went deep. “You’re right,” he said. “More than you know.”

She spoke to the hollow at the base of his neck. “I’ll take that as a down payment on restitution for last night.”

“I’m sorry.” He kissed her eye. “Sorry that being a prick is part of my job. I’m not wild about leaving the Netherlands. But our future’s going to change. And you’re going to love it.”

Was he gloating?

“So let’s eat,” he said, “and then see if Vienna has a decent place for us.”

Clarissa shook his shoulders like a scolding schoolmarm. “Tell me you haven’t forgotten where we started.”

“You mean Stanford?”

She flat-handed his chest. The echo bounced off the tiled surfaces of the kitchen. “We’re not discussing apartments until you remember your instructions. Say you don’t need me to write them out for you.” She nudged his belt with the soft mound of her belly. “And just so you know, we’re going there with no net. I am ready. Got it? Ripe. And you and my father need this as much as I do. Now take me upstairs and make love to me like you mean it.”

AFTER, CLARISSA LAY satisfied in body and soul, wishing his sperm Godspeed. But before they rose, she negotiated away some of her day. He had to write, he said, and proved it by looking at his papers on the makeup table. He needed privacy. Four hours. He was emphatic. And he had to call his editor at two. That still left them three hours for apartment hunting before going to St. Stephen’s with her father to light candles to mark four weeks since her mother died. “Fine. But know I’m taking you with me to inoculate me from that Catholic mumbo jumbo.”

So it was set. They got up this time the way she had seen it in her mind when he'd called from the airport and she'd hustled to the restaurant. While Finn wrote, she called around to apartment rental agencies and private owners. At two-thirty, they took her car to the northwest quarter of Vienna.

It would be some days before she realized her handicap in the search. Intuitively, she compared every apartment to the one-of-a-kind mansion her father bought right after the war when the dollar was king, a three-story stone house with a slate roof and swooping eves. It was set back from the street behind a small arboretum, the whole place a charming anomaly to the six-story buildings favored by nineteenth century city planners from Paris to Moscow. The cardinal who requisitioned that house also secured land across the street for a single-block park. Compared to that, none of the apartments Clarissa and Finn looked at stood a chance.

They got home thirty minutes late. Her father was pacing the parlor with a drink in his hand. Blue suit. Shiny black shoes. His mood wasn't good. Traffic and road construction delayed them more. They arrived minutes before the end of the evening mass.

As the recessional organ music played, her father grimaced. "Jacqueline deserves better." Chastened, Clarissa and Finn allowed him to walk them up the center aisle against the flow of worshippers filing out. He settled them in the pew fronting on the nave and disappeared, returning a few minutes later with the assistant priest. "Father Gabriel has agreed to give us what Jacqueline loved so much." The priest stood in front of their pew and launched into Latin with a German accent.

Clarissa whispered into Finn's ear. "Twenty-third Psalm."

Next the priest sang a German hymn in a beautiful baritone. Her father's shoulders dropped as if releasing a great weight. She was surprised that she'd never seen him carry it. Finn looked up as if following the notes into the vast recesses. He stroked her hand, and at one point, wiped the bud of a tear from her eyes.

The priest bade them kneel, spread his hands, and tilted his head back to pray. Her skin rippled with emotion when he called out Jacqueline Fortier by name and gestured to the vaulted space as if she were hovering there. Wondering if Finn was feeling anything, she glanced over. Amazed to see his head bowed and his hands in the prayer position, her frame jolted at the sound of a gunshot cutting through the reverberations and echoes.

Sweat beaded on her skin, and she warded off her worst fear: Finn dying in a foreign land. When none of the men seemed disconcerted, she doubted what she'd heard and focused again on the priest singing. She cast her eyes above the stained glass windows, hoping to find her mother. She saw only shadows.

BY THE TIME they left the cathedral, Clarissa had managed, with the voice of their therapist from Rotterdam in her ear, to dismiss hearing the gunshot as a mental upsurge prompted by an overwrought emotional state. At the house, she composed herself to cook dinner for the men. They would discuss events of the world in the parlor, the one situation where they seemed best suited to be alone together. She delivered a bowl of mixed nuts and lit the candelabrum on the little table between the parlor chairs where they sat.

She dry-mixed the batter for the dessert of crepe suzette, poured herself some wine, and tuned the radio to a recording of Mozart's Jupiter symphony. She put a salad in the refrigerator, prepared shrimp, garlic, julienne carrots, and parsnips to bake for the entrée.

After setting the casserole to cool, she slipped up the servant's stairs to her room. She put on the white silk blouse Finn had purchased for her before heading to Poland in advance of the talks. It was a rare gift, both in his buying it and in its design. The off-shoulder cut and the bowed line of the front drew the eye to some of her best features: her clavicles, her shoulders, and her cleavage—*the sacred triangle*, Finn called it. Before going down she stooped to look into her makeup mirror, rewound her hair, and pinned it up with needles Japanese-style, leaving the tail loose as was fashionable in other parts of Europe at the time. The block of Finn's papers sat there, so like him, organized and hidden. She manipulated the corner as if counting the sheets, then shrugged and flipped the stack over.

REDS CAUGHT RED-HANDED

Stalin's Imperfect Burial

The US State Department announced late yesterday it now has indisputable proof that, in 1940, Stalin's secret police, the NKVD, executed half of Poland's army officers in a Russian forest. American University Soviet scholar Joshua Blankfeld confirmed the authenticity of an original copy of Stalin's orders, which came through the New York Times.

"Stalin's trademark red ink signature is sprawled across the page," Blankfeld said. "We've finally nailed him." [Get Blankfeld involved ASAP/see if he'll okay this quote from himself.]

Though officials have not revealed how they obtained the document, those who have seen the text call it chilling. As if talking about slaughtering hogs for market, the two-page document gives explicit orders to murder 21,857 prisoners of war, which is a war crime under the rules of the Geneva Convention.

Nazi troops advancing on Moscow in 1943 brought the crime to light. On a tip from local people, they excavated seven deep trenches in the Katyn forest and discovered the bodies of more than 4,400 uniformed soldiers, from three-star generals down to sergeants. Though the rest of the officers were murdered in nearby areas, all five sites are known as the Katyn Massacre. Hitler and Stalin each accused the other of the crime. And until now, guilt has never been established.

Hitler realized pinning the crime on the Soviets could drive a wedge between them and the Allied Forces, giving advantage to his army. He invited representatives of France and England, along with a few American POWs, to see the butchery and to inspect the documents that had been found on the bodies. Unsent letters and diary entries indicate the soldiers died in early April, 1940.

Stalin insisted that when his army retreated toward Moscow in late 1942, they released Polish prisoners and that they set out west toward their homes in Poland and the Nazi lines. He enumerated previous Nazi massacres and contended the documents had been altered to obfuscate the truth. His testimony was strengthened by the discovery that the soldiers were shot in the back of the head using German-made Walther P38 pistols.

This set of orders proves beyond doubt Stalin was lying.

Lost in fifty years of denials has been the suffering of the officers' families in Poland who still mark the anniversary with marches calling for an impartial investigation of the event. Until now their pleas have fallen on deaf ears.

Could Square the Round Table Talks

According to __________ [get a quote from Kalmbach or Gooley] *of the Brookings Institution, the timing of this discovery couldn't be better for the Polish people. It could have a dramatic impact on the Round Table Talks in Warsaw, Poland. The Polish government of Wojciech Jaruzelski, a proxy for the Kremlin's intentions, is in negotiations with the Solidarity Labor Union, which is seeking basic rights offered in democratic societies.*

Clarissa drew a sharp breath and reset the pages. She'd meant only to read the headline to get a sense of where Finn dwelled when his eyes went fuzzy and was scratching with his pens. The story had sucked her in.

Without contemplating why he was writing this, she understood his hurry. The *New York Times* thrived because it demanded all its journalists to be first, to be respectful of sources, and most of all, to be accurate. She suspected accuracy was why he'd spent twenty minutes on the phone with Sam Rich before they'd gone apartment hunting, calling from her father's study. Sam, the old news dog, had an aura of omniscience, which still caused Finn to speak of him in revered tones.

Giddy from having peeked into Finn's world and from the wine, she returned to her project. She finished setting the table in the formal dining room, dressed the salad, and wet-mixed the crepe batter. In showers of joy her mind turned to his sperm, the waves of it twirling and pulsing at that very moment toward her egg, the bull's eye that floated in the existential dark.

When all was ready, she refilled her glass, slipped into her high heels that had waited for this entrance, and clicked her way down the wood floors to the front of the house. As the music faded behind her, she listened for male voices. Hearing nothing, she slowed and passed beneath the parlor arch. Confused that their chairs were empty, she scanned the room from right to left. Just as she located two figures by the bookcase, her mind, the room, and the night lit up with a brilliant realization.

Nine

FROM FINN'S POINT of view, his unleashed sex with Clarissa had burned off the dark cloud between them. Their cries and laughter had echoed off the hardwood paneling. For him, the tension of holding a secret about to become public supercharged his drive to communicate with her through the physical—mouth to mouth and pelvis to pelvis.

That release carried over into progress on his article. When he called Sam Rich in New York at 9 a.m. East Coast time, he was bursting with confidence. Sam grabbed his call as if it were the last blintz at a bar mitzvah.

"Waters, I have a brilliant Slavic historian from NYU in my office, and in spite of feeling intimidated by his brain, I'm trying to figure out our next move."

"He's translated it?"

"He knew what it was in ten seconds. But sad to say, he's had to spend the last twenty minutes walking me through some buried history. Bad pun! Bad pun! Something like this appears once a decade. It's an amazing document. The Pentagon Papers comes to mind. Before my time, dammit."

"The Pentagon Papers didn't just appear, Sam. Ellsberg smuggled them out."

"But, but, but, my little hero! You understand I can't print this until the State Department considers the policy ramifications." Sam paused. "Professor Menschev is nodding vigorously."

"I'm working on that with contacts from my end. Josh Blankfeld and I were at Stanford together. But if they dawdle, Sam, we can get around them if we have to. We only have to print a few lines to let the

Russians know we've got the orders. A photograph could show the top of the page and the date. The article is the thing. I've already drafted it. But hear me out. There's another crucial aspect to this story. Are you on speakerphone? Because I don't think the professor should be privy to this."

"I'm on a handset. Fire away."

"Get your mind around this. Both of my sources inside the Soviet Union—the prison guard who did the killing and the commandant of the camp—said the guns came from the Americans. I didn't prompt them. German guns came into Russia through American channels."

There was a long pause.

"Sam, do you realize how big that makes the story?"

"Huge," Sam said. "If that's true, it's political uranium. Gut feeling? We'll take it one part at a time. That thing you said could come out later, you know, through 'further investigation.' We'll need proof. Don't worry. I want this as bad as you do. I'll submit Stalin's orders to State within the hour, and I'll push them to decide ASAP. They're not stupid; they'll know what this is. My guess is they'll love it. It can only weaken the Soviets. State might hiccup on the second thing. I won't mention it to them until we have proof. Getting it wrong could get us long vacations in a federal prison in Nebraska. On the orders, if they object to some aspect of them, I'll find out what we *can* print. They may have national security concerns in the short term. Who knows what kind of cake they're cooking on the diplomatic front this week? But I don't think we'll have a problem. Let's talk tomorrow, or worst case, the day after."

"Don't leave me hanging, Sam. Remember, Solidarity needs this stick to keep the Russians home. So keep kicking State or it doesn't do Solidarity any good. It'd be god-awful if the Russians come in while State is weighing its decision. Solidarity wants something tangible before I head back there. We can't let them down."

"Got it, Waters. Keep your bias out of the way. Write your article. Better yet, write me several treatments. Let's be ready for anything they throw back. There's a Pulitzer in this. For you and, God love ya, maybe even for me, too. The executive editor's going to pas de deux."

Pulitzer. Sam had actually said it. Money would flow. He wouldn't have to take infusions of cash from Fortie any more to "properly care for Clarissa."

The apartment hunting turned out to be a bust; Finn hoped that would be a sign for Clarissa to change her mind. But during the visit to St. Stephen's, the priest's voice soaring into the dome had made the hair on his arms stand up. Even if there was no God, the designers had created a space where the existence of such a force could at least be posited without sniggering.

As a boy in Rockport, he had twice been in the poorer cousin of that cathedral. A wood-sided box with a bell tower and a door flanked by struggling rhododendrons. On both Sundays the sun reflecting off the Atlantic had illuminated the interior, as if God was a force of water, rather than of sky.

While Clarissa cooked dinner, he and Fortie settled in the parlor chairs that faced the bay window, the street, and the park beyond. Fortie greased their talk with an impeccable single malt. When Finn found an opening, he shifted the conversation to Soviet troops on the border.

"It will be tragic if the people of Poland get overrun yet again."

"I'm surprised, Finn. A journalist, taking sides."

"Point taken, Albert." Finn honored the criticism by raising his glass. "My mother's blood poking through. Anyway, give me some context from the war years. You were here."

Fortie looked at him with his closest approximation of fondness. "I came here in February of '38. My father's idea: Shove Sonny Boy onto the distant horizon. If he survives, bring him home and put him in charge of something important."

"Hardly. You were head of Fortier Enterprises in Europe."

"Not at the start. Just Austria."

"How would you compare the Soviet threat to Vienna in '44 to Poland today?"

Fortie stared into his glass. "It's hard to say. Jacqueline and I left for nine months in '44. That was the worst time here. Different types of players back then. So much change since. Failed policies, technological advances." He looked up. "My God, they're making computers now that you can carry around."

Finn yearned for one of those but didn't want Fortie changing the subject. "Is there something about the Russian psyche that makes tyrants?" he asked. "Khrushchev was presumed the opposite of Stalin, then he rolled into Hungary." He paused two beats, thinking of his father. "Here's my question: Does Russian weakness make Gorbachev duty-bound to rumble west? Is there anything that could stop him? And if so, what might it be?"

Fortie looked at him sidelong. "These aren't journalists' questions."

"It's for background. Books only give you so much."

Fortie shifted his hips in the chair. "I'm *sore* from the squash. Amazing how quick the body goes when you're old." He grabbed both glasses and refilled them at the hutch. Returning, he laid Finn's on the table by the candelabrum. "It's Poland you're really asking about. I never had a good bead on that country. I was young, and Austria isn't a neighbor." He ambled to the floor-to-ceiling bookshelf to left of the fireplace, where he lifted the official photograph taken at Yalta. Coming back, he laid it in Finn's lap and put his finger on the face of a young Albert Fortier in the back row. "Look at that boy. He was clueless."

Finn knew the photograph. He knew the story Fortie would tell.

"Harry Hopkins, Roosevelt's chief of Lend-Lease with the Soviets, wanted free enterprise representatives in the party. It was for show, and I was available."

Fortie sat again. Finn placed the photograph glass-side down on the table.

"Why downplay its importance, Albert? Your presence there stamped your ticket into the diplomatic corps."

Fortie shrugged. "Twenty years later, I suppose. But in Yalta? I was naïve about what was going on. That's why I can't answer your questions better than you can yourself."

The scotch was opening Finn's pores. He knew his father-in-law was about ready to be driven where he wanted him to go. "You credit my father with introducing you to the finer points of politics."

Fortie paused to watch a fabric-spangled horse and multicolored wagon of a Roma family pass by the house. Lanterns swung from the wagon's frame. Something about Romas always seemed to set Fortie on edge. This time he just clicked his tongue. "Your father and I both had some of what the other wanted." He pointed to Finn's favorite picture also on the bookshelf. A small black and white one, a little grainy. Two men standing on a grassy hill. A village in the distance. Fortie and Finn's father as young men facing the photographer, arms over each other's shoulders.

Fortie sipped his drink. "How's your mother?"

"About the same, I guess."

"So you haven't talked to her."

Finn's elbow connected with the hard plastic case in his coat pocket. "I almost forgot. When we were out this afternoon, Clarissa and I came across a CD of your favorite composer. It's the *Best Of.*"

Fortie turned the cover to the candlelight. "Chopin. One of the few 'Bests' Poland has contributed to this world."

If nothing else, Fortie was predictable. "It's the complete etudes and nocturnes."

"Austrian pianists, I see. Thoughtful boy. You're covering all your bases." He pointed toward a shelf on the bookcase that held sound equipment. "Put it in for me, would you?"

Finn hesitated, and then rose. The discourse was slipping away. "A new system?"

"A gift from our new ambassador. The CIA probably told him I wasn't up-to-date."

"If it's any comfort, Fortie, I'm out of my league with this equipment, too."

Fortie cackled. "I grew up with the windup kind. There's a button, sends out a whirligig that can hold more discs than a man should own.

You just drop it in and it does the rest." He rose and came up behind Finn.

Finn hit the power button. Writing too small to see came up on the readout. The reflection of candles made things worse. As he leaned forward squinting, he heard the kitchen door swing and Clarissa's heels striking the hardwood floor. His expertise with microphones and cameras made being ignorant about the latest audio components all the more humiliating.

She was going to catch him there. Not just him. Two grown men stymied by what most young people could do without thinking. He turned to look at her. Embarrassment and scotch pulsed through the capillaries in his face. She had removed her apron and changed clothes from before. The candlelight danced on the silk of her blouse. The one he'd given her. Her skirt was black and tight. If their lovemaking that morning had made her pregnant, he thought she might not wear that many more times. She was holding a goblet of red wine. She had just finished sipping when she came to an abrupt halt, mouth slack, brows scrunched.

She scanned the room and found his eyes just as a force drove his body toward the bookcase. The spines of a thousand books lit up in a harsh light. Fortie's body slammed into him from behind, pushing Finn's temple into the CD player. The explosion came like cymbals and drums together. Heat on his check. The wine from Clarissa's goblet lifted and hung in space as if it would never land.

Ten

FRACTURED IMAGES. Thoughts that refused to lead or follow. Twenty seconds passed, perhaps more. Grit on the floor, too sharp to be sand, Fortie on top of him, coughing. From the stratosphere, high-pitched peals: Clarissa.

Through his unclouded right eye Finn saw her standing, her shoulder pitched against the wall of books, fingers splayed. Wide-eyed, she was staring at her blouse, stained in the same pattern as the wine Finn had seen hovering. "It's ruined, Papa." Her jugular veins stood out.

He pitched Fortie off of him. "Clarissa, have you been hit?"

"My favorite blouse is ruined."

Hooking an elbow over a shelf, he pried himself to standing.

Fortie got up, stumbled toward her, and tried to take the flexion out of her arms. "I've got you," he hollered. "I've got you."

Finn's cheek was numb. He patted it. The skin was still there. He tripped on a carved box that had fallen from a shelf. His eyes met hers. Her breath left her. He reached for her. Her lips contorted. Her chin shot to the side like a beaten dog's. Thrusting herself away from him, her eyes rolled back. She went limp and tumbled her father with her onto the Oriental carpet.

Fortie pulled himself from under her. Finn knelt, searched her for blood and broken bones. Her limbs lay normal. Somehow she had escaped the flying glass. He put his ear by her mouth, mystified that he couldn't remember the basics of CPR. At last, she breathed, a gasp followed by panting. Sweat poured off her temples. He screamed for Fortie to call an ambulance and dashed to the kitchen.

As he turned the cold-water spigot, he wondered how Soviet agents had caught up with him so fast. Blood, not much, swirled in the drain.

As he soaked two cloths, he traced the drops to a shard of glass stuck in his sideburn. Racing back to the parlor, he glanced at the bay window, half expecting commandoes to be pouring in. Lead mullions hung like oversized chainmail in their casement frames. Fortie was still kneeling, leaning over Clarissa.

"What the hell is the matter with you? Call an ambulance." He dropped to his knees and laid the cloths on Clarissa's head.

"She's mine," Fortie hissed. He reached across Clarissa and shoved Finn backwards. His head hit the floor, knocking his brain loose. Struggling to stay conscious, he got to his knees. Fortie's eyes were flashing. His hands were hovering over Clarissa's breasts.

Clarissa opened her eyes. She punctuated her hyperventilation with cries and whimpers, until at last, Finn's strokes on her forehead settled her. She reached for his arm. Both men watched her gather herself to speak. "I'm not yours," she said to Fortie in a frail voice. "I'm his."

After half a minute, Fortie seemed more like his regular self. He nodded to reassure her. She wiped her face with her sleeve and sat up. "I think I'm okay. What happened?"

Then Fortie wheeled and vomited. After spitting his mouth clear, he said, "I couldn't bear to lose her, not with Jacqueline just . . ." He didn't finish.

Finn's mind assessed conditions in widening arcs. He blamed Solidarity for enlisting him. Behind that was the fear that once the Kremlin was provoked, nothing could make it stop. Clarissa shook her head repetitively. She kept touching the floor as if to confirm she was sitting on it. When faces appeared in the frame of the bay, her look turned vague as if the window and the room were not in the proper city.

Finn's first good breath came when he realized Fortie was probably the target. Any number of people he'd dealt with over the decades could have wanted him dead. He'd been overseer of the Marshal Plan in Austria. He'd made huge donations to the Vienna War Museum. And he'd been tireless in petitioning for Waldheim to become Secretary General of the United Nations. Those were just things Finn knew about.

A woman climbed through the bay with a medical bag. She knelt by them. "I am paramedic." She dabbed at the blood by Finn's ear.

"It's nothing," Finn said. "Look to her first."

The woman shined a penlight in Clarissa's pupils. She asked several times what Clarissa remembered. "Her heart is little quick," she said. "Generally, okay, but how to say? Foggy. We watch her." She examined Fortie. She took his orneriness as testament to his being near normal.

Finn's blood pressure was elevated, which explained his headache.

Outside, lights flashed off men in helmets. Two district constables charged through the front door. The first wielded a camera while the second—portly with a high forehead—gathered them around the kitchen island. The constable knew Fortie by name. In a thick German accent, he asked standard emergency responder questions. Somehow Fortie had recovered his ambassadorial cast—rich voice, eyes steady. Finn's ears were still ringing from the blast. Beside him, Clarissa stared into space. He rubbed her back.

The constable turned a page in his notebook and straightened up to his full height. "Please forgive the disrespect of my question, Ambassador. Who might want you dead?"

Fortie seemed prepared for the question. Expecting he was next, Finn zeroed in on how Fortie handled himself. "Some deranged person must have thought a strike against an officer of America would change the way our country does business. In my opinion, that's wasted ambition. America's carriage in the world is, on the whole, just and benevolent."

Finn lifted his shirt to air his armpits.

"What happened?" Clarissa said, looking at the chandelier above the island.

The constable stopped. "There was an explosion, Ma'am."

"Was anyone hurt?"

"What do you last remember this evening, Mrs. Waters?"

She gave her head a tip of recognition. "Dinner is ready." She looked at her blouse and giggled. "And I'm apparently a sloppy drunk." Distracted, she brushed the front of it.

The constable thanked her. “How about you, Mr. Waters? Who would wish you harm?” Just like that? No preliminary questions?

Finn flexed in his seat and avoided eye contact with Fortie. “In theory—excuse me.” He filled four glasses with water from the sink and delivered them. “Sir, I have no enemies in particular, but if a journalist isn’t irritating someone on a daily basis, he isn’t doing his job.” He glanced at Clarissa. She had drifted off again. “Clarissa and I live in Rotterdam. Except for the people in this room, only one person knows I’m in Austria, let alone at this residence.”

“And who is that?”

Fortie turned to listen carefully.

“My editor in New York.”

“We’re moving here, though,” Clarissa said, still staring into middling space. Her hands were balling the napkin they’d found on the island.

“We’re *thinking* about it, honey.” He patted her hand. “I came in last night from Warsaw. My articles there have all been recording simple events. So I can’t think of any reason for this.”

“Warsaw?” The constable scribbled on his pad.

“Is there something wrong with that?”

“No.” More scribbling. “But offended people have long memories."

He thanked Finn and looked at Clarissa. They all did. When she didn’t notice the room going quiet, the constable jutted his jaw and shoved his pad into the side pocket of his uniform. “Ambassador, leave the front room as it is. We’re securing the scene now. We’ll send a team of investigators over first thing in the morning.” He lowered his voice. “If your daughter’s memory still seems spotty tomorrow, or if you notice anything abnormal—” He struggled to be diplomatic. “Sometimes explosions can bruise the brain without any marks on the skin.”

“Concussions,” Fortie said.

“Exactly. Concussions. If she throws up or if you have any concerns, go to the hospital.”

The constable said his department was posting uniformed men at both the front and rear of the house. Another two would be stationed undercover in a car beside the park. Finn walked him to the door. A carpenter had already tacked a tarpaulin over the maw where the bay window had been. Coming back, he flicked on the parlor light and tip-toed through the debris. The books had suffered mild damage. Because he had protected it with his body, the audio system was still on and ready to play, but he couldn't find the Chopin CD anywhere. Finding the leather of the parlor chairs shredded, it was clear Fortie's desire to hear Poland's master composer had saved their lives.

When he reentered the kitchen, Fortie was hanging up the phone. "We're not staying here. I've booked us two rooms at the Wunderplatz. The embassy is sending an armed limo. Get her ready."

"You don't think being in her own bed will—"

"No, I don't. Use your head, boy. I've lived in Vienna for close to fifty years, and I've never been attacked, for God's sake." He wiped spittle off his lips. "Have you been playing out of your league? Because I'm damned sure this has nothing to do with me."

"You have no enemies, Mr. Ambassador?"

Fortie inhaled as if to fight but clamped his jaw shut.

"As I thought," Finn said. "When you convince me your past is crystal clear, I'll be sure to ask your forgiveness."

Fortie transferred pots from the stove to the refrigerator. "We shouldn't fight, Finn. It's the tension. Let's smooth this over." He poked his chin at Clarissa. "For her sake. She needs us."

"Stop talking like I'm not here," she said, standing up and making ready to leave. The color in her face was better. "My problem is I can't remember anything after coming back from St. Stephen's. Was that to-day?"

"We'll figure that out tomorrow," Finn said. "Can you help me pack a bag?

THE WUNDERPLATZ CONCIERGE met their limo in the underground garage. He whisked them to their adjacent rooms on the twentieth floor. Clarissa went straight to bed but was restless. They watched television then lay together in the dark. Occasionally, she raised her head as if remembering something. Each time she flopped back down, disoriented. Finn awoke to her battling in a dream, sweating and whining. As he rocked her, her crying exploded into punching and kicking. She pushed him away and grabbed the sheets to protect herself.

Fortie charged through their common door. His baritone voice settled her. Finn spent the rest of the night in a stuffed chair. His mind spun, wondering if his consequences were already catching him. Catching *them*. For an hour he cursed the babushka from the Warsaw airport. He plotted hunting her down.

When dead soldiers in trenches uncovered themselves and when a girl child whispered she was joining him and Clarissa from a distant star, he realized he'd fallen asleep.

IN THE MORNING Finn found a handwritten note shoved under the common door. *"I'm in the penthouse dining room."*

Fortie was wearing a coat and tie. He beat Finn to hold Clarissa's chair. He kissed the top of her head when she sat. "I'm counting my blessings this morning."

"I'm not," she said.

"We're all here," Fortie said, "and we can start over."

"Bombs don't plant themselves, Papa. Unless they prove it was an electrical transformer blowing up, we can't go on living there."

"Seems like you have your critical faculties back," Fortie said. "That's reason to celebrate."

"I hate it when you're condescending."

Finn put his hand on Clarissa's wrist. "It's a miracle none of us was hurt."

She squinted at him, dead serious. "Are you sure I wasn't?"

Finn could think of no reply.

"This will pass," Fortie said. "The Austrians are nothing if not good cops. They'll catch the guy."

"You're not listening. Why do I feel so damaged? So ruined?"

"I don't need to remind you we've just lost your mother."

She curled her lip. "Death I can deal with. It's being awake that's debilitating."

Finn could count on one hand the times she'd had her father off-balance.

"We should probably all get checked for concussion. Don't you agree, Finn?"

"You boys can if you want," she said, ever-so-slightly lifting her fork and slapping it down. "I need to see a therapist."

Fortie folded his menu with deliberation. "One thing at a time."

She hissed between tight teeth. "Therapy *isn't* quackery. It's time you know Finn and I have walked on the dark side."

"I know you have." Fortie was scrambling. "And if your mother and I had ever had serious trouble, I'm sure we would have tried that, too."

"Behold the perfect couple," she said.

Fortie's head jerked back. "That was cruel. Any perfection was because she put up with me."

"Which makes me imperfect, because I'm not buying it."

Fortie glanced around the room. "Keep your voice down."

"I think we should use the day to unwind," Finn said. "You took a shot, but you're mostly fine. Your memory will come back."

Clarissa huffed. "Since when are *you* Pollyanna? If not remembering a goddamn thing and beating your husband in bed qualifies as mostly fine . . ." She trailed off.

"You were having a dream," he said. He caught himself forcing a smile.

"Tell me, then," she said, "do your bruises feel dreamy?"

By coming earlier, the waitress might have saved them these indignities. Finn felt ill, though, at how they played the happy family when she took their orders.

After she was gone, Fortie laid his palms alongside his silverware. "I want to table this discussion."

"Which one?" Clarissa asked.

"The one where we're hurting each other more than that damn explosion did."

Clarissa collapsed back into her chair, her fight exhausted.

"We do have to deal with things,' he continued, "but let's keep to logistics."

"Do you have any news or revelations?" Finn asked.

"Not yet. I've made calls. I propose we go back to the house after breakfast and take stock."

Finn was itching to get there. Stalin's orders and his article were waiting to be discovered. "We should do whatever we can to help the authorities."

Fortie agreed. "I called Washington last night. They're sending a forensics crew to oversee the local one."

Clarissa addressed her folded hands. "Those skillful Austrian cops you mentioned?"

"I'm not ready to give up that house. I want . . . we all want to know what we're dealing with."

"There's enough property out front to build a fence," Finn said, "if you reconfigure—"

"I'm with you, Finn. I'm seeing a wrought iron one with tall hedges on the outside."

"Camp Fortier should have guard towers," Clarissa said. She grunted in self-derision. "I'm sorry."

"If nothing else," Finn said, "this is incentive to get our own apartment as soon as possible."

Clarissa cocked an eye. "Hark! Yonder husband makes sense."

"We can go looking again today, but I *have* to get an article out." Suddenly the fourteen hours until bed seemed too short. "Give me three hours to write."

Clarissa lit up. "I just remembered something about last night. I went up before dinner to put on my silk blouse."

Eleven

When the embassy limo delivered them home, a Vienna Polizei van was parked in front. A forensics team of a petite woman and two Aryan men with buzz cuts was gathering samples of glass and dust from the front room. They were running field tests to determine the explosive's chemical markers.

Finn dashed upstairs. He slipped Stalin's orders inside a book on Clarissa's shelf. When finishing his article proved difficult with the activity downstairs, he watched from the hall. Outside, passersby slowed to gawk. Men with rifles shooed them along.

The team found no place where a bomb had sat. They took scans and swabs of the stone. They took more pictures inside and out. They erected a ladder into a tree and drew diagrams. Finn joined their conference with Fortie in the front hall.

"We think we're dealing with a projectile," the petite woman said.

"A missile?"

"Fired from the park. Technicians are scouring the ground there for signs. Footprints. Where equipment may have been set up. They'll ask the neighbors for leads."

Fortie turned to Finn. "So much for a fence being a deterrent."

The woman, the lead investigator, pressed on. "What tipped us off were scratch marks on the finish of a car parked in the street and broken branches in your front yard. It seems the branches triggered the cap and saved you from the full force of the blast. We'll know for certain if our analysis turns up propellants."

"Do it."

"In the meantime, commandos will guard your house."

"Good. Has our embassy contacted your department about working together?"

The team members exchanged looks. The woman shrugged. "Of course we'll share our data. We'll call you when it's all right to contact the cleaning company."

FINN FINISHED TWO articles. The second was a kid-glove version of the first. Both would inform the Soviets of their situation. Before going to the embassy to fax them to New York, he stopped in the kitchen. Clarissa was preparing leftovers for lunch. They were discussing apartments when Fortie came in. He was stifling a strange look.

"I've found a therapist for you. The new American wife of the Austrian attaché to NATO. Good credentials from what I'm told. I've left her a message." He turned to Finn. "Don't worry. For now I'll cover the bills."

"That's very kind," Finn said.

Fortie grimaced. "Clarissa wants help. I want to make sure she gets it."

Clarissa clacked her serving spoon on the side of the pot she was stirring. "Perhaps you didn't notice me standing here."

"We've been put in our place, Fortie." Finn kissed her cheek. "I'll be back soon."

AFTER FAXING THE Katyn articles to Diana at the Foreign Desk, Finn filed Freedom of Information Act requests to various government departments regarding commercial and governmental shipments between Europe and the Soviet Union from 1938 to 1942. If Janis Semyonovich, the Katyn executioner, and his commandant, Andrei Kurishenko, were right that Americans had sent guns to Katyn, Finn would pen that story as the tip of the spear to bring legislation preventing future US administrations and corporations from supplying materials for use in war crimes.

Returning, he found the house quiet. The air was dense with dust of wood and stone. In the parlor, fragments of nineteenth-century glass would have to be beaten out of the rugs. The bound volumes in the shelves would always carry signs of the blast. For a large sum, the leather chairs could be saved, but the front of the antique Louis XIV table between them was scarred. The photograph of Fortie at Yalta that Finn had laid down there was undamaged. He looked at Fortie's picture gallery. All the pictures had been knocked flat. The one of his father and Fortie on the hill had crashed to the floor.

❖ ❖ ❖

HER FATHER'S VOICE in the downstairs hall knocked Clarissa out of a hard sleep. He was speaking German. She lay there trying to reconstruct her last twenty-four hours. She remembered the priest at St. Stephen's singing but not how they'd gotten home. Taxi or the Rolls? The Rolls, because they'd gone in the Rolls. There must have been a couple of hours after that before she came upstairs to dress. Out of the blue she flashed on lying on the parlor floor. She'd had her hand on some man's arm and told somebody else, "I'm his." Very strange.

She remembered sitting in the kitchen with Finn, a policeman, and her father, but there was no sound, like an old film. She remembered the basement of the Wunderplatz and Finn yelping when she kicked him.

Rising, she listened at the top of the stairs. The subject was wood and money.

"It will be three days to get you closed in," the man said. A carpenter, she guessed, from his laborer's speech. "And about ten for the finish work."

As always, her father was pushing. "Don't worry about the cost. Hire who you have to for the sake of speed. But I want it to look like it did before."

"Ja, ja, Herr Fortier. We will."

The front door closed.

She was about to turn away when she heard Finn's footsteps coming from the kitchen.

"He says it's worse than it looks." Fortie's voice. "They may have to remove most of the front of the house. We'll have to move out for a while."

"How long?" Finn asked.

"Most of a month."

Why would her father lie?

"Too bad we didn't find an apartment yesterday," Finn said. "We all could have lived there."

Both pairs of footsteps began walking away.

"It's not the best time of year to travel," her father said, "but I have friends who might take us in. Clarissa loves the Alps, and they'll still be in snow."

The swinging door to the kitchen pumped open and closed. She lost the definition of their words. In her bathroom, her silk blouse hung drying. Finn hadn't known how to care for it. The wine stain still showed.

She addressed her mirror image. "You look like crap, Clarissa." Remembering her mother's maxim that bad things came in threes, she counted: a dead mother, a husband who wouldn't make love to her on schedule, and a missile. She was due for some smooth sailing. *Has anyone ever come up with a rule for how many good things happen in a row*? she wondered. Maybe happiness was never more than random.

Finn entered the bedroom and called to her. Though the bathroom door was open, by not answering, she sensed she was fighting for a piece of high ground.

"Didn't you hear me?" He stood behind her in the mirror.

She feigned being startled. "Sorry, my thoughts are a little loud today."

Finn ground his hands together, a habit he had when he felt unsure. "Are your ears still ringing?"

She listened a moment. "No."

"Albert says he wants to take you on a trip for a couple weeks—"

She ran a comb through her hair and inspected for split ends.

"—but that tonight, we'll be back in the hotel."

"Are we going to sleep together?" she asked.

"Why wouldn't we?"

"Bring your hockey pads in case I wale on you again."

He rubbed his left kidney where she'd landed a knee the night before. "Love *is* a contact sport."

Her blush was genuine. Seeing it soften him, she turned and put her arms around his neck. "I'm scared. I can't remember anything."

Finn whispered back, "You still remember how to embarrass me. You'll be all right."

She felt whole when he let himself be held.

"I have to pack, 'cause I'll be leaving from there tomorrow."

She ran a hand over the white blouse. "While you do, I'll work on this some more."

AT DINNER IN the hotel, Fortie said he hoped they'd get an apartment close enough for him to walk over for breakfast.

"That will happen if it does," Clarissa said. "Right now, I want your help. I want you to describe being in St. Stephen's and the trip home. Maybe it'll jump-start my memory."

"You go first," her father said to Finn.

Finn's discomfort with religion made him endearing. He hated wrangling with her father about it.

"Promise me you'll forget I said this, Fortie. I got chills when the priest was singing. The harmonics and the resonance."

"It gets into you, doesn't it?" Her father scratched the air, palm up, to elicit more.

Finn tipped his head back, modeling William F. Buckley giving a pronouncement. "I think conclusive proof of God's existence would be . . ." and he let them wait, "if he'd left blueprints for cathedrals lying around."

Her father grunted and placed his glass down with disgust. "So you're saying, because he didn't, there is no God? That's a circular argument if I ever heard one. Remind me to cancel my subscription to the *Times*."

"Let's face it, Fortie. A desert wanderer pissed off the Jewish glitterati by dumping their money and got himself martyred. Nowadays they'd treat him for sunstroke and move on."

Her father crossed his legs, which angled his body on a tangent to the conversation. "I have to admit I had the same experience of sacred spaces when I was a little boy. My grandfather would walk me to the church in Hartford. A cathedral talks to that part of us that has no words."

Clarissa had never seen either of them give ground to the other on religion. "Was your father raised Catholic?" she asked Finn.

"No. I gather he loved my mother in spite of it."

"But he *was* religious," she said. "I have this strong image of him praying. Wow, it's coming back to me from yesterday. When I watched you kneeling in St. Stephens, it rang an old bell. You have the same profile he did." She grabbed her chin to remind Finn she liked his jaw.

Emotions flitting across Finn's face exposed her bad judgment. One of his greatest hurts was that she'd seen more of Jordan Waters than he had.

"You wouldn't have been more than five," Finn said. "Not old enough to know what prayer was."

Her father piled on. "Finn's right. Praying would be the last thing Jordan ever did. He was an *avowed* atheist and vocal about it. I met him right after he came from reporting on the 8th Army retreat from Ch'ongch'on in Korea. He said the desperation of those soldiers cured him of religion forever."

Having struggled with her memory, when this one came to her so clearly, she wasn't going to let them crush it. "You're wrong, Papa. Dead wrong. I *saw* him pray. I don't know where it was, but I can see him plain as day. He's on his knees and his hands are together and—"

She was modeling her memory when Fortie cut in, his tone clipped. "You're outnumbered on this one, darling. Mind is a trickster." He curled his shoulders, ready to pounce, a pose she hated. She said nothing, and he capped his argument. “I’ve remembered things myself that later proved absolutely untrue.”

She noted how both men seemed uncomfortable. And she wanted peace for her last night with Finn. “I’m just sorry he’s not here . . . for both of your sakes.” She stroked Finn’s thigh.

But she wasn’t done with this.

Twelve

AS FAR AS Clarissa was concerned, departure days were never long enough. Finn had last-minute errands to run before returning to Poland. To make matters worse, BethAnn Kerlingger, the therapist her father had recommended, called to offer her an early afternoon appointment.

Her father's goodbye to Finn was typically awkward. She and Finn spent a few hours touring various neighborhoods. He liked the area around the Diplomatic Academy of Vienna.

Finn dragged her into an antique bookstore in the old commercial district. The owner was an elderly Jew. His wool pants and eyes were both baggy. Hearing Finn was looking for something by a Belarusian, he led them to an alcove in the back of the store. He handed Finn a volume in Russian by Uladzimir Dubouka. Clarissa translated the Jew's spiel. "A good novelist, but a better nationalist. Stalin sent him to the gulag."

"Ask him," Finn said, "if he thinks there will be a problem if my friend crosses the border with it."

The Jew flopped his hand over and back to show things always change. "It should be okay now. Dubouka survived. Under Khrushchev, some of his books were allowed back in."

"We'll take that. Do you have others?"

Clarissa liked seeing Finn as a customer. The Jew scanned the spines, pulled out a fat one. She translated: "This is my favorite of what you seek. Ivan Melezh, the 'People's Writer of Belarus.' *The Polesye Chronicles* is three novels showing what really happened there in the '20s and '30s. I'll be sad to part with it."

The cost of the two books made Finn reconsider. He bought the Melezh, saying his friend was worth three books.

"Tell me about your friend," she said, as they waited for his change.

He stiffened slightly. "A fellow I met in Poland. He had amazing stories. He's right out of the mold of this guy." He tapped the book. "I'm going to write about him someday."

Finn writing! She saw herself at her makeup table turning over his stack of yellow pages. She was fuzzy about when. But out of that gloom, the title of the article surfaced as when a sunken ship is hauled from the deep: *Reds Caught Red-handed.* For a minute, that was all. On the way to the car, she remembered something about Stalin lying. It was before the missile attack. Her mind was putting itself back together. She inhaled to share her excitement. But stopped when she realized she'd broken Finn's "no reading" rule.

She navigated while he drove into the western part of the city. A six-story apartment building, nicely appointed. Four floors up, Frau Kerlingger welcomed them. She was a no-nonsense type, above average height. Hair dyed red, a small anvil of a nose, almost black pupils, and deep lines descending from the corners of her mouth. Yellow police tape cordoned off a corner of her office with a piece of furniture in it.

"That," Frau Kerlingger said, "is Freud's couch. It's still a major crime scene." She called herself a reformed California hippy. "I came into therapy the back way. Social work in the Haight Ashbury. Call me BethAnn." Finn turned to go wait in the car.

"Hold on," she said. "*Dis*-eases of the mind penetrate systems. You know, couples. Families. If anything's amiss here," she indicated Clarissa, "it's good to hear from all the people in the system. Think of people as stars and health as the galaxy that holds them."

Clarissa saw Finn shrink. She wondered what it would take for her father to ever climb those stairs.

"So sit, why don't you?" BethAnn said. "Unless you fashion yourself a comet in Clarissa's life." Her laugh was mischievous, infectious.

She reminded Clarissa of the history professor she and Finn studied with at Stanford the spring they became lovers.

After hearing Clarissa lay out her situation, BethAnn said, "Because you'll be an absent partner, Finn, it might be helpful for your voice to linger in the room—that is, if Clarissa likes what she sees enough to return."

She sprinkled questions to each of them. With Finn, she explored how his choice of profession might be related to his parents' relationship. "Are you aware of unresolved issues between them?"

Finn's confidence skipped a beat. "My father's dead."

"I'm so sorry. How did he die—that is, if you're willing to talk about it?"

"No one knows. He vanished."

BethAnn wrote her first note of the session. "In America?"

"No, Europe. He was last seen in Hungary."

"Do you think about that?"

Finn seemed astonished at the question. "His nonexistence hangs on me like a necklace. Maybe if I knew how he had died, I'd learn a little about how he had lived."

"And that will help you how?"

"I'm not sure."

"Interesting."

Clarissa was happy the light was on Finn. She gave the tactic another push. "Years ago, he filed a Freedom of Information Act for his father's papers of record."

"Your father being a journalist," BethAnn said, "I imagine his report is pretty thick. Was that helpful?"

Finn spread his thumb and index finger about an inch. "There's surprisingly little in it, though. And without the context, it's just ink. Dates and numbers."

"He knows the thing by heart," Clarissa said. "We joke about it being our adopted child."

"That's dedication. And what would you hope for Clarissa's time here?"

"She suffers." Clarissa liked the glance he gave her. "And I wish she didn't."

"You travel for work?"

"Yes." He said it as if verifying that water was wet.

"I wonder if there's a relationship between reporting from afar and your love for Clarissa."

"That's not a question," he said.

"It's not. Would you say you choose to be away from her?"

"Distance comes with the profession."

"All I ask, Finn, is that you look at the choice. Every day you wake up and go."

"It's a calling to get to the truth of things."

"The truth." BethAnn sucked her cheeks. "What is that, Finn?"

Damn, if he didn't seem ready for the question. "It's what happens before people package what happens, before they spin the details."

"So can anybody ever know it? Or is it just some ideal philosophical state?"

"I report details that time, distance, and people obscure, so the rest of us can see them."

"And why do people obscure them?"

"That's your department, isn't it?"

BethAnn's smiled acknowledged how sharp he was. "Do you tell the truth?"

Fearing she'd be next, Clarissa started to sweat. When he said, "Of course," she became agitated.

She turned to Clarissa. "Does he tell the truth?"

"Do we have to have this conversation now? He's about to leave."

"Then perhaps we should. Are you okay with this, Finn?"

Finn put on his *I-can-handle-it* look.

"He's given you the floor."

"He's passionate about the truth. The truth out there." She waved her hands at the world, then put them in her lap. "But in our personal lives . . ."

"Go on."

"I wish he would level with me sometimes rather than make me guess."

"So he doesn't tell the truth exactly?"

"Please, BethAnn, he's about to leave for I don't know how many weeks."

"So you keep secrets from each other." Her voice was quintessentially kind. "Look I'm not a judge. My job is helping people see things just as they are. What you do then, I leave to you."

Her tone calmed Clarissa, emboldened her. "Do you think a secret is the same as a lie?"

BethAnn looked at Freud's corner. "It depends on how it turns out. But it's not the truth."

"Then there *is* something I need to talk about."

"Is this okay for you, Finn?"

He folded his arms. "I guess."

BethAnn used the back of her hand to clear the space for Clarissa to speak.

"I want a baby." She glanced at Finn.

"Is that all you have to say about it?"

"I'm thirty-eight, and Finn isn't around enough to make it happen."

BethAnn waited for a siren to pass. She turned to Finn. "Do you want a child?"

Clarissa hated the seconds ticking by.

"I don't know what being a father looks like," he said.

"Fair answer. Do you think you're too old to learn?"

Clarissa couldn't wait. "You were willing in the restaurant, but not when we got home."

Finn scowled. "I'm in the midst of something very important that I can't divulge here."

"Secrets?" asked BethAnn.

Finn lifted his chin slightly. "Confidentiality is a much higher bar."

"The mother of secrecy." BethAnn pointed at the door of her office. "By the way, everything we say in here stays here."

"In this case, many lives are at stake. I can't even tell you how many."

"What about *my* life, Finn? Your *confidentiality* blew the front off my father's house."

Finn looked at her, aghast.

"You know what I'm talking about. The Soviets have operatives in Austria. When I went up to put on my silk blouse for dinner, your article was on my dresser."

"You read my article? What were you thinking?"

"Of course, I did. I had to find out what was more important than making love to me. Jesus, Finn, everybody knows Stalin was a liar. What's the big deal? I wonder how you'd feel if I'd died in the blast. Or my father had? I wonder if you would feel *anything*."

Finn's right foot flexed down as if accelerating a getaway car.

"You seem tense, Finn," BethAnn said.

"If you could have just waited a few more days, Clarissa. Do you have any idea how—" His hand thundered on the arm of his chair. "Of course you don't. That's why I kept it secret."

"Listen to me, Big Shot. It's time you get your priorities straight."

"Oh, yeah?" Finn said. "Most journalists get their priorities straight by being single."

Clarissa didn't breathe once in the silence that followed.

BethAnn put her elbows on her knees. "And is that *a truth*, Finn?"

"No way I should have said that."

"But you did, damn it," Clarissa said. "It's a good thing I know where I stand."

More silence.

"I suggest," BethAnn said, "that we all speak as if words are diamonds, as in *Diamonds are forever*. What we say here exposes our beliefs, our perceptions, what we want, and what we think we deserve. And we'll have to live with what comes out."

THOUGH THEY BOTH feared they had crossed the Rubicon, BethAnn said that wouldn't happen without getting all the cannons on the move. It was fortuitous they were going to be apart for a while. It would allow them to salve the fresh burns. And BethAnn didn't let them go until they had fashioned ways to reach each other.

"You must communicate. What I see here," she said, "is nothing like an ending. It could be a promising beginning *because* of the pain and your ideals. Particularly your ideals, Finn."

As she walked them to the head of the stairs, she laughed. "You two seem like beef and onions. It's an old saying of my mother's, meaning very different, but belonging together."

In the car they rode like deaf-mutes, Clarissa pointing directions to his last stop before heading to the airport, a small branch of the Oesterreichische Nationalbank.

Once parked, he said, "I can take a taxi from here, if it'll be easier."

BethAnn had helped Clarissa relearn something. *Dare to speak your truth*. "I'd actually hate that."

He replied by setting his briefcase onto his lap.

Fear gripped her. "If you're opening an account, shouldn't we do it together?"

He looked straight ahead, and sighed. "I'm going to get a safe deposit box. I have Stalin's orders in here." He tapped his case.

She remembered a line from the article. "I thought they were in New York."

"The article *implies* they were in New York. We want the Soviets to believe that's where they are, because that's where they have the most power over the Kremlin."

"So you lied."

"I've never told so many lies in one week in my life." He laid his outstretched arms across the steering wheel and looked at the floor mat. "Crimes poison everyone who touches them. Even the good guys."

"What difference does it make to expose the Soviets at this point?"

After warning her about keeping this information secret, he told her about the troops on the Belarusian border. He told her how international pressure could keep the Politburo from ordering them into Poland. "Gorbachev may have no choice except to do something decent."

"This isn't journalism any more, is it?" she said.

"I don't know what it is. I don't even care. I just know it needs to be done."

"At what cost, Finn? I haven't agreed to die for Poland. My father hasn't."

He deliberated a long time. He spoke softly. "Maybe divorcing me is the only way for you to stay safe."

She looked out the window and fogged it. "One day all you want is to honor your dead mother by having a child, the next you find out you're married to someone on a Russian hit list."

"I'm not."

"The front of the house is missing!"

"Look, somebody who wanted me dead would . . ." he extended his index finger, "one, be following us right now . . ." Clarissa couldn't help but take a paranoid look around the street. "And two, would have to know I have the orders. It's the orders they want, not me. Not counting you, only six people in the world know I have them. Three people in Solidarity, Sam Rich, me, and the man who no longer has them. And only Sam knows I'm in Vienna. Do you think he's a Soviet operative?"

"You're not counting right. Someone tried to kill you. That makes at least seven."

Finn grimaced. "Sam got a professor from NYU to translate for him. He's a Russian."

"Good God, Finn. What have you done?"

Thirteen

IN THE AIRPORT Finn checked to see if he was being watched. All seemed normal. After boarding his flight, he made a trip to the bathroom to see which passengers looked up when he returned to his seat. He noted one detail about each. During the flight, to ease his tattered ego after the fight with Clarissa, he cracked Melezh's *The Polesye Chronicles*. Horse-drawn wagons. Life without doctors or money. Acres of earth turned with hoes. His Polish roots felt satisfied.

The plane touched down in the smog—or was it fog?—of evening. Windrows of new snow lined the runway. His pulse raced coming through customs and all the way to the hotel. It was 10 p.m. The talks would be resuming in the morning. Happy voices of correspondents buzzed in the lobby, lounge, and restaurant. Cigarette smoke. Since all the single rooms were taken, he doubled up with a Hungarian reporter from the *Magyar Hirlap*. Downstairs, he surveyed the tables in the lounge. No sign of Annalisa, the woman he'd abandoned the night he found the note from Solidarity. He both wanted to see her and hoped not to.

"Waters, get over here." That boor, Eggelsman, from the *San Francisco Examiner*. He was better at explaining American football to foreigners than reporting. He was surrounded by tag-along Americans—new overseas, probably paid little or nothing—and the Dutch film crew that always liked a rowdy atmosphere. Finn saluted him and kept looking.

Marty Cisneros hailed him from a corner booth with a half-moon circular seat. Marty was a crackerjack journalist from Mexico City. Stanford grad, too, a couple years behind Finn. He was sitting with some of the more thoughtful Scandinavians and Alice Whatshername—the cute one from Britain.

To wash away BethAnn's assaults, he ordered a single malt—neat—from a passing waitress and pulled up a chair facing the corner.

"Where you been, Gringo?" Marty said. "New York? Filing something special, while we've been twiddling our digits?"

"Vienna," Finn said. "Clarissa's father lives there."

"The ambassador."

"Former ambassador." Across from him in the booth, a rocks glass marked an empty place between Marty and Svenson. Svenson had been hanging around Alice since the talks began. "By the way, Marty," Finn said, "the Black Market of Butter was a nice article."

"Thanks. I'm getting kudos from fans in Stockholm." Marty pointed. "Svenson translated it for me. A simultaneous release. I might get a byline in his paper. So my kids *can* start thinking about college."

"Ah," said a smooth voice behind Finn, "now we have most of the continents represented." That Malian accent—French and African—was sure to make Chantelle Mugatando's jump to television a near certainty once she'd earned her stripes abroad. That, along with a quick wit and her Swiss Chocolate skin. She had perfect ivory teeth. Tonight her lips glistened red like steamed lobster. Television. That's where the money was. Finn regretted he'd never get there.

"It's good you've come to join us," Chantelle said, leaning close. Scents of perfume and rum poured over him in equal amounts. "This group needs the seasoned professional," she said. Her dress was an ecstatic color of yellow, fashionable enough to go anywhere. Marty and Norland, the quiet Norwegian, stumbled over themselves to let her slide into her place. Men were always stumbling around her. "I learned a lot," Chantelle said to the others, "from Mr. Waters's questions to the Polish media minister the day the talks fell apart. You made him scramble. I liked that exceedingly."

Finn tipped his head at Chantelle's compliment. He toasted her to get more alcohol in. He was at least two behind everyone. "It's not hard," he said. "Trying to make tyranny sound reasonable scrambles anyone's brain."

Alice Baldwin, yes, Baldwin—how could he not remember such a simple name?—was sipping on the last part of her drink. She was fun to have at a gathering. She was sincere and inquisitive, a good student. And she was female. So far, her writing lacked depth; it often left several pins standing in the middle of the lane. He presumed Svenson had had her in the sack. He was funny and good-looking.

"What's the mood in Stockholm?" Finn asked. "If Poland goes free, might that change the balance of shipping in the Baltic?"

"Ja," said Norland. "We Norwegians aren't looking forward to a new player on the block. This recession's been harder on us than on you guys." Finn confessed he didn't have a good handle on affairs in the States.

The waitress came with seven shots. Finn looked around to see who was being generous. Eggelsman—his table now with half of the chairs empty—waved like a beauty queen. "Next time," he said pointing to Finn, "join me, and you won't have to pay." The guy must have had a trust fund.

The caraway scent gave the drink away as akvavit. The compliment was not lost on the Scandinavians. Norland and Svenson launched in on the proper way to drink it. They made Alice their star pupil. Svenson said it was to be drunk in a shot. He downed his with a theatrical batting of his eyes. With defiant erasure, Norland said that, no, most of *his* countrymen preferred to sip it even though it often came in a shot glass. Giddy, Alice started laughing. Chantelle, for whom akvavit was a novelty, was first after Svenson to shoot it. "Whew," she blew. "That licorice hides its punch. I'll take another." But she became distracted with the drink in front of her and with Marty's attention. He had his hand on her forearm. Their game seemed to be scouring journalistic metaphors for sexual innuendo.

While assessing how Marty's Mexican skin complemented hers, Finn felt the akvavit take hold. His body felt close and distant at the same time. Six days before, he'd been drinking with a Russian mass murderer. He sat back satisfied, cradling his third scotch on his solar plexus. In a day or two, his story would be published.

More drinks. He didn't rise when Norland left along with the Dane, whose name he couldn't remember. A few times he caught Alice watching him watching her. Sometime later he felt Alice's ankle sliding back and forth on his shin. A mistake on her part, no doubt, since she'd already played her chips for the night. She seemed to be ignoring her encroachment even when she looked right at him. Finn received her intimacy as one of life's unheralded graces. Still talking a smooth game with Svenson, she increased her rubbing.

Women unleashed were so vast, he thought. He looked to see how Chantelle was making out with Marty. She was staring Finn down. She showed him the foot was hers by lifting it onto his thigh and licking her lips. Marty was blathering, mostly in Spanish. Chantelle patted Marty's arm and told him he was ready for bed. He smiled a victory smile. "Not tonight," she said.

Marty was too far gone to mind his change in fortunes. He rose. Before wandering off, he drank from the Dane's empty glass. "A perfect end to the evening," he said.

When Alice threw up, Svenson hauled her off somewhere. Maybe the kitchen. The table now looked like the end of a chess game, most of the warring pieces off to the side. Chantelle eyed him as if she still had her queen and two rooks.

"You're onto something big, Waters."

She paused long enough for Finn to realize the alcohol must have emboldened him to tell her his whole secret strategy to save Poland. His mind raced for a scheme to cover his mistake. "What?"

"I'm onto something big. And I want it in me."

Without remembering how it had happened, he'd joined her on the leather seat side of the booth, and she had ahold of him through his pants. He made an effort to line up his thoughts. But when she stroked him twice more, surrender seemed an honorable response.

She leaned her nose into his cheek. "What's that saying in English? 'A bird in the hand will soon be in the bush.' "

He was perched on that edge of sexual encounter where the highly unlikely flops over to the inevitable, the unstoppable, the *why-would-I-ever-want-to-think-about-stopping*-able. That precarious state. Sometimes—okay, more than half the time—he'd lived to regret going over the falls. But . . . this connection . . . had so much promise.

The beige walls pulsated colors he didn't remember them having. He tipped his head back. A dim halo surrounded the ceiling light. He summoned his awareness the best he could to see which side of inevitable he was on. He thought about Clarissa—very briefly. Long enough to see they had as good as agreed to a kind of separation. They each had to make sense of who they were, who they were becoming. They hadn't made any rules about infidelity, but this hardening of affairs with Chantelle seemed in the acceptable realm. He could at least be gallant and make sure she got home safely.

"What's your room number?" he asked.

"That's more like it. Three-o-nine. No, what am I saying? Four-o-nine. Though I'm sure three-o-nine would be delighted with our company." She could have slid her beet-round hindquarters out to her right, but she crawled over him, smacking his legs with her purse and grazing his face with the curve of her hip.

Few people remained in the lobby to watch them supporting each other through it. Past the fake potted palm, the black-and-white chessboard floor tiles narrowed towards the lift. He loved the scene they were in. A black queen and a white king. The bell of the lift rang. The door slid open. "I love that sound," Chantelle said. "More so when I'm not alone."

Inside the lift, she cornered him, kissing him with abandon. Her mouth was windy and warm. He felt comfortable to be undecided about next steps and yet still the recipient of her largess. After a minute, she said, "I love slow lifts. Better for getting to know a man."

It *was* a damn slow elevator. With great effort he freed his face from hers. The door had closed, but they'd forgotten to push number four.

"Where were we?" she said, pulling him back. Her tongue was masterful. When the lift jerked to a halt, she dragged Finn left down to the last door on the hall. "Corner room means we can make all the noise we want."

He predicted she would drop her keys just before they fell from her hand. As he knelt, he remembered having dropped his keys returning from that first meeting with Dabrowski. Now he saw it: Lessons of life, important and not, circled until their meaning came clear. What was the lesson here? Grabbing the key, he decided the lesson here was—when faced with obstacles—grab the key and never give up. And of course, he was part of some lesson circling in *her* life. Everyone was part of the circle in the lives of others. The universe was beautiful in that way, even with genocide and poverty and the rich getting richer. He wanted to laugh. Maybe he did laugh. She was stroking him through his pants again. And her breast. He had his hand on her breast. She was kissing his neck.

"You do it," she said. "The lock is so far away and I'm a little . . . busy."

He was nonjudgmental about how long it took him to hook the key into the hole. Driving its ridges past the tumblers so satisfied him that before turning the lock, he had the thought that when analyzed, one way or another, everything in the universe was about sex, or about getting there, and that he was brilliant to see it.

The door blew open. Chantelle, graceful—was she thirty yet?—flicked the bathroom switch as they passed the door so they would have just enough light to see each other. She sat him on the bed. Using the dresser for balance behind her buttocks, she crossed her arms and slipped her dress over her head in one expert draw. Where he expected to see a bra, her breasts greeted him, nipples tight. And goddamn, she'd been at the table without panties; pubic hair trimmed short, in the shape of a heart. Finn looked at the light on her skin, wishing so much to lick her everywhere. He pulled back the sheets, hooked his arms behind her knees and around her back and lifted her in.

He sat with his hip next to hers. And because he had the key to life now, he trusted he could get away with saying whatever came to mind. "You are the finest drink in the bar, and I want every last drop of you."

Humming satisfaction, Chantelle arched her torso. She skated her thighs back and forth.

"I am so drunk," he said, "and drunk on you." She fingered the buttons on his shirt. So slowly, he ran his left hand from her throat to her thighs, and all the way down, she lifted her body to meet his touch. The gold band on his finger glinting in the light struck him as another lesson, one he saw because of his recent awakening to meaning. And he breathed. He breathed. He breathed hard.

He whispered her name. Working on the second button of his shirt, she didn't reply. "Chantelle?"

"Hmm?"

"You are blessed and . . ." he geared up his nerve, knowing this was his last chance, "and you'll have a river of men in your bed."

"I like *that*," she said. "Right now I'm getting into deep Waters." She laughed at her cleverness.

"No, listen. I have to tell you . . ." he waffled between wanting and regret. "I'm a little too married to take what you are giving."

She was slow to come to his meaning. She sought his eyes. "No one says 'no' to me." She said it as if stating a law of nature. She repeated the line again. This time it came with bewilderment. The third time, she said the words as if charging him with a crime. After a long silence, she put her palm to her forehead. "My God, I am swimming." When she rolled away from him, the white glow from the bathroom trimmed the perfection of her lines against the sheet and against the dark.

She extended her neck and cast her eyes on the ceiling. "I guess it's not so bad, Waters. Every river has stones in it. That's what makes it interesting, don't you think? Now get out of here."

He wove his way to the door, surprised and proud of himself to have doubled back—against all odds—into territory where his wedding vow had meaning. He turned the deadbolt, felt its satisfying thrust and click. There it was again, everything being sex and a circle. But the door wouldn't open. He had *locked* the damn thing. Now the bolt wouldn't throw the other way. It was a test. And like Lot's wife, he turned to look at Chantelle. At the sound of the lock, she had rolled face up. Fingering herself, she smiled.

"Congratulations," she said.

"For what?"

"For being so strong."

Strong sounded like a four-letter word. Like another crime. Was she mocking him?

She groaned. Her tongue licked the corner of her mouth. "Strength is good."

He tried the lock again. It definitely had a glitch in it. A fire hazard.

"Let me congratulate you in person." She swung her legs down. She walked toward him. By god, she could hold her liquor. She planted a kiss where his shirt opened. Sliding her hand behind his neck, she pulled his mouth to hers. "Congratulations."

He deserved congratulations. He had done it. He had had her where he wanted her and had walked away. A tremendous act of willpower. He knew now the pride of fidelity, the strength it took, knew he could manage it, so he accepted her kiss in the spirit it was given. And he gladly let go of the doorknob so he could wrap her properly. He enjoyed her congratulations even more as she freed his belt and unzipped his pants. He felt huge, like a king in control until like a wraith she was gone, slipped from his arms, vanished. He looked for her, found her not with sight, but with touch. Her head was in his hands, her tight wound hair so thick in his fingers, and she was sucking him with all the congratulations a man deserved.

For a second she stopped what she was doing and looked up at him. "No one says 'no' to me."

That night, at least, she was right.

Fourteen

IN THE MORNING Chantelle didn't stir as Finn dressed. When he got to his room, the hot showers were long gone. The cold one got him to the briefing in the Presidential Palace on time. The spokesman for the government's negotiating team showed that the eleven-day hiatus hadn't improved his charisma. His tone was somber enough to announce the death of a head of state.

"Gentlemen, the talks will commence at 10 a.m. with the introduction of members of both parties. After lunch, the individual working groups will initiate proposals that could lead to an agenda . . ." It was Groundhog's Day, Polish-style.

"Verbal gangrene," Marty whispered to Finn, who was looking a little green himself.

Viktor outlined the same five-point plan Solidarity had brought to the table February 6, but each point had a new name. His excitement supported the fiction that Solidarity had reinvented itself. Journalists from around the world scribbled madly. The parties retired into the big room. The waiting began.

At 11:30, an underling from Solidarity's support staff handed Finn a folded note.

Article needed, it said. It was signed with a large D. It reminded Finn of Stalin's signature. He asked the staffer to wait. On the back he wrote *Written and submitted. Expect any day. Excited. Please present this book to Mikolai.* He drew *The Polesye Chronicles* from his briefcase and signed the frontispiece *Your Co-pilot on the Vodka Mission.* The staffer departed.

The noon statement from the government spokesman: *Introductions are complete and the session was cordial. Have a nice lunch.*

Finn's colleagues headed for the food establishments across from the University of Warsaw. Finn grabbed wiejska kielbasa from a street vendor and walked back to the Bristol Hotel. He ordered coffee in the lounge and composed the follow-up pieces Sam Rich would want as soon as the article on Stalin's orders hit the street.

He woke the first time when his writing pad hit the floor. He snapped awake again when Chantelle wrapped her knuckles on the bar. "Juice. Orange, if you have it." The clock over the mirror read two-thirty. She wore a brown and earth-yellow bogolan and leaned both elbows on the bar. She hadn't seen him.

Finn went to her. "They made no progress this morning." He slipped some bills to the bartender before she could open her purse. "My article will be about forty words."

She brightened. "Promise me more nights like that, Mr. Waters, and I don't care if the talks *never* end." She bumped her shoulder into his chest.

He saw how easy it would be to leave Vienna and not look back. His words were for himself. "You know what they say. 'Nothing lasts.'"

"You know what we say in Mali? Eat fruit while it's fresh." She showed her grille of teeth.

"I pronounce you to be in the persimmon family," he said.

She stretched her hand on the bar and looked at her nails. "Give me some time to come up with what *you* are."

He bumped her shoulder in return. "I've got to get back to my writing."

"Your article is finished. Is it a book then? You look like the author type. A novel maybe. Agents and killers."

If he planned on being effective at all that day, he had to get away from her. "If I ever write a book, it will be about all the circles life throws us." He waved. The bartender slid her orange juice toward her.

"I'll circle up with you later then," she said.

AT THREE O'CLOCK, he dictated his paragraph to Diana in New York. "I'll update it before deadline if need be. May I speak with Sam?"

Sam came on. "I've got about a minute, Waters."

"Then I have three questions: You got my message about the remodeling in Vienna?"

"Yes. Not the kind of fresh air a man wants close to home."

"It opens new possibilities," Finn shot back. "When's the article coming out?"

"We've got major constipation. As I told you, the background's deep on that one."

He felt brass-knuckled in the ribs. "What kind of constipation?"

"Plumbing problems, of course. They need time to look for leaks." Sam was ad-libbing the code.

"Time is critical. Lean on them."

"I have already, like Killer Kowalski. What's the third question?"

Nothing would salvage Sam's bad news. "Can I take a side trip on a related story?"

"Where to?"

"Walking around this city, you'd never know the Warsaw Ghetto was only half a mile from the palace. How about a piece on the status of Auschwitz and the other German camps?"

"The Israelis have already been there. Pick something more interesting."

Finn had been nurturing an idea along the lines of Hitler and Stalin using the same playbook. If he dug deeper, he knew there'd be something profound buried with all the bones. "The trip will be research for I what sent you."

"We have no room for fluff," Sam said. "The budget's tight. Corporations buying newspapers is strangling the industry."

"I don't do fluff. And I just gave you gold. What do you say?"

"Two days. If you miss anything in Warsaw, I'll have you back here working the City Desk."

Sam pulling rank on him was out of character. Suddenly he doubted his idea. "Let's work on a suppository for that plumbing problem. I'll call Diana tomorrow with my itinerary."

AT FOUR, CHANTELLE begged off getting together that night, and the government floated the first glimmer of hope for its people: a path for Solidarity to achieve status as a trade union fifteen years into the future. It would have to wage no strikes or demonstrations over that time. People expected Wałęsa to hit the roof, but he said, "No. It's a sign that dialogue is working toward a solution for all Poles. Something to build on." The electrician was becoming a savvy negotiator.

Finn skipped dinner. At the university library he asked for books on the Holocaust. Students behind the desk gave him blank looks.

"World War II," he said. "Prisoner of war camps." They pointed him to the military section, all of twenty books. There he read how Russians rescued their good cousins to the west, the Poles. Only two referred to camps and the 'difficult' conditions Germans created for their prisoners. Finn made a list of names and locations.

When the talks let out for lunch the next day, the same Solidarity underling handed Finn another note.

At 12:25 catch State Taxi 3518 across the street from the palace. D.

To keep warm in the light rain, Finn danced his feet on the sidewalk. Now that gas prices had doubled, traffic was down. Taxis stood with their motors off. A military helicopter labored across the sky. He entertained himself with the day's front-page story, Jaruzelski inspecting huge hoppers at a milling plant. He looked ridiculous in a baker's hat.

Taxi 3518 pulled up. Finn got in the front seat. "I'm headed where you are."

"My condolences," the driver shot back. "Poland's on the long slide down." He had folds of blotchy skin around his eyes and smelled of cigarettes. Peels from an orange lay at his feet.

"How old are you?" Finn asked.

The driver thought before answering. "Sorry, no interview. I can't afford to end up in the paper."

"At least tell me where we're going."

"I'll let you off at the bus terminal and pick you up on the other side. When I drop you on Krasinskiego, walk two blocks toward the Arch of the Brutal Shrimp and turn left down the alley. You'll find the back door of a restaurant held open with a red barrel."

On Krasinskiego, Finn walked around the block and affirmed he wasn't followed. Heading north toward Stalin's Victory Arch, he found the alley and slipped into the kitchen of the restaurant. No one was there. Hearing music beyond, he entered the dining area, a dark space with low ceilings. Several people were eating by the light of the bar. In the far corner, dim light outlined a stevedore hat.

"No article," Dabrowski said as a greeting.

Finn laid his shoulder bag on the seat between them. "The pictures flew to New York the day we got back, seven days ago. I sent my article two days later from Vienna. My editor says the State Department, the department that—"

"I *know* what that is. Tell the truth. Does your editor dislike Poles?"

Sam and Dabrowski would be good pair in a boxing ring. "Not at all. But the US has a . . . a complicated relationship with the Soviets."

Dabrowski fiddled with the last of a cigarette in the ashtray. "If you have a *simple* relationship with Soviets, they have pictures of you with a prostitute, or you're dead."

Finn realized he needed someone else to help him get through to the State Department. Fortie had the muscle, but he would be Finn's last choice. "I have someone working on cutting through the red tape. I expect news any day now."

"Two days ago, you said 'soon.' More troops are arriving at the border." He stubbed out his cigarette. "We're making progress in the room. But you know about Hungary in '56, and Prague in '68."

Finn's stomach clenched. His father had disappeared in Hungary in '56. "Of course."

Dabrowski made him wait. "I don't want my grandsons remembering Poland in '89."

"I understand."

"Maybe you'll have to go to New York and jump on some desks."

"My editor wants this story as much as I do. I can't imagine what's wrong."

"Will you go to New York?"

"If it will make a difference."

Dabrowski lifted a book from the seat beside him and slid it across the table. It was the Melezh.

"I want this to go to Mikolai."

The shadow cast by Dabrowski's hat made him hard to see, but his face was taut. "Mikolai Begitch can't read."

"That's nonsense. He was trained as an editor."

"Open it," Dabrowski said.

Inside the front cover, Finn found two photographs. In the first, a body hung from a tree, limbs trussed up behind in a way that would make a man agree to anything. The head was hanging oddly. The other was a close-up of the same head. It looked vaguely like Mikolai. Finn looked to Dabrowski.

"Mikolai can't read," Dabrowski repeated.

For all his time abroad working in papers, Finn had never come close to murder. The ground fell away. The images Finn had nursed of Mikolai with his grandnephew fell with it. "God!" He pulled his lips back from his teeth. "When?"

"Two days ago, maybe three. His nephew found him . . . and the boy."

Finn looked at the closeup. Mikolai's mouth had been extended double with a blade yanked through the corners. "They left him in his own yard?"

"They wanted to send a message."

"Do you suppose he talked?"

Dabrowski scribed the line of the knife on his cheek. "Usually that means they couldn't get him to. But at the end maybe he did."

"What about the first contact we made? Janis Semyonovich, the guard at Katyn? Is he still alive?"

"We're checking. Getting there's not easy. As for Mikolai, you know his history. Maybe his death is unrelated."

"What did you mean 'and the boy'?"

"They spare no one who sees them." Dabrowski lit a fresh cigarette. "That's how they are. That's why we need the story now."

Everyone needed the story. Maybe even Gorbachev needed it.

"I'll get it in print, I promise you. Or I'll die trying."

Dabrowski waved at the book. "There's something else there. You may need it."

Under the photographs was his passport as Karol Sobczak. The pages with the Belarusian and Russian stamps had been removed.

"Take care with it," Dabrowski said.

Finn knew he could pass for Karol Sobczak, but in most cases, being journalist Finn Waters was a get-out-of-tyranny free card. On the other hand, getting caught with two passports together meant a trip to the gulag or a hole in the ground. Finn pushed it to Dabrowski. Dabrowski pushed it back. "For an extra one of these, people here borrow money they can never repay."

"But if I'm stopped—"

"Carry the two together. Give me your passport sleeve." Finn fished the lanyard from around his neck and tossed the fabric wallet over. Dabrowski modeled with his hands. "Cut the sleeve along the edge and remove the cardboard. Slide Karol in. When asked for your passport, be sure to hand over the right one. Polish guards don't look at faces anyway. They go through the motions in case their superior is watching." He slid the passport and wallet back. "I suggest you travel to Silesia some time soon, in case a guard who sees this happens to be from there."

"I would plead stupidity. I'd tell him I just got hired."

Dabrowski showed his first smile. "That's how we do it here."

"And if Soviet guards check me?"

Dabrowski stood and gathered his cigarettes. “You’re on your own . . . unless you get that story.” And without turning back, he made his way out the front door.

Finn sat long enough for the cook to offer him food. Busy assessing his next moves, he ate without tasting. The bill came to 70,000 zlotys. With his wallet out, Finn asked, “If I give you 200,000, can I take your hat?”

The cook didn’t hesitate. Wearing it, Finn felt safer walking back to Krasinskiego. There he flagged a taxi that dropped him two blocks from the American Embassy.

Fifteen

CLARISSA WISHED SHE could drop Finn at the airport all over again. Given a second chance, she would quash the awkward silence. And she wouldn't apologize to smooth things over. Hoping a beautiful place might remind her that she, too, was beautiful, she pulled into a park along the Danube north of the airport intending to watch the sun set behind the hills. But as the temperature dropped, fog formed over the river. All she witnessed was an amorphous orange glow.

On impulse, she passed the turn to the Fortier mansion and stayed on Wallensteinstrasse. It brought her to the area she and Finn had liked before the meeting with BethAnn. At the Arts and Music University, she turned left and became lost in a warren of tree-lined streets. The buildings still sported the stucco of prewar days. Windows had the same leaded diamond mullions as her parents' house did. Stopping to admire the light coming from a third-story apartment, she saw a *For Rent* sign in the window above. She parked and perused the line of buzzers in the building foyer. Apartment 4C had no name tag.

With a shrug of her shoulders, she rang 3C. Within minutes, she was seated on a Berber wool upholstered chair with stainless steel frame, sipping wine and swapping stories about school and relationships with Anika—single, Swedish, a year younger than Clarissa. She drove home knowing she would live there as soon as her possessions could be shipped from Rotterdam.

An armed US marine posted to the rear of her father's home asked her for identification before letting her go in the back way. The house was quiet, eerie. She parted the curtain covering the front door sidelight. Two Austrian commandoes walked back and forth on the side-walk.

The next morning, when her father still hadn't returned, she fixed herself some coffee. To be near the phone, she sat on the bottom stair across from the parlor that had been taped off from the house with plastic sheeting. She weighed which situation would upset her the most: Her father being in the emergency ward or morgue, or him having spent the night with a woman. While waiting, she twice walked what must have been her steps the night of the missile attack coming from the kitchen in high heels. Still, nothing of that part of the night came to her.

At quarter to nine the garage door opened and closed. She listened to her father suppressing his movements as he came through the kitchen.

"It's okay," she said, as he tiptoed into the hall. "I'm up."

He appeared happy to not have awakened her. "What are you doing there?"

"Trying to understand all the changes."

When he asked her to enumerate them, she avoided mentioning his recent whereabouts, wanting a baby, the canyon opening between her and Finn, and having found an apartment. A death in the family, a missile attack, and memory loss seemed enough to bring anyone seeking solace to sit on a bottom stair. But she became annoyed, and then incredulous, when his eyes wandered and he excused himself to get a cup of coffee.

Rising, she eyed him through the crack in the kitchen door, heard him muttering to himself, cheerful and verbose. "I'm sorry," she said, opening the swinging door. "Were you talking to me?"

"No, darling. Just encouraging myself to keep putting one foot in front of the other. I share your mystification with all we've had to endure."

"I didn't say I was mystified. I said *frightened*. Things happen for a reason. And whatever the reason for this is, it can't be good."

"I see it differently," he said. "Things are bound to turn around."

She wanted to hit something. "Needless to say, I wondered if you were all right."

"Me? Of course." There was a chortle in his voice. The lines by his eyes became pronounced. "I went out last night for dinner with Ambassador Britcher. Ended up staying the night. His wife is lovely. We discussed a slew of subjects, including theater and—if you can believe it—the ivory trade. When we looked up, it was two-fifteen in the morning. They gave me their guest suite." He pushed the plunger on the French Press and watched it work. "How I miss being in that man's shoes."

"So you've said."

He pulled a large cup from the shelf. "I'm expecting a visit from forensics, otherwise I might have accepted breakfast on the Britcher terrace. The mourning doves are back. Have you heard them? They're early." He took his coffee and turned to back through the swinging door. "Would you mind translating for me? If they send who I think they will, the man has a lisp. If there's anything that makes German more difficult to understand, it's a lisp."

"Only if you let me listen in."

That stopped him a moment. Then he winked.

"You're buzzing like the old Albert Fortier. Doesn't it bother you that we can no longer feel safe here?"

"We have to go on living, Clarissa."

He disappeared. The door swung like a hand warding off foul odors.

HERR SCHOFELD, THE forensics administrator, was a rail of a man who tottered. Twice leading him down the hall, Clarissa lunged to steady him. Both times he ignored his need. For a moment, he stood in the doorway of her father's office, squinting, the back of each hand feeling for the doorjambs. It was the darkest room in the house. The underside of the stair winder cut through one corner of the ceiling. A small window looked out on the building next door. Lore had it that this was where the bishop wrote his letters and sermons. Clarissa assumed he'd designed it to remind himself of rooms in the Vatican. Settled in the chair opposite her father's desk, Herr Schofeld opened a folder holding a trim clutch of papers. She leaned against a bookcase to his left.

"Ambassador," Schofeld said, "please forgive my appearance this morning. They've just taken my daughter to the hospital."

"I'm sorry," her father replied. "Will she be all right?"

"It was a horrible decision." He tapped his temple. "A hospital for the head. She's been tormenting her husband and the children. But never mind."

He indeed had a pronounced lisp. Her father looked to her, then to him. "My German is only fair, so I've asked Clarissa to translate. Do you have results?"

"We do. First let me express we're all mortified about this . . ." he paused, "incident."

For an explosion that could have laid waste to them all, his choice seemed antiseptic. Her father sloughed it off. How many times had he had to dismiss tragedy? she wondered.

Schofeld traced a few lines of text with his finger. "We've tested for both missile accelerants and explosives. The results of those tests and the type of copper used in the missile head all point to this being a terrorist group."

"My God. That makes no sense. How—?" Fortie shot Clarissa a glance. A rare instance with some of his armor missing.

"We have nothing conclusive yet, but our national security experts have been on the trail of a copycat group to the Red Army Faction."

"The German leftists? I thought Germany had them under control."

Schofeld nodded. "The group here only has a few members and is centered in Graz. But a few weeks ago we got signs they'd been to Vienna. This missile that struck your residence had identical markers to weapons the RAF have used. We worry they are getting outside support. I've informed President Waldheim's chief of staff. Our government contacted Interpol this morning. Our police are in full readiness mode. The Interior Ministry is checking immigration records."

"Preposterous!" her father said. "Isn't the RAF's main focus ousting former Nazis from government there? Anyway, Austria has solved its Nazi problems quite nicely. They've been reabsorbed into society. In any case, that has nothing to do with me. Are they Jews, these people?"

"I can't answer that, Ambassador." Schofeld reset himself in his chair. "But President Waldheim's service for Hitler's SS *has* been getting a lot of news lately outside Austria."

As Clarissa translated, her wheels churned. Recent investigations had exposed Waldheim's lies about only having been a low-level officer in the SS. And it wasn't long ago that her father had lobbied hard against America banning Waldheim from traveling to the US. The Jewish lobby in the States wasn't about to let Waldheim whitewash his past.

"As for why your house," Schofeld said, "we can't say. The RAF makes no secret of its opposition to American military bases. Maybe *this* group is looking to prove its stature by making a similar statement, attacking an American target here. Who's to say what seems logical to deranged minds?"

"Herr Schofeld, there are other forces that can be brought to bear. I may no longer be a servant to my country, but I think I'm able to help coordinate between our governments."

"And we'll work with them, Ambassador. It seems these demons never rest."

Clarissa let Herr Schofeld out. When she returned, her father's door was closed. She heard him speaking in that voice she knew was raising hell with officials somewhere.

THIRTY MINUTES LATER, dressed in a tight blue skirt and a teal blouse, Clarissa drove to what she hoped would be her new neighborhood. Within the hour, she had secured the apartment by paying three months rent. She lingered in the vacant rooms *listening to their voices*. It was on a high enough floor to catch good light, and she took in views of the neighborhood: trees on the sidewalks and the tiled roofs, the hallmark of the city. In a matter of minutes she became convinced she didn't want furniture. Just a bed and a table would do to help her enter this new stage of her life. Scouting for markets and cafés during the noontime bustle, she encountered many women in their thirties carrying or pushing little ones. The message of time passing her by was clear.

Back at her father's, finding him and the Rolls gone, she took her phonebook into his office to be more comfortable. Leaving the door open so she could hear him return, she made calls to the Netherlands. She arranged for clearing out their apartment and shipping their belongings. If Finn wanted to separate further, he would have to deal with her on her terms. She called Yvonne, her closest friend there, and spent an hour catching her up on all the changes. After the worst of the news was out, she put her feet up on his desk and allowed herself to laugh. Just as she hung up, she sensed shadows and movement in the alcove outside the door.

"Is that you, Papa?"

"I've just come in. Sorry if I cut you short."

"Were you eavesdropping?" She hoped she'd masked her irritation enough.

"You're not to use this office. There are Top Secret papers in here. There's a phone in the hall."

"How about you install phones for adults in the rooms upstairs?"

"Say you understand."

"I don't have to. I'm leaving. I've got an apartment."

"So I hear."

"You *were* listening." She walked past him into the hall, unwinding the last part of her conversation with Yvonne to determine what he might have heard.

"This is the wrong time to move, Clarissa. Staying together will improve our safety."

Her back was to him. "I think you're more interested in my making meals for you."

"You don't understand the gravity. Terrorists aren't predictable. Did you happen to look to see if you were followed when you left here?"

"No." She felt a chill. "You said yourself, you're not a real target."

"Maybe not, but all it takes is one careless act."

She rather liked watching him squirm. Her mind leapt to Finn's discomfort during the session with BethAnn. "At least Finn is vindicated."

"Finn?"

"The missile has nothing to do with Poland or the Soviets." She was partly aware of speaking out of bounds, but was taken by more of her memory returning—details from Finn's article, not in a coherent body, just phrases, and images her mind made when reading it.

"My first thought was the Soviets, too," her father said. "But he denied it. What has he been up to?"

His question showed he was on the same level as her and offered her the chance to demonstrate that she was well and knew something he didn't. She turned and took a few steps towards him. "Nothing much. An old document about a massacre."

"During the talks?"

"No . . . in Russia." She spoke the thoughts as they arose. "And, oh! Twenty thousand officers." When her father jerked his head to hear her better, she felt close to celebrating. "Katyn. That's the name."

Her father fiddled with change in his pocket. "Just in case, I'll call the CIA and see if they have anything from that part of the world."

"Why bother?" she said. "They've got the drop on this group."

Her father entered his office and closed the door.

Sixteen

During Clarissa's second session, BethAnn seemed more casual, which helped Clarissa relax. She told BethAnn about renting the apartment.

"And what does Finn think?"

"He'll find out eventually."

"So you're striking out on your own. How does it feel after all these years together?"

"That's what I'm worried about. Striking out, in the other meaning. And having no one to care when I do."

"Have you ever lived alone?"

"He's gone more than half the time these days."

"I guess I meant in your development years."

"For about six weeks once in San Francisco. Finn was off training for journalism."

"And what were you doing?"

She looked at the ceiling. "Waiting, mostly."

"Was that your major at Stanford?"

"No, history. Finn majored in Russian language and culture. Our plan was to get jobs in the same university and teach and travel. A shooting on campus turned Finn's life—" She finally got BethAnn's joke and laughed.

"You strike me, Clarissa, as a strong woman who's got a broken tie rod." When Clarissa showed her confusion, she said, "The gizmo that holds a car's front wheels together."

"Sometimes I do feel like I can't steer straight." Grief surged in her chest. If nothing else, her mother was steady at the wheel.

"Has that always been the case?"

"No, Finn wouldn't have married me if I had been like this. He told me that in therapy in Rotterdam."

"And you let him get away with it?"

"Actually, I didn't want to let him get away at all."

BethAnn nodded and made a note. "So you shrank a bit."

"I wasn't aware of it happening. I was very confident. I turned down a lot of men."

"Let's take another angle here. When a man in his thirties senses he's already lost the prospect of becoming the leader of the pride, his wife begins to shoulder the blame when he misses the kill. The good men run a little harder, hoping for a last chance. And because we women love seeing our lions run, we facilitate that." BethAnn paradiddled her pen on the page. "But it comes at a price."

"I wish I knew what he's chasing."

BethAnn smiled as she wrote a long note. "He's almost forty, right? But youthful in a way, like he can't help himself."

Clarissa harrumphed. "I have a question. Is it *okay* to keep a secret from your husband?"

"With Colonel Kerlingger," BethAnn said, with a straight face, "I find it absolutely necessary to keep secrets."

"When Finn and I got angry with each other in our session, remember?"

"Of course."

"Minutes before the missile hit, I read his article about Stalin. That memory vanished along with everything else. Then right before we came here, I remembered the headline. It must have been on the tip of my tongue."

"I was surprised at the stricture he'd put on you to not read his work."

"He said the lives of many people depended on the secrecy, though I don't know how it can go from that to headlines around the world a few days later and not jeopardize those same people."

BethAnn nodded. "As I see it, you have no secret there."

"Now I do. The other day, while arguing with my father, I remembered some of the text."

"That's good. And?"

"I told my father."

"Oh! So you told your father the secret your husband asked you not to tell anybody. Do you know why you did it?"

"To make up with him. Things have been rough between us."

"So you sacrificed Finn. At least, you gave away something he thinks is important. And now you don't want to tell him."

"You saw how on edge we were. I've already broken his rule about this goddamn thing once. About his article. An article that isn't coming out, so far as I can tell."

"Here's what I think: Things always have a way of coming back around. If it's important, there will be a time to tell him what you've done."

Seventeen

Finn put the Melezh and a change of clothes in his bag. He boarded the early train, heading not west toward the German POW camps, but east to Bialystok. There he boarded a train for Minsk. In the lavatory, he practiced pulling out his Karol Sobczak passport. Now that birds really were arriving in their spring numbers, he had little trouble convincing Belarusian customs agents of his plans to study them east of Minsk. But because the last fifty miles to Dyedna had no train or bus service, he rented a room in Mogilev, the last town of any size nearby.

He purchased second-hand country clothes and set off on foot. He walked many miles but also rode in two cars, a flatbed truck collecting scrap metal, a state grain truck, and a horse-drawn wagon. He walked the last long stretch to the home with the bright yellow chicken coop. As he knocked on the door of Janis's house, he saw Mikolai had been correct: paint applied in the cold of early March doesn't fare well.

He hoped for only one thing: to see Janis alive. Mrs. Semyonovich answered in her kerchief and apron. When she called over her shoulder, Finn's heart almost broke with gladness. They hadn't had a walk-in visitor in many years, she said—somehow she discounted Mikolai as one—as she washed the only two cups they owned. She sprinkled chamomile leaves into them from a bundle hanging near the stove. After expressing pleasantries of surprise and delight, Janis—come of age in the world of lies—asked if Finn had had 'success with his project.'

"Yes. Thanks to you, we found your old friend. He gave us everything we needed." Mrs. Semyonovich pretended to not be listening as she carded wool. But the timing of her strokes gave her away.

"And your friend is well?" Janis asked.

"He went home, and I haven't heard from him." Finn struggled with a sense of not deserving their hospitality. He shifted his awkwardness by presenting Janis the Melezh book as thanks for risking so much. That wasn't how he meant to say it, but Mrs. Semyonovich trotted to the kitchen and slammed the door behind her.

Janis sat unperturbed. "As long as she doesn't know *what* I did . . ." he shaped his hand like a pistol, "she'll get over it. She's a good woman who let me drag her into this empty land to live under an uncompassionate sky."

"What will you do when—?"

"When I get older?" He pointed to the kitchen. "Isabel has children, two daughters. The elder isn't married any more. He died." Janis raised a make-believe bottle to his lips and drank heartily. "We could live there. If she leaves me here in the ground, she will go live with one of them."

In Finn's mind, Janis was now the one standing on the edge of a trench, showing grace about what was coming.

"I just came to deliver this." He touched the book, his feelings mixed. Finding Janis alive supported the idea that Mikolai's other adventures had caught up with him and that he had gone nobly without speaking of Janis. So perhaps Finn's family was safe too. But the question lingered: Who would be in danger when the story of Stalin's orders came out?

His business complete, Finn rose and knocked on the kitchen door. He thanked Mrs. Semyonovich for her trouble and wished her well. Standing on the porch, he donned his hat. Janis walked him to the road. An hour before, the surface had been muddy. Now, with the sun being past mid-afternoon, it was freezing again.

While at one time Janis might have wished he'd chosen to die at Katyn rather than slaughter bound prisoners, in the end he had tried to rectify the horrific bargain he'd made with staying alive. In farewell, he said, "Be careful walking across this land."

BACK IN THE MOGILEV train station, Finn changed his plans. He asked the ticket agent, a woman with green eyes set above copious jowls, how to get to Katyn.

Her brows peaked into a triangle. She spoke in a voice deep from cigarettes. "You young people haven't seen enough cadavers, I guess."

Finn flexed to keep his head from snapping away from the window. "I'm writing a book on Sov—" he caught himself—"on German atrocities. If you must know, the SS killed my grandparents in Poland."

"You're Polish?"

"A professor."

"You don't sound like you're Polish. Not at all."

Not liking how her mind jumped, he felt desperate for Mikolai's craftiness. What would the master say? "You compliment me, comrade. I've been listening to the bullfrogs in the Kremlin my whole life." At that moment he realized his left hand, with his wedding ring on it, was in her line of sight. He laughed loudly to cover withdrawing that hand and slipped it in into his pants pocket. "Within one generation," he said, "all the peoples in the USSR will be speaking one language." And he took the Russian word for frog and melded it with the word for Russian. "Lyagruski yazik."

She laughed and shot back, "Within one generation, we'll all be eating grass. And I don't mean like the dead at Katyn."

"In that case," he said, "I best get there soon."

With a jab of her chin, she acknowledged that the people in the line behind him were grumbling for Finn to shut up and move on. "You can't get there by train," she said. "You have to take a bus to Orsa. There, you catch another to Arzhipovka, then take a taxi to Katyn."

"How far is it?"

"Not far." Her smirk expanded. "Unless you're taking the bus. Then sometimes the train is faster."

BLESSEDLY, THE BUS used paved roads, none of its tires went flat, and the heater stymied the Baltic wind that blew through the windows that wouldn't quite close. Finn spent the night in an Arzhipovka boarding house, alternately scratching at bed bugs and plugging his thumbs in his ears. The metal workers who were dismantling a factory for shipment on trucks to Minsk snored around him like a Russian chorus.

Standing on the street at sunrise, fate chose for him a taxi driver whose blood alcohol level hampered his ability to keep to the right side of the road. He dropped Finn by the gate that blocked a one-lane track marked with a humble sign. *Memorial - one kilometer.* There, Finn had to face the truth that he had no clear idea why he had come. He stashed his bag under a winter-killed bush and headed up the road.

The sun was weak and low. Islands of snow huddled on the north sides of trees, spindly things, all the same species, a kind of lodge pole pine, straight as arrows but with sparse branches. In his visions of the place, that forest had been dark and mature with romance enough to counterbalance the crime that had occurred there. Several hundred yards on, he realized he was walking where the voices that were rocking the Black Marias in song fifty years before had begun to falter.

He entered their world. The bumps in the road made them press their faces to the windows to look into the night. They saw lights. At some point, they heard the roar of diesel engines and the pop of pistols. Veteran soldiers exchanged morbid looks. They were not going home. When the headlights of their buses panned the scene where each of them would take their last walk, the cries and fury began.

The road Finn walked bore no recent tire tracks. There were no farmers in the fields that bordered the forest. The land held just a Polish-American lost to himself, at odds with his wife, and searching for a soapbox on which to stand and shake his fist at a world, a world that favored denial over most every version of reality.

So often had he imagined the horror that had taken place there that he expected to come upon remnants of the mounds left over from the Wehrmacht's exhumation. But the whole area had been bulldozed and replanted. The condition of the trees seemed a purposeful insult to what had happened there.

The road ended in a gravel turnaround flanked by an upright piece of rose granite, some ten feet wide and four feet tall into which words had been chiseled. "In memory to the victims of the Hitlerites." Nearby, a small building that might someday serve as a token museum or a souvenir shop stood unfinished.

From there, a path of flagstones led to the largest of what had been seven trenches. A flat stone marked the site. On it was a brass plaque giving the number of bodies and the names of a few generals. The quality of the path deteriorated beyond the second trench. *You've seen one mass grave, you've seen them all*, he grumbled.

Coming to the site of the third trench, Finn stood long enough to see it open up in front of him. He placed his hands behind his back, felt the wire bite into his wrists. He imagined the *pop-pop* down the line, the diesel smell, and the realization of having only seconds to accept that his life would end in this bleak place.

He wanted to die better than this. No doubt, the Polish officers had as well. Angry, he opened his eyes. The leveling of the site had reduced its strength to a whimper, had obliterated its lessons. The trenches, the uniforms, the undelivered letters home and the bones should have been left exposed for all to see. School children should have been dragged there. Army recruits should have been forced to sleep among the remains. When he picked up his bag at the end of the road, he vowed to set the record straight once and for all.

BACK IN WARSAW his second stop was the US embassy, which is where Sam Rich's note at the hotel had told him to go. Sam had sent a post under diplomatic pouch, dated March 29, 1989. Two days before.

> *Finn, I order you to stop pursuing the story and to dedicate yourself to covering the talks. The State Department has shut us down. (And off the record, I feel it's "us.") My source there says their teams weighed Stalin's orders carefully. They were almost ready to go with it. Then late last week another advisor close to the presi-*

dent convinced him too much was at stake. He decided this revelation must only come out through "a concerted international exploitation of Soviet vulnerabilities." Please confine yourself to other news. Sam

To rebuke the directive Finn shredded the page, then tramped around city blocks, contemplating his next moves. The Roundtable Talks had stopped for the day when he arrived at Solidarity headquarters. Dabrowski made him wait an hour in the outer office. And he stood behind his desk to signal their meeting would be short. He pointed to the plaster casting on the ceiling to remind Finn of KGB microphones.

"There will be no baby," Finn said.

Dabrowski's tongue drove hard into his cheek. "You couldn't get the woman pregnant."

"I'm not in . . . I failed."

"So is there anything more we need to talk about?"

"We've been shut down." He waved his hand over his head to show it was coming from on high.

Dabrowski leaned his massive frame over the blank pad on his desk. He scribbled a note and spun it for Finn to see. *"You said you would die trying, but you're still alive."*

Finn lifted his foot for Dabrowski to see, then wrote, *"Fresh dirt from the site is in these treads."*

Dabrowski spread his hands and mugged insult. "Souvenirs don't interest me."

That was the kick Finn needed. It got him wondering which papers might take his story without him being under contract. Did he have credit with some publisher he could cash in? Thinking Clarissa wouldn't stand by him if his career pulled him to another city, he thanked providence for the wedge already between them. He crossed off American papers. The Cold War wouldn't allow them integrity. British papers couldn't be relied on either, except perhaps for the *Guardian*. But their budget was so low their correspondent at the talks had to hole up in a cheap hotel across the city. Finn resolved to track him down. "I'm not finished," he told Dabrowski.

Dabrowski lifted a report from his desk and waved it to send Finn to the door. "If we talk again, you will be convincing me we didn't lose a good man for nothing."

DETERMINED IN THE short term to keep his byline hot, at the hotel Finn buried himself in the AP reports filed in his absence. They revealed why Dabrowski had reason to be surly. The talks were in a delicate stage. Wałęsa was incrementally pushing for Solidarity to gain access to governing. Later, Finn's friend Marty told him Wałęsa's plan seemed to be to stay at the table until Jaruzelski agreed to contested elections, something unthinkable in the Eastern Bloc for forty-five years. Tensions were high.

That night after dinner alone, he sought out Chantelle. He pulled her from a gathering of French-speaking colleagues, saying he needed to talk. It was her grace that got her up. She shrugged ignorance to her friends and followed him to the dark lounge, the one abandoned and awaiting a remodel, where the piano sat locked and dusty. Kapok fibers bled through the fabric of the bench seat they found.

"Would it be all right," he asked, "if I unleashed the greatest hurt I've known in my fifteen years on the job? And if you agree, will you understand if I don't tell you the 'who, what, or where?' "

"I was hoping you were going to tell me why you disappeared for a few days."

"I was working another story."

Chantelle sucked her lips. "What do I get in return?"

He hadn't thought that through, he said. He apologized and rose to lead her back.

Not rising, she reached for his hand. "No, Waters, you didn't say *no* to me. If you need it that bad, I won't say no to you, either." And they shared a look, dating back—what was it—ten days? He got them drinks. In the shadows and the chill of that space, he described the extent of his defeat, how he was now lost in his career, soon to be a has-been. In nothing did he give her any information that a torturer could extract from her in a case to be made against him.

"I haven't been around long enough," she said. "Or maybe I'm just too much of a pond skimmer to find the kind of prize you're talking about. I doubt I'll ever know what it's like to lose one."

"Well, take this with you," he said. "If you don't make your mark early in this business, age comes faster than you can believe." She seemed to lack context for what he was saying. She was only a decade younger than he was, which proved his point all the more.

"You know what we all see in you?" she said.

"I have no idea."

"A man using his wounds for good cause."

He was not aware his wounds showed. "It's that obvious?"

She shook her head. "I shouldn't have said."

He rocked his frame in agreement, hoping to make the subject go away.

"Why are you talking to me, and not to Marty or Eggelsman?" she asked.

"Because I don't want to lose them as friends. Men get nervous talking about failure."

"And women?"

"Tell me if I'm wrong: They get closer."

"You're not wrong," she said.

"I need to prove I'm not used up."

"No one thinks you're close to—"

"I want to be with you tonight, Chantelle."

She turned her jaw sideways to him, then pointed to the ceiling and raised her eyebrows.

"Yes," he said.

She ran her tongue under her top teeth. "Tonight is fine. But I don't think I want to make you a habit."

Eighteen

ALONG WITH PORTOBELLO mushrooms, spices, shanks of lamb, and new potatoes from Lebanon, Clarissa packed a bottle of her father's favorite Claret. She chatted with the guards outside his house. Masons had poured footings for the seven-foot iron fence they would erect along the sidewalk. It would be wired with sensory equipment, cameras, and alarms. The carpenters greeted her on their way out. They had completed the exterior finish work. As soon as the plaster and the painting were done, life could return to some kind of normal.

The aromas of garlic, rosemary, and meat filling the kitchen made her happy. But as the hour for her father's return approached, she poured herself a generous glass of scotch. She rehearsed her lines. They flowed better than earlier in the day.

"I didn't know you drank scotch," he said, coming into the kitchen. He swung two silver-papered bags onto the island. Bottles clinked together. He was cheerful.

How could he not know me that well? she thought. They pecked the air by each other's ears. "Now I know why *you* do."

"Am I late?"

She hoped the drinks he had in him meant the evening would go well. "You can't be late to your own house."

He poured a scotch for himself and backed through the door into the hall. She heard the rustle of plastic sheeting that covered the parlor archway. The front door opened and closed. She lit the candles in the dining room.

Her father pushed back into the kitchen. "It finally *looks* like a house. Gotta love the Germanic will to win. They're right on schedule."

She pulled warm bowls from the oven, ladled in the stew, and led him to the dining room.

He sat, looked around. "I've never noticed how big this room is."

"It was fine for you and Mother."

He shook his head. "Wood paneling only glows in the presence of laughter."

"Have you been reading poetry?" she asked.

"No. These walls cry out for another voice. Don't you sense it?"

"Papa, may I? That's not what I want to talk abou—"

"Laugh with me," he said. He swirled the cubes in his glass. "But first I have good news."

"Can't it wait?" To prove she was not drunk, she watched how fluidly she spooned stew into her mouth. The spices were perfect. She groaned pleasure.

"I think you'll want to hear it. They captured the terrorist band from Graz hiding out in the wetlands near the Flugel Hof. They killed the leader."

She stirred her stew.

"I'm the only citizen the police called about this."

"You're not a citizen of Austria."

"I'm . . . Clarissa, you're not grasping what this means."

"Perhaps I'll be more intelligent after you've allowed me to say what's on my mind." There was a slight growl in her voice.

"Christ, Clarissa. Listen. Interpol and the Austrian police have been chasing these people for two weeks. He's the wacko who tried to kill me." He slurped another spoonful of stew. "Kill *us*."

The wood paneling wasn't glowing at all. They put down their spoons almost in unison. "I hope he didn't have children," she said.

"That's a strange thing to say. If they're right, we can send the guards back to base and get on with living. If he had kids, they'll be better off without him."

She leaned forward and raised her brows. "I thought it was *beautiful* thing to say."

He sighed. "Is this about your memory? Are you making progress?"

"You mean with Frau Kerlingger? Yes, we're making progress."

"I meant you. Are *you*?"

"BethAnn seems to think you and I never separated properly." There. It was out. Clumsy, but it would have to do.

"What's that got to do with why you're seeing her?"

"Why does it matter? Let's look at it."

He leaned back in his chair. "I didn't know there *was* a proper way to separate. You went off to school in Switzerland when you were sixteen. As I remember, we both cried. We both got over it. It's never changed my love."

"Separation has nothing to do with distance or ability. It's not like balancing a checkbook. Children have to grow strong in certain ways."

"Let me say, this is not a time to assail your mother's childrearing skills."

"You're not hearing me. This is about *you*."

"I grant you," he said, "you've been edgy lately, but we've always had a good relationship." He drained his drink. "But if irritation is a sign of not separating properly, I suspect we'll get there in short order." His glass smacked the table.

He'd been a decent father. Though he had traveled for work, he lived at home in equal amounts. She loved that he would bring his drink and sit on the floor with her in front of her dollhouse built in the mode of Noah's ark; twos of each animal. He had read books to her in the bay window the missile demolished, pushed her on the park swings. She remembered the joy that accompanied Sunday nights in Switzerland when she was free to write him letters. They marked the beginning of her getting his attention as an adult.

"We'll never know now," he said, "but I wonder if there was something that you didn't finish with your mother. Because when she got sick, that's when everything started to get away from you."

"Everything has *not* gotten away from me. And my mind *was* rickety before then."

"Have you stopped to consider that your problem is with your husband and not with me? What do they call that? Transference?"

Clarissa wasn't sure what shook her more: Finn being the problem, her father knowing they had problems, or him knowing even one psychological term.

"You are having trouble with him, no?" When she balked, he softened, "We should be able to speak of these things, especially now with Jacqueline gone. Tell you what, I'll fashion myself into a listening post. That's what an ambassador is mostly; someone who pays attention to every nuance of speech and affect of the other party to figure what they are really trying to say, what they are trying *not* to say, and then reaching back to help shape their message into what my boss wants to hear."

"I think I have that in BethAnn."

"The point is, darling, we have to stick together now. And with Finn making mistakes at work, you need to have a fallback—"

She slapped the table. "Mistakes? Do you know what he's dealing with? Do you even read his articles?"

"As a matter of fact, I do. And I have been reading them more carefully since you told me about this mess with Stalin's orders. I can see a man who's trying to speak almost in code to readers. I'm so glad you told me, because it—"

"I mentioned the massacre, sharing it in the context of the bomb blast. But it's none of your business or mine."

"I've done a little checking, Clarissa. You seem to be hot on the trail of the truth about him."

"Dammit, Papa. This is what I'm talking about. You're trying to tell me what I think, the logic that goes with it, what time of day I should think about it, and how I should feel happy for the privilege."

He put both his hands on the table as if it were a lid to his emotions. "That's unnecessarily harsh, Clarissa. You know your best interests guide me. If I were in your shoes, I'd want a lot of the kind of support you just outlined, though I'm sure I'm nowhere near as tight as you make me sound."

"Don't you see my point, Papa? I'm deathly afraid of failing at something that is unnamable. There's a black hand somewhere. And if it doesn't kill me, I'm afraid it's going to beat me silly and take away everything I love."

She saw, by his even demeanor, how he must have handled heads of state.

"I think," he said, "that hand has already done its duty. Several times."

❖❖❖

AFTER THAT SECOND night with Chantelle, Finn slept alone. And enough time had passed since hearing Clarissa's voice that when the phone woke him, he felt genuine interest in what she'd been experiencing. He looked at the clock. Eleven thirty-nine. "Are you in the downstairs hall?"

"You didn't get my message?"

"No," he said.

"I'm in my new apartment."

He rolled onto his elbows "One of the ones we looked at?"

"We'll get to that," she said. "I think someone is following me."

He flashed on the eavesdroppers. "Following you in Rotterdam?"

She hesitated. "Is it okay to talk on this phone?"

"Of course. We've been assured no one is listening in."

"Then, yes. Here in Rotterdam."

He was pleased she'd caught his lead. "What have you seen?"

"A blue sedan. German make, darkened windows."

"What's special about it?"

"It's got *no* characteristics. Shiny. No personality. That's what makes it stick out."

"When did you first notice it?"

"Today, both times I went out."

"And did you try to alter your route the second time?"

"I should have, but I thought of it too late. I just hurried."

"Does your building have another exit?"

"Um, yes."

"Then tomorrow go by taxi and do your makeup on the way. Use the compact."

"I get it," she said.

"Is your building secure?"

"The landlady went on and on about security."

"Have you told your father? He might know somebody who can tail the tail."

"I'm reluctant to do that right now."

"I understand," he said. But he didn't. "I look forward to talking about that. Are you . . ." Now he rethought. ". . . Making good friends with BethAnn?"

"We're fine. Her health is back."

Good girl, he said to himself.

"Is she calling you every week like she said she would?"

"Are you alone, Finn?"

The thought roared through his mind that this had all been a diversion to set him up. Not hesitating was the best message. "Way too much, as you know."

"Good. Because if you can get away from there, I have something you need."

In their courtship days, that was how they asked each other for sex.

"You remember the reference?" she asked.

"I do."

"Good. Anyway, something came for you at my father's house tonight. In a black package, no markings except for a Washington address. I nearly broke my ankle on it in the dark. It must have been too big for his mailbox."

"A box or an envelope?"

"A huge 9 by 12 envelope. Unrippable fabric."

"Great."

"Do you want me to open it?"

"You know what it is, don't you?"

"I think so. Should I send it to you?"

"Nothing's that important." He was already plotting how to get to Vienna.

"I'll have it whenever you get here."

In the silence that opened in the line, he faced the pain of not knowing his future with her.

"I'll check my schedule and let you know."

"I guess that's the best I can hope for," she said. "Here's something you should take down." She gave him eight nouns that he recognized stood for digits, the way to reach her on her new phone.

Nineteen

TWO DAYS LATER, April 2, the press gathered in the briefing room for an important announcement. The Polish government's spokesman waited on the dais until Viktor trotted into the room and up the stairs to join him. Viktor was wearing the kind of smile Poles would see a lot of in days to come. Both men confirmed there had been breakthroughs. The official joint statement said it was in the best interest of the people to allow for new elections. When Viktor took the microphone, he explained that Solidarity had successfully negotiated for party status and *real* elections, not just exercises that replaced one set of dour faces with another. They could fill slates of candidates for the lower house and for 40 percent of the seats in the senate. Viktor seemed unperturbed that this precluded Solidarity from achieving a majority stake in the government. "In two short months," he said, "Poland will have free elections."

Finn thought of the troops on the border, but Viktor said one of the conditions of the agreement was for the troops to leave. "The first convoys began pulling back at noon." He looked at his watch. "Two hours ago. If all goes well, representatives for both parties will meet here in three days and sign papers that fundamentally change the government of Poland."

The clicking of cameras sounded like hail on a tin roof. Looking for Dabrowski, Finn saw Annalisa on the photographer's platform, saw Chantelle next to Marty, saw the Swedes, Alice Baldwin, Eggelsman, and Norland. Their faces abandoned the professional distance their editors were proud of. This was justice. Dabrowski wasn't there.

That day, the ground shifted. For a month, Finn had linked bringing Stalin's orders to light to an eruption of Polish joy. Walking back to the hotel, he saw in the faces that they had no room for additional happiness. Again, outside events were burying the story of 22,000 cadavers.

His article tempered the legalese of the provisional accord with descriptions of the celebration in the streets. He included Wałęsa's optimism that the authorities wouldn't dare derail the process. "I knew going into the talks that the government had no option but to collapse," Wałęsa said. "The future is always hard to know, but please return again and again to see what people who long for justice can accomplish."

After filing their articles, his colleagues retired to the lounge for good cheer. Finn wasn't much in the mood. Regret often swept over him when coverage in a place wound down. He knew that in a decade's time, new leaders would have converted the fresh start into riches and power for themselves. He, or some journalist on the rise, would return to this place to file stories of the country's pain. Political scientists would connect the dots. But the people who were being fleeced would ignore the reports until it was too late.

IN THE MORNING, the Bristol Hotel looked like a theater after the show has closed. Decorations were gone. An army of cleaners plied the elevators. Painters moved lobby furniture into the basement. Cabs and trucks parked in front at all hours to haul people and tech gear to the airport. Sam Rich told Finn he'd earned a few days off. "Tamara Schell, our rising star, will arrive on the weekend," he said. "She'll cover through the June elections and the swearing in of the new government in July. It's fitting, don't you think, that the first country overrun in 1939 is the first to slip the yoke of tyranny? Six months short of fifty years. You're heading back to Vienna, I suppose."

Finn saw no reason to let Soviet apparatchiks know where he was planning to live. Sam had no reason to suspect the truth or Finn's lie. "We're returning to Rotterdam."

"Okay, call me from there. This isn't the end of Communism. The whole Eastern Bloc is about to learn how to polka. Mark my words, we're going to be busy."

Clarissa and Finn's phone answering machine was in a truck somewhere on the European continent. Finn called before he left the Bristol, later from Okecie Airport, and again from Vienna's Flugel Hof. Not reaching her, he began to worry. He didn't know the address of her apartment. With no options, he left a message on Fortie's machine saying he was coming in.

He found the house lit up. An iron fence with sharp points ran along the edge of the property. Too high to reach, a camera stared at him. He reviewed his agenda. Find Clarissa and avoid the following subjects with Fortie: his marriage, his fidelity, her sessions with Beth-Ann, and any mention of where he'd been. He rang the bell.

Fortie's voice came over an intercom. "Welcome, Finn. You're the first guest to see the completed project." The rise and fall of his speech let Finn know he was what Gloucester fishermen called *three sheets to the wind.*

Finn deposited his bags in the foyer and shed his overcoat. Fortie led him into the parlor. The workmen had done a good job. The space just needed living in. "The fresh paint smell requires an antidote," Fortie said. He turned to the liquor hutch.

"Scotch will do. I'm looking for my wife."

"Join the club."

Dammit, he was too late. Was the old man drinking to flatten his sense of alarm? Had she told him about being followed? Or maybe he was referring to Jacqueline and gearing up to do his morose widower thing. "I'm serious. Is Clarissa all right?"

"That depends on what you mean by *all right*. Drink this and we'll talk. It's good to have you home. We need to work together."

The proposal set Finn off balance. "You've got my attention."

"That's never been hard." Fortie sipped and shook his head. "I meant that as a compliment."

Finn had already taken it as poison. "Tell me, is she safe?"

"Maybe not from herself. Certainly not from that woman."

"Have you seen her?"

"Of course. She left just before you called." Fortie's laugh was inappropriate.

Finn scratched off the fear of her being followed. "Then why didn't you pick up?"

"I was on the toilet."

"And what woman isn't she safe from?"

"Kerlingger. What's-her-name."

"BethAnn," Finn said.

"When was the last time you talked to her?" Fortie asked.

"Five days ago. She told me she'd just rented an apartment."

Fortie exhaled exasperation. "To get away from the old man, no doubt."

"Are we talking about the same woman?" Finn asked. "Five-seven, strawberry blond, beautiful, Daddy's favorite girl?"

"We are. But unless you intervene, I'll have to start editing her résumé."

"Come on, Albert. Put down the drink and talk to me."

After sucking the life out of what was left, Fortie did as he was told. He came away with a cube in his mouth.

"She's missing, Finn. The old Clarissa's gone. A sharp-tongued she-devil has taken her place."

"I like that part of her . . . in the right season. So she's all right?"

Fortie spit the cube into his fist. "Not when she accuses you of 'father-daughter cluster.' "

"What the hell is that?"

"So you don't know? Good. Something about being too close, that we didn't separate properly. I didn't know you could ever get too close to your own family."

Incest never crossing Fortie's mind was a real possibility. But then, incest was an even blacker secret than mass murder. At the thought, Finn avoided Fortie's eyes. What he would do to the old man if he *had* damaged her! Fortie interrupted him.

"This BethAnn creature is feeding her all kinds of . . ." his mind ranged, "merde. It makes me damn mad. I've been paying her bills."

"Stop it, Albert."

And Fortie did stop. Like he'd run into a door.

"Let's be fair. Less than a month ago my wife—your daughter—was inches from losing her face not ten feet from where we're sitting. And somehow it peeled back a layer of her putting up with you."

"I haven't been controlling her."

"Then why bring it up? Get real, Albert. Jacqueline was a lovely woman who—"

"I didn't deserve her."

"Be that as it may, she made all objectionable things look and smell good."

"May I have another drink now, please sir?" Fortie mimed Oliver Twist.

Finn ignored his antics. "What's the big deal?"

"Thank you," Fortie said, rising with his glass and making for the hutch. "She's saying something is wrong in our past." He grumbled. "As if I didn't know our past. If she doesn't come back to her senses, I'll fight this to the death. And I'll tell you what," he shook his glass at Finn, "I'm done paying for the pleasure of . . . the source of my displeasure." He stopped, both bitter and amused. He poured himself a double and then some more. "That Kerlingger woman has to go."

"Everybody's got stuff buried, Albert. Why else do we drink?" If men drank amounts commensurate to what they buried, Finn guessed Fortie had a cemetery named after him. For the moment, he ignored gauging the extent of his own burial grounds.

The old man sat again. He tongued the corner of his mouth, gathering a strategy. "That's what you do for a living, isn't it? Digging up dirt."

Finn dodged his wish to tell somebody new about Katyn. "I'm part of the balance in the universe, yes."

"That makes you a dangerous sonofagun to some people."

"Only to the corrupt."

"Ah! One of the good guys. So, Marshal Waters, tell me what's the next big thing?"

"I'm interested in Clarissa tonight."

"Humor me."

"All right. Other communist regimes may fall."

"We can thank Reagan for that. The man was a genius."

Finn looked at the floor. "With your permission, I'll abstain. In any case, Hungary seems to have the hiccups."

"I'm worried about that step, Finn. Hungary isn't Poland. There's no story there worth your talents. What your career needs is to make a coup somewhere."

"Maybe so. Right now, I'm here to help Clarissa move in. And to apologize for being a jackass." He immediately wanted to punch himself in the face for veering off his agenda.

"She's told me," Fortie said matter-of-factly. "But look, if you help me with her, I'll develop amnesia on your account. I need you to stitch us back together as a family."

"What has she told you?"

Fortie bit his lower lip for a long while, long enough for Finn to wish he hadn't asked. "What you do is hard work. You come by it naturally, and I admire it. I always have."

Finn searched for his father's picture in the gallery. The shelf was bare.

"Look. You help me with Clarissa, and I'll help you find the big stories. You think we in government don't know what's coming better than the media?"

"That's why our job is so damn hard."

Fortie thought with pursed lips. "It's no secret I've always been hard on you. It's just that having you around reminds me of your father and . . . his disappearance." He sighed as if about to act on a huge decision. "I'll tell you what. I'll keep my ear to the ground for you. I'll feed you things in ways that keep us both clean, hmm? And you see what you can do to bring Clarissa back to where she was. I love that girl. That woman. And she loves you. She'll listen. What do you say?"

Twenty

FINN PUT ON his coat in the Fortier mansion hall.

"She hasn't even given me her new address," Fortie said. "Can you believe that?"

Finn thought he'd test the rules in their new arrangement. "Sounds like she's breaking the father-daughter thing. Give it time." He called Clarissa from the hall phone. Clarissa seemed groggy. Finn checked his watch. It was only 10:15. When he told her he was in Vienna, she didn't ask where he was. "It'll be good to see you," she said. He heard water running. "But don't come here assuming anything."

It was the scotch that pressed him to have her say more.

"I mean anything about our relationship."

It was the same scotch that kept the blow from knocking him down. Until that moment, he'd assumed he was in control of the distance between them. In one sentence she schooled him that she would be loved at her consent. "I won't. I mean I'll try. I'll stay at a hotel tonight."

She said, "There's no need."

"I'll go to the Richter," he said,

"He's standing nearby, right?"

"Yes."

"Promise me you won't tell him the address."

"Of course not."

She gave him the street and number.

Finn looked at Fortie. Even if he'd overheard, he was past the point of remembering much. "I'll call you tomorrow from the hotel," he said into the phone. "We can meet somewhere for breakfast. We'll start talking then."

"I'll see you in a few minutes," she said.

In his mind, that was as healing a conversation as they could have had. When he pushed the button in the cradle for a dial tone to call a taxi, Fortie said, "That went well. Did she give the address?"

"Let's see what tomorrow brings."

CLARISSA HAD LANDED on a pretty street, a couple miles north of her father's mansion, four blocks from the Donaukanal. It was tree-lined and narrower than many in the city. Four floors up the windows were dark.

Clarissa responded to his buzzing 4C with a test. "What's the date we first made love?"

She would have known he'd remember, but he wondered how long an interview she would put him through. "April 7th, 1971."

"Were you followed?"

"Not that I could tell. I had the cabbie checking, too."

"I'll leave the door unlocked."

A minute later, he pushed into 4C. In the light that slipped over his shoulder from the hall, he saw wet footprints on the floor. He couldn't find the light switch. He made out curtains in the big room, then tracked a faint glow down a hall. The room blazed with candles and incense. Water was dripping into a claw foot tub. Only Clarissa's head was visible above the bubbles, hair piled on it, face glistening with perspiration.

"Sit." She tilted her head at a stool she had set there.

Finn took off his shoes and sat cross-legged.

"I thought things were upside-down before," she said.

He nodded. "They've been at least sideways for a while. I'm so sorry for the trouble I've caused."

"We all cause trouble, Finn. We all find it. And we'll get to yours." She stared at the wall over the foot of the tub. "I had a tough session today."

"With BethAnn?"

"Yes."

"Is that why you went to your father's?"

"She warned me not to go."

"You're the bad girl now?"

"Shut up and listen." She took her time. She drank water from a glass perched on the radiator. "BethAnn has been—no, BethAnn *and* I have been uncovering some shit."

"I'm listening."

"I'm not the person I've ever thought I was. She's asked me to look if I experienced some tragedy way back." Several times Clarissa tried to form a sentence. "I have no idea what it is, what it might have been. It's coming up like a hole in my heart. That's not what BethAnn says. That's how it feels to me." She wiped her forehead with her wrist. "Are you comfortable?'

Finn said he was.

"It doesn't make sense that a person can't remember what happened to her . . . unless she was unconscious or very young . . . and even then it's rare. It so happens BethAnn's doctoral thesis explored this topic. I asked her if rape was one of the things. She said studies show it is linked to this kind of suppression. Particularly if it was violent or by a relative." She waited a long time for words to come. "Are you with me?"

"Barely." His visit with Fortie took on a whole new dimension.

"Me, too," she said. "I'm barely with me. But I had to find out if he was hiding something." Her voice strengthened then faded as she continued. "I was determined to avoid tipping him off or getting into the whole thing."

"That explains why he was drunk off his ass. But he wasn't talking about incest. He was blathering about something called—what was it—'father-daughter cluster.' "

"That was more than a week ago."

"Do you think your father was . . . like that?" He wanted only one answer.

"I want to know where my mother was."

"I can't see it, Clarissa. Not with him. It's got to be something else."

"Without a memory of it, I can't, either. But incest happens, Finn. It happens where no one suspects. But if my mind did that, if it scattered the details, it protected me. It worked."

"What do you mean?"

"All these years I've lived free of it."

"But you said you have a hole here." He put his hand on his chest.

She laid her arms over her breasts. "The image I've been sitting with here tonight is my heart is like a geode, you know, crystal on the outside, beautiful and durable. But there's nothing on the inside, just space where flesh and spirit are supposed to be."

He knelt by the tub, took her head in his hands, kissed her hair. For a second she let go into his gesture. "What did he say? What did he do when you told him?"

"I never mentioned incest. I said something really bad happened to me when I was young, and I needed his help to find out what it was. I wanted to see if he would offer anything that hinted at it. Or hinted at *anything*. I'm pretty sure I started out low-key, but he went cold and headed for the liquor. I think that's when I began raising my voice."

"You *think*?"

"Actually not until after he deflected me with every trick in the book. You know how he is. He wanted to tell all the good stories, the family lore stuff. And I kept cutting him off, saying that somewhere I was violated. I said BethAnn wonders if this may be the root to my nervous chaos and if something's causing it to bubble up now. I had to tell him, *no*, for the umpteenth time, it wasn't Mother getting ill. When he went off about missing her, that's when I started to lose it. I asked him point-blank if he knew anything or ever suspected anything had happened to hurt me. Did my mother know anything, or had she ever said she was worried? He looked me dead in the eye and said she never spoke about anything."

"Maybe she didn't know."

"What happens if it was one of my mother's brothers or a guest?"

"What does BethAnn say?"

"She wants to see me tomorrow. Will you come with me?"

"Two days in a row?"

"She says the day after like the one we had can be a critical time."

Finn thought about the bills her father wouldn't be paying now. They had some money saved. "Won't I just end up being a distraction?"

"I need a friend, Finn. Do you think you can muster yourself to be one?"

SHE MADE HIM sleep in the living room. At dawn, he woke like a shot, stiff from having only a carpet as a mattress. He reminded himself the Polish officers had slept on concrete while waiting for Commandant Andrei Kurishenko to ship them 'home.'

The black-wrapped package from Washington that he'd come for lay by the door. A brick of three bundles—over 500 pages in response to his Freedom of Information Act requests from the departments of Commerce, State, and Trade—detailing all transactions of American companies with Germany between 1938 and 1941. Each department used the same cover letter explaining the redactions were to protect state secrets. With security clearance, they assured him, he could request to have the redactions removed.

He hoped those listings would reveal evidence of armament transports headed for the Soviet Union, including the pistols used by the NKVD at Katyn.

The first page was a deed of purchase for a parcel of a 1.37 square kilometers in Molsheim, filed January 2, 1938. The font was small, complete with typos. As promised, there were blacked-out words and phrases as well as one long sentence toward the bottom. Finn was stunned with the effort clerks and higher-ups had made to assess the risk of every word in these pages.

There were long documents of company prospectuses; lists of materials ordered, sent, checked, and paid for; letters of concern from company headquarters to international missions and their replies.

Mounds of boring details and still, no document escaped the censors' pens.

❖❖❖

CLARISSA LOOKED IN the mirror. A little makeup and breakfast hadn't covered her haggard look. Finn had their taxi come to the back of her apartment. She rode to BethAnn's with her head in his lap. He didn't think they'd been followed.

BethAnn said Finn's showing up was perfect. Clarissa didn't fault him when he said not to read too much into it. When she confessed she'd gone straight to her father's, BethAnn got a pained look. She took notes and interrupted when Clarissa talked about screaming at him. "Did you sense he might call the police or a doctor?"

"He said there wasn't a problem, and we should deal with whatever it was ourselves."

"And this is the same man who drags in American forensics and the marines when a missile flies into his living room?"

Clarissa looked at Finn. "It doesn't fit with him, does it?"

BethAnn thrummed her pencil on her pad. "Clarissa, we have to be very careful at this stage to not misidentify *or* label anything. If we're going in the right direction, what we're trying to do is summon your mind to assemble pieces that want to remain isolated. Some children can't process the damage. The details scatter, hiding themselves in different places in the consciousness. That means we don't know the *what* of it and we certainly don't know the *who*. If we are kind to you and make you feel protected, and if we are determined, little by little, things may start linking up, kind of like a puzzle putting itself together. After a while, we may see whole sections. Then we go for the next round, trying to see the picture." She gave Finn a tender look. "And we'll be relying on you, too."

"For what?" he said.

"You've been together twenty years, right?"

"Eighteen."

"So here's *your* line of inquiry: When did you first notice things change? What did they change from? How did they move and manifest? Did you ask questions? Did you keep a diary?"

"I get that we shouldn't label it," he said, "but I think we can scratch incest and rape off the list. Don't they ruin sex for the victims?" He tipped his head toward Clarissa. "I would never say she has problems in that department."

Clarissa stared from one to the other, pleased for the moment. For some reason, he was overlooking the times she refused him.

BethAnn shook her head. "We're in a theoretical stage. No one is saying it's sexual. But to answer your question, it might *not* ruin sex if the crime was perfectly buried."

Finn pointed to Clarissa. "She *is* a perfectionist."

Clarissa leaned back hard, nodding. "Nothing's ever good enough. I always have to fiddle with things."

BethAnn made a note.

"What did you write?" Clarissa asked.

"It's my way of remembering things."

"But I said something that made you think. I thought we were working together. Your ideas may spark mine."

BethAnn weighed the moment. "I was just wondering in which situations your perfectionism is geared to fix things and in which to hide them." After an edgy silence, BethAnn suggested they relax with free association. "Red?"

"White."

"Tympani?"

"Viola."

"Flute?"

"Gong."

"Horses?"

"Jell-O. No scratch that; jumping."

BethAnn eyed Clarissa and wrote a note. "Sex?"

"Hammock." She flashed on herself and Finn falling out of one before a successful insertion. Laughing about it lasted long after the bruises disappeared.

BethAnn gave her twenty more before she pruned her chin, nodded, and shifted focus. She had Clarissa choose what kinds of things she would want to put in her boat if she knew she would never return to her former life. Pens, yes, Oranges, yes. When the list seemed long, Clarissa quipped they'd need a bigger boat.

But after a while, she grew restless. "What's the point of this?"

"We're looking at the pieces," BethAnn said, "For now, none of us should analyze too much. Let's just see where they are. To do that we'll need to be patient."

Twenty-One

RETURNING FROM THE session with BethAnn, Finn and Clarissa found the moving van from the Netherlands waiting on the street. They hired two men from a local café and while moving everything up four flights, he wondered if he would ever live there. Afterward, hunger got them started with the boxes. Putting china in the cupboards, they fell into their old teamwork, she standing on a stool, delicate pieces moving from his hands to hers. At last she took a wine glass from him, caught his hand in her free one, and sat on the counter. Her foot slid the stool to the side. Her thighs stayed spread. He found her looking at him, clear in a way she hadn't been since before Jacqueline's illness. In the next minute, tears were plunking onto her jeans.

"Jesus, Finn. How did we get here?"

To answer her properly—and she deserved it—would require untying every nuance of intent, every accident and coincidence, and every stupid thing going back and back. He pursed his lips and shook his head one slow time. Her hands came to his jaw. There was something about the hands of a woman who had learned about lovemaking with him, who had suffered loss and defeats with him that no other woman's could match.

Their foreheads met as if trying to answer her question. They kissed, their mouths locking into the best parts of their history. Then he carried her through the doorway and down the hall.

THEY ATE LATE, a tablecloth on the floor, candles perched on a box. Their talk wasn't small; there wasn't enough of it to make an assessment.

Finally, he said, "Your father enlisted me to help bring you two back together."

She took the corner of her mouth in her teeth. "See if you can do it."

"I don't have to. Only if you want. Maybe I can play him."

"You're forgetting he's an ambassador. Opaque and smart. Do it. I don't want to live like this."

"You sure?"

"BethAnn's right. We don't know anything."

"Is there anything I should know before I see him?"

"Don't go out on a limb. Make it about him and me."

ON THE WAY to initiate the rapprochement, Finn upgraded his passport at the US embassy. Then, using their secure phone, he called Sam Rich.

"You were right about other countries following," Finn said. "The opposition in Hungary is demanding talks."

"I tell you Finn, if they go the way of Poland, I wouldn't want to be in Gorbachev's boots. I want you to go there, talk to the trade unions and ordinary people. Pen your insights from the street-level. You're good on the regular-person aspect. What happened in Poland has people here reading and thinking. I'll put $650 into your expense account. See if you can make it last a week."

"I need two more days here."

"Two days is perfect. We doubt the lines will be secure, so use spook lingo from the hotel. Let Diana know when you get settled."

It had been one of Finn's life's goals to go to Hungary, to walk the streets of Budapest, streets his father had walked before disappearing. The prospect inspired him to call both the *Christian Science Monitor* and the *Boston Globe* to have their archives resend all the articles his father had written. In the fifteen years that had passed since he'd first pursued this track, he'd often wondered if the computer age might turn up more of Jordan's work.

Feeling satisfied, he walked the two miles to Fortie's and rang the bell.

"Well?" Fortie asked, when he'd brought him into his office.

"I'm heading off to Hungary and don't know twenty words of the language. Sure you don't want to tag along and be my interpreter?"

Fortie rattled his lips in disappointment. "Not the place for a man to shine his career, as I've said. But that's not what I'm asking about. Have you've managed to rope our wild buffalo?"

"Signs are good. Say, did you tell me everything that went on between you?" As soon as the words were out, he realized he was breaking Clarissa's advice.

"If you can do that for me, I'll be in your debt."

Fortie not answering the question got him off the hook. "She wants us all to have dinner tomorrow night, neutral space, to clear the air. What do you say to Michele's?" Fortie's restaurant of choice.

Fortie got up and walked to his little window, patted his coat pockets as if looking for cigarettes.

"You're not smoking again, are you, Albert?"

He dropped his hands as if caught in the act. He'd quit when Jacqueline got her diagnosis. "Sometimes I'd sure like to."

"I'm no mediator. I'll listen in, maybe interrupt if one of you is being stupid."

Fortie fingered his tie. "I'm not the one who's on the edge of delusion."

"I think you're going to have to be more gracious than that. She's hurting, and you don't want to blow it."

"That's true. So where is she?"

"At home."

"Smart aleck," Fortie said, scooping a pen from his desk. "What address?"

Finn ignored caution. "Did you know she's being followed?"

"Good Lord, no. Are you sure? They said they caught all those guys." He reached for the phone and dialed a number by heart. Finn's German couldn't keep up, but he grasped Fortie was talking to the Vienna Police. After a minute, he put his hand over the receiver. "They're going to need the address."

"I'll run it by Clarissa," Finn said. "Here's the deal: If Austrian Police can't clear their streets, I doubt she'll want to come to dinner."

Fortie nodded, spoke into the phone, and hung up. "They'll put a detail on the house as soon as she allows it."

"She would rather wait before telling you her address. Can she call it in herself?"

"I don't see why not."

"It's that easy for you? Just a phone call?"

"I've been in this town for fifty years."

Thirty seconds passed.

"What are you thinking?" Fortie asked.

"I appreciate you passing stories to me, but there's something I need even more."

"Money? Because if so, the change in tone makes me willing to keep paying for that Kerlingger woman . . . for now. I just want to be first to know if there are any more cockamamie ideas coming."

"Thank you, and I accept that gift. But that's not it. If you can pick up the phone like that, I have a favor to ask."

Fortie sat. He appeared smaller behind his desk. Funny, Finn hadn't noticed that before. "I can't guarantee anything."

"How well do you know Secretary Baker?"

"So-so. He was at Treasury. Shultz was my boss. What about him?"

"I want to find out why State crushed a story of mine." And he told Fortie just the minimum about Stalin's orders and Katyn. Nothing about going to Russia, or stealing anything, or any names. Just that he'd gotten hold of the document and that State hadn't allowed the story to be printed. Finn couldn't tell if Fortie was riveted or concerned. He paid attention to every detail and Finn glimpsed his value at the elbows of power. He asked appropriate questions about the crime and what else Finn knew about the history.

At last, Finn concluded his argument. "I want to know why the US can't stand definitively for justice here. Maybe in the sweep of history, it's a small story. But if it's released, its meaning and precedent are huge. Think of how it might prevent other massacres in the future. Think of how it might hobble the Soviet Union right now. State's got to have an interest in this."

HE LEFT FORTIE'S house convinced it had been a good day. He'd been on the attack and hadn't lost more than a couple of pawns. When he told Clarissa that Fortie had accepted the dinner invitation, she fidgeted. She said she'd need the whole twenty-six hours to prepare. And because it was on his mind, he told her he'd asked for Fortie's help at the State Department with the Katyn story. When she seemed at a loss for words, he apologized. "I shouldn't have brought it up. You have enough on your plate."

AGAIN THE LIVING room floor woke him early and he worked on the FOIA documents, this time at the table they'd set up in the kitchen. When Clarissa came in to make her tea, he found his face in a drooled puddle on the page he last remembered seeing. She handed him another that had fallen to the floor.

Finn blinked it into focus. Animals destroyed in experiments with various compounds, a joint venture, both company names redacted, except for the second ending in "Benz." A censor's mistake. It begged the questions: Why would a car company experiment with animals, and why in 1939 after Germany had invaded Poland would an American company be involved?

"I need to be more like a cow," he said.

She seemed amused. "Because?"

"Because when she eats through the haystack, the needle ends up in her tongue."

THANKS TO CLARISSA'S frittering and ambivalence, they arrived late at Michele's. Bent at the waist, gracious, the host named Justin greeted them. "Bon soir, Madame, Monsieur. Monsieur Fortier est déjà a table. S'il vous plaît, suivez-moi." Justin led them toward the raised section in the back where the high and mighty gathered. It was quieter there. Over the years, part of Finn's education on how power was wielded had come from eavesdropping on the negotiations at tables here.

Clarissa slid her arm into Finn's. "I'm nervous."

"Two things in your favor, Clarissa. He's a diplomat, and underneath he's your best booster. I've never told you, but when he was walking you down the aisle, I had this fear you both would just keep walking right out the back of the cathedral, and everyone would applaud."

For a second, dimples broke through the tension by her mouth. "You *did* marry up."

Fortie, in a black suit reminiscent of mid-century nobles minus the sash, stood and reached for her hands. After they kissed the air, he steered her to the chair on his left. "My better ear," he said, tapping that side of his head. "I'd prefer we don't talk about unpleasant things. Good food and tense conversation don't go well."

Clarissa prodded Finn with the toe of her shoe and he spoke. "You're the pro, Fortie, but my understanding is superpowers have to at least mention the issues between them. Am I wrong?"

"Superpowers," he said to Clarissa. "Your husband has potential as a diplomat."

They ordered, then Clarissa launched in with the slightest waiver in her voice. "Since I don't know what happened to me, I'm not accusing you of anything."

Fortie steadied his breath while using the pads of both thumbs to adjust the butt ends of his flatware. He drank from his crystal water glass. "That's nice of you to say. I'll take that under consideration."

"Under consideration?" she asked.

Finn nudged Clarissa back.

"If something traumatic did happen to me, you'd want me healed, wouldn't you?"

Diners at the next table turned to look, then returned to their conversation.

Fortie spoke just above a whisper. "How could I not?"

"Exactly. And . . ." she paused, "if I get dirty in the process of getting clean, if you do, and if Finn does, I think Mother would prefer that to the status quo."

Fortie looked to Finn and pointed at her. "Classy, don't you think?"

"Take some of the credit," Finn said.

"BethAnn advises me to— All I ask is that you stand by me." Justin approached with a bottle of wine. She waited while it was opened and poured.

"Here's what I want, Papa. If you remember a situation where I was hurt but couldn't express it, help me. I'm not in a hurry. BethAnn says patience is the key."

Fortie's nostril's flared and his eyes began to water. "This whole thing is very difficult . . . coming on the heels of losing your mother."

Finn disappeared into the scene of his mother yelling at him that his father was never coming home. In that moment, he realized he'd always taken the blame. When he came back to Michele's, Clarissa was saying, "The little girl in me that needs—" Her breath came in short sighs. She traced her index finger around the silver frame of her bread plate. "I can't finish anything until this gets resolved." Then with little more than air from the back of her throat, she said, "Anything."

With that statement, it seemed the goal of the meeting had been met. Fortie and Clarissa shared a long look that Fortie ended with a loving nod. Poking at his crab cake, Finn sympathized with Clarissa's need to finish things. Like her, he suffered from being incomplete. Seeing Fortie's frame curling under the weight of time and loss, he realized the old man wasn't whole either. Finn's mother Brygitta's favorite proverb sprang to mind: *Leave this world with nothing in your heart left to give.*

Why, he wondered, *had she then engaged every part of her life with clenched bitterness*?

A classical guitarist began playing on the lower level. Waiters came and went with a rack of lamb, escargots, and coquilles St. Jacques. They came again to clear the plates.

Fortie asked when Finn was to go to Budapest.

"Tomorrow."

"And you'll be there how long?"

"Until the Hungarian Communists wise up to help the people they profess to care for."

"It's a pretty trip by train," Fortie said, "along the river there."

"We went there, didn't we, Papa?"

Fortie hesitated, then nodded. "Yes, once. I took you on business when your mother was out of town. After the war, Finn, those huge bridges over the Danube hung in the river like party ribbons left out in a rain." The corners of his mouth drooped. "Bombing."

"I've seen the pictures," Finn said.

"But I worry for you. May I? I don't think the next Pulitzer's coming from there. Hungary's halfway out of the Soviet compound already." He dropped his voice. "I've thought about our talk. You want to know where the next great story will be?"

Finn leaned in.

"The Baltics."

"Why the Baltics?"

"Because they're right in Russia's mandible. If Lithuania leaves, Kaliningrad will be cut off from the Motherland. *That* will trigger the war that marks the end of the century."

"Kaliningrad?" Clarissa asked.

Fortie leaned back into his teaching posture, one hand on the table. "The Soviet's only frost-free port north of the Black Sea. Shipbuilding, their navy, troop facilities. Poland and Lithuania surround it." He addressed Finn. "The Lithuanians were treated worst of all. I don't think they'll stand for another invasion. It's a powder keg. I'd tell my boss to send me there."

For punctuation, Clarissa spilled her water. Waiters came with towels. When they were gone, she told her father, "I worry about him in places like that." Then she hoisted her wine and Finn was struck with the contrast of red against the same white blouse she had worn the night of the missile attack. "Thank you, Finn, for helping me and my father this evening. And here's to you staying in Hungary, far away from all powder kegs. Which has the added benefit that when we need to see each other, the trip won't be too long."

At her words, Finn's hope jumped. She had as good as said that they would see each other, that she wanted to see him. She sat, shoulders up, full goblet of red wine in hand, the vibrant woman he'd seen enter the parlor while he was kneeling before the CD player trying to get the Chopin to play. Fortie standing close behind him. As if time had rewound itself, he heard the blast, saw her wine lifting into the air, saw her fainting, and her rabid looks trying to escape his touch. He remembered running to the kitchen, blood swirling in the sink, and his returning to the parlor with damp cloths. Then an image that had eluded him returned full force: Fortie kneeling over Clarissa, the buttons of her blouse *undone*, her bra exposed, and his hands frittering in the air as if they didn't belong to him.

Book Three

Budapest

Twenty-Two

Before boarding the morning train to Budapest, Finn purchased a strap for his briefcase to prevent his getting separated from the FOIA documents. Even on board, he wore it bandolier-style across his chest. No doubt many of the trains carrying the materiel catalogued in those files fifty years before had rolled down these very tracks. The State Department may have killed his chances to get Stalin's orders out in a timely fashion; Sam Rich's attention may have moved on; Poland might be temporarily distracted by real elections; and human propensity to forget history might be against him; but if Finn could prove an American company sent the guns Russians used at Katyn, *that* story was beyond state department censure. In the national chaos and soul-searching that article would surely cause, Finn would push Sam to release Stalin's orders. If he worked fast, it might come out in time to help other countries wiggle free of the Soviet yoke.

Because his father had last been seen in Hungary, Finn had projected himself crossing that border countless times. He longed to feel a kinship with the place. Looking south from his train compartment, the farmland on the Hungarian side differed not in the slightest from Austria's. Whatever language humans spoke, whatever their national or ethnic passions, they all dug the soil the same way. They inserted fence posts into the ground the same way. They left marginal land for forests. It was rarely survival that drove countries to war.

Several times over the hours, he entered the train car's corridor to observe the magnificent Danube River on the train's left side. A wide highway of water, barges chugging up and down, villages and towns on the Czechoslovak side resembling the Hungarian ones, though here and there he spied a mosque's minaret.

That morning's conversation with Clarissa had left him restless. Seeing her more relaxed after the meeting at Michele's, he'd hesitated to bring it up. If he had *imagined* Fortie's hands over her open blouse, *that* would have been one thing, but his contemplation through the sleepless night only intensified the images. It was the indecision in Fortie's hands that had called attention to them and that shook him now. And wasn't it right after that when Finn berated him for not calling a doctor that Fortie had cried out, "She's mine!" and shoved him over backward? He thought it irresponsible to leave for he-didn't-know-how-long without telling her.

Sitting across from her at breakfast, he waited for the right time.

"I'm happy with how it went last night," she said. "Are you?"

"I am . . . in general."

"But?"

"I think there's more to come."

She frowned.

"Like you," he said, "I don't remember everything that happened when the missile hit."

"That again? It's basically solved. And I must have imagined being followed, which is a good thing. I can't carry any more tension *and* keep up the work with BethAnn."

"Then I'll wait."

"No, I cut you off. Tell me."

He made her push him a second time before telling her what he'd remembered. Describing it out loud made it more vivid than before.

She wrapped her hands around the coffee mug and stared into it. "Under pressure, people do strange things."

"Yes, maybe that's all it was."

"And his hands shaking? Maybe he thought the wine was blood and opened my blouse. He was probably embarrassed that you saw him. He's from an older generation."

"But why did he push me away? My head slammed the floor."

"Because you yelled at him. You told him what to do."

"Maybe."

"In any case, it doesn't prove incest." She slapped her head. "And I'm overlooking the most obvious evidence. I bled the first time I had sex. We have to be looking for something else."

Later, as he mounted the railroad car's stair, she called out, "Don't go off on any jaunts."

The thought flew through his mind those might be her last words to him. At least as his wife. She was clawing her way to freedom, one that might lead to divorce.

NEITHER MAPS NOR photographs had prepared Finn for the full force of Budapest's grandeur, even in the dilapidated state that four decades of Communist rule had left it. Coming around the hills to the north of the city, he caught sight of spires and domes of every possible design. Closer in, the facades of buildings were so dense with arches and ornamentation they were hard to take in. No doubt Viennese planners and builders had spent much of their creativity trying to keep up with this downstream city.

It was a relief to hear Russian in the train station because he found Hungarian unintelligible. He settled into the Parliament Hotel with other early birds from the international press. As usual, paperwork to register with a foreign government was the order of the day. On his first walk around the town, though, he was struck that he felt free to go anywhere. Soldiers took note of him but made no move to intercept.

He described this in his first article to distract from the fact that nothing was yet happening on the political front. The significant difference here versus in Poland was that Hungarians had no counterpart to Solidarity. It was Communist workers versus Socialist ones.

❖ ❖ ❖

CLARISSA ENVISIONED HER apartment as trim and beautiful, but the ambiguity between her and Finn disturbed that. To set symbolic boundaries, she gave his things their own room.

Next, while gathering art books stored in her parents' attic, she came across notebooks of stories she'd written long ago. She grabbed them too, thinking they might offer insight into a girl hiding a buried trauma. On the way downstairs, passing her parents' bedroom, she spied the shelf of her mother's diaries. Forty-five volumes in varying sizes and colors. Her mother had always downplayed them. "Just the drivel of a sentimental creature," she had said.

Clarissa knelt and because it was her age, she pulled number thirty-eight. The entries Clarissa read supported her mother's assessment, but she'd written something every day. She took the book with her.

BETHANN HAD SET up two chairs back to back.

"Some of my California colleagues have been trying this," she explained. "They have reported interesting revelations. The idea is to awaken the part of our minds that relies on hearing alone."

Within a minute, Clarissa launched into her memory of the dinner at Michele's.

"Great," BethAnn said at the end. "Regardless of what happened in the past, keeping the door open with your father can only be helpful. If your trauma came from the outside, it would have affected the whole family, even if none of you knew it at the time. To heal, both you and he will need to engage it."

"I doubt he'll do that . . . without being medicated."

"Good for you for laughing. And things with Finn, how did you leave them?"

For the first time with BethAnn, Clarissa felt that she wanted to—if not lie—at least obscure the truth.

"You don't have to talk about him if you don't want to."

Clarissa exhaled. "Remember when we said that lies have consequences?"

"Of course."

"I haven't yet confessed to him that I told my father he'd found Stalin's orders. Now it's more complicated."

"Between you and your father?"

"No . . . well, yes, with him too. Wanting to find out why the State Department shut his story down, Finn also told my father about his having the orders. He wanted my father to find out why. When Finn told me this, I had a golden opportunity to confess my father already knew. But I didn't. So now I'm in a double lie. At dinner, I watched to see if they had a side deal not to mention it. It's the most important story in Finn's life, but I didn't sense a twitch from either of them. That worries me."

"You brought this up talking about consequences."

"Right. If my father had told Finn that I'd already told him about the orders, Finn would have killed me. You were here when he told me not to tell anybody. It makes me think my father's got something going."

"Are you sure he wasn't just protecting you?"

"I'm never sure of anything with him." Suddenly, she wished the session were over.

"Do you have plans to see Finn?"

"Nothing concrete. He called. He'd forgotten some papers. But I'm not his courier."

"Good. You're thinking independently."

"It feels spiteful," Clarissa said. "These are really important to him."

"His father's papers of record?"

Clarissa broke the rule and turned to look. The back of BethAnn's head revealed nothing.

"You brought them up on your first visit here," BethAnn said. "You said he'd practically memorized them."

Clarissa bounced between resentful and sad. "Can you teach me to do that?"

"What?"

"To remember things."

BethAnn moved her chair to face Clarissa's. "Look at me. Your memory is fine. Something in your heart is protecting you."

Twenty-Three

THE NIGHT OF April 23, Finn's light was off when Diana called from New York. "Sam wants you to join Barristof in Beijing."

"Has Deng died?" A dumb question. Barristof was the *Times*'s shining boy. He could handle a state funeral on his own.

"No," she said. "The pundits were wrong. China isn't immune to revolution after all."

She brought him up to speed. A march honoring the death of the one Politburo member students found sympathetic had, over the course of a few days, inspired major government blunders, including police beatings. "A movement has started, Finn. The number of people in the streets is beyond comprehension. Students have occupied the heart of the empire, Tiananmen Square. Sam wants all hands on deck. This could be the story of the century. I've already booked your flight through Tokyo."

The change caused Finn regrets. The slow progress in Hungary's talks had allowed him to keep working with the FOIA documents for his Katyn story. He had also been touring Budapest and interviewing a raft of people, from officials to cab drivers—anyone who knew Russian. But the message was clear: Hungarian society didn't share his interest in looking back at 1956. Researching his father's past was going to be a lonely business.

In the morning, half of the international press corps swelled the ticketing lines of the four airlines that served Ferihegy Airport.

THOSE EARLY DAYS in Beijing, Finn was certain students and workers would take over the city and then the country. They were respectful and determined to earn the freedoms of speech, assembly, and free elections. Their numbers were too many to subdue by any means. When Politburo member Zhao Ziyang stood in Tiananmen Square with a bullhorn to reverse Premier Li Chen's denouncement of the demonstrations as unpatriotic, people around the world expected the fight going on in the leadership meant China would follow Poland's lead. The question was only how much blood would be spilled.

Sam Rich cheered how Finn wove the students' euphoria and discipline into the deadpan reporting of demands for democracy. He also conveyed a message from Clarissa. She had been unable to get through the international phone lines into China. "She says to tell you she's booked a room to meet you in Hong Kong." Sam sang the first line of *Simple Gifts*. "This is the last time I'm going to be your marriage secretary."

On May 7, during a lull in the standoff in Beijing, Finn's airplane landed on the tiny island that shepherded much of the wealth of the Far East. Clarissa was waiting for him at the bottom of an escalator. She hugged him with all her strength. In the taxi she didn't seem herself. She took every skyscraper, every ornamental garden, and every glimpse of ocean as an opportunity to chatter in describing it.

But having traveled for two days, she was as exhausted as he was. He had just enough stamina to hold her hand, sign in at the front desk, and follow the bellboy. The view from the suite she'd booked was of the ocean to the south, flanked by hotels taller than theirs. They fell onto the bed, made love quickly, and didn't wake until the sun had set. Batting his eyes open, he had a vague idea of something he wanted to ask her. She shushed his lips with her finger. Then with her mouth.

She was asleep when he woke. City lights played on the ceiling. At dawn, when he woke again, she was standing naked in front of the plate window, looking through the silk drape at fog and overcast. The city had never stopped churning. She came to the bed and made love to him a third time.

Many of the breakfast diners were European. Listening in with the half-dozen languages they knew between them confirmed the passion for the miracle happening on the mainland. She praised his article about the memorial to Hu Yaobang. She said it dispelled the notion that the Chinese were unfeeling.

The boat on which they toured Hong Kong's outer harbor was crowded. Her arm around his waist and the wind in his hair reminded him of the simple joy of being married. On shore again, they couldn't make their bodies abide by a local schedule or even by each other's. They napped. They had dinner in the room, struggling to find things to talk about. Later on a whim, they showered, dressed in their best clothes, and commandeered a taxi driver to take them to his favorite places. Beside a fountain gushing water in purple light, she kissed Finn and wept.

He asked what was troubling her.

"We'll talk tomorrow."

Had their moods been music, passersby would have heard sparse contrapuntal studies that ended without resolution.

The last morning, they left their bags in the hotel and got dropped at a hilltop Buddhist monastery built in 1533. The gate was open. Through several arches, a courtyard beckoned. They passed two old monks and a young one washing their robes in a stone sink. With gestures, they invited Finn and Clarissa to move about as they wished. For a seat, she chose an artful arrangement of rough boulders under a cherry tree.

Finn found his mind clearing. He caught her blinking away emotions and smoothed the round of her back. She was sweating, though the ocean breeze was cool.

"I think I'm worse rather than better," she said.

"Worse?"

"My moods. They're worse than before you went to Poland." Her expression was bitter as if she was defying an inner voice. "Remember back when I first started having trouble? It centered around being born a Fortier, thinking I didn't deserve my good fortune."

This wasn't the time to point out she'd forgotten even earlier signs of her pain.

"And I wanted my life to be a bridge to help the less fortunate cross to new lives."

"That vision has *always* been part of who you are," he said.

"Well, if I'd been a bridge, all those people would have drowned." She waited for the pounding of a tourist helicopter to fade. "I hate my therapist."

"Three weeks ago you loved her."

"Don't you get it? My father needs me. It's cruel to break away from him."

"Can't you see BethAnn and still be his daughter?"

"He says we're in no shape to have a baby right now."

"Whoa! Last I heard we weren't trying." The images of making love to her turned dark. "Where are you in your cycle?"

"But not because I'm unstable." She inhaled two quick breaths. "He says a baby needs a father."

"Sonofabitch. He's a counselor now? Give me a break. Are you trying to get pregnant?"

"He says you're gone too much. He has a point."

"What point?"

"He says your father ruined your family."

"Is this coming from him or from you?"

"Listen to you," she said. "Will you never become vulnerable?"

"You've heard him, Clarissa. He's been pushing me to pursue bigger stories. He said he'd help me. He cheered me getting out of Hungary and heading to Beijing."

Clarissa reared back. "He said he'd help you? How? By making it easier for you to leave the country?"

"You know what this is? He's worried I won't ever be wealthy, won't be in his class."

"That's not it. And keep your voice down."

In this courtyard where time stood still, he saw his emotions erupting as if they were colors, dancing like ribbons in a wind. Across the way, the youngest monk was sweeping the walkways. Finn ached to be able to carry himself like that. Life without desperation.

"What are the drugs for?" he asked.

Clarissa glanced at him, averted her eyes.

"I needed a swab and they were in your bathroom bag."

"They're to settle me," she said.

"Did BethAnn—"

"No, she doesn't know. Fortie's doctor wrote the scrip."

"And you're smoking again."

"Sometimes. Not a lot. But as you've seen, I've stopped drinking."

"You're all over the map, aren't you?"

She lowered her voice as the monk came near. "You said yourself I was getting better."

"And you just said you weren't. So who should we believe?"

"Take me out of here." She stood and wiped the seat of her dress. "This place is repressive. It makes me want too much."

"Do you really hate BethAnn?"

"No, I hate the work." She made fists and released them. "I just know I have to do it."

"Then let's pay for two sessions a week. Let's get on with it. Are any of your old friends still around for support?"

She sighed. "A few from school, but we're so different now."

Just then Finn would have given a lot for a true friend. The traveling, the stress of competition, and an involuntary move to Vienna for a marriage that was swirling the drain didn't make having friends easy. "Has your father said anything about the State Department?"

She stiffened. "I don't know why he would. Our visits have been cranky lately. BethAnn calls grief the Black Bugger."

Finn saw walking as a way to change the subject. He slid his arm through hers and turned her toward the waiting taxi, sure that neither he nor Clarissa nor Fortie was seeing half of the mess between them.

Twenty-Four

FINN RETURNED TO Beijing to find students on a hunger strike and China's leadership bewildered about how to respond. That political vacuum allowed him and the rest of the foreign press corps to wander the streets unhindered. The wide boulevards, parks, and back alleys were electric with the prospect of students and workers showing the Politburo that China's future would be different from her past forty years. When the pictures and stories flying around the world inspired Chinese leaders to call in troops, a million ordinary Chinese—mothers and old people, too—clogged the streets. The rulers backed down.

Overnight, on May 29, art students smuggled a hastily made plaster and Styrofoam statue of "the Goddess of Democracy" into Tiananmen Square. They erected her facing the twenty-foot tall photograph of Chairman Mao that hung over the main gate. For five days they followed the Chairman's instructions: *Live the Revolution*.

In the end, the government played its only card. After dark on June 4, the thirty divisions of the 27th Army advanced with orders to empty Tiananmen "by any means necessary." Most of the deaths occurred in the northwest of the city, where students, workers, and pensioners fought troops with stones, Molotov cocktails, and desperation. Defying orders for journalists to stay inside the Beijing Hotel, Finn ran alongside two photographers who snapped pictures of tanks breaking through the barricades into the square and toppling the statue. Students scattered, but not before hundreds were killed. With tear gas filling the air, Finn limped back to the hotel. He wrote and retched as the rebellion petered out.

The leadership expelled foreign journalists. In Bombay, Finn bought an English language paper. Only then did he realize the Chinese military had crushed their citizens on the same day Poland had held its first free elections. Solidarity had taken all but one of the seats available to them.

VIENNA WAS AWASH in summer storms the morning Finn's flight touched down. He took a taxi straight to the Fortier mansion. If there would be blood, he didn't want Clarissa seeing it.

"Why didn't you call first?" Fortie asked, taking Finn's coat like a butler.

"This is what first-strike capability looks like."

"Are we at war?"

"We'll know within the hour."

Fortie pulled his cuffs down over his wrists. "Until then, I'll pretend we're going to resolve what's on your mind and part friends."

Finn followed Fortie into the parlor. A fresh flower arrangement caught his eye. At the hutch, Fortie set up two glasses.

"I've read all your articles from Beijing. The *Times* was smart to send you." Finn didn't reply; his mind was running over the collage of hope and death he'd seen in China. "And it's a shame about the kids in Tiananmen."

"A shame, Albert? From my hotel window, I saw students being shot down in the street. Two hours before that, I saw a young woman crushed by a tank."

Fortie handed Finn a glass with more than two shots in it. "My sources tell me it was worse than any newspaper will print. I've been in war zones, too, you know."

"I'm here to get some things straight with you, Albert."

Fortie hummed concern and sipped his drink. "Let's sit."

Finn did, but balanced his glass on the arm of the chair. "I assume you know Clarissa joined me in Hong Kong."

"I told her it was a lousy idea."

"Did you think she wouldn't speak to me about how you're playing me?"

"Playing you? Really, Finn. If you knew half of what I do to keep things together."

"Oh, trust me. I'm getting the picture. In our last heart-to-heart . . ." he made a face, "you enlisted me to help keep your family together."

"Clarissa is all I have left."

"Stop it. You said—no, you *pledged* to help tip me off on news before it happened."

"Yes, I did. And you were happy about it."

"Do you think I'm stupid, Albert? You proposed to keep me on the rise in my career. And at the same time you tell Clarissa I'm gone too much to be a good father. You told her my father ruined my family because he was gone all the time. You have balls the size of—"

"I respectfully and completely disagree. You're gone a lot, so you may not see the swings in her behavior that I do. About a week before she left, she came in here all set to fix her marriage with you by having a baby, for Pete's sake. If she's getting that from Frau Kerlingger, the woman is a disaster. I did caution her. Anyone would have. She's in no more condition to have a child than I am."

"The way you did it undercuts me."

"I did not phrase anything as you just did. That's part of the problem. She's making stuff up as suits her."

"Apples and trees, Albert."

Dots of perspiration appeared on Fortie's temple. "You don't know the half I've done for you, Junge."

"I am *not* your 'boy.' "

Fortie apologized, picking at his pant crease. "I never thought I'd tell you this."

"Then don't."

"I will, goddammit. You need to be informed." Fortie glared at him. "You can't imagine how devastated I was for you and your mother when your father passed."

"My father didn't *pass*, Albert." Barking felt cathartic. "He was either killed or kidnapped."

Fortie rolled his glass from hand to hand. "He put himself in the middle of the revolution." His voice was softer. "There is no record. But he never came home. Never checked in with his paper. The State Department—long before my time there—sought answers with all the pressure it had to bear. They offered a pretty sum to the Soviets, so you and Brygitta could have closure."

Finn turned to the picture shelf. The one of his father and Fortie was still missing.

Fortie pointed to its absence. "It was ruined in the blast. I'm paying an archivist to go through my papers to look for the negative. Anyway, I checked the state department files decades ago. The CIA also went deep undercover to resolve his disappearance. And they offered the Soviets two double agents for information on him. The Soviets said they didn't have any."

Finn's copy of his father's CIA files had no such information. "You searched his files?"

"I had clearance. I was amazed how few there were. Someone has seen fit to hide those negotiations and stages. Can't say for a fact, but it points to the possibility of your father being an agent." He shook the ice in his glass. "But that's not what I wanted to tell you. In fact I'm sorry I did. I never meant to."

Finn stopped drinking. If what Fortie had said was true, he needed to reorder his father's papers. Were there fewer now than when he gotten them twenty years ago? "Albert, as an ambassador—someone working with CIA spooks—you know damn well US law forbids spies from taking cover as reporters. We value speech so highly we'll never put our reporters at risk. And the rest of the world knows it. That's why I'm comfortable to go the places I do. When CIA recruiters came to Stanford, they never set foot in the journalism school."

"You're wrong on one count, " Fortie said. "I grant you embassies in darker places *have* agents, but Austria's a true ally. We don't do spycraft here." His voice shook. "My staff was all career diplomatic service officers. The best America's got. And if Waldheim ever caught us at it, he'd throw us out. But there's one hole in *your* story."

"I doubt it."

"One word: Katyn. You went a reporter and came back a spy."

Finn was sure he hadn't told Fortie about actually traveling to Belarus when asking for his help with Stalin's orders. But to fight it at that point could cut all his momentum. "That's a story welded to truth. Not to mention justice."

"Finn, I'm sorry. I've let us get way off the subject. Here it is, what I thought I would never have reason to tell you. I felt so . . . *ruined* for your mother that I set up a fund to take care of your schooling. I had her tell you it was grants and life insurance." He shook his head as if he were on stage and wanted people in the back of the theater to see. "It wasn't. All that private schooling your father told me he wanted for you but never could save for, I paid for it. Stanford, too. I'm afraid that's how Clarissa found out where you were going. Thinking how sweet a story it made, Jacqueline told her, and . . . well, you've heard her tell it. She was in love with you before you ever met. She applied there straight off. With her résumé, they snapped her up. She had been headed to my al mater."

"You're afraid?"

"Not at all."

"You just said 'I'm afraid that's how she found—' "

"It's an expression, Finn. How much love do I have to give you to let you know I am honored to have you in the family? Some people would think sixteen years of education might carry some weight."

THE REST OF their meeting was a blur. At the door, Fortie thanked him for his help with Clarissa. He renewed his pledge to shuttle news in the making. Then he hugged him. A first.

In the taxi to Clarissa's, Finn changed his mind. He had the driver drop him at the US embassy. First, he filed another FOIA request for all the State Department and the CIA had on Jordan Waters. For a return address, he put Clarissa's apartment. Next, he faxed a 1,500-word article to New York that he'd written on the plane. In pen across the bottom he asked if Sam wanted an article comparing China and Poland.

As was her habit, Diana faxed him back that she'd received it. Above her signature she wrote, *Will ask Sam re: China/Poland.*

In a street-side café, he roughed out a longer piece that he thought might go well in *The Atlantic* or *Esquire*. He didn't care that it could damage his chances of ever being allowed back into China. At three o'clock, he returned to the embassy and called New York. Sam was raging about what had happened in Tiananmen. "I'm thinking of a series written by my best journalists. Some guest historians, too. I'll call it something like 'Century of Slaughter.' With Generation Xers sticking their heads in the sand, we need every hook to get them to read."

"What about a story on the counterpart in the US?" Finn asked. "The dysfunction at State? It's Foreign Desk related."

"Something to ponder. In the meantime, look for jewels in Hungary."

"I'm not optimistic," Finn said. "Six weeks have passed. The talks are set for their formal opening in two days, and they're still debating how to distinguish the parties at the table."

"You sound tired, Finn. Don't forget how history surprises. Find the causes before they break."

Finn waited out a hard shower in the embassy lobby, then headed at a good clip for the streetcar. A full block from the embassy, someone close to his elbow said his name. The man was young, sallow-skinned with short black hair made to stick straight up with some hair product. Finn thought of Russian taiga as seen from above. A section of the man's halter for embassy credentials was visible around his neck. Finn tried to remember his name. Bridge. McBain.

"Did I leave something?"

"No, Mr. Waters." The man pointed them to continue walking down the block. "Mind if we have a word?"

"You're . . .?"

"McBride, Sean McBride." He stopped at a doorway with patrons behind plate glass. "Can we get a coffee?"

At the table McBride leaned and lowered his voice. "I shouldn't be here. It's just that I like your work, and you seem like a nice guy."

Finn played with a sugar packet. Even in Austria men were starting to hit on men.

"I don't know how to say this. I overheard your call."

"The one to my editor? Was I yelling?"

"I'm low-level here."

Finn scanned McBride again. "Are you CIA?"

McBride fidgeted. "No. A tech geek. I keep things running."

Finn encouraged him to continue.

"Sir, I think you should know . . ." He checked out the window. "I think you should know your conversations in the embassy are being recorded."

Finn laid his cup on the table without a sound and leaned in. "Go on."

"There's a system that can be switched on and off."

"I'm a goddamn American citizen and I—Who gives the order?"

"I can't say. I mean, I don't know."

"Which is it?"

McBride batted his eyes. "I don't know. The order comes from upstairs. I'm the guy who implements it. I waited for you to leave. I thought you should know."

McBride was placing his job in jeopardy. "What's in it for you?"

"For obeying orders? A paycheck. For telling you? Nothing. It's painful, that's all. You want to investigate the State Department, and you speak about it on a monitored line in a State Department building. What you were talking about is none of my business. But somebody is making it theirs. You deserve to know you're not getting the confidentiality you go there for."

Finn laid his hand over McBride's fist. "I have to thank you. You've given me—I don't know what to say. Somebody wants me . . .

wants me, what?" Finn stopped and considered the young man. "Are you safe by telling me this?"

McBride's Adam's apple bobbed down to his clavicle. "I have no sense that I'm not."

Grateful for more information to include in his article on the State Department, Finn jotted Clarissa's telephone number on a napkin. "Except with column inches I can't help you, but if they fire you, call me. And if you find out who gives the orders, I'd love to know. A *lot* of people would like to know."

McBride's eyes were pinging all over the shop. "Thanks. I suggest you continue calling from there. If you stop, it might tip off whoever it is."

"Got it," Finn said, tossing a bill onto the table. He went to the door wondering how many of his phones were tapped. It was raining again.

Twenty-Five

AFTER FINN CALLED from the airport saying he had landed, Clarissa fretted over simple things. He'd said he had several stops to make, but when he hadn't arrived by five o'clock, she put her dinner prep into the refrigerator. At 8:30, he walked in the door exhausted and drunk. She ran a bath that he lay in until the water turned cold. She woke him and piled him into the bed. Long after daybreak, he lay there torpid.

Remembering BethAnn's encouragement to be her own woman, she left the house. She chose a secluded spot on the Donaukanal and read his article on the last days in China, which had made page 3 in the paper. His balancing truth and journalistic ethics softened her to him all over again.

She bought fresh croissants. The smell of coffee greeted her at her door. Finn was on the couch. "I have a vague memory of you welcoming me last night."

She faked a smile and went to prepare the food. When they sat, the sun was no longer streaming into the breakfast nook. A light breeze from the high pressure that cleared the skies came through the open windows. Birds chirped in the little courtyard all the apartments shared in the back.

"Let me start again. Thank you for taking care of me last night."

It felt like a tiny gift. "How long are you home?"

"A few days. Then back to Budapest."

She sipped her tea, not knowing how to raise the subject.

"I hate this work," he said. "I may never be all right again."

"I read your article in the *Times*."

"It made it into today's edition?"

"I feel sorry for the Chinese," she said. "Even people here seem heartbroken by it."

"Maybe it'll light a fire under the Hungarians," he said. "They need one."

"What's their problem?"

"They can't trust the future."

"I can relate."

It had been a long time since she'd drawn him up short. He raised his croissant to his nose and smelled the dough.

"My period is late."

He bit into his croissant and settled his elbows on the table. He chewed. He swallowed. He poked his tongue into the spaces between his teeth. He laid the croissant down. "I wish all of life could be this simple," he said.

She scrunched her face in disbelief.

"A table by a window, a breeze, something good to eat. Then there would be no wars."

"Did you hear me? I may be pregnant."

He looked her in the eye with no surprise or regret. She felt herself withering.

"In a world like that," he said finally, "a woman having a baby would be an ordinary thing, a blessed thing."

She wanted to shake him. "Are you saying we don't deserve a blessing? Or that you won't *allow* one?"

Looking at the wall over her shoulder, he took another bite. When he was done, he turned his chair to face the open window. "Your father may be right about me."

Her shirt got sticky. Did he think he could just skate away from this? "I don't give a damn what my father thinks. There's a story developing right here, Finn." She put her hand on her stomach, making sure he saw her do it.

Even that didn't reach him.

"I confronted him for saying my father ruined my family."

"He loved your father. Anyway, I'm not the counterpart to your mother. I won't say anything against her, but no one could be normal after living through what she has."

"Did you know he paid for my education? All sixteen years of it?"

She took a minute to process it. "Really?"

"Yesterday. I stopped in to see him on my way here. Truth? I went there to whip his ass for trying to break us up. I think the sonofabitch wants you for himself."

There were too many issues flying around. "See it for what it is. He loves you."

"So he has only himself to blame."

"For what?'

"For my being a journalist."

"That's his joy. He's trying to help you, isn't he?"

"He's resisted me from the beginning. I think he never wanted you shackled the way my father did my mother."

"Stop it. Yes, we carry our parents' legacies"—and she thought of her mother's diaries; she was slogging through the fifth one, working backwards through time—"but we chart our own courses."

"I had no model, Clarissa. How can I be a parent?"

"Is that it? Is that what this is all about? You were robbed of the chance."

He rubbed his arm to make a tremble in it go away. It jumped to his cheek and he blinked. Too many times for a man. He used a knuckle to wipe the corner of his eye. "That's not all that's wrong. Everywhere I turn—"

When she rose to get a paper towel, he said, "Don't."

She sat, then regretted it. Almost in defiance, she said, "I haven't gotten a test. But I'm pregnant. I just feel it."

His look confirmed he'd heard her.

"Yes," she said. "Which means we have our work cut out for us."

"What's *your* work?"

"The most important is with BethAnn before I become a mother. What's yours?" His face went blank. "You have to know what your work is if we're going to go through this together."

He folded his arms. "All right. Mine is to bring the truth to light."

The opening she needed. "Then it's time I join you there. I have something to confess."

His forehead jumped with wrinkles. "Haven't we had enough thrills for one day?"

"I told my father about Katyn."

Finn opened his mouth, then closed it. "He already knows. I asked for his help on it weeks ago."

"You're not listening. I told him *before* that."

"When?"

"When you were still in Poland."

"Did you tell him I went there?"

"Yes."

Finn's nostrils flared. "You both disgust me."

"No. I won't take that. You know I'm not the hiding kind."

"What's with you two? I told *you* not to and apparently *he* played dumb about already knowing when I told him. You put me at terrible disadvantage."

"I needed purchase on him for something. And it just came out."

"And now you expect me to trust you?"

"It hasn't hurt you. You went to him yourself. And now I'm begging for forgiveness."

"That may take a while."

"Fine." She stood and in the doorway to the kitchen and threw up her arms. "Take the whole eight months. But only if you convince me *you* have nothing to hide. You know, women *friends*. Otherwise, forgive me. And do it before dark comes. Or sleep on the couch."

Some object hammered on the floor above them. A voice in German yelled, "Shut up!" Clarissa pointed up. "She's right. We don't need to scream. I'm done. My conscience is clear. Better, anyway. The ball is in your court."

Twenty-Six

FINN DRESSED IN traveling clothes—pressed slacks and a tweed coat that could double as a pillow. On his way out of town, he went to pick up something Fortie said he had for him. If there was time, he was going to excoriate Fortie for being dishonest about Katyn. Finn caught him in his kitchen having a late breakfast.

"Make sure the *Times* sends you to cover the Warsaw Pact meeting in Bucharest."

"It's on my calendar."

"Good. With your Russian, you might hear something it takes the State Department a couple weeks to get actionable. Hell, your reports could help them drive policy. How do you think news anchors get their jobs, anyway?"

"Thanks, but I'd have to get over being on the business side of cameras first. I'm more interested in why my calls out of the embassy are being monitored. Do you know about that?"

Fortie didn't bat an eye. "That's routine. It's to get some sense of what goes through those phones."

"News is the fourth branch of government, Albert. I should have been told."

"Except when it comes through a government agency. How did you hear about it?"

Finn had prepared for the question. "I'm expert at tapped phones."

Fortie walked his dishes to the sink.

"So it's not special for me? They monitor everyone?"

"As far as I know, it's random."

"I don't buy it. They've done it every time I've been there."

"If it'll make you feel better, I'll look into it. In the meantime, regarding our conversation the other day, my archivist found these." He tapped two thin file folders on his table.

"Don't forget," Finn said, "harassing the press makes an even hotter story in the West. You can pass that on to whoever might be interested." He opened the top file. A fresh copy of the picture of Jordan and Fortie on the hillside. A bigger print. Finn stooped to see the faces. "You found the negative?"

"No, that must have been enlarged way back. Take the ones in the bottom folder with a grain of salt."

Eight by tens, black and white. In the first, his father was sitting on a barstool locked in conversation with a young woman dressed like a hooker. Both were smoking, elbows on the bar, drinks in front of them. They seemed unaware of the camera. The woman's rocks glass was full and had ice. His father's was empty. Finn recognized the thick head of hair as his own. The clock read eleven and a poster in Hungarian reflected backwards in the mirror, which would have made the year 1956 and Jordan thirty-one. The woman's purse glittered with studs. Its strap flopped off the bar and onto her bare thighs.

Under that were several others of Jordan on a street corner near dusk, looking like he was choosing from a crop of hookers ready to go to work. In one, he stared into the camera with his arm over an old hooker's shoulders.

Finn had a sensation of falling. "These are from Hungary. How did you get them?"

"I pulled them years ago from the file the CIA had on him. I broke the law, Finn. I didn't want anything ever coming back on your mother. I'm sure these girls meant nothing to him."

"So did the CIA have *more* information on him?"

"Not that I'm aware of. They're for you to take. And I destroyed the negatives. I debated showing you, but after our talk the other day, I decided you should know all about the man. He was plenty good, too. Don't forget that. Don't ever forget."

Without pleasure, Finn slid the folders into his briefcase.

"What comes naturally for men," Fortie said, shaking his head, "seems criminal to women. I have to say I've dipped into that pool from time to time." When Finn didn't reply, he said, "I'm sure you have, too."

Finn barely registered the question. "I've never paid for sex."

"But you've had affairs, or you hardly belong at the table." Fortie laughed and when Finn didn't respond, he said, "I thought so. Which is good because I'm going to need your help."

"I can't help you, Fortie."

"On this you can. I've started seeing someone. She's an old friend."

"Don't tell me you need me to drive you around."

"No. I want you to tell me when to break the news to Clarissa."

"You're not sane. There's never going to be a right time."

"Think it over, Finn. I'm trying to be your friend."

"So you say." He fiddled with the buckle on his briefcase. He breathed out his anger. "I didn't thank you for sending me to school."

"No, you didn't. But we both were *stolper betrunken*." At the sink Fortie filled a glass with water, turned, and rested it against his chest. "You have your father in you and now a glimpse into the whole man. And I have my daughter, who's worried I abused her . . . or at least, let her be abused." He curled his lips against his teeth. "It's fitting that we learn to love them as they are."

"If we're going to be frank, I want to know why you unbuttoned her blouse."

Fortie cleared his throat with a swallow but otherwise didn't move.

"You know what I'm talking about. The night of the missile. It weakens the ground you stand on when you say you haven't abused her."

Fortie studied the floor. "I was hoping you hadn't remembered that. Not because I'm hiding any wrongdoing—if there's one thing I want, it's to convince you that I'm not guilty of what it looked like. But that moment is something I can't explain."

"You pushed me away and—"

"Did I?

"—even now, I want to knock your head off."

"I don't remember doing that, Finn. Believe me, I don't."

"It's going to take much more than your word for me to get past this."

"God, I have prayed that wouldn't be so. I think I just must have been out of my mind from losing Jacqueline."

"If she were alive, Fortie, I'd ask her what she knew that you're not telling."

ON THE TRAIN to Budapest, Finn squelched his mood by focusing on the Hungarian the three businessmen in his compartment spoke. When they disembarked at Gyor, he pulled out Fortie's folders, then thought better of it, preferring instead to run through his memories of his father one last time. He knew from that day forward they would never be the same. Time had pared them down to a few. Finn had replayed them so often, he wasn't sure of their chronology or how much about them was true.

Several involved sailing on his father's little yawl, day sails out of Rockport. In each his mother wore a look of terror. She hated the boat heeling over in the wind. He remembered his father laughing when waves drenched them in spray. The memory came fused with the taste of salt water. Of those sailing times, Finn's favorite—probably from the summer of '56, which would make it his last memory—was holding the helm in his little hands, steering that wild thing.

His father guided him from behind, his thighs holding Finn in place. His breath smelled of cigarettes. At one moment, to share his joy, Finn let go the helm to hug his father's legs and the boat veered hard into the wind. Had he made up what his father said? "Love is important, son, but never let go of the wheel."

In other memories, his father was hunched over his desk in his writing nook, the air rattling with the clack of his typewriter. His father pushing a wheelbarrow into the garden shed. At the breakfast table, his father slapping Finn's face. Finn couldn't remember the words he'd said, but he knew it was a just punishment. An early one of his father pushing him in a handmade swing tied to the apple tree—the double joy of flying to freedom and his father always being there when he swung back. He had a black collage of nights lying in bed hearing his parents fighting. There was crying and things thrown, though Finn never saw the damage in the morning.

Unbidden, the deep sea fishing memory plowed its way in. It had no business being included in that group. He was a fatherless boy of eleven, jerking the line hard and releasing it the way the boat's captain commanded, to set the hooks deep in the marlin's gullet. Even from the distance of a hundred and fifty feet, Finn saw—or imagined he did—the fish's outrage as it leapt out of the water. It looked up the line that tethered the two of them—the young boy trying to find a place to enter the marketplace of men, and the sleek, free spirit from the underwater world realizing its mortality.

The cheers of passengers and the captain's bark swirled in one ear. The panic of the fish and his own voice crying for justice roared in the other. *Pull*, they said. And he did, wishing he could flip the line like a ringmaster's whip and somehow free the hooks. He'd grunted as if with the effort of hauling in the prize. In reality, he was raging against his father for not being there to tell him why he should go through with this. The picture taken of him on the dock with the fish hanging from its tail was a portrait of conflicting emotions.

To purge that humiliation, Finn slapped open the first folder and saw his father and Fortie on the hilltop above the village. Having not been exposed to the light for decades, the picture was brighter than the one that had sat in Fortie's parlor. Finn was able to better discern the chemistry between the men. He'd always wondered if their wearing lederhosen held some special significance.

He decided to forego looking at the hooker pictures. Instead, he pulled the one of his father he'd saved from the trash. Years before, the tape he'd used had yellowed and let go, but at the beginning of their marriage, he and Clarissa had given it new life by gluing the pieces onto white card stock. As Hungarian farms flicked by the window, he laid it alongside the one with Fortie. They'd been taken within a year of each other. Perhaps prompted by the pictures of the hookers, he realized there was another person in each picture he'd never considered.

The photographer. Had a woman come with them? Or were there two women? Was the bond between his father and Fortie forged around married men being randy? Perhaps that was why Fortie pushed that morning to have him admit to infidelity. He was testing Finn's mettle, his heritage, trying to graft an old bond onto the next generation. The photographer who'd captured his father smoking under the streetlamp was highly skilled. He could research if there were any woman photographers in the press corps in the early 1950s.

Perhaps there was an elderly woman photographer somewhere who could help him know Jordan Waters. The notion of his father being a philanderer shifted his understanding of his bright eyes and happy face. If his father had had lovers on the Continent, how important to him was the little boy living in Rockport? And if his father's dalliances had made him happy, why did Finn struggle with his own?

THE TRAIN EXITED the hills and streamed toward Budapest. Many of the city's streets had no lights. The station, though, was well lit. Even at eight-thirty, the quays bustled with travelers, the poorer folk mixing with entrepreneurs, soldiers, and Party members. The Parliament Hotel was busy, too, with press crews returning from China. In Finn's mind, the excitement didn't compare to Warsaw in the early days of Poland's talks. Perhaps it was his sense that the conclusion was foregone. Hungary's communism under Kadar had long been steering a gentler, more human course than Moscow wanted. But older Hungarians who had fought in the revolution weren't glib about the presence of the 15,000 Soviet troops stationed in facilities east of the city. Thirty-four years earlier, they had seen their ecstasy at overthrowing Soviet domination crushed when Khrushchev's tanks roared into the streets.

Finn found himself berthed on the fifth floor among crews from South America and Australia. In the hotel's main lounge, cigarette smoke wafted out the door. He drank a beer near the waitress depot, eavesdropping on languages he knew and surveying tables. He saw the top of Chantelle's head. Alice Baldwin was clinging to Svenson. *Good for her*, he thought. A hand gripped his bicep. "We can squeeze you in at our table," Marty said.

Finn avoided Marty's *how-are-things-going* question. With Clarissa in the family way he wasn't sure how they were going. Instead, he leaned into the typical journalist free-for-all fare of discussing personalities, the latest gaffes made by famous people, and the ever-changing face of technology.

A fork pinging a glass hushed the room. It was Lombardo from the *Italian Daily*. He wanted, he said in a preamble, to honor all the people from the press who put their lives in danger to bring stories to the world. He wore bandages on his left arm and ear from the burns of a Molotov cocktail when the Chinese Army took control of Beijing. Since he was Italian, Finn thought of Annalisa and how in one night a life can change, and how things that seemed good could become anything but. He spied her with her back against the far wall, sedate, statuesque.

A British journalist Finn knew in passing offered a moving prayer for his colleague, Killian, who was still in a coma from the blow of a Chinese soldier's baton. Svenson stood and in his best Swede-inflected English asked everyone to join him with a raised glass. "Poets and writers," he began, "speak to the conscience of humanity, sometimes beautifully. And they're praised for that. But they do it in their garrets. We journalists and cameramen, we put our bodies where history is made. We are the eyes of the world. Any tyrant, rebel leader, or corporation that hurts any one of us risks the greatest good that has come out of civilization. So for this one night, let's support each other . . ." and he paused with a sly grin, "knowing that tomorrow we'll revert to wolves, all eager to be first to get the killer story and the picture shown 'round the world."

Through a scattering of embarrassed laughter, glasses were hoisted.

Twenty-Seven

WHEN SLEEP WOULDN'T come, Finn rose and pulled the state department's brick of information from his bag to begin again where he'd left off when he was sent to China. *Why*, he wondered, *would the same department that wouldn't let his story be printed send him such a trove of material*? Perhaps State was so large and its branches so disconnected its bureaucrats couldn't cross-reference its priorities. But the underlings who had prepared the work had made his task Herculean.

Since some documents were lists and tables, while others were narrative texts, he needed multiple strategies. For each, finding patterns would be key. For the lists and tables, he tried to determine which redactions were names of companies and individuals, and which were materials, quantities, and currencies. For each narrative document, in the hope of intuiting the redactions, he looked at the grammar and shape of the sentences to capture the thinking and style of the composer. To approach the task from every possible angle, he used a small ruler he'd brought and above each redaction, he wrote in pencil the number of missing letters.

Needing a master list to organize what he gleaned, he pulled a shorthand pad from his stash, but no sooner had he opened it flat than one of his stacks of papers fell to the floor. Cussing at the token desk the hotel provided, he looked at the stuffed chair and with a groan, made up his mind to sleep there in order to free up the bed for use as his work surface.

HIS MIND RATTLED awake to discover his hand was already groping for the phone. Marty was calling from the front desk. "Have you overslept?"

"I've hardly had any," Finn said. It was 7:50. The talks were scheduled to begin at nine. The steam radiator was blowing in the corner. His body stench rose from the collar of his shirt. The shower water smelled of sulphur and turned cold before he could rinse off the soap. Breakfast was the cold version of communist gruel and unsalted bread. The coffee, though, cleared his head in a shot.

At the Parliament building, he ran the security gauntlet for press people, unpacking the contents of his shoulder bag. He signed the pro forma confession for whatever the Party might choose to convict him of, if the need arose. Foreign journalists had broad immunity . . . except those caught with things like Stalin's orders.

The atmosphere was chaotic, because overnight a second group, the National Association of Trade Unions, had abandoned the government's side. It now seemed to be holding a wild card, though its name presaged the lack of creativity it would contribute to the talks. The bright spot was that newly seated president Pozsgay had convinced Moscow to change its rhetoric regarding the 1956 revolution. For decades, the official line throughout the Warsaw Pact had been that *Hungarian* forces had restored law and order after a minor *uprising*, meaning that the revolution had never happened. Now under Gorbachev's experiment of openness, the Kremlin acknowledged twenty-two divisions of Soviet troops had crushed a *popular revolt*. History was being rewritten. Again.

The promise of it being a low news day was born out in eye-rolling fashion. Finn and Marty dined at a small place some blocks away—there was only one other table of customers, and the meal lacked color. Marty seemed to have lost the thread of what was driving him to talk so earnestly when they had walked over in the morning. Now he wanted to learn all of what Finn knew about Chantelle. Finn felt his smile begin to stink and begged off, saying it was his night to call Clarissa.

When she answered, he heard it in her voice. "What's wrong?"

"I'm not sleeping."

"Why?"

"The dream I told you about with the nuns. I've had it twice more since."

In the dream, she'd found herself in a dark courtyard surrounded by nuns praying.

"I can think of worse dreams."

"Three nights ago, they were clapping in unison like in exorcism. Last night, they encircled me, along with an old man on his knees singing the Lord's Prayer, but singing like he was pleading for his life."

"You saw BethAnn today, right? What did she say?"

"That I should let them sing. That nuns are a symbol of purification. That prayer is my subconscious trying to go deeper. But I'm lying in bed wired."

"Have you heard from Fortie?"

"Why do you ask?"

"I wondered how he felt about the visit I had with him."

"He called but didn't mention it. He wants to take me to Salzburg."

"What for?"

"A change of scene. He says time together might get us on a better footing."

"I think you should wait until the feeling passes."

"How are the talks going?"

"Slow, so I'm working on the material . . . the stuff you held for me."

He heard her pause to remember their call might have a wider audience. "Any revelations?"

"Parties were in cahoots that shouldn't have been."

"I hope Sam will print this."

"We'll see. Did you take your question to the drug store?"

"Yes."

"And . . . you got an answer?"

"Positively."

"No doubts?"

"Uh-uh."

He played his thumb through the corner of FOIA documents three times, four times.

"Are you there?" she asked.

"Sounds like the nuns better get busy while there's still time."

She thought a minute. "We all should be praying for that."

AFTER WORKING ANOTHER night on the FOIA papers, Finn realized he needed a bigger book to keep track of his theories and all the details. When the talks broke up that afternoon, he filed his report with Diana, followed directions away from the government district, and entered a stationery store. The place smelled of old wax, and the floorboards squeaked. The shelves were half-bare; the merchandise seemed to date from the '50s. He asked the craggy-faced clerk if he spoke Russian.

"It's mandatory to be in business."

Finn spaced his hands eighteen inches apart. "I need a ledger. Twenty columns or so."

The clerk secured his tie behind a button of his shirt and limped to the wooden ladder that had its top end attached to a rail. He wheeled it halfway down the long wall. "How many?" he said, as he climbed. "They're twenty-thousand forint."

Cheaper than Finn thought. "I'll take two."

The ledgers were wider than they were tall, their covers were faded. One hundred pages each and twenty-four columns wide.

"Do you have colored pencils, by chance? I need as many as I can get."

The clerk scratched his wiry hair and coughed a smoker's cough. He held up his finger and walked to a trunk that sat against the back wall. From it, he produced a broken box of eighteen used colored pencils.

"Are you going to start a bank?"

Finn laughed. "No."

"Too bad, I need a loan. Preferably one I don't have to repay."

"I trust my money will help."

"I'd prefer you pay me in chickens. Their value doesn't inflate before they reach the pot. You're not Russian, are you?"

"No, I'm a journalist here to cover the talks."

The clerk frowned and flapped the fingers of both hands against his thumbs to signify mouths talking gibberish.

"I know," Finn said. "But look what Poland did."

The clerk huffed. "I doubt they have more chickens than before." He smoothed the cover of the top ledger. "Look at me. I was a professor once. Now I'm a clerk. When I come home, my wife greets me with sad eyes."

"What is your field?"

"That's nice. Hungarians ask me what my field *was*. My field *is* government."

"Then you should be at the talks."

The clerk shrugged and touched his head. "I'm old. The hair in my family doesn't go grey."

Finn laid the money and more on the counter. "If I bring you chickens, can you help me?"

The clerk brightened. "I'd like to see my wife smile."

"I'm looking for records on businesses. Company names and what they shipped."

"That sounds like a sentence in Hell."

"Records from before the war. Not just here. I intend to do this all over Europe."

"Before the Soviets came then?"

"Yes."

"You may be in luck. Unlike conquerors in the old days that burned the cities they lusted after, Stalin kept all the records regardless of whose they were. They came in handy when he felt like having you shot. Whatever the Nazis didn't burn as they left, the National Historical Museum and Archive is a place to look."

"I don't read Hungarian."

"For another chicken, I'll translate."

Finn patted his wallet. “My newspaper isn’t paying for this.”

The clerk frowned. “Too bad. I was starting to dream of a hen house.”

“I’m tracking who’s accountable for a particular mass murder.”

“Then you must not have a family.” He drew his fingers across his neck just as Dabrowski had done at their first meeting.

“I’m American.” He regretted waving entitlement. “I hope to publish the results in the West first. But it’s for European dead.”

The clerk sighed disappointment. “Do you know what you’re looking for?”

“Companies that ran from here to there as if there was no war going on.”

The clerk looked at his watch. “The archives just closed for the weekend. They’re only open between ten and two. Government cuts.”

“I’ll use the days to prepare. Can we go Monday?”

The clerk put Finn’s money in his wallet. “You’ll find me chickens?”

“I’ll do my best. Are you safe being seen with me?”

“I won’t give you my name. Meet me at City Park. Come in from the Ajtösi Dürer side, and we’ll walk over from there.”

“Wonderful. Call me Karol. Karol Sobczak.”

Twenty-Eight

FOR THE NEXT three nights, Finn worked on the FOIA documents, collapsing asleep in the chair when he could no longer function. First, he arranged the documents by date and dedicated a ledger page to each. Tackling them one at a time, he gave a line for every company, transaction, person, and result. The columns tracked various data: dates, materials, type of transport, costs, destinations, and so on. With the colored pencils, he linked families of information to facilitate review when an idea for research struck.

Arising in his ledger was the organized record of American companies doing business with Germany after Hitler attacked his neighbors. Starting in fall of 1939, a host of companies—GM, Ford, General Electric, Shell Oil, DuPont, Kodak, and their subsidiaries—retooled factories inside and outside of Germany to supply the Wehrmacht war machine with troop transports and war materiel. There was nothing ambiguous about it. As the list got long, Finn fumed at the blind eye the US government had turned to the business strategy of exchanging mayhem for profit. It had all the markings of abetting war crimes.

During the day, coffee became his crutch and lifeblood. As perceived from his manic state, his colleagues disappeared into the grey walls of government buildings. The fear Hungary's negotiating parties had in opening new ground emboldened him to inform New York that he wouldn't be filing a report the next day.

In the morning, Finn found the stationery store clerk at City Park feeding pigeons. For a while they sat on a bench like two spies and agreed to present themselves as a teacher and his student. They walked several blocks to a huge eighteenth-century building. Its original arched windows had been bricked in and skinned over with concrete. At the main gate, Finn flashed his Polish passport. The guard bobbed his head and said in passable Polish, "Nice going, you Poles."

Because all Hungarian eyes were on the Parliament Building, the only footsteps that echoed in that cavernous atrium that morning belonged to Karol Sobczak, visiting professor of ornithology, and an old limping clerk who had given his name at the entrance as Wilmot Pokorni. Most of the light at the floor level filtered down from wrought iron clearstory gables high above. Sad to say, microfiche technology had not yet come to the National History Museum and Archive. Cabinets housing the documents stood in rows that on each floor filled a space half the size of a football field. On the third floor, Wilmot leaned to read the handwritten labels taped to the top of each cabinet. "These here are all Commerce. What are we looking for?"

"I'll know it when I see it," Finn said.

Wilmot pursed his lips in skepticism. "You've brought chicken in your bag for my lunch, I hope?"

"All I could find was duck and some fresh bread. But there is plenty to take home."

Wilmot smiled, a trait he underused, considering how warm his was. "I guess I can't complain if you treat me like a Politburo member."

If German pistols used at Katyn had been delivered by boat through the Black or Baltic Seas, there was little chance of tracking them. But if they had come overland by rail, Budapest was a choke point. The invoice for them might be filed right here. Finn's mind hummed in anticipation of turning history on its head and tearing down the myth that World War Two had been a simple struggle between good and evil.

As soon as Wilmot began pulling drawers to their length and translating document titles, two things were clear: Budapest *was* a primary transportation hub for every imaginable commodity and product, *and* companies of every flag were facilitating shipments from one enemy to another.

Gradually it dawned on Finn a case could be made that the Nuremburg Trials had been a sham exercise. Corporations of the victorious Allies had exerted their influence over the judicial process to cover their culpability. Blame was strictly assigned to the Third Reich and only a few players at the top. Another story begging to be told. The real test would come from documents dated after December 11, 1941, the date the US declared war on Germany. What changes did Washington then enforce?

The crackling voice over the loudspeakers announcing the closing of the archive caught Finn off guard.

But Wilmot sighed with delight. "I hope you've found what you needed today, Karol, because I doubt you can find foie gras and caviar enough to get me to bend over for hours tomorrow. Or any other day. My knees can't take it."

"I need at least another day, Wilmot. I'm just beginning to understand how the files work." Finn ran his hand over the drawers from 1940 that they hadn't yet opened. "I'll look for caviar. Perhaps we could do a morning next week?"

"How much are you paying me?"

Finn gave him a figure half-again as much as he had planned.

"I think someone else would be better. I have a girl in mind."

"You're invaluable to me." He heard the pleading in his voice.

Wilmot raised his eyebrows. "This is no ploy to distract you. She's over fifty-five."

Finn did a quick calculation of when the woman was born. "This woman is too young to know anything. You were in Budapest in 1939. You know a lot about what went on back then."

"I was only in my teens," Wilmot said.

At the exit, Wilmot spoke to the guard.

"What did you say to him?" Finn asked as they headed down the granite steps outside.

"I told him you would be here tomorrow with a woman."

Reluctant to part with Wilmot's company, Finn followed him back to the park.

"Does this woman speak Russian?"

"Better. She speaks English."

"What if I brought pads for your knees?" Finn asked. "Or a folding chair?"

"These are not the knees of old age."

"What do you mean?"

Wilmot gave a mysterious smile. "How old are you?"

"Thirty-nine."

Wilmot tapped his left knee. "Shrapnel."

"You fought the Germans?"

Raspberry flesh showed in Wilmot's throat when he laughed. "I survived the war in perfect health."

"The Revolution, then?"

Wilmot nodded. "At least you know about it. The Russian people were never told."

Finding all the park benches occupied by women watching children at play, Finn sat on a low wall and splayed his legs. Wilmot sat beside him. Birds gathered at his feet for crumbs he'd saved from lunch. With the sun out and with no troops in sight, Budapest seemed delightful.

"In my life, Karol, I've had two good weeks."

"Only two?"

Wilmot shrugged. "More than some people get. We thought it would be longer."

"You and your wife?"

Wilmot snorted. "We Hungarians. We were so close to freedom."

"But too close to Russia?"

"The Americans would have crushed the Soviets."

"How do you know?"

"They would have had an ally in every house."

"Life was that bad?"

"It got worse after."

Finn recognized a bird from Karol Sobczak's notebook. "You mean after the two good weeks?"

Wilmot leaned back and opened his shirt to the sun. "We students protested for better conditions, and the government collapsed. At first Khrushchev promised no intervention and pulled his troops back into the countryside. Within days, we had set up a new government and everything in the city was getting done without problems. We were going to succeed. But Khrushchev's rivals made him change his mind. In the Kremlin, your most dangerous enemies are sitting right next to you." Wilmot laughed a bitter laugh. "And he *swore* he was gong to be different from Stalin."

"That's who I'm pursuing, you know?"

"Nikita?"

"No, Stalin. Actually, the whole system."

"Good luck. Russians prefer tyrants."

"Were you in the fighting?"

"They attacked our buildings with tanks. My knee got in the way." He gave a wry smile. "I was on the national football team. The wound made me a better student."

"So nothing I can say will make you go back there with me?"

"I can't spend that much time away from the store. I'll have her meet you here tomorrow at 9:45."

THAT NIGHT HE WAS preparing for another day in the archive when Chantelle opened his door.

"Aren't you going to ask a woman in?"

Finn looked to see if his chair was clear of debris. It wasn't.

"You know what they say, don't you?" she said, closing the door behind her. "He who hesitates doesn't catch the worm." She tittered a laugh, stood on one leg, and raised a heel behind her. The fabric of her dress parted to expose the calf. The skin was smooth.

For a second Finn was interested. "You're mixing your aphorisms."

"I'm hoping to mix more than that." She pointed at the bed. "But that's not inviting."

While he looked at the spread of documents, her purse clunked on the floor. Needing support, she groped for the wall behind her. Impatient, he stood to usher her out, but she intercepted him, laid her forearms on his shoulders, and tagged him with a whiskey-laden kiss.

She showed no offense when he pulled away. “You weren’t at the talks today.”

“I’m working on something else.”

“Is this what you told me about the last time we were together?”

“No, this is different.” It was a good enough lie.

“I stopped by to tell you how much you missed.” She rolled her eyes. “My readers at *Le Monde* are begging for more. Marty told me he’s filing the same piece every day. What is it with these communists, Waters, that they can’t even laugh?”

“Tyranny is serious business,” he said.

“What would tyranny do with this?” She tipped her head back and offered her neck.

“I’m busy, Chantelle.”

“Thank you for using my name. Men avoid it when they plan to forget me.” With the pads of her fingers, she brushed the fabric around her breasts as if about to go in front of cameras. “But they never quite can.”

“Look, you have been good to me, but I’m—”

“Nice picture,” she said, thrusting her chin at his desk. Finn had leaned the shot of his father smoking under the streetlamp against the books. “For a minute, I thought it was you.”

“No, my father. I don’t smoke.”

She approached it and leaned down. “What happened to it?”

“It got torn up once.”

“And you put him back together. That’s what most parents want their children to do.”

“Chantelle, I need to work.”

“If that’s the story you’re working on, I hope he appreciates it.” She seemed pleased with herself.

“He died when I was six.”

The information hit her as he intended. She had no comeback. Her smile gave way to a look of utter loneliness.

“Let’s talk another night,” he said.

“I need company. I gave it to you once when you needed it.”

The phone rang. He looked at his watch. "This is my wife. You've got to go."

She crossed her arms. "I'm a reporter. I'll stay to report on how loyal you are."

"Please go."

"If you don't answer, she'll guess you're with someone like me."

He jammed his finger at her as a warning to stay silent.

"Finn, glad to catch you." Fortie calling was worse than Clarissa. He waved Chantelle out. She didn't move. He waved with more force. "Am I catching you at a bad time?"

"No, good to hear from you. Is everything okay?"

"I've got news . . . for your ears only."

"What?" He turned his back and pushed the phone to his ear.

"There's a protest planned in Minsk for the day after tomorrow. The Soviets have a news blackout on it. My sources tell me several groups with a history of violence are planning to show up. In response, they've mobilized three armored divisions from Kaliningrad."

"Which sources?"

Fortie laughed. "If I told, they'd have to kill me."

"I should've known."

"Keeping my ears open for you is the least I can do."

"Is Clarissa okay?"

"Seems to be. She's been more to herself since you've been gone. Jacqueline went soul-searching, too, when she became pregnant."

Clarissa was supposed to have kept it secret. "Just so you know, we're still processing it."

"Congratulations—that is, if you're going to go through with it."

"Jesus, Albert. How did you ever handle negotiations with mortal enemies?"

"You're right. It's not my business. Except it's my blood, too. Anyway, good luck." He hung up.

Chantelle batted her eyes. "You've got—how to say—a little sugar daddy for the news?"

"I think you misheard."

"Riots and armored divisions, Monsieur Finn? I have ears like a fox." She pulled up the tips of her ears to give them points.

"Then why are you asking me?"

"Look. We can cover more ground as two than alone. I'll be ready first thing in the morning." She shook off most of the effects of being drunk. "I'll meet you downstairs at six-thirty." She slipped out the door.

Finn went to the journalist's phone bank and caught Sam in New York just before closing time. After congratulating him on his choice of father-in-law, Sam gave him permission to fly out.

The bad news was that flights to Minsk went through Moscow. He would be flying into the belly of the beast.

Twenty-Nine

BECAUSE OF THE summer heat, BethAnn arranged to meet Clarissa in a park near her apartment. They settled on a shaded bench facing a duck pond. Children were hollering by the water.

BethAnn leaned her umbrella between them. "If those thunderheads open up, we can take refuge in my cathedral. St. Charles. It's a block away."

"I wouldn't mind getting drenched," Clarissa said.

BethAnn looked at her over the tops of her glasses.

"I feel stuck. Cold rain might clean me out."

"Good. Then my change in thinking may be well timed. Searching for something buried often leads to dead ends. Your bleeding in your first intercourse pushed us to consider *different* kinds of sexual trauma. But you don't use the coded language victims perfect to hide it. The exercises we've been doing for tapping into your subconscious don't show those markers."

"But didn't you say the nuns in my dreams were symbols of purity? I assume you meant sexual purity."

BethAnn nodded. "Dear, we must always be willing to dump assumptions."

"So where does that leave us? Back at the beginning?"

"No doubt you *were* traumatized." BethAnn pulled her blouse away from her skin and blew between her breasts. "But I think we should revisit if you were you ever in an accident. Think carefully."

"You mean with broken bones or a hospital stay?"

"Did you ever take a blow to the head? Perhaps you could check your hospital records."

Clarissa thought of her mother's diaries.

BethAnn patted her arm. "We just want to rule it out. On the other hand, it could be something else entirely, something disturbing you saw."

"Why would something like that upset me so much I couldn't grow out of it? People forget things all the time."

"A good question. If we just had something to go on, some kind of event or pattern where your memory wants to disintegrate."

"We have one. The missile attack."

"No, if that's related, it was just a trigger. Maybe you witnessed an explosion, an airplane crash, somewhere that people were hurt. Do you startle at fireworks?"

"No more than most."

"You've put together most of what happened the night the missile struck?"

"Yes, all except walking into the parlor."

"You went to St. Stephens. The priest sang for your mother. You came home. The men were drinking." BethAnn turned, excited. "Has your father ever been attacked? Are you afraid of losing him?" She sucked her pen, then jotted a note.

"Of course. Aren't we all afraid of losing people close to us?"

"The only other thing is you went upstairs to change into your blouse—"

"Yes, the white silk one."

"—and you read Finn's article."

"I've been meaning to tell you. That exercise you gave me of relaxing into the past? I've remembered most of what I read."

"Take me through it again, then."

"Finn wrote that the *New York Times* was in possession of Stalin's orders of a mass execution."

"Have you ever seen a mass grave?"

"You mean an open pit with bodies in it? I'm sure I never have."

"Humor me. Can you visualize one? Hold up your hand when you do. Good. Now jump your mind to your father."

Clarissa was annoyed, but she raised her hand again.

"How do you feel about him right now?"

"Pretty good. We've been getting along better."

"Would he mind you asking about your travels? We're looking for something that might seem ordinary to an adult, but that a child could misinterpret."

"Do you think I've made something up? If so, I hope those clouds shoot lightning right here." She thumped the tips of her fingers on the top of her head.

BethAnn looked at the clouds and checked her umbrella. "I apologize, dear. Your experience is *real*. To you it is, and that's all any of us have to go on."

"But I don't *know* my experience. That's what drives me crazy."

BethAnn clustered her fingers like an Italian might when pressing a point. "Let's pursue this. Your homework this week is, one, check hospital records. Two, buttonhole your father. *Nicely*. Ask about places you've been. It doesn't have to be places you've gone with *him*, of course. Maybe you were with your mother or relatives. Did you visit relatives in faraway places?"

And so the session went. Clarissa left hopeful of finding the start of the right path.

She drove to her father's house and let herself in. Getting no response to her salutations, she mounted the stairs and entered the master bedroom. Instead of picking the next diary back in time, she pulled number seven, sat on the floor, leaned back against the four-poster bed, and read. July 6, 1955. The tone made it seem as if it had been written by someone other than her mother.

She awoke to a woman's heels clomping in the downstairs hall. The voice was foreign to her, fluent in German, and laced with a giddiness that made her heart sink. The gold light that precedes sunset was splashing the buildings across the park. The diary lay open on her lap with only a few pages left to read.

She was of two minds: Bellow from the top of the stairs, unseen, to drive the woman out of the house, or eavesdrop to learn about whom her father had charmed. She chose a middle course. Marking the diary page with her finger, she walked downstairs as if her being there was normal. The sudden silence that greeted her told her most of what she needed to know; the rest she could see. The woman was comfortable in fine clothes and jewelry. She had manners and bleached hair. She was skilled at sucking the cream off the top of life. And this was not her first day with her father.

The pair stood stunned, their backs against the coat closet like children awaiting punishment. A gash of lipstick framed a crease in her father's mouth. With bravado she hadn't acted on in years, Clarissa slipped the woman's handkerchief from the wide belt that held her midriff in check and handed it to her father. She mimed where he should wipe.

While he obeyed, she introduced herself as the child who had grown up in the house. "I lived here longer than any woman could hope to before she dies. That, ma'am, should clarify my rank. My father and I need to have a conversation. You're free to stay if you want, but you'll have to keep quiet."

The woman did her one better; she went stiff.

"Wait a minute, Clarissa. You will treat Mrs. Krueger with the—"

"I will treat Mrs. Krueger with more courtesy than you afford my husband on most occasions, which is with condescension and a drink to mimic affection. No doubt, Mrs. Krueger, you already know where the hutch is." She directed her, not unkindly, and Mrs. Krueger escaped into the parlor. Sounds of her clearing her throat and the clink of glasses on the top of the hutch.

"You're wrong," her father said. "Finn and I are getting along well. We've teamed up to care for you."

Clarissa weathered the hit with nothing more than a blink. She barreled ahead. "How kind," she said. "I've been upstairs reading Mother's diaries. BethAnn has suggested I—"

"Has that woman put you up to this?" Fortie inhaled as if to dress her down, but then clenched his jaw, realizing the poor timing of doing so. "I've informed Melody—Mrs. Krueger—about your condition, and I'm sure you'll find her quite supportive when your mood is over."

"That's bull!" Clarissa withdrew the Fortier house key from her skirt pocket and dangled it before him. "I came from Rotterdam to take care of *you*, because you couldn't handle the house, let alone Mother's illness. You remember *Mother*, the woman who used to live here? I made the meals. I listened to your practiced simpering of love, and since she's died, of your loss. You're a cad with an ambassador's pin. What's your guess, Papa? Was Mother on to you?"

Having cut her father's forward motion, she turned and walked triumphantly toward the kitchen. Halfway there, realizing she'd already set the agenda to talk, she wheeled around. And in any case, if he refused to sit for that, her car was out front. She strode back, leaving embarrassment behind. "So are you ready to talk? Or do you need a drink first?" She came to him and hooked his arm. Her exhilaration exploded into a broad smile that disarmed him even more.

The parlor's new arrangement of furniture made her stutter step. She fired a look at Melody, who bowed to take the credit. Clarissa shrugged. "Change is good, isn't it, Papa?"

Her father's silence emboldened her to begin. "It's not complicated. Something went on in this room three months ago, and I want to know what. And I want to know why. Have a seat, the both of you. I'll stand. I might need to pace."

The two reupholstered leather chairs now faced the fireplace. The couch that had been there for decades was gone. Melody brought her drink and one for her father. And they sat. "Something has just occurred to me, Papa. All along, BethAnn—and of course, *I*—have been thinking that the missile attack reminded me of something like it that happened somewhere else." She had both of their attention. "What are the possibilities that whatever it was happened right here?"

Her father drank but started shaking his head before he finished swallowing, which made his negative come out garbled.

"No?"

"Honestly, Clarissa, if anything happened here, I wasn't party to it. I was away a lot."

"Fortunately, we can check it out. Mother catalogued everything. Every last detail. Some might say she was trying to make her life seem more secure." She raised the diary and, though she'd already announced having read it, it seemed her father just grasped the fact. He turned to Melody as if blindsided.

"It's very interesting reading. I mean she wasn't a wordsmith. And she had a habit of telling the pages what time the noon whistle sounded. But here and there are clues to her pain. What do you think, Papa?"

"She was a dear woman."

"Yes, and I hope you spend hours telling Melody all about her gifts. Have you ever met my mother, Melody? Shake your head yes or no."

Melody shook her head.

"That puts you at an advantage. You won't have to compare yourself to the royalty that preceded you."

"Have you ever considered," her father said, indignant, "your mother wrote those things for herself alone?"

"And left them on a shelf in your bedroom?"

Fortie took another pull on his drink.

"Obviously you haven't read them. Still, how thoughtful of you to guard her privacy! I've found things that would interest you, that may interest BethAnn." As Clarissa flipped pages back looking for a particular line, she realized the longer she made them wait, the more uncomfortable they were becoming. She read the line to herself several times. And then aloud.

"*The suffering a woman married to an ambitious man goes through!* Exclamation point." That says a lot, don't you think? Would you like me to read the lines before that?"

"I thought you said we were going to have a talk," her father said. "You know, an honest exchange among people who care for each other. This is an interrogation. And quite frankly, it's beyond rude. Please, Melody, understand she hasn't been herself."

Clarissa put her finger to her lips and stared Melody down. To her father, she said, "*Quite frankly*, I wonder what having 'Clarissa being herself' would look like. It didn't take me ten pages of something written in"—she turned to the first page of the book—"1955 to realize I grew up in a world with a whole lot of theater scrims as backdrop, not one of which was related to reality." She held up the book to read. " '*Albert insists his overnight meetings with women—who make me feel like a Dachshund at a field trial for golden retrievers—are work related. I feel dirty when washing his clothes.* ' " She skipped down to the line that had brought tears to her eyes when reading in the bedroom. " '*I wish Clarissa had been born a son, so I wouldn't have to hide this from her.* ' "

Clarissa saw how extending the silence would be more productive than reading more.

Her father finished his drink. His brow was a mangled mass of lines. "I haven't been perfect. But my sloppy days are long behind me." Melody blew him what she must have thought was a surreptitious kiss. "You, on the other hand, are in the middle of making your way through life, and you will come to regret this day. I will not, however, celebrate your humiliation when you get there. You have been a good daughter to both your mother and me."

Clarissa had her first moment of doubt, and he must have seen it, because he gained height in his chair. "I've learned, darling, that it isn't so much doing wrong that is the problem, but not acknowledging it and thus avoiding penance. I want to use this opportunity, which is public, to give you a blanket apology for my mistakes as a father and as a man."

His eyes were steady. He seemed as open as was normal for him. Damn him. His off-the-cuff statements always came out like they'd been written beforehand.

"All right," she said. "All right. I guess a woman needs to blow off steam once in a while. All this stuff," and she faced Melody, "is my response to finding *you* in the house. It's a lot to take in." She looked again at her father. "Here's what I came to explore with you. Are you willing?"

"I will answer that as we go," he said.

She rapped her thumb and two fingers on the book. "You've got to wrack your brain about what happened when I was young. Be advised, I'm reading Mother's diaries cover-to-cover. And we're going to come back together to compare notes. And when that's done, when we've turned over all the stones, I promise you I'll allow you to live your life however and with whomever you choose. Call this the last payment of responsibility you have to make on my growing up."

Thirty

FINN WAS UNABLE to sleep. From speaking to Barristof and others over the years, he knew getting a press visa to Moscow was more of an ordeal than to places Finn had already traveled. There was a double interview process in which the reasons for travel and accommodations had to match exactly. He and Chantelle had not agreed upon a narrative and even when she wasn't hungover, he didn't trust her to keep to one. Before the sun rose, he zipped through the lobby carrying only his briefcase with a clean shirt and socks in a side pocket. He woke the driver of the single taxi parked out front.

The airline didn't think twice about selling a ticket to Moscow to a Polish professor of ornithology. No visa required. With several hours to kill, Karol Sobczak disappeared into another part of the airport terminal and hunkered behind a pillar with a two-day-old issue of *Pravda*. At the third announcement for his flight, he marched straight to the gate without looking left or right. Even so, his peripheral vision picked up the animation of Chantelle's red dress in front of the visa desk. She would be too late for his flight, in any case.

He muscled on with the bearing of an actor as he was taught by his mentor-in-crime Mikolai Begitch. When she started calling his name, heads all around him turned to see the spectacle. Imitating them, he turned, too. A large man in uniform was grabbing her arms and when people saw her eyes looking beyond them, they turned, hoping to see whom the beautiful black woman was hailing. Like them, Finn turned as if to see beyond himself. Not twenty feet away, a trio of soldiers were sliding machine guns off their shoulders. As any traveler would, Finn looked at his ticket. With a shake of his head and a smirk, he walked by them onto his plane, pulse high, sweat running under his arms.

Three hours later, he disembarked in Sheremetyevo Aeroport. He ate a plate of blinchiki in the terminal while scouting out who the observers were. After studying the information kiosk, he boarded an express metro to the Belarusky Train Station. There, he caught an overnighter to Minsk.

A BELARUSIAN AGENT backed by an inspector in a Soviet uniform detained him at the Minsk station exit. His Polish passport was a flag. Finn explained he was to give a lecture on hawks at the university. When the words were out, he prayed the agent wouldn't ask him which one, because he hadn't bothered to learn the names of any in the area.

"You have just the one bag?"

"I'll be leaving on the evening train. I have a clean shirt for the presentation. You know how it is. Hotels cost money."

They let him through. In the taxi, he said in Russian, "I don't have a reservation."

"This isn't Moscow," the driver said. "You don't need to reserve taxis in Belarus."

"No, for a hotel. I want to spend the night within walking distance to Victory Square."

The dark brows of his driver appeared in the mirror. "Going to the march?"

"I've heard about it, but I'm on other business. How big is it going to be?"

The eyes in the mirror narrowed. "What *is* your business?"

"A professor of ornithology."

"That's some science thing?"

"Birds."

The cabbie nodded. "I take my granddaughter to the lake to watch the gulls."

"How lucky she is."

"She's all I have to live for."

"I expect to be here two nights. Do you know of a place?"

The cabbie responded by shoving the car into gear and pulling into the traffic. When he slowed at a hotel with Soviet guards in front, Finn suggested someplace smaller.

The cabbie understood but didn't press for details. He drove to an older neighborhood of three-story buildings and stopped at a dimly lit corner where the air smelled of burned lard. Through the open door of a bar, light spilled into the street. He waved a finger to indicate the upper floors. "The rooms are over. The food?" He gestured to show he'd eat it if he had to.

Finn had the cabbie wait until he knew he had a room. They placed him in the attic, with a window looking east, though the square was beyond view.

After a chilly shower, he went to the bar. It was early, and having his choice of tables, he settled at one near the kitchen door. He'd learned the service was often better there. And sometimes he'd catch gossip of the staff to enrich his articles. But he'd miscalculated. At least in this part of town, Belarusians spoke their native tongue. And the cabbie was right about the food. Still, not having eaten since morning, he polished off a plate of kalduny and two beers.

As night deepened, people came to drink. Their glances and talking behind their hands to their friends showed they identified him as an outsider: a Russian speaker in clothes better than they could afford hanging around the night before a demonstration. What else could he be but a government snitch? He liked the earthy faces, liked how a joke told somewhere made its way around the room, the laughter snowballing until they had all shared it.

As he prepared to go upstairs, a group of seven rough-cut men and two women came in. They pushed two tables together as if they owned the place and ordered drinks. The way they huddled made Finn order another beer. Noticing him, they spoke with their heads together. A scraping of chairs. Four of the men came and stood by his table.

"Please, sit," he said in Russian. They did with their elbows on the table. They didn't say anything. One of the men had soft lips too big for his face and a fresh welt under his eye. He brushed blond hair back and in Belarusian asked who Finn was.

Thinking they wanted to know who he wasn't, he laid his Karol passport open.

"Polski, eh?"

"Da."

The man switched to Russian. "Why are you here?"

"Are you KGB?" Finn asked.

They repeated his question to each other loud enough for the whole bar to hear. From the cynical laughter, Finn knew things would be okay.

"We want to know the same thing. What are you doing here?"

"I write."

"What do you write?"

Finn mimed opening a newspaper. "About what people want."

The man with soft lips considered this a moment. "We want what Poland has."

"I hope you get it," Finn said.

When this circled around, the bar assumed a different tone. Some brought their drinks closer, others turned to watch.

"We're going to try tomorrow."

"I see a lot of troops," Finn said.

It became quiet enough to hear meat sizzling on the stove beyond the swinging door.

"They can't hold us all," the man said. "We'll make our break soon enough."

"You mean they can't hold all the satellite countries?"

"Yes."

Finn raised his glass to the patrons, and they drank with him.

"You know about Latvia?"

"No," Finn said.

"They're going on a hunger strike, like the Chinese students."

"That didn't work out so well," Finn said.

"Maybe not. But they didn't have Gorbachev. He's okay, you know."

"His coming to power," said a man with a thin torso, "means it is our time."

"When are the Latvians going to start?" Finn asked.

"They started yesterday," the soft-lipped man said. "Two hundred and fifty people in the square. They were sitting down and being filmed by the news before the Soviets could get there. They have women bringing them food and water, setting up tents. It's a standoff." He smiled.

Finn wondered if he could get there in time. "Are you going to the march?"

"That's why we are drinking. Since you're from Poland, you could be our mascot."

"What about the troops?"

The man extended his right hand as if to shake another and slapped the wrist with his left—the continental sign of *fuck you*. The others at the table growled a laugh and copied him. In their minds, they might as well have been watching soldiers running away, or better yet, defecting to their side.

"What time are you going?" Finn asked.

The man looked at his watch. "Whenever we're done here." His mates raised their glasses. Come *with* us, they said.

THE MARCH NEVER got going. Early in the morning, Finn stood in the rain a block from the square and watched the hearty souls of Belarus come face-to-face with several hundred well-armed soldiers. Each protest leader came with his entourage of ordinary people—men and women, laborers and retirees—carrying signs with slogans demanding that the big bear let them go. The few that had walkie-talkies tried to gather the crowd outside the square to march to the parliament anyway, but as the crowd reassembled and began to move, trucks filled with more soldiers, roared in from side streets—two flew by Finn—causing the would-be marchers to take refuge on sidewalks and hustle down alleyways.

Finn took every opportunity to drift back, but stayed close enough to see the confrontations—the taunting of the protestors and the implacable response of the soldiers, advancing shoulder to shoulder. They raised their rifles. The first volley took out windows and ricocheted off walls above him. Seeing no fallen bodies, he presumed they had orders to aim high. But people started running.

Squads of soldiers followed them in disciplined ranks. They used the barrels of their rifles to push protestors forward and the butts to deck those—all young men—who confused indignation with invincibility. Knowing that to be caught with both American and Polish passports would be dangerous, Finn ran, too. One time he found himself in an alley with troops coming from each end. He followed two boys who disappeared into a culvert that led to another alley still free from the fray. On a main street, he slowed to help an older woman who had fallen. He got her seated in a doorway, then feeling his luck was running out, he sprinted east past his hotel into streets made crooked in the time before city planning. As he ran, he had just enough wherewithal to reflect on how fortunate Poland had been. He found a small place in his heart for appreciation of Poland's president Jaruzelski.

When he ran out of breath, he shared an alcove out of the rain with a couple that had missing teeth. A blue silk kerchief adorned with flowers covered the woman's hair. The man wore a wool suit coat. They hadn't heard of the march or of the trouble that had erupted. Finn listened again. Over the din of rain on the street, he heard neither gunfire nor screaming. When an armored vehicle rode past with its full complement of troops on board—boys, now that he looked at them—he shielded his head with a newspaper and walked west to his hotel.

ON THE OVERNIGHT train to Warsaw, Finn wrote his article—in shorthand—about Soviet soldiers crushing the march, complete with an eyewitness feel. After breakfast in the Warsaw station, he took a taxi to the American Embassy and filed his work with Diana. The piece came out the next day under the byline 'Guest Reporter.' It was the only one printed about the event until later in the month when several Belarusian underground newspapers released their accounts.

From the embassy, Finn went to the hotel where the press corps had lived for two months during Poland's talks. In the lounge the few customers—native Poles—laughed with a relaxation he hadn't seen before there. He booked a room and set out to find the new headquarters of Solidarity. Because their parliamentary strength all but guaranteed they would take the presidential elections in December, they were setting up proper offices down the street from the Parliament. The front hall was imposing. A pressed flag of Poland—lacking hammer and sickle—hung from the top of the atrium and reached almost to the polished stone floors. There was a long line of people—Americans and Brits among them—standing in front of the receptionist's office, hoping to do business. But the mood made him miss Solidarity's old quarters and the time just past. Finn told the young clerk whose job was to organize the chaos he was there to meet with Mateusz Dabrowski.

The longer he waited to be called, the more uncomfortable he became. In part, it was that the kinds of propositions people were petitioning for hadn't changed: recognition of this or that group, a new transportation line, jobs for family members, loans for medical emergencies, better street lights, and to be excused from things everyone was expected to pay for. Also, the response they were getting also hadn't changed: *Come back in a week. Here's a form to fill out. You're in the wrong office. These things aren't a priority with this administration.* He had no desire to see Dabrowski caught in those gears.

Finally, he was asked him to wait in a room upstairs. An hour later, an earnest fellow with a large clutch of keys on his belt and a burn scars on his hands came for him. He led Finn to the Office of Interior Ministry and introduced him to Viktor Hablinski, the same Viktor who had worn bolo ties during the talks. Now he wore a silk one secured in a Windsor knot.

"Have a seat, Mr. Waters." The door closed. Viktor rested his flank on the corner of his desk.

"We are very busy. What do you need?"

"I want to see Mateusz."

"Mateusz?"

"Mateusz Dabrowski."

"He's not here."

Finn felt like slapping him. "Is he in the building? Is he alive?"

"Alive, yes, but not in the building."

"I expected him to be part of the government."

"He's still close to Mr. Wałęsa, but his job is more behind the scenes."

"I'm here overnight. Can you set up a meeting?"

"He's not available."

"Can you get him a message?"

"Yes." Viktor didn't reach for pen.

"But not today, it seems." A non-Polish speaker would have thought they were negotiating the price of a casket.

"It will be a few days before he returns."

"Tell Mateusz I am still working on the . . . story."

Viktor's eyes flickered the slightest bit.

"Tell him I *will* expose that Soviet lie."

Viktor seemed too uneasy to smile. "He'll be pleased. We all will be." His handshake was limp and quick.

What had happened to these people? Finn backed up two steps and beat a retreat.

Thirty-One

DISEMBARKING FROM THE Warsaw flight into the green swelter of Hungarian summer, it finally dawned on Finn how distracted be'd become; he'd flown to Moscow the morning he was supposed to meet Wilmot's friend in the park. Four days passing without word or apology had probably burned his bridge to the national archives.

Still, he had his taxi drop him at a public market. It was a little past noon. The vendors were packing up. Because he didn't know the Hungarian word for chicken, he mimed one, complete with clucking noises, first to a cabbage seller, then to a vegetable farmer. They gave him looks reserved for mad men. Nearby, a little girl pulled the skirt of a woman packing up her display of fruit and said a word that sounded like *circus*. The woman pointed a gnarled hand toward the far end of the plaza where a farmer was packing crates into an ancient convertible sedan.

As Finn trotted there, the little girl ran alongside. "Csirke," she said to the farmer.

Wanting two, Finn put his palms together and said, "Két."

With no discernible emotion, the farmer unpacked part of his load, and one-handed, pulled two live chickens from a cage. Taking Finn's fifteen thousand forint, he shoved them into Finn's arms.

While Finn dug for a coin for the girl, the birds pecked his hand and beat their wings in protest. He hadn't walked twenty paces before regretting that his Rockport education hadn't included handling livestock. But Finn found the girl still attending him. Without being asked, she seized the legs of a hen in each hand, turned them head down and held them high enough to keep their heads from dragging on the granite cobbles. "Where are you going?" she asked. A phrase Finn had heard many times.

"Taxi," Finn said. When she handed the birds to him in the back seat of the taxi, they squawked louder than the driver. They quieted when Finn rolled them in his jacket. The driver shrugged and nodded when Finn gave the address of Wilmot's store.

Unlike Warsaw, where life seemed to stop during its confrontation with Communism, Budapest lumbered on. From the Chain Bridge, the river smelled of diesel—the price paid for barges traveling night and day. Runoff from a thousand upstream miles of cities and farms turned the water opaque green.

Through the glass in his shop's door, Wilmot watched Finn's clumsy exit from the taxi. One of the chickens was trying to make a getaway. Wilmot wagged his finger to show him he wasn't welcome. Exasperated, he was making ready to free the birds to do whatever hens in a city would do, when Wilmot opened his door with a wide grin. As Wilmot wrung the neck of the birds one at a time and wrapped them in paper from a large roll, Finn reviewed which Russian apology would be most appropriate.

But Wilmot spoke first. "I thought you'd been disappeared. It's only right I give one to Eva."

The word *disappeared* exploded in Finn's chest as longing and dread for learning his father's fate. "I don't deserve forgiveness, but do you think your friend might still be willing to translate documents in the archive?"

"Go to the park on Tuesday. I will have her meet you there."

IT WAS FRIDAY night. Journalists were swarming the phone bank making personal calls. Finn made a beeline for the elevators. As his lift arrived, Marty grabbed his arm. "Not so fast." He dragged Finn into an alcove beside the lifts.

"Where have you been?"

"Buying chickens for a source."

"Don't try to play me, Waters. For the last four days."

"Lying low."

"*Lying* is right."

"Back off, Marty."

"Do you know what happened to Chantelle?"

"I don't."

"She was recalled . . . at the request of the Hungarian government." Finn had never seen Marty's eyes flash. "And if you play dumb, I'm going to break your head."

"Slow down. She's gone?"

"They pulled her visa because of what you did."

"What *I* did? She came to my room drunk, overheard a private phone call, and invited herself on a trip."

"She says you've got a CIA sugar daddy."

"That part she made up. Here's all I know: I saw her in the airport as I was boarding. She was already apprehended and making a scene. Not cool. I couldn't have helped her and would have missed my flight. Where'd they send her?"

"She said you set her up."

"Marty, I know you've got a crush on her. It's hard not to. But we have certain ethics and she was over the line."

"Ethics, Finn? Heal thyself."

"Wait a minute, Marty."

"Zip it. I may be the last friend you've got. Chantelle heard you were going to Belarus. Not my business how she heard. You disappear and voilà! A police action in Minsk that nobody hears about ends up in your paper. Guest reporter, my ass. No rocket science required." He faltered. "You're right. I've got it bad for her."

Both men snuck a look into the lobby. "And Mrs. Cisneros feels how about this?"

"Don't change the subject."

"What is the subject? That I got a story you didn't? That I—"

"That you're to a point where you'll sacrifice a woman—no, another reporter—to get what you want. I thought you were better than that. Chantelle told me you've been on the story of your career. Well, get it out there, so you can stop acting like the biggest asshole in the corps. What's wrong with you?"

What indeed was wrong with him? "What can I do to get her back?"

Marty shrugged. "*Le Monde* has her on probation. She was bound for the TV desk. Now she may have to go back to cabaret."

"She sings?"

Marty ignored the question. "She's a wreck."

"Marty, I told Chantelle something in confidence. What does it say that *you* know about it?" He laid his hand on Marty's shoulder. "Twenty years from now, while she's interviewing presidents, you and I are going to be reporting triple-A ball in towns no one's heard of."

"Not if we don't—if *you* don't do something." Marty took a deep breath. "And Mexicans don't play baseball."

Finn had no chance of helping her. "As soon as I get out of my current mess, I'll do what I can."

"I wish *I* had your mess. A career story. My twins have dreams, and I'm still going month-to-month."

"Marty, whatever I thought I had just won't fall into place."

"Is it something about your father?"

The jab caught him looking. "What do you mean?"

"I shouldn't have said anything."

"What do you know about that? Come on, tell me."

"We know about your father."

"*We*?"

"Everyone in the corps, Finn. We've all been trying to cut you a little slack. I'm sure being here must be driving you crazy, wishing you could solve his mystery."

Finn sniffed back a surge of emotion. "There's no goddam trail to follow. What's creepy is I might have sat on the same barstool he used when writing those stories about the Revolution.

"I'm sorry."

"The whole corps knows? No one's said anything."

"We can be decent if we have to."

The heavy click of heels approaching distracted them. It was the service desk assistant everyone called Betty, because her name was hard to pronounce. It was harder still to not be taken by the fullness of her breasts. Her English was passable. "Mr. Waters. You have package, waiting couple days."

"Go," Marty said. "I'm done for now."

CLARISSA HAD SENT Jordan Waters's *Boston Globe* articles via special courier. In his room, Finn unpacked two hundred and sixty two-sided sheets with the font reduced. They'd been printed directly from microfilm. In his two years with the *Globe*, Finn's father had been prolific. He thumbed to the back. Included either through oversight or courtesy, the last pages were letters on *Globe* letterhead: one a request to the CIA, the second a response to the FBI, and the last a condolence letter sent to Brygitta Waters in 1957.

The Boston Globe
Office of the Editor-in-Chief
289 Boylston Street
Boston Massachusetts
September 7, 1957

My Dear Brygitta,

Though we don't know each other well, we share a love for your husband Jordan Waters. Even after all these months, I can still hardly bring my hands to write about him in the past tense and perhaps I should be more patient. But as you have been informed, there is no record of him since November 3 of last year and it seems we, the various agencies of the government, and even the Office of Refugees in the United Nations have exhausted the avenues open to us. I write in the hope of consoling you and in some selfish way of easing my own pain and that of all of our readers.

I can only imagine how difficult it has been for you to endure the total news blackout on his disappearance imposed by our government. As a newsman I find this silence particularly painful. Yet I am resigned that this was the best way to bring him home safely and at the same time to prevent totalitarian governments from censoring all newsmen through intimidation, which would make our futures very dark. I believe Jordan would have agreed with this, and I admire you for your restraint.

I am sure that until I become too feeble to understand simple sentences, every story or anecdote that I read from or about Eastern Europe will quicken in my mind's eye because of images Jordan forged in his work for this paper and for the Christian Science Monitor. His love for and insight into the lives of people living under oppression is what made my livelihood not a job but the foundation of a treasured life.

I hope that in the enclosed collection of his articles, you, too, will find solace. Please know that whenever you come to Boston, it will be Marjorie's and my honor to host you either at our home in Quincy or here in town.

With the Warmest Heart for your Great Loss, I am Faithfully Yours,

The letter was signed in a flourishing hand by Solomon ___________ and followed by the postscript: *Do take care of your wonderful little boy, Finn. It is my hope that someday, perhaps with the help of the enclosed, he will come to appreciate all that his father was.*

Nineteen years before, Finn's previous request to the *Globe* had yielded ninety articles—he had fingered them in Clarissa's apartment while going through one of the boxes that had come from Rotterdam. But this package held close to two hundred and fifty.

He looked again at the date of the editor-in-chief's letter, September 7, 1957. Laying the pages on the little desk, he settled in the armchair that was his bed, closed his eyes on twilight, trying to imagine where he'd been that day thirty-two years before. September 7 was probably a workday in the first week after Labor Day. A simple calendar check would settle that. Finn would have been six and a half. Summer was over, school was starting, and for Finn, it would have been the week he entered first grade, a year he cherished because of the grace of the teacher.

Miss Cummings's touch planted in him a standard of feminine comfort, so much so that he cried when he learned he would have to go on to second grade. The schoolhouse was a block from the Atlantic tide, an easy half-mile walk from his house, in a time when a kidnapped child was an anomaly reserved only for wealthy, famous aviators.

Insight into his troubles from that distant time came in bundles. His father had been gone so long the promises of his return had lost all credibility. The week school opened, September's heat made the ocean air oppressive. Finn remembered his clothes sticking to his skin. On the second day, he wrote all the letters of his name, and Miss Cummings praised him and stroked his hair. After school, eager to show off his work, he tromped home through the heat and into the traumatic scene of his mother raging in his father's writing nook. She must have just received Solomon's letter.

She hadn't heard Finn enter. Never comfortable with her moods, he had stiffened in the unadorned vestibule of the house. Right away, he noticed the unbleached spot on the wallpaper above the stair transom where the picture of his father smoking under the streetlamp had hung. The floor between Finn and his mother was strewn with torn notebooks and items journalists of that era treasured; pens, spiral pads, scotch tape, newsprint, a magnifying glass, scissors, pictures of every size and style, and of course, paper of all kinds. Typing paper, lined paper, yellow pads, myriads of notes—all with writing on them, that secret code the young Finn was starting to crack. When Brygitta started in on his father's books, tearing off the covers with grunts and slinging the carcasses into the living room, he waited for her to turn her back to him and scurried like a mouse to his room and stood with his back to the closed door.

No.

That was not an authentic memory.

Finn batted his eyes open to catch the Hungarian twilight. He hadn't run upstairs undetected. He had wanted to, but in the middle of a throw, his mother had seen him there. It was that look that had made him fear anger ever since. Half her hair had broken out of its side comb and had become stuck in sweat or tears to the skin of her face. She seared him with contempt, and he pictured himself a sorrowful sight.

That was when she yelled that his father was never coming home. That she'd warned him to not return to the evil world that had killed so many of her family. That he was to blame for his own damn death, for seeking it, for tempting fate.

The next morning while his mother slept, attempting to erase the damage, Finn had taken armload after armload to the basement, and on one of those trips had seen his father's right eye staring at him from the bottom of a trash can. Ever since he had prided himself that as a six-year-old he found all the pieces to the photograph. But of course, without an inkling of the value he would place on them years later, the papers he had sifted through for that one icon were his father's writings.

The stack from the *Globe* would hold the answers to many of his questions. But when he tried to read the first article, no amount of blinking or willpower could cover the onslaught of his emotions. To calm down, he took a hot shower. Then needing a drink, he went to the lounge and had two Irish whiskeys straight up. Intoxication lent him a semblance of an even keel. He looked around hoping to find Marty so he could apologize. As usual, most of the corps was taking Friday night off and had dispersed into the city. Only half the tables had patrons. Some journalists were eating alone; a few were writing. Scattered laughter and debate. Marty wasn't there.

Across the room, a pillar concealed all but the hem of a skirt and a woman's legs. He leaned to look. By the modest platform for musicians that never offered music, Annalisa sat alone at a round table for two.

Seeing her reinforced the commitment he'd made in the shower to learn how to apologize. There was Eva that he'd left in the park. There was Chantelle to whom he would never be able to apologize. There was Marty who had caught him in a lie. And here was Annalisa whom he'd embarrassed at the beginning of this wild and narcissistic ride of trying to capture the truth, the night the note from Solidarity appeared under his door. And under everything, were his failing Dabrowski and the Poles and his infidelity to Clarissa. With a series of gestures to the bartender, he communicated he wanted to buy Annalisa's next drink. A few minutes later, he carried a martini to her table.

Over the months, harmonics from the hurt of their encounter in March followed them. That night though, she must have sensed his contrition.

"I regret treating you badly in the Bristol Hotel," he said, setting the new martini by her old one.

She straightened her posture and waited.

"The fault was mine," he said. "It *is* mine."

She dropped her gaze into the drink.

Inspired by the eloquence of the *Globe*'s editor, he said, "And I admire your restraint."

She cleared her throat and looked up. "I not have been gracious as you think." How easily truth came to her. "Actually, I have cursed you at some of my friends."

"I deserve it." The warmth of the whiskey carried him through the awkward moment. "That's all really. I'm sorry." With a self-deprecatory shrug, he returned to the bar.

In the minutes that followed he felt well. His self-condemnation ceased. He listened to the piped-in music and to the staff speaking Hungarian. The bartender signaled he should look across the room. Annalisa was beckoning him with a finger. As he approached, he saw half of the new martini was gone. "You are able to sit if you like."

"I hesitate to gamble away my one good moment."

"I am not a plate for dinner," she said. "I will not break."

He stood with his hand on the back of the chair. "I envy you."

She sighed as if she had to give up saying one thing to say another. "You are not bad, Mr. Waters. I hear things of you making you more human." She gestured at the chair.

He sat, bracing himself for criticism.

"I hear-ed of your father."

Because of his intoxication and the lack of judgment in her voice, the sadness he usually blocked rose up. He thanked her.

"It is not same," she said, "but my papá has . . . sickness with Parkinson." She gazed left across the lounge, seizing one hand in the other as her father might to hide his tremors. Then she shook her head, vulnerability giving way to a smile. "But I have him. I have him a long time." She looked at Finn expectantly.

"I wasn't quite six the last time I saw my father."

She cooed. "Very young."

"It's not the age I lost him that hurts," he said. "It's the not knowing how he suffered or how long he lived. Someone told me once"—he was thinking of Fortie—"that technically he could still be alive. In a way, that hurts even more."

"Oh," she said. Her hand touched his forearm.

With no prompting, she confessed to being in love with her news chief in Italy. He had shipped her off to Poland and now to Hungary to protect his standing. "He is . . ." she couldn't find the English word, "onorevole. You know, good. But not so much to be easy to move on."

Finn placed his hand on her arm. In no hurry, she lifted it off with her free hand, and he understood her to mean he had gone too far. But she surprised him by leaning and kissing his fingers. "Thank you for listening."

"Annalisa, you don't seem hard-boiled enough for this work."

She dismissed his opinion. "Actually, it is better here than Naples. No bodies in the streets on the mornings." She inhaled, her fingers over her mouth. "I am sorry how I am uncaring."

Without her response, Finn might not have made the connection to his father. She was so bright. "I don't know why you're not with some-one and—"

She groaned and raised her palm.

He gambled. "The last time," and he pointed over his shoulder to indicate Poland, "it was you who asked to come with me." She softened. "This time I'm asking you. Will you let me make love to you?"

Thinking about it later, he was amazed how, with good timing, the right forces could mend hard feelings. He took her to her room and they did not hurt each other with what they did. But after, the fraud of his earlier apology to her overwhelmed him. He thumped his fist into his temple, harder and harder until she reached his hand and wouldn't let go.

"What is?"

For the first time ever he found the words for it. "All my life I've been mistaking comforting myself for love."

"But you are married." Annalisa fingered his ring. "So you are some lucky, no?"

"I've treated my wife like a vault of precious metals."

Annalisa nodded, as if in solidarity with a woman she had never met. He thought himself a mid-level rogue in the thieving class.

Finally she spoke. "In my country, women talk to each other. Much of it is about love. But"—she fluttered her fingers to imitate something fleeing—"men and women see only part of love, not half even. Me, I keep open for married men, hoping their luck will stick on me."

"I'm really scared," he said. "Clarissa is pregnant, and I'm—"

She pulled back from him, saying, "Oh," the way a crowd does when a matador is gored.

"—not fit to be with her."

She released his fist. "To Italians, love of man and woman is one thing . . . but family is different, bigger. You are not," she groped for the word, "thin, Finn. But I think you must not be here."

He couldn't enter his room just yet. He paced in the hall, bidding unconscious salutations to his late-returning colleagues. At last, in a fit of exasperation he went in, tugged Fortie's 8 x 10 prints out of his briefcase, and leaned them against the base of his worktable lamp. In the one of the girl in the bar, Jordan Waters was almost a decade younger than Finn was now, yet his face had lost all boyishness. The lines were rough-hewn, the cheekbones and the jaw were of a man who worked outdoors.

Finn knew little about his father's upbringing—as part of her grieving, Brygitta had cut off relations with the Waters side of the family—but he never imagined his father doing farm work or cutting trees. Still, he had that advanced-before-his-years-look that people from the '40s and '50s seemed to have. Maybe it was the film back then, the way it caught images. Maybe it was the wars and the cigarettes smoked with abandon. Maybe it came from marrying young.

In its way, it was an extraordinary portrait. It captured the world of Jordan and the hooker at that moment, the microcosm of two people connecting. They were framed beautifully, the right side of his face highlighted and at the angle to catch the power of his eyes, which were clear, capable of seeing deeply. And they were kind. In fact, in contrast to the meaning of the encounter, the whole aura seemed one of joy. A man hooked and happy to be so. He was good-looking, made almost of the stuff of film stars, or at least the photographer knew how to make him appear so. And the hooker, though clearly a woman for sale, had an aspect of pride. She was in her physical prime. A light source behind her etched her profile platinum white.

Finn imagined that her skin must have appeared more yellow to his father and that the darker space in the hollow of her cheek was rouge, but with the break in her lips of a smile coming on, it could have just as easily been a blush. Yes, that was it. She was glowing, happy to be there, happy, independent of the half-hour of horizontal work that was to come and the wad of bills in her purse to take home. In '56, food in Hungary wasn't a given. She might have been working this way to help feed her children or her siblings. The angles of her right breast jutting into the space between them also caught that backlighting and from the camera's point of view, it was a powerful tool of seduction. And among the shadows created by her hair and her dress, a patch of lighter skin announced her cleavage.

Maybe she was smiling because her beauty was rooting this man to his stool. He may have just commented on this and taken a drag on his cigarette. His other hand held the rocks glass like a pro. In it, Finn saw his own hand when he drank. His father was dressed in ordinary clothes. He was no dandy, at least not that night, so perhaps this was a chance encounter, a fly landing in a spider's web. Finn visualized him in her bed wrapped in her arms, she sucking the blood out of him. He was stung how like this man he was, pulled by feminine power when he had responsibilities at home—in his father's case, a son to teach the ways of the world to.

Maybe there was music in the background, welcoming two attractive people from different worlds. He from a free country, recently victorious in a righteous war, with its best twenty years about to come. She a city girl, or maybe she was from a farm nearby, choosing, perhaps needing, to place a price on her flesh. In the mirror over the bar a sign in Hungarian read backwards. The clock was frozen at 11:01. How close, Finn wondered, was this to the end of his father's life?

Now that he'd moved into the frame with them, he was disoriented by the sense of wholesomeness. Part of him wanted to take his mother's side, which he'd never done with the photograph he'd rescued from the trash. Her tirade in destroying it always arose in his mind.

But his sympathy stirred for the woman in the bar, and for the man who was captured by her and captured by the photographer, and for the wife he'd left at home in Rockport, and for the boy there, and for the man the boy had grown to become. Last, his sympathy stirred for Clarissa who suffered in Vienna with an inner shadow she couldn't fathom and an unfaithful husband who wasn't there.

Thirty-Two

ON MONDAY AFTER attending the talks through the morning break, Finn walked the ten blocks to the government police building and took a place in line. The clerk behind the desk was a crisply dressed mid-level public servant, about Finn's age. His Russian was excellent.

"I'm an American journalist hoping to investigate an old crime."

"Our files are government property, limited to Hungarians with clearance."

"This is from before our time. Before the Revolution."

"Are you a historian?"

"In a way. But this is personal."

"You have Hungarian relatives?"

"My father died here."

"In the war? I'm afraid those records are all gone."

Finn knew *that* wasn't true. "No, during the Uprising." The Soviet name for the Revolution in '56.

"I see. Still, we have strict regulations."

"I'm willing to be monitored. In fact, I would love your help."

"Perhaps I can try."

Finn waited in a functionary's office for most of an hour. When the Vice Principal for Special Requests finally appeared, he struck Finn as someone in need of a humor workshop, but past the age in which he might benefit from one. His skin bore heavy creases from cigarette smoke.

"You have a request?" His Russian had an accent that didn't seem Hungarian.

Finn explained his desire. The Vice Principal cocked one eye and looked at his watch, dissatisfied, perhaps, that it was too early for his lunch break. "Tell me what you're looking for, but not so much that I have to ask you to leave."

"I lost a relative in your country thirty-three years ago."

"How do you know he was here?"

"When last heard from, he was a journalist who was filing reports from Budapest."

"Was this during the Uprising?"

"Yes."

"Records from that time aren't very good."

"Didn't the police want to keep records?"

The Vice Principal's expression told Finn he'd struck a nerve. "We had a few weeks of confusion."

Finn poked again at the spot. "Sometimes mass graves are the only option."

The Vice Principal bristled. "We worked strenuously to record all casualties."

"I'm happy to make it worth your while if you can assign someone to do a search."

"I can't say yes, but you *would* have to wait. We're very involved in governing."

"Of course. How long?"

"Months, probably."

"Are the records in this building?"

The Vice Principal blinked three times. "I'll refer you to Records. Come back at 2:00 and go to the third floor."

Finn waited in the third floor hallway until 2:20. A corpulent woman in a coat that may have fit her once arrived with a clutch of keys and opened the door to the office. He explained he was looking for a deceased relative. She seemed relieved to make short work of him, saying her superior needed to give that kind of permission. He sensed he was getting close.

Her superior drafted a note almost as soon as Finn had finished speaking.

"You're in the wrong department," he said. "This note will get you into the police files. Perhaps someone there won't be too busy." He gave Finn an address some blocks away on Barcsay Street. "They close at four." It was 2:30.

Finn's taxi dropped him at a plain building still bearing marks of shelling. The ten-foot door was locked but he tugged off a shoe and beat on it. A thin man with hair parted in the middle read Finn's note. "Come." Finn followed him through empty rooms to a desk placed in the middle of a cavernous space. Phalanxes of shelving fifteen-feet high lined the walls. Hundreds of cardboard boxes. Beside the desk was a lone chair. The man told him to sit.

At thirty minutes from closing time, an older fellow in gold wire-rimmed glasses and an exhausted wool suit took his seat behind the desk. He read the note. Finn asked him in Russian if he was in the right building to find records of a deceased foreigner.

"It depends," the man said, his voice a whisper. He didn't explain what it depended on. "What's the name?"

"Jordan Waters." The name echoed in the room.

The man wrote down what he heard and turned the writing for Finn to see. "You mean like this?" He'd chosen the wrong vowels. Finn wrote the name in English. "Ah! Jordan Vatyerz. Follow me." They entered an adjoining room that housed card catalogue cases. The man flipped through cards.

"This is no record here. When did Mr. Vatyerz die?"

"Nineteen fifty-six. In the fall."

The man brightened. "In Budapest?"

"Yes."

"You're not sure, are you?"

"No."

"If we *have* a record, you're probably in the wrong building."

"Where should I go?"

"The problem is the Uprising Museum is closed."

"The Uprising Museum? When does it open?"

The man peeped like a chipmunk escaping a predator. "It's been closed for ten years."

"How can—?"

"There's no money. And it's a Soviet record. Not for ordinary people."

"Can you get me in?"

"Who is Jordan Vatyerz?"

"My father."

"I thought so."

"Can you understand my situation?"

The man's tongue tapped his upper lip. "My father went out for meat during the war and didn't come home. That's how it was." He closed the drawer as exclamation point.

"Are the keys to the Uprising Museum in Moscow?"

"No, the Government Police. Our police."

"Which is where I started the day."

"Be grateful they didn't turn you away."

"Who is the person I should speak to?"

"Chief Danko. Chief of the whole department. Maybe he'll let you in."

"And when do they close?"

"You'll miss him today. The best time to catch him is early in the morning."

FINN HAD OTHER plans that next morning. He waited in the same park where he had met Wilmot almost two weeks earlier. Because of the rain, women and children were indoors. Gaunt dogs dug through trash barrels. They bared their teeth when finding a morsel. Behaving like nations, he thought.

"Gospodeen Sobczak?"

The rain on his umbrella had hidden the woman's footfall. She had taken a seat on his bench at a respectful distance. High-heeled boots disappeared under the hem of her shiny green mackintosh. Her hands were buried inside the sleeves of the other, and she had been careful about her makeup. Her lips were full. The lipstick was the color in which red meets brown. Her wide-brimmed sun hat was drooping in the rain, which finished her with an element of comedy. If she were fifty-five, Finn would have *eaten* her hat.

"I believe you need an interpreter for the archive, hmm?"

Attempting to cover his astonishment, he said, "Your Russian is perfect."

"I was raised there. But don't worry, I'm Hungarian. My father was an ambassador."

Another Clarissa. "What shall I call you?"

"Eva is good. Shall we go?"

"Not yet."

"Excuse me?"

"Why are you here?"

"The man you called Wilmot is my uncle, not by blood, but it feels like that. A friend of my father's."

"It doesn't look like you need money."

"Money? No. I understand you lost your father."

Finn tried to remember if he'd mentioned that detail to Wilmot. But it didn't much matter. If this woman was an agent, he was already caught. Best not kick. "It's true."

She turned to show her face. Her eyes were set wide apart, the color of cocoa. "Two of my uncles died in the Revolution."

"Were you born yet?"

"Goodness, yes. I'm forty-three. I remember the gunfire and tanks rumbling through the streets. Just the sound of them made you afraid. The squeaking of their tracks."

"I thought you said you were raised in Russia."

Without missing a beat, she said, "We were sent back because of the troubles. To deal with them. You have a right to be cautious, I suppose, but hopefully that won't be necessary much longer."

"Is *your* father alive?" He peered at her to see if she was being genuine.

"Barely." She grimaced as a daughter might. "It seems his regrets could be the death of him."

"Regrets?"

"Secretly, he favored the Revolution. When Khrushchev found out, he had Kadar put him in prison. Two years later, they rehabilitated him and stuck him into his old position. But he was never the same. It was like they had something on him."

"I don't understand politics on this side of the Curtain. Is there such a thing as loyalty?"

When she turned to him, a rivulet of rain ran off the brim of her hat. "Mr. Sobczak, so many men died that to fill the government, anybody who could hold a pen had to be rehabilitated. You see it all the time here. The revolutionaries who didn't die took jobs in the government they were trying to overthrow."

Finn thought of Mikolai. "I'm sorry about your father," he said.

"What are you looking for?"

"I'm trying to find if German war materiel got to Russia during the war."

"During the war? That seems odd. Though probably some was stolen."

"No, not stolen. Ordered and delivered. It's just a theory."

"Your paper is paying you to do this?"

Finn stood. "No. Shall we go?"

The archive was busier that morning. Voices hummed beyond the checkpoint. Eva charmed the entry guard. Finn waved Karol's passport. In the commerce section, they used the top of the cabinet as their desk. His recent nights with the FOIA papers had yielded many entries, so he had her start again with 1938. In that year, factories in Germany and France were sending loaded trains to Eastern Europe. The bulk of them headed to destinations in Russia. Automobiles, trucks, farm equipment, and military vehicles. The goods included inventories of replacement parts manufactured in Ford Motor Company's European plants. A number of trains carried precast pieces for the foundry and conveyor lines for Ford's automobile plant being built in Gorky. German companies that were household names in 1989 were ubiquitous in the files as well. In his ledger, Finn jotted the case and carton numbers of interesting listings to crosscheck later.

Then like magic, in September of 1939, when Hitler invaded Poland, all traces of the Ford name disappeared. A new player emerged named Hamlin International with the same points of origin and destination as the Ford shipments had used. After Austria joined with the Nazis, trains from Berlin and Leipzig came through Prague and Budapest on their way to Vienna to supply the armies gathering there that would soon stream east and north to conquer those same cities. Traffic in both directions swelled as other countries got involved.

Eva's vigor made her more proficient than Wilmot. By noon, they had gone through all the drawers he and Finn had. For her lunch, Finn had brought a small can of caviar to go with the bread and cheese. Eva slipped the can into her pocket.

When they attacked the files again, Finn had seen enough Hungarian script to recognize the names of many manufacturing firms and shippers. With Eva translating, Finn filled in redactions in the FOIA papers. Over time, a pattern emerged of which companies, people, and goods the US government agencies hadn't wanted Finn to see. The web of commercial players lorded above the fray of army campaigns and war crimes. It even lorded above nations. Entrepreneurs traveled back and forth in official delegations led by well-known politicians. The whole enterprise facilitated soldiers in killing each other with supplies manufactured and traded by ostensibly mortal enemies.

Fifteen minutes before closing time, they came upon yet another Hamlin International shipping order. The train cars had left Frankfurt loaded with raw shells for tanks, casings for grenades, crates of bayonets, and small round blanks stamped out of tin for campaign medals to pin on soldiers. The cars of machine guns, rifles, side arms, and ammunition were to stay in Vienna. When Eva read down the list and said, "Valter," Finn's heart stopped. "Something called P38," she said. "And then there are four cars at the end of the train carrying gunpowder and chemicals—"

"Walter P38? And it says they're staying in Vienna?"

"Yes, it gives the numbers of the cars. Z102G and BF339."

"What about boxes? Are there numbers?"

"Three hundred crates of Valter P38s, forty kilograms each."

"What's the arrival date in Vienna?"

"February 18, 1940."

"That's the key," he said. "We're looking for P38s bound for Russia."

Finn pulled a wad of documents dated after February 18, and they both scanned them. On the 20th, a company named Trèana Furasta sent cars to Minsk and Moscow, including seventeen tons of military uniform fabric made in Istanbul, seventy crates of ammunition, and fifty crates of side arms identified as Walther P38s. The link was circumstantial, but German guns went to Russia via Vienna.

There was no way of telling if the Germans had intended them for the Russians or if fifty crates had been misdirected in Vienna, but since Hamlin and Trèana Furasta worked together, either option seemed possible.

A voice crackled over the loudspeaker announcing five minutes for people to leave the building. As Eva put files back, Finn slid the Trèana Furasta invoice into his ledger. Now he possessed Stalin's orders and the invoice for the guns.

Walking back to the hotel, he admitted to himself he was a serial thief. But only a thief of pieces of paper that in themselves had no market value.

At least for now.

IN THE HOTEL reception area the desk clerk waved him over. "A number of messages, sir," he said in Russian, knowing Finn preferred the anonymity it afforded. He handed him five small slips of paper. Finn took them up to his room.

The top one, the most recent, was from Sam Rich, fifteen minutes ago. *What the hell is my crack journalist doing? Three days without a filing? According to the Washington Post, things are heating up at the talks and you're F-ing silent. Call.*

The other four were from Clarissa. All with the same message. *Call.*

Sensing her news might influence his conversation with Sam, he called her.

Hearing his voice, she said, "BethAnn's dead."

Finn sat on his bed. "How?"

"She fell in front of a subway train."

"Fell? How'd you find out?"

"My father told me." Clarissa was close to hysterical. "Colonel Kerlingger is a colleague. Or was."

"Are you all right?"

"I'll never be all right."

"Then I'm coming home right away." His conversation with Sam just got more complicated. "Do you have any sedatives?"

"I've taken one."

"That's enough. Keep your head clear."

"I'm not stupid, Finn."

He told her he'd be on the next afternoon's three o'clock train.

Next, he went to the phone bank to call Sam. The *NYT* operator patched him through.

"This better be good, Waters."

"I wish I could say there's anything good."

"Don't tell me you've gotten the paper into a lawsuit."

"No. And I'll write a story on the train. You'll have it by tomorrow night."

"Give me another story about life *around* the talks. Bring readers into Hungary."

"I know my job, Sam, for Christ's sake."

"The train? Where are you going?"

"Vienna. Clarissa's therapist turned up dead. She's already under a lot of stress."

"You've told me."

"I've got to be there for her, Sam."

Finn heard Sam rummaging through papers on his desk. "It's just that I hate being beaten up by the *Post*."

"I do, too." Finn visualized the *Post*'s rotund, nerd, Budapest reporter. He and Finn had never had a meaningful conversation.

"Our investors watch the ratings. The board reminds me I'm replaceable at any time."

"They'd be stupid. You're the best there is. But I need three days off."

Sam hesitated. "They're yours, but let me know where you are, in case I decide to fire you."

IN THE MORNING Finn made sure he was first in line at the Government Police building. He reminded the desk clerk he'd been there two days before and presented his note from the man at the police files. "Mr. Szala advised me this might help set up a meeting with your chief."

The clerk's call ascended through the hierarchy. At last, he read the note aloud, hung up, and handed the note to Finn. "Chief Danko's secretary says to go up. Top floor, number 501."

The furnishings on the top floor were the same make and color as in the offices of the underlings. The chief himself came out, took Finn to his office, and closed the door. Chief Danko moved like an old athlete. If he had ever had the wound-up nature of his underlings, it was gone now. He had a blaze of wrinkles by his eyes, salt-and-pepper hair, and a big jaw.

"It seems Mr. Szala at our files building wants to help you," Chief Danko said, lifting a piece of paper from his desk. "He had a message sent over early yesterday morning to verify the one he wrote for you."

"That's unusual, isn't it?"

Danko pondered that. “Yes. But I count on him to make good choices.”

“I don’t have much time today. I’m returning to Vienna for an emergency. But I want to find my father’s file, if there is one.” He waited for acknowledgment. “Just so you know, I’m a journalist, but this is for me, not for any paper.”

“Mr. Szala explained this already.”

“Because my father died in fall of ’56, Mr. Szala thinks his record might be in the Uprising Museum.”

“One of the odd things Khrushchev worked out with our president Kadar after the Revolution,” Danko said, “was that though it was to be a Soviet museum, its jurisdiction belonged to Hungary. Specifically to the police.” He laughed. “I *am* the police.”

“What do I have to do to get in there?”

“Give me a day’s notice. I’ll see what I can do for you.”

“I hope to be back Friday. What I want to learn is if my father’s body was ever found.”

Danko wrote a note on his stationery and signed it. “Present this when you come; it will get you in to see me. But keep in mind if the government changes,” he pointed towards the Parliament building, “someone else may be sitting here.”

Thirty-Three

FINN'S TRAIN REACHED the Austrian border in early afternoon. Since he was new to the customs agents coming through the cars, they put him through their full line of questioning. When they were checking the stamps in his passport, it hit him: no files in the National History Museum and Archives carried any mention of shipments from Vienna by Fortier Enterprises. Fortie's corporation must have been using a subsidiary.

CLARISSA DIDN'T MEET him at the Vienna Bahnhof. He found her curled asleep on the couch. The air coming with him through the door roused her as surely as a gunshot. Seeing him, she sighed and collapsed back down. "What took you so long?"

"Traffic."

"No, I mean to figure things out."

A handful of unrelated mysteries winged through his mind. "Figure what out?"

"Dammit, Finn. You're the investigator."

He knelt by her. "If you're talking about Katyn and the guns, I've had a productive week."

"That's not what I'm talking about. I'm running out of time."

Her pupils weren't dilated, so she hadn't taken too much medication. "Time for what?"

"I can't do this without BethAnn." She lunged and roped his neck with her arms.

It took him a few seconds to let go into her embrace. "How's your—how are you feeling?" He laid his hand on her stomach.

"That's the one thing that seems fine."

"You don't look pregnant."

"He's only that long." She held her fingers about three inches apart.

"It's a boy?"

"While I still can, I change her gender every day."

"Have you heard from your father?"

She got a pained look and shook him by the shoulders. "Did you make some kind of deal with him?"

"A deal? No. When I stopped on my way out of town, he had a proposition. But it wasn't about keeping an eye on you. He wanted me to prepare you for—"

"For his having a girlfriend."

"So you've heard. I told him I'd have nothing to do with it."

"I caught the two of them the other day. She's disgusting, the opposite of Mother."

"Should I have told you?" he asked.

"It would have been hard to hear it on the phone. Anyway, I let that broad have it. I let them both have it." Her look turned sarcastic. "He told me he's not seeing her any more."

Finn realized Fortie had been testing his loyalty. If he had told Clarissa about her father's affairs, there was no way she would have been silent. "You don't believe him?"

"Your mother had dignity," she said, "never remarrying."

His mother had spent years staring out to sea. "She's never been with a man that I know of. Promise me, you won't be like that, if I die first."

She jerked to face him. "Are you in danger over there?"

"No, Hungary's safer than Poland was. But I've been thinking about death this week."

"That's not new."

"I went looking for records of my father."

She sighed like a mourning dove.

"I've always wondered," he said, "if he had any inkling he was about to die."

"BethAnn sure didn't." Clarissa rose, and hugging her elbows, stood in front of the large windows overlooking the street. "Is there any chance my father . . .?"

"Your father, what?"

"Do think he could have had BethAnn . . .?"

"Christ, Clarissa. Granted, he doesn't believe in therapy, but murder?"

"Yeah, but his irritation with her bordered on hatred."

"He's the one who found her for us. He paid her bills. Is he going to the funeral?"

"Yes. He wanted me to go with him. I told him I'm taking my own car."

"Does he know I'm here?"

She shook her head.

"Let's keep it that way. I have something I want to ask him before he has time to think."

"What about?"

He rose and stood behind her, put his arm over her shoulders. "Old history. Do you happen to know if Fortier Enterprises had any subsidiaries and their names?"

Nothing came to her. "I was eleven when he sold Fortier. I can ask him after the funeral."

"Good. If it comes from you, he'll still think he has me as an ally."

CLARISSA WAS ASLEEP before twilight. After eating, Finn flipped through his pile of mail, hoping for his father's articles from the *Christian Science Monitor*. What *had* come was something he'd almost forgotten about: the FOIA package of his father's papers. But the heft of them wasn't right. Pages were missing. If anything, after all these years there should have been *more*.

The beginning pages were as he remembered them, even the same redactions. The middle looked the same as well. It was the pages that might have shed light on his father's last months that he'd hoped to find more of. Instead there were fewer. He resolved his next investigation would examine who controlled the Freedom of Information Act requests. If Sam Rich wasn't interested, he'd find a paper or magazine that was.

CATHOLICS KNOW HOW to send off their deceased. It didn't hurt that right after BethAnn's funeral service began, sun broke through the downpour for one minute, bathing her coffin with the hues of stained glass. What affected Finn most was the vibration of the organ's bass pipes rumbling their pew. Fortie sat stone-faced on Clarissa's far side closer to the aisle. All around them, BethAnn's friends wore funeral finery.

Ten minutes in, when the priest asked the worshipers to pray, Finn got onto his knees. Beside him, he felt Clarissa resisting. Fortie turned from his kneeling position and tugged her wrist to get her down. "Please," he said. "Your mother would want it."

She tried, inching forward on the bench. Then she popped her head up, hyperventilating and looking all around. Sweat beaded her temples. Her heel rattled on the stone floor. A second later Finn felt her breath in his ear. "Get – me – out of here."

They were caught in the middle of a long pew, and the priest had just launched into song. "Can't you wait?" Finn asked.

She was dabbing the front of her blouse, distraught. "It's ruined." She looked at Finn, distraught. "Ruined." She jumped to her feet. He rose, too, and got his arm around her, guiding her toward the center aisle. Fortie ignored them squeezing behind him. The other seven people, though, stood to let them pass. The sound of a prayer bench toppling on the floor turned many heads. The priest and the pipe organ carried on.

In the center aisle, Finn held her close to prevent her from running to the rear of the cathedral. Once there, she blew through the huge doors and clattered down the stone steps into the rain. She positioned herself between two trees, tilted her face to the sky and rocked her head left and right. "I saw it," she said.

"Saw what?" A car going by hushed its wheels through a puddle.

"I really saw it. I saw the stuff in my dream . . . but I wasn't dreaming."

"What dream?"

"The dream with the nuns."

"Slow down. You're okay." But she was not okay.

"Remember the man in the dream praying for his life?"

He remembered. "What about him?"

"The man in the dream was *you*. And over your head, hanging all the way down from the top of the cathedral was a fire escape with its bottom ladder pulled up. It had a red towel hanging on it. It's a premonition, Finn. I'm worried about you."

"There's no fire escape in there, Clarissa. It's just a dream, a weird dream."

She froze. "The fire escape is right above you . . . all the time. You need to look up to get away. Someone should lower the ladder."

She was there and not there. "Were you in a fire once? Is that what happened when you were a child?"

When she seemed not to hear him, he grabbed her in his arms. "Stay with me, Clarissa. It's August. We're in Vienna, and I've got you. We're standing in the rain on whatever-it-is Strasse. You're my wife, and you have our baby in you. Can you hear me?"

His skin was hot, and the rain in his eyes blurred his view of her face. He had no idea what she needed, but his loneliness these past months erupted with a new cause. It was time to be there for his wife. Be completely there.

"Choo-choo foresta," she said aloud.

"Choo-choo what?"

"Choo-choo foresta. That's the name you're looking for."

"The name for . . .?"

Wherever she had been, she came to him now, not like a deranged person that people in the cathedral must have seen, but as the bright woman he'd fallen in love with by a fountain in the Stanford Quad. Her mouth curled in satisfaction. "That's the name of the subsidiary for Fortier Enterprises. I think it's Italian. It means 'Train of the Forest.' "

The music of the phrase *train of the forest* rang a bell. He repeated it half a dozen times. But Clarissa had said something different. Choo-choo foresta. "Choo-choo," he said aloud. "Choo-choo. Train." He wheeled. "Do you think it might have been Trèana *Furasta*?"

She gave him a quizzical look as she took his inquiry back in time. At last, she beamed. "Yes! *I'm* the one who called it Choo-choo Foresta. It made my mother laugh."

Finn didn't know Italian. Perhaps Furasta meant forest. "Are you sure?"

His gut wanted the homonym to be an ugly coincidence. But redactions of a two-word company in the State Department FOIA matching arrival times on the stolen invoice would resolve the issue. He prayed that if Fortier Enterprises had shipped the Walther P38s to Russia, Fortie had been too removed to know. Perhaps the Nazis or Hamlin workers had buried the crates deep in the rail cars.

"I'm sure," she said. "Absolutely sure." She was exhausted, emptied out. Her breath was returning to normal. She grabbed his arm for support. "Take me home. Throw me into the tub.

Thirty-Four

As Clarissa soaked, Finn prepared a meal for them. Their front door intercom rang. Finn called down. "I've got a gift for Clarissa." It was Fortie.

Finn kicked himself but by answering, he'd already exposed her. "Give me one second."

He padded the few steps down the hall and listened. Keith Jarrett piano was coming from the bathroom. He stuck his head in. She was asleep.

"It's not a good time, Albert. Clarissa's . . ." he debated how much information to give. "Really tired."

"Hell, Finn, *I'm* really tired. Seventy-two years will do it to a man. All I want is to leave a gift for her and to let *you* know people are concerned and help is available if you need it."

"Let's do this tomorrow. She's had a rough couple of days."

"Let her stay in bed. I'll just hand this to you and be off."

"No, I'll come over to your place—"

"Finn . . . son. Let's not let the team thing fall apart."

He was asking for such a small gesture. But after Finn hit the buzzer to let Fortie in, he realized he'd been had. And there would be consequences. It wasn't a hard decision to lock the apartment door with the deadbolt. He deliberated a little longer before hiding a butcher knife in the drawer of the hall table. He turned off the house lights, so he could spy out the fisheye peephole hole to see Fortie coming.

Fortie carried only a bottle of wine. Finn realized he had allowed Clarissa's emotionality to unseat him. Fortie reached under his coat and withdrew a baguette. He tapped the knocker with the bottle.

When Finn opened the door, Fortie laid the muzzle of the bread against his chest and said, "Bang. How is she?"

Finn made no move to let him in. "Resting."

"Can she hear us?"

"She has music on."

Fortie handed him the bread and wine. "That was very difficult . . . in the service. After, people were . . . I was embarrassed not to be able to say anything."

"Thanks for these, Albert."

"Before I go, I just wondered if you've ever seen her come apart like that before."

"You were there the night the missile struck."

"Just barely there," Fortie said. "But that's ancient history."

"Was Clarissa ever in a fire, Fortie?"

Fortie's head jerked. "What do you mean, 'in a fire'?" Then he smiled and softened his voice. "I'm willing to talk, but let's not do it in the hall."

Thinking he seemed harmless enough, Finn flicked on the living room light, opened the door wide, and took the gifts into the kitchen. He returned carrying a glass of water.

"Are you controlling my alcohol intake now?"

"It's in case you're thirsty."

Fortie handled the glass as if it held medicine. "What were you asking?"

"Inside the cathedral, she had a flashback of being in a fire. When was that?"

"Could be an idea rammed into her head by . . . by Mrs. Kerlingger."

Finn observed Fortie's every twitch. Something about him made it seem he wasn't holding his gloves up like a fresh fighter. "Having just come from her funeral," Finn said, "I think we could be more charitable."

"Yes. The colonel gave a nice eulogy at the reception."

"Did she suffer trauma related to a fire?"

"I'm no psychologist."

"But you damn well know if she was ever in a burning building. Maybe a car accident. Don't you want this cleared up?"

"I don't understand this, Finn. I thought we were working together."

"Your idea of working together is like collusion."

Fortie threw up his hands. "As far as I know, she was never in a fire."

"Good. Now both after the missile and today, she said, 'It's ruined.' What goes through your mind when she says 'It's ruined?'"

"I don't remember it from either occasion. She said that today?"

"*What* was ruined, Fortie?"

"I've no idea. And I'm feeling like a punching bag. Mind if I sit down?"

Finn answered by sitting. "BethAnn thought Clarissa was close to a breakthrough."

"Nonsense," Fortie said. "Her erupting like that shows she's far from it."

"That's like blaming the tide for making the moon full. Something's pushing to come out."

"You're making things up."

"What happened long ago, Fortie?"

"I can't answer that."

"You mean you won't."

"Can't. And I resent your tone."

"She's got some infection inside. Only after she gets it out can we all move on."

"Widowers never move on. We sit in the station waiting for the train to . . ." His voice trailed off. In the silence, the bathroom door clicked. Bare feet treaded down the hall and the bedroom door closed.

"Nice job, by the way, on the Minsk article. See? I'm not all bad."

"True, but I'm undecided if I should thank you for the pictures of my father."

"Why not? I thought you'd love having them."

"They feel like the work of J. Edgar Hoover. Who took them?"

"His photographer, I presume."

"Was he being blackmailed?"

Fortie balked. "I have no way of knowing. Who do you think I am?"

"What do you know about how Freedom of Information Act requests are handled?"

"Judas Priest, Finn. What is this?"

"I'm a journalist. I ask questions."

"What is the question, really?"

"I don't think you want to know, which is why you keep changing the subject."

"I think the question is, 'Am I trustworthy?' And I'll answer it for you. I was the youngest person at the Yalta Summit, present at the request of Harry Hopkins."

"Good ol' Harry Hopkins. The driver behind Lend-Lease with the Soviets."

"I know where you're going with this. Fortier Enterprises happened to be in the right place at the right time."

Finn gave caution a sidelong glance and barreled on. "And you moved goods back and forth."

"That's what shipping companies do. After that, I implemented the Marshall Plan in Austria, working full time and raising a family. I was friends with Truman, as much as anybody could be. And Eisenhower liked what I did enough to encourage me to move into the State Department. These are not things that happen to scoundrels, Finn. A stint in the UN as deputy assistant secretary. The list goes on and on, and you know the last twenty years."

"If your conscience is clear, you won't mind me asking a few more questions. I'm working on pieces from the war years."

"You've told me. The Katyn thing."

"The *thing*, as you call it, is where thousands of Polish officers stopped by a woods on a snowy evening."

"You're quite poetic when you're angry."

"I'm not angry."

"You're wrong, Finn. You're always angry. You have an ax for everybody." He lifted his water glass and reset it with precision. "That's why I worried about you marrying Clarissa."

Long silence.

"Good, Albert. This meeting has yielded at least one truth."

"I love her and because she loves you, I've gone along with it."

Finn looked up and smiled. For the first time in a long time the air between them felt fit to breathe. "I could do this all night," Finn said.

"Unfortunately I can't. I'm meeting some people later."

Finn saw the just-opened opportunity about to close. "Indulge me a little more. Harry Hopkins came under suspicion of filling FDR's cabinet with Soviet sympathizers. Posthumously, he was charged with being a high-level Soviet agent."

"That was all debunked. You know it was."

"Ah, yes. 'Debunked.' Buried in the hope it would rot before anyone cared. Like Katyn."

"Weaselly opportunists made those charges against Hopkins."

"And companies got in line to make bundles from the money pouring into Europe."

"Grow up, Finn. After hostilities cease, the games begin."

"Do they *ever* stop, Albert? Mind you, Republicans went after him. Your party."

"Mistakes were made."

"I hear the echo of our recently unemployed faultless President Reagan."

Fortie stopped. He took a drink from his water glass, laid it down with a wry smile. "You *are* your father's son, all right. I'm just out of practice. We used to fight like this until we broke into gales of laughter."

Clarissa appeared in her nightgown. "What's all the commotion?"

"Finn and I are just clearing the decks a little. In some ways getting to know each other. I've learned what I need to know for now. Glad to see you up."

For his part, Finn felt full to bursting with leads for his theories. Fortie was in perfect position to facilitate legal and illegal commerce at the bidding of powerful people in business and government, and he was rewarded handsomely for it. The Hopkins and Yalta episodes meant Fortie had been present to forge ties with Soviets that could have easily continued in his work with the UN and as ambassador to a country bordering the Warsaw Pact. His work at the State Department meant he had clearance to archives and any paper trail he wanted, even his own. Finn's next question would have to wait until he gathered more information. Did Fortie have allegiance to any country or ideal?

Clarissa came in sweet as a pet and hooked her father's arm. "Do you have to go?"

Fortie looked at his watch. "I'm later than I want to be."

"Darn," she said. "I wanted to ask you one question."

"I've brought you some little things. I was worried about you."

"Don't worry," she said. "I'm determined to come out of this thing."

"That will make us all very happy. You have a question? Fire away."

She flashed a look at Finn. "I just want to know if I'm right about something. And you're the only person who can tell me." She waited for his attention.

"Yes?"

"The name Trèana Furasta. That's Italian, right? What does it mean again?"

Thirty-Five

IT WAS HOURS before Finn and Clarissa could sleep. Their adrenaline was pumping and they needed to talk. He told her everything he'd been discovering, including the realizations he'd had right up until the moment Fortie left. And along with everything else, they fought about the secrets they'd kept from each other. In the end, though, he saw her bravery toward everything she feared. He wanted her to be his partner again and to learn how to start being hers.

Losing BethAnn was kicking Clarissa into a higher gear; she seemed determined to hold her head above water. As soon as Finn saw Fortie climb into his Rolls four stories below, he praised the brilliant timing of her arrival in the living room. She'd cornered her father and hit him with that question out of the blue. Fortie's face had shifted through surprise, pique, and a hint of anger before righting itself behind the opaque ambassador's mask. As if it were of no consequence, he'd said, "No, honey, it's Gaelic. It means The Easy Train. It was your mother's idea."

"I can't believe you pulled that off. How did you know to come in?"

She was still trembling when he put his arms around her. "When the music ended, I heard your voices and remembered what you wanted. I listened a bit, then made sounds like I was going into the bedroom."

"So you were in the hall listening?"

"I'd never heard you be like that with him," she said. "You were a junkyard dog."

He kissed her once and began to pace. "I'm through being the orphaned son. I don't have to make nice any more. You heard him yourself. He didn't want you to marry me."

"That answers many of my questions, too."

Over the hours, Clarissa began to accept the possibility of her father's proximity to past crimes. And it was impossible to ignore that Fortie now knew they were on to something about him. To avoid threats to Clarissa's safety, they plotted to travel together to Budapest on the early train. From there they would improvise new lives.

Exhausted, they lay down together.

And they overslept. Undeterred, they packed for the afternoon train, using the time to fill larger suitcases in case they were away for quite some time.

But at noon, the police called. Something BethAnn had written in her personal notebook the day before she died had mentioned Clarissa. The police wanted to interview her that afternoon. Finn knew he couldn't stay another day without risking his job. They made the excruciating decision to travel separately.

At 2:00, she loaded him into a taxi in the back of her apartment building. The plan was she would call his room from the station a little after 3:00 the next day to let him know she was boarding. She leaned her head through the window into the back seat. They kissed like young lovers.

The die was cast. In one more day, they would embark on new lives. Finn boarded the 3:20 as optimistic about his story as he had been since first returning from Russia with Stalin's orders. He and Clarissa would get a suite in the hotel. Or maybe an apartment nearby. She would research a new city in which to raise their child. In the near term, after attending Hungary's talks in the mornings, Finn would spend two hours poring over the commerce files in the archives.

Following that, he would write and submit his article for the *Times*. After dinner he'd cross-check that day's archival data with his ledgers and unravel more redactions in the FIOA materials. When completed, the ledgers would build a powerful case exposing the system of corrupt wartime corporate commerce. He would take it all to print. The Walther P38s and Katyn would become the capstone, the cautionary tale sealing the story into the minds of the public.

The guns were a potent symbol of capitalism's failures. And those who had conceived of the crime and requisitioned the guns deserved more consequences than even the shooters. Fortie was merely a bit player. But if he *were* in the chain of greed and hate that had killed Poland's best and brightest, he hoped the Poles would decide his fate. The grand prize would come when philosophers, journalists, and policy makers around the world convinced the UN to label this wholly toxic aspect of commerce a war crime.

Finn called Eva from the Budapest station and set up a meeting for the next day. Then over a late dinner with Marty, he learned *Le Monde* had worked something out with the Hungarian government. Chantelle was coming back, though she'd be on probation. They drank a toast to her. Finn had just returned to his room to call Clarissa when she called him.

"I messed up."

"What's happened?"

"I made the mistake of seeing him one last time."

"Your father? Why?"

"Because sometimes in life you have to finish things. He wants to take me to Switzerland. I'm bluffing, saying I'll go, but I've got to get out of here."

"Yes, you do. Where is he now?"

"In the wine cellar."

"Can't you just get out the door?"

"He knows all the cops in the city, so I'm pretending I'm his old Clarissa. Damn, he's on the stairs!"

"Whatever you do, get on the 3:20 tomorrow. Call me before you board." He heard Fortie's baritone in the background.

"I'm coming," she said, her voice a whisper.

"I'll call you in the morning." He held the phone, unsure if she'd heard him.

She didn't answer his call at midnight when she should have been home. She didn't pick up when he called in the morning. He waited until 8:30, hoping Fortie wouldn't suspect anything was amiss by him calling and as casually as he could manage, said, "I'm just looking for Clarissa. Is she cooking you breakfast, by chance?"

"I wish. She *was* here last night for dinner," he said. "But she left around ten."

"She wasn't drinking, was she?"

"What's the problem?"

"I don't know if there is one, but I called last night and this morning."

"No, she's quit drinking. The baby, you know. But now you've got *me* worried. Tell you what. I'll call over there right now. If it turns out she's missing, I'll follow up with the police."

"Do that, Albert, and call me back."

He waited a minute. When he dialed Clarissa's number, the line was busy. Just maybe Fortie was doing what he'd said he would. Just maybe everything was okay. A minute later Finn's phone rang. "She's home, though she said she was just stepping out. It's the first I've heard about it, but she's planning to go out of town for a few days. Did you know about that?"

"Yes, she said something about visiting a friend, but I don't now where. BethAnn's death has upset her a lot." He wished his hand could reach through the wire and grab Fortie's throat.

"I know, the poor dear. But I'm surprised she didn't mention it when she was here."

For a minute, Finn listened to Fortie breathe. Finally, Fortie said, "Well, I think we've got it covered for now. Call me whenever you want or need."

Finn tried again to reach Clarissa. The phone rang and rang. She must have gotten out of the house to avoid Fortie. His only option was to wait for her call before boarding. If she didn't, he'd head to Vienna immediately—by taxi, by airplane, by whatever means he could find.

At the archive, his insight on his days away made his work easier. Eva was beginning to anticipate his leaps of intuition. He was back in his room in plenty of time to get Clarissa's call from the station. The phone rang at 3:15. He leapt for it.

In his ear, he heard the blessed sounds of a train station: the clunk of cars engaging their couplers as a train pulled out, the drag of the brakes of another pulling in, the train dispatcher over the loudspeaker announcing the arrival of the 106 from Salzburg. A symphony of steel in Vienna.

"I'm at the station," she said, breathless. "They're already boarding."

"I'll meet you at 8:30."

She said nothing.

"Are you okay?"

"There's no way . . ." she seemed distracted, even angry. Maybe juggling her tickets and her purse. "Yes, and I've got to run. And the fire escape with the red towel . . . three men . . ."

"Say that again."

Her receiver clanged onto the hook.

She'd said what he was hoping to hear. But her line about the fire escape threw him back to her delirium in the rain outside the cathedral. Maybe she *had* been in a fire. Perhaps she was getting close to solving her mystery that had been buried so long.

He had five hours to kill. He lay back in the chair and dreamed the journey into Hungary with her—the farms, the Danube, and the city lights. Later, he woke to the disaster in his room— papers all around, laundry by the door. He called the front desk and reserved the only room available, a suite on the top floor. He couldn't afford it for long, but she would appreciate that it marked the renewal of their marriage. He jumped into the shower.

At seven-thirty on the way past the dining room, he ran into Marty, and while telling him about Clarissa coming, Annalisa and Chantelle strolled by chatting; Chantelle raised an eyebrow at him.

It was a beautiful night to walk. With the air off the hills and twilight masking the disrepair of the city's once-grand buildings, Budapest was as pretty as Paris. Yellow light from the train station reflected on the cobblestones. He smiled in anticipation.

The station spun vignettes of humanity. On the stairs, a huge family overtook him, boys and girls surely out of the mold of the parents, uncomfortable in formal clothes. Standing beside him at the schedule board, a wiry man and his obese wife—he, eyeing the schnapps concession and she, using her arm as a leash. The Vienna train was on time, it said, coming in on track lucky number seven.

On the platform, a beatific nurse minded an empty wheelchair alongside a gouty fellow with a stethoscope around his neck. *How civilized*, Finn thought. *A medical team there to collect a traveler*. The voice of the announcer rumbled in the same hertz range as a train arriving on track number one. The release of compressed air as the doors blew open. Further down the quay, two crones holding hands peered to the west. Surprised to find himself out of breath, he leaned for a moment against a column. A woman with two balloons on a stick; a foursome of workers with rumpled pants; a single pensioner in ethnic dress, hands clasped behind his back, worry beads swinging.

In the distance, the headlights of the train from Vienna curved into view. A moment later two huge engines crawled past and came to a stop.

Clarissa wasn't among the first to rush out. That big suitcase was probably slowing her down. As the numbers of those debarking dwindled, Finn trotted along the quay, peering in windows. Maybe she was being swallowed by another mood and didn't want to get off. One by one, conductors exited their cars and signaled "all clear" down the line. The doors closed. Lights in the train dimmed and went out.

Hoping he'd missed her, he jogged back toward the gate. Passengers had queued to have their passports checked. He came upon the nurse and the gouty doctor, making their way to that same exit. As he slowed to catch a glimpse of who might be in the wheelchair, they turned to look at him. The nurse had porcelain skin and Slavic cheekbones. The doctor had a confident cast to his mouth.

The nurse shook her head. "It seems *your* friend didn't come, either."

Arrested by her awareness, he came to a walk and peered around the doctor. The wheelchair was empty. As Finn raised his eyes to hers to express sympathy, a sharp prick lit his shoulder by the neck. "Perhaps," she said, "you could come with us."

He realized two things: She was speaking Russian, and he was wobbling as if struck by a 2 x 4. He started to form a question, but a honey-cream sensation of heat rolled through his chest. A tingling scurried up the back of his skull. He forgot his words. His breathing slowed. He felt grateful they were there to take his elbows and lower him into the chair. The nurse's cool palm running over his forehead seemed divine. "It's all right," she said, as she put a hat on him. The doctor squatted and placed Finn's feet onto the footrests. Then the wheelchair was rolling. Lights overhead drifted by. He was pouring sweat.

One minute, four? He didn't know. A face under a custom agent's hat leaned down and spoke to him. Or at least his mouth moved; sound seemed to have vanished. Finn tried to explain to him about Clarissa not coming, but his jaw felt huge. He saw passports being opened at the level of his eyes but had no memory of giving his to the nurse. The agent waved them through. The chair rolling. Fresh air, the moon, the doors of a van opening and his chair being lifted in and secured to a wall. And then sleep.

Thirty-Six

A RIVER OF DREAMS. Breathing. Not his. Very close. Violation to his left eyelid. Odd, but not painful.

"Nothing yet." The voice seemed perched in the air.

"Give him the shot." A tetchy male. "He's slept long enough."

"Are you sure? It'll make him combative."

They were speaking Russian. Finn felt his head snap hard to the left. His right cheek stung. The rest of his body lit up with sensation.

A cruel laugh. "That will be fun."

Finn was sitting, restrained across the chest. Legs numb. Hands cold. Wrists bound to the arms of his chair. A thumb peeled back his eyelid again. A bright light reminded him of the train from Vienna coming into the station.

"He's responding."

"Move aside."

Finn blinked. Deep-set eyes loomed too close. Nearby, a man looked on. The doctor at the station.

"He's not your friend, Waters." The speaker's face, dull ivory skin pulled tight over bone. "It's me you're interested in."

Finn's words came out as gibberish. With a cackle, the bone-faced man worked Finn's jaw up and down. "What did you say?"

"Who are you?"

"Call me Vladimir," Bone Face said. "All Russians are Vladimir, aren't they?"

Finn shook his head. It felt heavy. "No."

"Speak up, or we'll be here all day."

"I said, no, Vladimir."

"Good. What day is it?"

Finn looked for windows. There were none. An empty chair faced his. The light was dim. A floor lamp in a corner cast long shadows. Every sound made a quick echo. This was no hospital. "I don't know."

"That's right. And you never will again unless you work with me."

"I'm an American citizen."

"I don't give a shit."

"What do you want?" Finn asked.

"Say it again. Clearer this time."

"What do you want?"

Vladimir moved into the path of the light. He was fit. He had the bearing of a soldier. "No, Waters, tell me what *you* want."

The number of his wants frightened him. "I want to take a shit."

Vladimir laughed. "Go right ahead. Most people who sit where you are shit in their pants."

Finn's nose awakened to the smell of feces. Vladimir wheeled. Finn wasn't prepared for the blow. His head slammed to the right. When his eyes cleared, he peered into the shadows on that side of the room. He was in the middle of a space about the size of handball court. High ceiling.

"Is it coming, your shit?"

Finn's teeth had cut the inside of his cheek. He tasted blood. "What do you want?"

"Tell me who you work for."

"The *New York Times*."

Vladimir mimicked his answer with disgust. "No, you don't."

"Call my editor." A headache was spiking.

"You've been fired. You work for me now."

"Then it's back to you. What do you want?"

Vladimir belted Finn in the stomach harder than he had ever been hit. His breath hurt coming and going. When he straightened up to see what might be coming next, Vladimir was still massaging his fist. "I want to communicate."

Finn spat a little blood."Your mother must be proud of you."

Vladimir sneered. With a flourish, he unzipped his fly, shook his dick free, and thrust his hips forward. Finn ducked and pinched his mouth closed. Warm piss rolled down his cheeks.

"I'm disappointed, Waters. It can go better than this."

Finn rubbed his cheeks on his shoulders. "Give me something to go on."

"I'll give you this: Next time I see you, I want to know what you did with the orders." Vladimir turned and barked, "Get him out of here."

A hood dropped over Finn's head. He fought for breath as his chair rolled out a door.

He heard two sets of footsteps. They pushed him along several halls. A service elevator dropped, clicking past two levels. They wheeled him past diesel oil and hay. They stopped. Keys jangling on a ring. A key in a lock. An iron door swinging open. Four hands released his restraints and shoved him forward. The floor clobbered him on the face. Cold and damp.

The door slammed. Finn heard another door close farther away. After a few minutes, he sat and pulled his hood off. He was in a place equally dark. It took great effort to get onto all fours. He crawled to a wall and rested against it until he felt it sucking the heat from his body. He heard the faint passing of air. He wasn't alone in the cell.

He called out the one Hungarian greeting he knew. His voice was weak. No response. He tried Russian. He tried English. Still no response. Crawling toward the sound of breathing, his hand landed on a man's leg. Something smelled foul. The body did not move.

He located the man's chest. It rose and fell under his hand. Gently, he rocked the body to see if he could rouse it to consciousness. "Hello," he said again in Hungarian.

"Nye dót-tik-ai!" *Don't touch*! The voice sounded shredded from screaming.

Finn removed his hand. "You're Polish."

"Tak." *Yes*.

"What's your name?"

"I want to die."

"They've hurt you."

"Tak."

"Can you sit up?"

" Kill me . . . please . . . I beg you."

Candles offering hope to the future were snuffed out. "My name is Waters. Who are you?"

A huge sigh. "A coward." The man turned his head and coughed. He lacked the force to clear his lungs. "You understand?"

"Understand what?"

He coughed again. "How bad it will be."

"How long have you been here?"

The man wheezed for some fifteen seconds.

"Do you need water?"

Long pause. Scratching sound. The man was rubbing his head on the floor. "Yes."

"Do you have any?"

"In the corner past my head."

Finn found a metal pitcher, half full.

"He said you were coming."

"Who did?"

"Vladimir."

Finn helped him sit up. Guiding the pitcher for him, Finn felt bandages on his hands.

The man drank, waited, and drank again. He exhaled hard. "I'm Dabrowski."

"Dabrowski! Mateusz? No!" Something deep in Finn's heart broke its bindings.

"Tak."

So after all, the Soviets had managed to fell Solidarity's big bear, the man who had sent Finn to Russia. That explained Viktor Hablinski's evasion during his visit to Solidarity Headquarters. Finn jettisoned his resentments toward Viktor. "Where are we?"

"Russian troop barracks, east of Budapest."

"Why are you in Hungary?"

"I came to help the workers in the talks."

Finn began hearing the voice as Dabrowski's. "The Hungarians?"

"Tak."

"Do they need it?"

"Tak. Tak."

"And how long have you been *here*?"

"Time disappears."

Finn considered this. "What are your injuries?"

"They beat my feet."

"Are they broken?"

"They feel like Kielbasa. And my shoulders. They hung me from behind."

Dabrowski's weight would have ripped muscles and tendons. "Jesus."

"Did they burn your hands?"

Dabrowski sighed but didn't answer.

"You don't have to tell me."

Dabrowski's voice pitched into a whine. "They cut off my thumbs."

"Off? The bastards. Why?"

"To get me to talk."

"What do they want from you?"

"The same thing they want from you."

Finn imagined life without thumbs. "Katyn?"

"The orders."

"You don't have the orders."

"Logic isn't logical to them."

"If *I* give them what they want, *you* can go free."

"They want me for other things, too." A little pride snuck into Dabrowski's voice.

"If you live, you can go home to your wife."

"I'll have *her* kill me."

"Because you have no thumbs?"

"I gave . . . I gave up a man."

"What do you mean?"

Dabrowski half-rolled, half-collapsed onto his back. "When I still thought living was important, I gave them Janis's name."

"Janis? The guard at Katyn? The one who gave me his story?"

"Tak. I'm a coward."

Finn saw the KGB breaking down Janis's door. "Everyone has a limit," Finn said.

"Wrong. I watched Stasi torture my grandfather. He didn't say one word as he died."

A long time passed. Dabrowski's breath became shallow. When he woke, Finn asked him, "How come I never saw you at the talks in Budapest?"

"I was advising the opposition off the site. I listened on the radio."

"Do you remember the date they seized you?"

"Mid-July." In only three weeks, they had destroyed this man.

Dabrowski squeezed Finn's arm. The hand felt like a flipper. "The infection is spreading. Next time I sleep, find it in your heart to strangle me. Start and don't give up."

Thirty-Seven

FINN COULDN'T BRING himself to kill Dabrowski.

Later—it might have been the next day—guards threw in a thin mattress and left a cold bowl of barley soup with one spoon. Finn imagined Vladimir observing them through an infrared camera, hoping to see them battle to the death over supplies for one. Motivated as much by spite for Vladimir as by kindness, Finn slid the mattress alongside Dabrowski, rolled him onto it, and fed him from the bowl until it was gone.

Over the hours, Finn distracted himself from the thundering pain of his headaches and his bruised organs by tracing his route to this cold concrete room. A simple note slipped under his door, then the trip with Mikolai Begitch into Belarus and Russia, to the villages of Dyedna and Mosalsk, where he met the shooter Janis Semyonovich and his commandant, Andrei Kurishenko. Then after Solidarity succeeded in the talks and he had delivered the Melezh book to Janis, he'd traveled through Mogilev, Orsa, and Arzhipovka to Katyn. Against what he thought possible, visualizing the road into the forest and hearing the cries of Polish officers when they realized all hope was lost banished many of his fears about what lay ahead for himself.

When sleep wouldn't come, he found ease riding the train to Budapest in his mind, over and over along the Danube. The humor of the would-be revolutionaries in Minsk balanced out their failure, and his hour of running for his life from Belarusian boy soldiers. He acknowledged Beijing and Hong Kong, but did not linger on them. When he felt a little conviction, he conjured the faces of those to whom he owed apologies. Noble Annalisa, wild Chantelle, Marty Cisneros. At last, when he realized his motive was to avoid thinking of Clarissa and all that he owed her, he wept into his sleeve.

They'd had a great escape plan. Only the two of them knew of it. She was going to leave Fortie quietly, so they could be together, finally away from their pasts. A reenacting of elopement. Sitting in the dark, he conceded the Soviets or someone in league with them had grabbed her at the last minute. They'd broken her and forced her to the phone in Vienna station, setting Finn up for the kill. He strained to make sense of her lasts words on the call about the fire escape, the red towel, and three men.

In the middle of wondering if Fortie could have prevented any of this, he had to conclude Fortie was in on kidnapping her. He'd never wanted Clarissa to marry Finn. Was his motive for sending Finn to Minsk for him to be caught or killed? Perhaps Fortie was hiding more than Trèana Furasta's shipments of the Walther pistols to Kaytn. His heart stopped. Perhaps Fortie was a Soviet mole.

WHEN NEXT ROUSED by the door opening, Finn found himself wrapped around Dabrowski's bulk to fight off the chill. Light from the hall hurt his eyes, but in it, he saw the black shapes of two men and the wheelchair. They ordered him to don the hood. Dabrowski hadn't stirred when the door opened and wanting to see him at least once, Finn turned. He lay like a broken bag of flour. When hooded, Finn got hit with vertigo.

To the delight of the guards, he stumbled and bashed his chin on the metal of the chair. As they wheeled him back past hay and diesel, regret came easily. At any time over the last months, had he obeyed Sam Rich's demand that he drop the Katyn story, Clarissa would still be safe. And if someone as tough as Dabrowski wanted to die here, Finn would soon want to do the same.

Whatever the case, rising in the service elevator, Finn believed he would meet the same fate as countless others who had died at Soviet hands. If Vladimir had gotten Dabrowski to talk, Finn had no chance of holding out. From his one short session, he already had the highest regard for torture.

As they wheeled him along the corridor, he realized if they were going to torture him to extract information only to then kill him as they did Mikolai Begitch in his yard, he might as well invite death. Play this bastard Vladimir somehow, light the fuse of his evil so deliberately that he would delight in murdering him. The irony was Finn would have to conduct the interview of his life to bring Vladimir to that point.

The slap-back echo and smell of feces told him he was back in the torture room. He sat hooded and bound, listening to the sounds of equipment being set up. Then without the manners of removing his hood, Vladimir punched him right between the eyes. For a few minutes, sun flares shot from the place he'd been struck. As his ability to think returned, it was clear manipulating Vladimir enough to kill him would take more than a simple decision. He'd have to call death with all his might.

To practice how that might go, he settled on the strategy of accepting the blows. He raised his head inside the disorienting dark of the hood, as good as offering his nose. But Vladimir let him sit there. At length, he spoke not to Finn but to someone else, asking what kind of drug he had to keep blood from coagulating. A voice rattled off two medications Finn didn't know. Vladimir's change in strategy brought another insight: committing to die at the hands of someone in complete control demanded ultimate flexibility.

The next blow caught his left ear. It came with enough force to lift the wheelchair onto its right-hand wheel. The ringing in his head rivaled an avalanche of icicles. After most of a minute, he righted himself.

Vladimir pulled the hood off. Seeing Finn serene, he whipped him across the face with it. Three quick strokes. Through water pouring from his left eye, he saw Vladimir's lips move.

"I can't hear you," Finn said. His lower lip was swelling.

Vladimir leaned close and laid his palm flat on Finn's clavicle, almost a lover's touch. "You must be CIA to not be blubbering like a baby. I look forward to breaking you."

So it was time for the interview with death to begin. "I'm a reporter."

"So you say."

"I could write a story about you."

Vladimir smiled and turned to show off his profile. His nose had been broken. "Will there be photographs?"

"If they are ever published," Finn said, "you'll have to find honest work."

"You will soon discover, you little shit, nothing feels more honest than being beaten."

"Then my assessment is that neither of us has been beaten enough."

Vladimir slid his hands around Finn's neck and drove his thumbs into his larynx until his eyes felt like they would explode. He tried to let go of life, but his lungs fought for air. His throat emitted a pathetic garble. Each step getting to the dying point placed the goal farther away.

"That's better, Waters. I hate bravery. It tells me I'm not good at my job."

Finn's throat was on fire. He took another blow to the face before clearing his vocal cords enough to get the words to come. "What do you want?"

"Yes, it *is* about what we want. We know you went to Russia. And we want what you stole."

"That's it?" he whispered.

"*Da, moi horoshi droog.* That's it."

He remembered his first glimpse of Stalin's orders. The paper itself had an aura of inevitable evil about it. The commandant had kept them enshrined. Finn, too, put them in a shrine in the bank. Instead of respecting the document, he'd become a slave to it. He'd defied his professional code *and* common wisdom. How stupid he'd been to think he could handle—that *anyone* could handle such poison without unleashing severe consequences. Everyone had been telling him so for months

—Sam, Fortie, the State Department. And now Vladimir. It was definitely too late to avoid consequences. What strategy could hasten their arrival? "I confess."

Vladimir laughed. "I know what confession sounds like. That's not it." He backhanded Finn's cheek.

"What do you say now?"

The ligaments in Finn's jaw burned. "I still would like to confess."

"Confess to what?"

"I'm a thief."

"Tell us something we don't know."

"I need water."

Vladimir tossed a cup of coffee into his face and belted his right ear. It rang in a different octave from the left one. Vladimir was releasing the pipe organ in his head. Set on joining Mikolai, Finn smiled as much as his mouth let him.

"I'll give you water."

At Vladimir's signal, the guards unbuckled the restraining belt that held Finn upright. They undid the bindings on his ankles and wrists. He let them drag him to a low gurney, let them bind him face up and cover his face with a terry cloth towel that they tucked behind his head. A last strap ratcheted across his eyes locked his head in position. At nose level, water poured steadily onto the towel as if from a samovar or a hose on low flow. By the time Finn realized what was happening, he was short of air. He took a ragged mouthful into his lungs. He writhed on the gurney. More water came. Choking, coughing, sucking for air. Fire and water in his lungs. One minute, two.

His head wanted to crack, but he was getting his wish. He would die today. This eased his desperation. He lay back and let it come. A minute later he was jolted awake. His throat was raw and the water came again. He waited until he had to breathe and inhaled whatever water he could. Each cough allowed more water in. No power of mind would help. He was in rapid convulsions when purple light radiated in his brain.

LIKE A DREAM that would neither cease nor resolve, the door of his cell opened, and the two guards held the chair. Finn had no memory of being brought back or of sleeping, but his throat burned. The hood was beside his head. Dabrowski was sitting up.

"I'm going the slow way," Dabrowski said. His voice sounded distant, not because of Finn's lack of ability to hear, but because of Dabrowski's depression.

"Where are you going?" Finn asked him.

"No talking," a guard commanded. "Put the hood on."

"Infection is taking me. Good luck. When they come at you with the cleaver, change your tune."

Finn sat in the chair. "I'll get you clean bandages." The hood came down.

In the room Vladimir came at him with a short piece of pipe. Instead of striking him with it, he placed one end on Finn's sternum and belted the other with a steel mallet over and over. The blows left Finn longing for the straightforwardness of punches to the head. "I thought of this myself," Vladimir said. "Lying on my bed with nothing to do, I wondered if my CIA reporter would appreciate something different. I think I'll call it the *Vladimir*."

"Dabrowski's dying."

"You expect me to give a shit?"

"Let me clean his wounds. He needs new bandages. Then I'll talk."

Vladimir abandoned his invention for a conventional blow with the pipe, striking Finn below his left shoulder. His arm went numb. Then like a dancer Vladimir unclipped the flap of the holster on his hip—odd, Finn thought, that he hadn't seen it there before—and drew the revolver.

"Up."

Finn didn't move.

Vladimir stuck the barrel of his gun in Finn's mouth. It was cold, huge, and hard as diamond. His teeth felt brittle against it. Steel in the mouth felt less intimate than being beaten. Less dangerous, too. Hemingway had chosen this way to die. He was in good company.

"Then we'll do it here," Vladimir said.

Finn looked Vladimir in the eye. He sent apology to Clarissa for never getting his priorities about their marriage straight. He couldn't decide, though, in those seconds if he regretted stealing the orders. He would die without a story told, but he'd come close.

"Vladimir," said a male voice in the room, a presence without volume. Vladimir's boss? Finn felt the pistol turn as if it had lost concentration. "Think of the mess."

After a minute, Vladimir withdrew the barrel. "Put the hood on him," he barked. "Wheel him out."

Though Finn was free to fight, he sat as the hood was lowered over his head and the drawstring pulled. He counted three sets of footsteps and the first turn was away from his cell. After a long hall, they turned right, rolled down a ramp and into a cooler place, across concrete. When they stopped, a pair of hands on each bicep lifted him forward and shoved him onto his knees. The steel of the pistol barrel connected with his skull where the spine goes in.

Beating this Vladimir character had been so easy. Finn straightened his torso, and in solidarity with the Polish officers at Katyn, he put his hands behind him. He only wished he could stand and die with their same dignity.

"You Americans like to pray, don't you?"

Finn thought about Clarissa, and if she lived, of the hollow story she would have to tell their child about her father gone missing in 1989. He grieved for that child.

"Pray. I want to hear you pray."

"To what?"

Vladimir racked the pistol to bring a bullet into the chamber. "I don't know. Entertain me."

It would be lightning quick. Having brought this fate upon himself, Finn let everyone go, all the forces and characters in the chain of events that led him to this moment—his ambition for greatness, the Solidarity

Poles, the Soviets, the Belarusians, his mother, Fortie, and Clarissa. He perched upon the image of his father, in the pieces he'd taped back together to make him a whole man. He recalled Clarissa's dream of the nuns dressed in red and Finn on his knees praying, pleading for his life.

No, he would not plead. *It's all right*, he thought. *It's all right*. He leaned back into the barrel of the gun.

Thirty-Eight

When they returned Finn to his cell, he had won both ways: He had relaxed into death, and he was still alive. Waiting for him was a large pot of freshly boiled water, some disinfectant, a roll of bandages, a portable light, and a slightly intrigued Dabrowski.

As a result of Vladimir's last blow with the pipe, Finn couldn't move his arm, but by pressing that elbow to his ribs he was able to use the hand. Over the next hour he stripped Dabrowski's putrid bandages and washed the stump of each thumb. Both were infected. The left one was gigantic with puss. Finn milked it into the feces bucket. No matter how Dabrowski cried out, Finn insisted on getting fresh blood to flow freely from the wound before squeezing to stop it.

When the guards had come for him, Finn hadn't seen Dabrowski clearly. Now in the light, he seemed a decade older than he had in March. But the bear was visibly touched to have this attention to his life, a life that—if it were not to be short—would be difficult in every way. They didn't speak except about what was best to accomplish the task, but sympathy passed between them. Afterward, Dabrowski collapsed into sleep and Finn prepared to lose his thumbs.

On the next visit, Vladimir removed his hood first. Finn sat upright and received his welcoming punch to the stomach. He guessed they hadn't seen each other for a few days. Still, the pain made it clear his organs had not recovered from the previous blows.

For a few minutes, Vladimir busied himself at a stand that Finn had never had a good look at. Eventually he came over and rubbed Finn's head as a father does to convey love to a little boy. "I trust you slept well."

Finn realized kindness was part of torture, too. "Thank you for the bandages."

"Dabrowski was happy?"

"He still has no thumbs."

"It's been a few days since we talked about the main subject."

"I've forgotten what that is."

"The orders."

"Which orders?"

"The false ones you wrote to embarrass a former leader of the Soviet Union."

"Let's call him Stalin."

"A great man."

"You're taking that on hearsay. He died before you were born."

"Greatness is like diamond. Indestructible."

Finn had thought about this, though at that moment he couldn't recall if it was before he came here or since. "There are no great men," he said, "only great narratives constantly rewritten to spin mirage."

"You're mistaking greatness for truth, which is fluid. But I'm not here to debate you."

"Then beat me or kill me. I accept both."

"I'm here to work *with* you."

"You mean, *on* me."

"You have one thing we want."

"If the document you say I have is false, it shouldn't interest you."

"Stalin's greatness is unchanging, but that document *creates* a story that confuses it."

"So documents are never true?"

"Let's test your point." Vladimir walked away and returned, rolling the stand at which he'd been working earlier. He thumbed through a few pages in a stack and brought one for Finn to see. It was from the FOIA documents, the Commerce section. Finn knew it well, a particularly redacted page. He had wondered when the Soviets would clean out his hotel room.

"So where is the truth here, Waters?"

"Underneath the black strokes."

"Precisely. It's not here. So why would these interest you?"

"I'm looking for what's not there."

"Ha! That proves journalists create 'truth' out of nothing. In short, you are liars."

"Documents can prove both lies and truth," Finn said.

"Correct. They're unreliable, which is why things written down are bullshit."

"If I give you Stalin's orders, will you black out the numbers of people he slated to be murdered? And mention of the Poles? How will that help the story of the Great Leader?"

"You don't understand me. Words on a page mean nothing. For instance, your Bible says Jesus walked on water. That is not true, and no one *believes* it. But your stance is that if it was blacked out, it could *become* true."

Finn's mind couldn't keep pace. "Stalin's officers *believed* his orders were true, and 22,000 Poles are truly dead."

Vladimir was ready for him. "That kind of fallacy gets courts all over the world to twist justice any time they want. Innocent people get convicted all the time."

"And guilty ones walk."

"Good, Waters. Now you agree with me."

Vladimir shook the page with redacted text. "You yourself said truth is not on this page." He pulled a lighter from his pocket and set flame to a corner of it. When the heat threatened his fingers, he tossed the page into the air. "Now I ask you, is there more truth or less than before?"

"It's unchanged."

"Then we agree again. Truth doesn't depend on documents. They are fabricated to support whatever people want to believe. And *that* is the crime. The real crime. I'll show you where your belief trumps the truth." Vladimir picked up another page from the stack and burned it. And another.

Then he asked, "Do you feel anything yet?"

"Irritation at your confusion."

"But if you write your irritation down as if it were true, it can be burned. Your defense is that if it is blacked out it becomes more real. Still not true, but more real."

"You should listen to Dabrowski; he's right about you."

"Poles are never right about anything, written down or not."

"He says the logic of tyranny isn't logical. I want to throw up."

"Logic can be changed to support any point of view, but throwing up is very close to reality." Vladimir lifted a book Finn recognized as one of his ledgers. A wave of defeat closed his eyes involuntarily. "I see," said Vladimir, "that you would prefer we hadn't found this. Given how paper lies, we can't figure out why all this nonsense interests you." Betraying no emotion, he tore out a page and burned it. When Finn held still, he burned a whole sheaf. The light revealed a blanket of smoke sinking towards the floor. "Where is the truth now?"

"Unchanged. The Polish officers are dead, and Stalin ordered it."

"So you agree that giving me the orders will not change anything."

"It will confirm your insanity."

"But it won't change *your* conviction. This is where we differ, Waters. Conviction is a poison. I refer you again to Jesus walking on water." He lifted a small booklet, a passport. "Karol Sobczak is not a real person, wouldn't you agree?"

"But he found truth."

"It defies your own logic to assert that a phantom person can find truth." Vladimir lit the passport and set it to burn on a copper tray. He flipped open another passport. "Finneas Kumiega Waters. And is this a real person's?" He shook it. "How is it different from Karol's?"

"You know exactly how."

Vladimir flicked the lighter again, and while watching Finn, held the passport too high to catch fire. "You say some documents are true and some are not." He raised the flame, then lowered it. "And you also say truth is unchanged whether a document exists or not. If I burn this, will you cease to be? Or will you be unchanged?"

"My story will be harder."

"And that's the point of your false orders. They confuse reality."

"You're insane, Vladimir. The confusion of Stalin's orders has been their absence."

"Let's see, shall we?" He raised the flame of the lighter again. "Do you feel the heat of truth? And if so, where is it?"

Finn saw it in a flash. The only way corrupt governments succeeded was on the inherent goodness of the people they damaged. The tick lived on the dog. The plantation owner on his slaves. The tyrant on the oppressed. Finn watched his passport burn. If he were to soon be dead, this presented no problem to him. It would be a hardship only to others who might want to find his legacy. Then it came to him what else lay on the table.

Vladimir was watching him closely now. "Perhaps you think a photograph is closer to the truth," he said. He raised the black and white 8 x 10 of his father with the woman in the bar and turned it for Finn to see. "Is this someone you find interesting?" He set the photograph alight, laid it in the tray, and brought the tray close. The image of the woman and his father bubbled, turned brown and became ash. Finn wished his sadness was burning with it. From that point of view, Vladimir's argument had merit, too.

Finn was the only person on the planet who would be moved by this document and by its transformation. Was the photograph true or false? He had idealized his father only to find out he was a common man. So was his father true or false? What was the difference between a memory remembered and a memory misremembered? And did it matter in the long run?

"In the same way," Vladimir said, "perhaps you are also a hidden truth. A redacted man. A hidden truth that some other journalist needs to rediscover. Perhaps someday someone will make you true by writing your story in a book." He laughed. "But if those books get burned, I'm afraid you'll become untrue again."

Finn thought of Sam Rich. By now, Finn's disappearance was reverberating through the halls of the *New York Times*. In this day and age, a journalist couldn't vanish without creating an international incident. Or could he? Would the government shut down the investigation to protect its broader interests? Marty and others had seen him leave the hotel that night, knowing he was going to pick up his wife. Times were different than in 1956; the world was bound closer together. And bodies always turned up, didn't they? Documents always turned up. Stalin's orders would turn up, at least during an inquest to adjudicate his estate if he was never found. If Clarissa was alive, she knew the bank where he'd put them.

While Finn had been watching his father vanish yet again, Vladimir walked out of the light and returned waving at the air with a cleaver as if to rid it of things they'd said. In his other hand, he carried a heavy cutting board.

Finn wondered how Dabrowski's conversations had gone the day he'd lost his thumbs and if Dabrowski would say that his thumbs were real. He ran through his priorities now. "You don't need Dabrowski anymore."

"He's getting what he deserves."

"Like Lenin, he fought to free his people—"

"He's a criminal—"

"—except he has no blood on his hands."

"—and he's a traitor to the Union." Vladimir rolled his shoulders as if to regain his advantage.

"The Union!" Finn said, wanting to spit. "An involuntary union is madness."

Vladimir strode to Finn's chair. "Where's the *proof* of that?"

"Deniers burn truths. They cut off fingers to change the story. Talk about being a slave to conviction."

Vladimir nodded to his associates. The sound of chairs scraping the floor. "Chairman Lenin forgave mistakes others made in his name. That cleaned up history." He handed the board to the guard who had a face as flat as a refrigerator.

"If documents aren't part of history," Finn said, "tell me why you Soviets keep such detailed records of your exploits. The records show Lenin blamed others for his crimes and had them executed."

"You weren't there." Vladimir backhanded him across the face. "Are you right-handed?"

Finn knew where this was going. "Does it matter?"

"Then I'll play the odds. Free his right hand."

The guard with the flat face did.

"Now extend his index finger."

"I'll offer it myself," Finn said. He straightened the finger he used to hold his pen and laid it, pad down, on the board. Letting Vladimir take him by inches was just another means of dying.

At the sound of someone clearing his throat, Vladimir and the guards turned.

"You should reconsider, Vladimir."

"I am close."

"If he coaxes *you* to violence," the man said, "he's beaten you."

"I wasn't going to cut it off. It's just a technique."

"Don't you see? Mr. Waters has nothing to lose."

The man was positioned behind Finn and in the shadows, but Finn called out to him. "You won't find it written on any document," he said, "but in my cell, there's a better man than me who's missing both thumbs."

Finn heard a tongue click. "Think of the consequences, Vladimir. The Union is standing on the precipice. The last thing Russia needs right now is another bad story."

"But if he dies, no one will know."

"Not in my country, Vladimir. Not again."

The man entered the light. He was wearing his officer's cap. Danko, Budapest's Chief of Police.

"If this man had Stalin's orders with him," Danko said, "you'd have found them. After all, you found the note I wrote for him, which is why you called me here. He seems willing to die to keep them from you. Save yourself the trouble of having to dispose of another body." Danko thought a moment. "*Two* bodies, with his cellmate. Four, counting my driver's and mine."

"Chief, I outrank you."

Danko huffed. "Only because Russia has its boot on Hungary's neck."

There was a long silence that the second guard sought to end by moving toward Danko. Vladimir waved him off. "The chief and I disagree on that point, but we have to remain somewhat neutral while the talks are going on."

"I'm going to take this man with me," Danko said, putting his hand on Finn's shoulder. "You will either have to let him come or hold me, too, which will pose a greater problem. I wasn't so foolish as to come without informing my department."

Vladimir raised himself to his military best, eyes forward, hands clasped behind him. The twitching of his fingers was the only sign of his mind working. In bold steps, he exited the room.

When he returned, resignation tugged the corners of his mouth. "The Kremlin says take him." Vladimir signaled with his chin. The guards undid Finn's bindings.

But Finn stayed in his chair. "I'm not leaving without Dabrowski."

"I anticipated that," Vladimir said. "Unless we get the orders, Dabrowski stays."

Finally Finn was ready. "You can have them. They've ruined my life."

"When you bring them, he'll go free."

Danko said, "The swap will happen in the Polish embassy."

Vladimir bobbed his head one time. "No press. No pictures."

Finn ran through steps in his head. "You've burned my passport. Dabrowski won't survive long enough for me get my paperwork straight and get back here."

With a glance at the tray of ashes, Vladimir confirmed the status quo. He walked to the table where the rest of FOIA papers sat, lifted Finn's press credentials, and tossed them to him. "Make these work."

With his good arm, Finn draped the band around his neck. "I need a passport."

Perspiration greased Vladimir's face. "You had your chance."

Finn put his arms back on the chair. "Then send me back to the cell."

Vladimir resisted looking at Danko. "Our position is this is a matter of theft. The orders for Dabrowski."

Danko pointed at Finn. "Are the orders in Austria?"

"I'd rather not say."

"I understand. What if we can get you across the border?"

"If you do, I can send a diplomatic pouch within hours."

The chief turned to Vladimir. "Good enough?"

Vladimir gave a curt nod.

"All right. Put your prisoner, your Polish prize, in a proper bed. Bathe and feed him. We'll stay to see that you do." He raised his finger like a monarch. "If he dies, you'll visit my jail."

"WHAT DAY is it?"

Chief Danko pursed his lips and blew out through his nose. "Thursday, the seventeenth."

Finn was grateful for the thunder and the rain. Sunshine would have presented too severe a change from the windowless rooms of his incarceration. The road and the leaves of corn on both sides of it glistened silver. Danko's driver eyed him in the rearview mirror.

"I've been in longer than I thought," Finn said.

"It's hard to keep track of time in places like that."

Finn shot Danko a glance. The chief was massaging his molars with his tongue. "You have experience?"

Danko let half a mile go by. "This is off the record, right?"

Finn agreed.

"I spent a year in captivity."

Finn tried to gauge his age. "The Germans?"

"No, I helped form a workers committee in the Revolution. We ran a free country for a few weeks. Before Soviet tanks rolled it."

"In Budapest?"

"In Hatvan, just northeast of there."

"But now you're a loyal Communist."

Danko didn't show offense. "I am a Hungarian, and I run the police department."

"But you're part of the government."

"Safe streets are important. Beyond that, I'm an ordinary man."

"What you just did wasn't ordinary."

Danko curled his lip. "I know too well the mind of people like Vladimir Shugin. His mistake was to call me."

"Does he believe his nonsense about truth?"

"Never mind about that. Your troubles with him aren't over."

"Why?"

"You have to get out of here, and Soviet troops are everywhere."

"You said you could get me out. Can you make me a passport?"

"You must know by now having one is no protection."

Finn thought of Fortie. "I may not be welcome in Austria, either."

"You're like a hemorrhage at 30,000 feet," Danko said.

"I believe my wife has also been taken hostage."

"Here in Hungary?"

"No, in Austria. By the Soviets. Or by her father."

"That's not in my jurisdiction." Danko was quiet for quite a while, then said, "Maybe we can get you there on Saturday."

Finn imagined himself smuggled in a box. "How?"

"A unique picnic is scheduled on our border with Austria, for local people on both sides to celebrate their common heritage." He paused. "Near a crossing in the town of Sopron. There will be lots of goulash and wine. Very local, no passports required. If we get you there and you mingle with the Austrians, you may be able to go *home* with them."

"I don't speak either language. It'll be obvious I don't belong there."

Danko smiled. "We expect there to be some confusion. We're actually planning on it. See, for years, East Germans have been gathering in summer down the road at our Lake Balaton. And lately Hungary has been allowing their West German family members in to visit them for reunions. It's become very popular. East Germans love the freedom they have here. Many try to stay. Every fall we have to pay to round them up and ship them home. We can't handle the cost.

"So somehow," he winked, "flyers have appeared in Balaton inviting East Germans to the picnic. Officially, it's to be strictly supervised. But at a planning meeting yesterday, I heard our president say he wouldn't object if a few East Germans happen to mingle with the crowd of Austrians as they return home. Unofficially, both nations see it as a test of Gorbachev's commitment to perestroika."

"Given the delicate state of the talks, isn't it stupid to create a row?"

Danko showed amusement. "Stupid, maybe, but not out of character for us."

Thirty-Nine

AT A MARKET ON the outskirts of Budapest, Chief Danko bought coffee and tins of nuts. The nourishment made Finn more aware of his pains, in particular the bruising to his stomach.

"I'm as interested in our next stop as you will be," Danko said. A half hour later, they arrived at a walled compound. Years of leaves had piled around an iron gate to which sheet metal had been screwed to frustrate those who were curious about what lay beyond. Danko had the key.

A sign in need of paint hung from the roof: *Felkelés Múzeuma*. Hands on hips, Danko stood in the middle of the courtyard surveying the grey stone walls and red tile roofs. Boards covered missing panes of glass. "A few years after the Revolution," Danko said, "the new government tried to dampen people's anger by creating a museum to honor those who had died and those who fought." He pointed to a carved sign hanging over the double doors. "That says 'In the spirit of healing old wounds.' "

"It's dismal," Finn said.

"The Kremlin diverted the funds dedicated for it to suppress revolts elsewhere."

Raindrops began splattering on the cobblestones. "The electricity's off. Let's use the daylight we have. Imre, bring the flashlights."

A score of dust-covered glass cases were crammed in the front room. The rest of the building was used for storage.

"It became a dumping ground for many departments," Danko said. "But if the records area is like I remember, we should be able to see what's in them."

He led the way to the right-hand wing, past stacks of crates and piles of worn-out office furniture. They took a circular iron stairway to the basement level. The concrete floor reminded Finn of the building he had just left. The first room held used plumbing supplies—piping, pumps, broken toilets. In the room beyond, a single window in the far end let in light.

Cartons and piles of junk blocked file cabinets that lined the walls. "Let's see," said Danko, "if bureaucrats can organize drawers alphabetically."

"I know the Magyar alphabet," Finn said, "but can't read."

"Then clear paths to the cases."

Starting on the cabinet on their left and working with his good arm, Finn dragged things to the center of the room. When Danko pulled a drawer, a cloud of spores floated in the beams of their lights. Orange and black mildew splotched the files. Silverfish scuttled off the pages.

"It's *A*," said the chief. "The double-*V*s will be on the other wall." He shook his head. "It won't be long before these turn to dust."

Finn cleared an aisle in front of the case that the chief estimated was the other end of the alphabet, but though the label inside looked like a *W*, it turned out to be a Cyrillic 'Sha.' It held files of Soviet soldiers who hadn't gone home.

Danko kicked the drawer closed. "I should have expected them to give their boys the same deference as our own." He waved his hand down the line of cabinets. "Somewhere down there."

Finn dug three paths into the row, the pain in his arm easing with the work. On his third foray, Danko got sucked into looking for a friend of his who had perished. He became overwhelmed when he hauled the man's file into the light of the window and pored over the details. Finn offered support by standing near.

"*Buried in a common grave*, it says. In prison, I used to think of him every day. His sister came to visit me, brought me cakes and fine things, because they hardly fed us. She and I even talked of getting married." He lowered the file thinking now of a woman. "When I got out, our love lost the magic it had when we couldn't touch. Katalin. I don't know what became of her."

Imre hooted. He'd located the double-*V* drawer. They gathered around it while Danko examined the files. "It's not here. Maybe they put it under *V*." That search, too, came up empty. Danko leaned against a case, defeated. Imre wandered off. Taking the mind of a put-upon file clerk, Finn eyed the last cabinet in the room right by the door they had entered.

The glue joints of the desk blocking it broke as he pushed it aside. These cabinet drawers held the files of foreign nationals, each in some order of their native alphabet. There were about twenty in Roman script. It was touching that an effort had been made to give community—if only in death—to people who might understand each other.

Waters, Jordan was the last file in the drawer. His father was truly dead. Finn glanced around. Danko was digging into another cabinet. Imre was gone.

As Finn lifted his father's file, something metal fell out the end. It clinked on the drawer, hit his foot, and skittered across the concrete. Finn knelt to retrieve it. He prayed it was a key to some locker full of answers. Or perhaps to clues that would lead him to people who had known his father.

His hands found a small cylinder and brought it to his flashlight. A bullet, misshapen. He clutched it in his fist and closed the drawer with his good shoulder.

"I've found the file." His words died in the space. Danko, too, had disappeared.

No matter. Skin tingling, Finn walked to the window and laid the file open on the wide sill. The first item was a small envelope, rotting. The bullet had slipped out its end. He placed it aside. How foolish he was to think the forms would be in English! But police reports are the same everywhere, blank boxes to be filled.

The date of the report was November 10, 1956; the day the Soviets broke the back of the revolution. Halfway down the form was a second date, November 3, 1956, the day before Soviet tanks rumbled in. If this was the day his father died, Hungarians were celebrating victory over their own government. Finn had always blamed the Soviets for his father's disappearance. This date killed that narrative.

He thumbed the edge of the sheaf of papers. The flow clunked at the photographs. The first was a picture of a lane flanked by buildings with no sidewalk, an alley through a block. On the left side, at the base of the building and near some barrels lay the body of a man.

The second picture was one his subconscious had wrestled with for years; the close-up of a body, face down, hair matted. The stucco above the head carried a dark splatter-pattern typical of assassinations. Finn opened his fist to look at the bullet. Lead, not a large caliber, about 33, mushroomed where it had hit the wall. Someone had taken care with this crime scene.

The hand showing in the last photo had rolled the body to expose the face. Except for the line of the jaw, the man there was nothing like the debonair one in the shots Finn had coveted. The right cheek had conformed, over the days, to the ground. It was black and flat. Part of the forehead was missing and one eyelid was open. But Jordan was gone. The lips had shrunken, which made the teeth protrude, giving the corpse the look of a demon about to bite. There was more in the file to examine, but Finn closed it and tucked it under his arm. *Who*, he wondered, *would his father want to bite*?

IMRE AND DANKO were waiting upstairs. Danko, too, carried a file.

"We thought you should do that alone," Danko said.

Imre, who wasn't proficient in Russian, nodded, kept nodding.

"I never imagined I would find it."

Danko put out his hand to shake. "You need a vacation," he said. Imre, too, shook Finn's hand. They exited onto the stoop, locked the museum door, and waited for the shower to let up before dashing to the car.

When they were underway, Danko said, "We have a word for *vacation* in Hungarian." He paused like an old comedian. "We just don't use it anymore."

In spite of the tension, or perhaps because of it, Finn laughed out loud. Pleased to entertain an American, Danko laughed, too.

"Here's what I think, Mr. Waters. Tonight you're safest in a jail cell. Not at the main station. The Soviets would expect that. The town where I grew up has only three policemen. I know them well. I got them their jobs. They'll understand keeping your presence secret. Just in case, Imre's going to drop us at headquarters and we're going to use his car to take you there."

"Just in case means 'Vladimir?' "

"Yes. In the morning, we'll load you on a bus for the border. If you can get to your embassy in Vienna, you'll be all right."

For Finn, the American embassy was no longer a safe zone. "Is the phone in your office a secure line?" Finn asked. "I've been thinking of another way to free Dabrowski."

IT WAS LATE AFTERNOON when Finn reached Viktor Hablinski by phone at Solidarity's office in Warsaw. When he explained where Dabrowski was and his plan, Viktor became ecstatic. He said he would arrange it with Lech Wałęsa right away. Finn told him he wouldn't be there.

Next he called Marty. "A special tip," he said. "Wałęsa is flying in secretly in the morning. If you want to break the story with one other journalist, say, from *Le Monde*, to help her career, tell her I send my regards. Here's the crucial thing: If you want to save Dabrowski's life, have Chantelle call the AP *after* Wałęsa leaves the airport. Have her get the word out that a huge story awaits at the Soviet barracks east of Budapest. You want them to arrive after Wałęsa's been inside for ten or twenty minutes. My guess is the Soviets will back down when they see the whole corps coming."

COMPARED TO THE cell he shared with Dabrowski, Finn's accommodations in the Dunakeszi jail were luxurious. He prayed Vladimir was caring for Dabrowski as he'd promised. One of the policemen helped Finn with makeup to keep his face from drawing too much attention in public.

In the morning, Imre provided him with farmer's pants, sunglasses and a hat. He took Finn in his own car to the bus station, bought him a ticket to Ferotboz, and gave him nine 2,000 Forint notes. "From Chief Danko," Imre said. "He apologizes that it is so little."

Finn ate a bowl of goulash and climbed aboard. The noon hour found him in a bus station bar in Bicske staring at a television, nursing his first scotch in weeks. He watched Chantelle narrating footage of Wałęsa traveling with a Hungarian police escort to the Soviet military compound. In another clip, his colleagues were arriving en masse outside the barracks. He broke away to board his bus.

At sunset in Ferotboz, he found a single room in the attic of a guesthouse. His hostess said the forecast for tomorrow's picnic was promising. In the morning, Finn ate hearty breakfast fare alongside East German men and women who had been vacationing at Lake Balaton. All of them were young and excited. Their luggage consisted of backpacks. The couple from Weißwasser, ethnic Poles whose city had ended up in East Germany after the war, translated that everyone had interesting plans for the afternoon, but not one of them dared mention specifics that could be used against them. A skill perfected by oppressed peoples.

They had no room for Finn in the cars they'd driven from East Germany. And since the town's normal public transportation had been commandeered to carry supplies for the picnic, Finn set off on foot. He carried a shoulder bag with the few things left to him: the remains of his ledger, the bulk of the stack of the FOIA documents, his father's file, and the pants and shirt he was arrested in. His hat had a large brim and he tucked his press credentials into an outside pocket of his bag. Unlike towns in Eastern Poland, the streets were paved and the houses cared for.

Once out of the village, nervous gaiety spilled out the open windows of passing cars. And though there were Hungarian military vehicles parked at intervals, their soldiers seemed uninterested in him and the traffic.

Around 10, two personnel carriers jammed with Soviet troops clipped by at great speed. As Mikolai had taught him, Finn waved. Three miles on, he came to their checkpoint on the outskirts of Sopron. They had chosen a spot where the fields had been harvested, so there was no cover to walk around it. Every car that had passed him was stopped. The occupants were out, showing documents. They were unpacking. Even from a distance the stress was palpable.

Vladimir wasn't the kind to lose well. When embarrassed by Wałęsa freeing Dabrowski, he would hunt Finn down. Finn was hanging back, considering his options, when a Soviet soldier accosted him.

"Local?"

"I've never been to Sopron, if that's what you mean."

"What brings you here then?"

"The picnic. Sounded interesting."

"Papers?"

"Didn't bother to bring them. I'm here to write a story for my newspaper in Dunakeszi. Seems like a fun afternoon. Maybe they'll offer you some food. I see some pretty girls going by."

"A long way to come."

"I took the bus."

"You're a writer then?"

"I hope to be, but if I were any good, would I be walking, and dressed like this?" Finn laughed. "Say, any chance I can get a ride back to Ferotboz afterwards? My legs are going to be exhausted by then."

"We don't carry Hungarians. You should have made better plans."

That judgment was true about so much of Finn's life. "Thanks for the advice. Is there a problem ahead?"

"Just making sure the right people get through."

"Running an empire is tough. May I go?"

The soldier gave him a look. “You’re fine. Tell you the truth, I hate the phony stories these people are telling. Germans are such bad actors.” He called ahead, “This old guy with the hat is fine. He’s walking through.”

Finn walked past all the cars, through Sopron, and into the countryside. Eventually cars he recognized passed him with tooting horns. He came upon them a third time, empty, parked bumper to bumper beside the road as far as he could see. The doors were unlocked. Keys were left lying on consoles, gifts to Hungarians if the drivers did not return.

At the gates of the park, a throng of jittery people waited for noon. Austrian and Hungarian flags hung side by side. Balloons added cheer to hastily constructed picnic tables under the trees. Hungarian soldiers in the park behaved like staff at a huge outdoor cinema. Someone explained that the double row of barbed wire visible on the far boundary of the park was actually the border between East and West. Beyond the fence lay farmland in Austria.

At last, with smiles disproportionate to the event, the organizers swung open the gates to the park. Soldiers on the Austrian side were letting groups of eight or ten Austrians at a time through a gate in their barbed wire. In the privy, Finn changed into his old clothes. He slung his press credentials around his neck. When he came out, the grounds were bursting with people too excited to eat. Pretending to mingle, the East Germans made their way to the feared Iron Curtain. Finn joined them. The wire was brittle with rust. The concrete posts were flaking. Late arrivals on the Austrian side snipped pieces of their wire and handed them across to the East Germans as if they were bouquets. Austrian news photographers fired away. All the while, the real power on the scene—the gunner in the tower down the way—ignored them.

Pretending to be a Russian-speaking American journalist, Finn presented himself to everyone who would talk. Those he presumed were Austrians were really West Germans come to spirit away their East German friends if the opportunity arose. Local Hungarian officials seemed glad enough to give him a few minutes of their time. The mayor of the Austrian border town of Klingbach spoke good English. During his conversation with him, Finn drifted towards the fence. It was when officials from both sides were making speeches from a dais that Finn saw Austrian guards open their gate to allow groups to "return to Austria." Hungarian soldiers wished them well. Once through, those people hugged and wept.

As three o'clock approached, the Austrian gate peeled back and a stream of people holding hands, hundreds of them, ran through the fence and down the hill, never once looking over their shoulders, a jubilant snake of color against the brown grass. Not wanting to be last, Finn pretended to be looking at notes in his ledger book and slipped to freedom.

Forty

HOPING FOR A miracle, West Germans had chartered buses to carry their estranged countrymen to Vienna en route to new lives in the West. Finn didn't qualify for this group, but their elation scooped him up as one of their own.

The emotions around him on the bus—people cheering, crying, embracing each other at their good fortune—drove home the point that he was the odd man out, rescued, but not saved. In those two hours, as Austrian farmland, glazed in afternoon colors, streamed by the windows, the extent of his obstacles became clear.

Since it was Saturday and he had only press credentials and a small amount of Hungarian Forint, he faced at least a day and a half of improvisation: He didn't know where his wife was; records and actions implicated his father-in-law in international crimes, or at the very least, despicable motives; Finn's mission of six months had run him headfirst into ruin; having been out of touch with his boss for twelve days, he was most likely unemployed; KGB agents in Austria had reason to find him; his calls and faxes from the US embassy had been flagged for monitoring; and he had no friends in Vienna.

So when the bus delivered him to Vienna's Resselpark, he walked. Past jolly restaurants that catered to the financial district; past buildings that housed all things international; past memorials to dead soldiers topped by statues of pompous men who had sent them to their deaths; and past clubs that thrummed the brains of young people so desperate for identity that they dyed their hair, shaved their heads, dressed as ghouls, and pierced their bodies with stainless steel hooks and ball bearings. At last, he entered the district where the professional class lived.

Twilight was fading when he reached Clarissa's apartment building. He had no key and the landlady didn't recognize him. His second grand victory of the day was that she accepted his narrative of half-truths and led him up. Swinging the door open, she didn't turn on the light, but she did see the chaos inside and beat a quick retreat down the stairs. He hoped she wouldn't call the police. And in case Vladimir had people on the ground, he didn't turn on the lights.

Whoever had dumped the apartment upside down had done so with a fine-tooth howitzer. The fact that the rugs had been turned over first meant he was dealing with trained agents. Things he and Clarissa had put on shelves and in drawers were scattered about. The destruction in the kitchen was hard to take. He hadn't eaten a bite at the picnic. He found a flashlight and gorged on the moldy guts of a loaf of bread. Next, he scooped jelly from the inside of a broken jar, sifting through it with his tongue for pieces of glass. At last he found the can opener and ate processed fish.

In the bathroom, glass vials had been broken on the hard surfaces. Tins of body powder had been emptied. Slipping as he turned to leave, he belted the top of his head on the artisan sink.

HE SPENT THE night in a nest he'd hollowed out in the debris. Sunlight woke him. Because it was Sunday, the street was quiet. He wore galoshes into the shower to keep from cutting his feet. He found underwear and jeans in separate rooms. After piecing some food together, he sat on the stairs, listening for activity in the apartments below. When he felt safe to knock to ask if they had heard anything unusual from his apartment, the interview did not go well. The third time the woman said no, she had already slammed the door.

In time, he found enough shillings in the rubble to afford a taxi to Fortie's neighborhood. Clarissa had left her car by the park. Finding it was more disturbing than leaving Dabrowski.

He looked out the taxi's window at the house where Clarissa had been raised, where her mother had died, where Fortie had held court, where the missile had exploded. People passing that grand edifice would think those who lived there were happy. Fortie appeared in an upstairs window. A woman in a nightgown squeezed herself next to him. Finn slid low in his seat and asked the driver to roll on.

Sunday was never a day to catch Sam Rich at the office, but Finn called New York from the apartment and left the most garbled message of his career on Sam's machine. The one clear thing he said was that he would call the next day and explain everything, hoping by then he would know what to say. Then he spent hours, setting things to order and, at last, found what he was looking for: Clarissa's spare set of keys.

He opened his father's file from the *Felkelés Múzeuma* and gleaned what he could from the police report. He studied the photographs: the lane, the blood splatter, and the cadaverous face. The images took him back to when he and his mother had walked like ghosts through their lives in Rockport.

HE WOKE THE next morning in a reactionary state of mind, disbelieving the only story about Fortie that made sense. The man had paid for all his schooling. He had given him money when Finn was short. Finn was as an ungrateful fraud. After an hour of contrition, he grabbed the phone and called Fortie to beg forgiveness. But at the sound of Fortie's voice, bitterness welled up and muted him. He listened to Fortie breathing and twice more saying, "Hello?" In the background a woman asked, "Zie ist, Leibling?" Finn drew in a breath that sounded like a wave hitting sand and hung up.

If he could know Fortie by his breath, Fortie could know Finn by his and could postulate he'd made his way back to Vienna and to the apartment. Which meant he had to leave. Within minutes, he took the back exit, wearing a wide-brimmed hat over Clarissa's brown costume wig, and caught a taxi to the Oesterreichische Nationalbank.

His disguise aroused the attention of guards on the main floor as well as the fellow monitoring cameras upstairs. But it accomplished what Finn wanted. As luck would have it, the bank officer who pulled him into his office was the same one who had set up his safe deposit box. Finn removed the wig and showed his press ID.

"Something strange happened regarding your box," the officer said, smoothing the folds of flesh under his chin. "I can't remember how many days back. Two weeks? Please follow me to the safe."

There, he rolled log pages backwards in time, running his finger down the lines. "Yes, here it is. On the ninth. A gentleman and woman came to the bank with the key to your box. They said you had had an accident and had requested they come in your stead to gather some important items that would help you afford your care in hospital."

"My god, I hope you didn't let them open it. What did they look like?"

"A beautiful woman, blond, a nice figure. She said she was your wife, but her discomfort led me to think she was lying, which is why I remember her. The gentleman was older, also good looking, well spoken though with an accent. My assistant brought their request to my attention. We hold our regulations very strictly."

"Did you let them in?"

"I mean if she is your wife, we would be—"

"Christ, man, did you let them into the box?"

"She wrote 'Clarissa Waters,' but I informed them that since she had not signed the card when you opened the account, she would only be welcome if she brought a certified note from you or your lawyer."

"So you didn't?'

"No, we didn't."

"I am afraid I've lost my key. Actually, my apartment was ransacked. I'm guessing by people looking for the key."

The officer nodded. "As I say, the lady did seem very ill at ease."

"I hope your regulations allow me access to the box this morning."

The officer presented Finn with a clean sheet of paper and asked him to sign his name. Finn was both cheered and depressed at how easily a simple comparison of the signatures defeated the bank's protections. All he had wanted to do for the last six months was show the world Stalin's signature affixed to the death warrant of 22,000 Poles.

The officer led Finn into the vault and using his own key and a duplicate for the one Finn had lost, opened the box. "Take all the time you need, Mr. Waters." He left the room.

And blessed be! Stalin's orders were there. His arrogant hand in red ink proved he had destroyed many lives. It proved also that many forces *in absentia*—governments, corporations, investigators, policemen, and foreign agents—had become allies to keep that truth buried.

Finn used the safety of the vault to affirm his state of affairs, chief among them that he would have to find Clarissa on his own. Vladimir would certainly have alerted Fortie to Finn's release. Fortie's standing in Vienna would preclude Finn from getting help from local and US authorities. His call to Fortie would trigger the goons who had ransacked the apartment. And knowing where the orders were, Fortie could have sent someone to the bank to watch for him.

The officer allowed Finn to withdraw 30,000 Austrian schillings without having to appear in the main lobby. Then Finn boarded a taxi at the bank's rear entrance, and again on the strength of his press ID, managed to talk a hotel concierge into giving him a room. He called New York.

After keeping him on hold for many minutes, Sam Rich said, "I'm sure I don't have to tell you what's coming, Finn."

"Yes, Sam, but I hope you'll hear me out."

"It happens in this business, Finn. I've seen it before. Not everyone's capable of—"

"Sam, I was taken. Held and tortured by the KGB."

Sam breathed into the phone for a long spell.

"Did they beat you?" Finn had never remembered Sam asking a tentative question.

"That and more."

"Will you be able to work again?"

Each allowed a long space before talking. It seemed a respectful rhythm. "I'm counting on it."

"That's good."

Finn didn't like the finality of Sam's tone.

"It won't be with us, Finn."

"Sam—"

"I've covered for you long enough." The words of Finn's mentor at Stanford came to him: *Journalism is a small world. If you want to work again, when the boom comes down, go gracefully.*

"You have grounds to let me go."

"We were the only paper that didn't cover Wałęsa popping into Hungary and freeing that guy. That was a great story."

Finn hadn't heard the result of his plan. "His name is Dabrowski, Sam. He and I were cellmates. I'm the one who set up his release."

Long pause.

"Then you should be a diplomat."

"Don't you get it, Sam? That's the reason I've been silent. I was held for twelve days. I've spent the last two escaping from the country."

"Escaping? You could have called and flown home."

"Sam . . ." Finn wanted to chide his boss for living tethered to a desk in a safe country, but thought better of it.

"What?"

"They burned my passport. I'm lucky to be here at all."

"How'd you get out?"

"Now it sounds like I have a story, doesn't it?"

"For *Adventurer Magazine*, maybe."

"My wife is missing, Sam."

Sam exhaled long and slow. "She called here."

"Clarissa?"

"Yes."

"When?"

"About five days ago. She left a message on my machine. A strange one. I ignored it because of what you've told me about her condition. Truth is, I felt sorry for you."

"Do you remember what she said? Did she leave a number?"

"My secretary keeps a log. Let me get it."

Finn heard a door open and Sam barking to Sheila.

"Here it is. Word for word, ready? 'If someone asks, tell them I'm vacationing in Sisters of the Saintly Shepherd Convent outside of Salzburg.' "

"And?"

"That's all. I played it back myself. She hung right up."

"You're firing me, Sam, but I'd hire you in a minute.

Book Four

Salzburg

Forty-One

FINN'S GOAL WAS getting to Salzburg and finding the Saintly Shepherd Convent. From there, he would improvise freeing Clarissa. In the process, he hoped to atone for all he had ruined. Given his multidimensional outlaw status, his personal fortunes looked bleak. But he decided his safest option would be for the Austrians to capture him. For that, his action needed to be swift and colorful. Western press following a rogue American could draw lawyers to Clarissa's aid. Perhaps Fortie would get swept up in their net. But if Finn dallied, Soviet operatives would find him.

He took a taxi to St. Stephen's Cathedral. The day priest directed him to the administration office. There, reading from a large directory of Catholic churches and missions, a nun translated the listing into English: *"The Sisters of the Saintly Shepherd Convent, situated in Hinterwinkl east of Salzburg, is a strictly enclosed abbey of the Cistercian Order. In keeping with the needs of modern times, the convent serves dual functions: First and foremost, is the training of novitiates in the contemplative life. Second, is maintaining an onsite ward specializing in Godly treatment of disturbed women and girls. Mother Superior Aloysia and her staff of thirty-one embrace the wishes of the church as well as families committed to the faith. Set in the serene hills above one of Austria's most revered cities, the convent is open to the public on Tuesdays from 10 a.m. to 2 p.m.."*

She consulted a directory map. "There it is," she said. "Hinterwinkl is a half hour southeast of Salzburg."

Finn's next move required the cover of darkness. He killed the daylight hours in the basilica, learning about emperors, bishops, and princes who had been laid to rest there. At last, the parallels between wars of faith and wars of territory wearied him. Sitting in a pew, he conjured a world in which the officers resting in the soft soil of Katyn were afforded honors similar to those buried in Saint Stephen's. To his left across the aisle, a dowager in grieving attire was teaching a boy no older than six how to pray. The boy tugged her black shawl, whispered, and pointed to Finn. She gestured for Finn to show her charge that men also kneeled.

Going through the motions, Finn recalled the night he, Clarissa, and Fortie had gone there to honor Jacqueline. The priest's singing voice had resonated in the spaces. And wasn't it the night after the missile attack that Clarissa recounted having seen his father pray? He was embarrassed how he and Fortie had ridiculed her. Perhaps his father had been a secret believer, and she alone had seen him atoning for his sins. Sins Finn now knew something of. Then for the first time ever, Finn prayed. Or rather, he begged universal justice for one more chance to make things right with her.

Later, after a meal in a disco bar, he walked west and north. In the dark he watched Fortie's house from the park across the street. When the lights came on upstairs, he unlocked Clarissa's car and drove off.

OUTSIDE OF SALZBURG he roused the owner of a guesthouse and paid cash for a bed. Too few hours later, he covered his facial bruises with makeup and ate a breakfast of croissant and cheese at the communal table. To lay the groundwork for his capture, he visited the police station. He presented himself as a tourist with a medical need. They sent him to the university hospital. There he slung his press ID around his neck and with the help of a translator, he interviewed the chief resident under the shade trees planted in their atrium. He asked about their emergency unit and their mental health services. He scribbled notes and mentioned his next stop was the Sisters of the Saintly Shepherd Convent. The chief resident sucked his tongue inside his ample cheeks.

"What can you tell me about the care there?" Finn asked with the ease of Mikolai.

"Science," the chief resident said with a snort, "flourishes best when both hands of religion are in casts up to the armpits. Particularly when it comes to illnesses of the mind and heart."

Finn returned the chief resident's laugh. "I've heard good things about their programs with depression and . . ." he made it personal, "troubled dreams."

The chief resident worked his tie. "It's hard for depressed people to treat depression."

"I'm sorry," Finn said, meaning, *Could you say more*?

"In my experience, many of their patients' illnesses are products of the church itself. The diagnosis their *health professionals* practice is limited to finding causes in the world outside. Most patients would do better on vacation than with prayer and heavy medications."

"Doctor, I would love to bring you there and record a debate. That would make good theater."

"Fine theater," the chief resident said, "if you like Greek tragedy."

His translator rattled off a quick burst and the doctor sniped some words back at him.

"The doctor," said the translator, "understands what he is saying here is off the record."

"Of course," Finn said. "I'm sure you have to work with Mother Superior Aloysia on occasion."

The doctor frowned when he heard the translation. "At least three times a year I have to put Shepherd patients on suicide watch. We expend great resources rehabilitating them."

ON THE DRIVE UP to Hinterwinkl, meadows and fir trees on Alpine slopes pulsed green in the sun. Snowfields graced mountain peaks. The bells of Guernsey cows clanged. Log barns tilting with time mocked the newer, more sterile Tyrolean homes, with their overhanging roofs and decorous second- and third-story porches. Streams crossing under the road ran fast.

The white stucco complex of the convent sat back in a meadow below the confluence of two snow-filled ravines that cut down the south slope of a mountain. The roofs of its twin buildings spread like great wings, which together with the wood-shingled tower joining them, created the appearance of a great bird landing.

Having timed his arrival for a little after ten, Finn returned the wave of the nun who was posted by the iron gate. He drove over a stone bridge built in a previous century and parked in the shade of fir trees next to a beat-up news van. A light breeze rolled off the mountain. Steps in the path were made from logs. The wood door was open. Like the exterior, the inside walls were simple stucco. Honey-colored beams supported the floor above. In the small front room a man was filming with a shoulder-mounted video camera. Two cheerful women carrying media gear were speaking to a middle-aged nun seated behind a desk. The nun wore a white tunic and black veil. A striking white band of buckram framed her face. A taller nun in a less elaborate veil looked on from behind. Her shoulders were still and tight. When Finn's tension escaped in a sigh, she found his eyes.

The seated nun scraped back her chair and invited the journalists into the hallway beyond. Seeing Finn for the first time, she turned to her sister. "Bitte," she said as she left, "kümmere dich un diesen Mann."

When they were alone, Finn asked, "Do you speak English?"

"A little," the nun said. Except for one mole perched on her cheekbone, her skin was unblemished. He guessed she was maybe thirty.

"I'm here to see my wife. She's a patient."

She let go a plaintive, "Hmm," sat at the desk, and opened a large book. "The name?"

"Her last name is Waters."

The nun flipped through pages to the back. "Sorry," she said, "we have no Waters here. You are certain she is in this Kloster?"

Finn bluffed confidence. "Try Clarissa Fortier. She would be a new patient, long blond hair, thirty-nine."

The sister smiled. "Ah, Clarissa. Yes. Her hair was beautiful."

"Was? What's happened to her?"

The nun's shoulders lifted. She glanced toward the hallway. "Who are you?"

"I'm Finn Waters, Clarissa's husband." He whipped out his press credentials. She read them without registering the weakness they presented.

"You didn't come before?"

"I've been out of the country. This is the first time I could get here. Her father told me she was here."

Her look softened. "She's my patient *am Nachmittag*— Sorry. Afternoon."

"So she's all right?"

She tapped her head to discreetly indicate Clarissa's malady. "We are helping her. I like her."

"What were you saying about her hair?"

"Many patients," she put her hands to her veil, "can't comb the hair, so we cut off. It's the rule."

Finn mimed an Auschwitz cut. "You *shaved* her head?"

She smiled a little. "No, more like a boy's."

"What is your name?"

"Rahel."

"Rahel, I've come a long way, and I'd like to see her."

Rahel patted the desk. "Someone must stay here." She walked to the front door and looked out. "But no one comes now. I take you." Her voice dropped to a whisper. "Most people leave them. Never visit. Come with me."

The hall jogged left, then right, and was longer than he expected. In the distance, the media crew was filming through a doorway. A cluster of nuns behind them peeked in. Finn wondered if they were documenting another patient tragedy.

As if channeling his thoughts, Rahel said, "You are journalist, also." She opened a door into a stairwell with landings going up four floors. "All visitors are journalists today." Balling folds of her habit in her fists, she hammered up the stairs. As they were approaching the third floor landing, a door opened on the second. "*Rahel,*" a voice called up in disapproval, "*Nicht Laufen.*"

"*Verzie mir, Mutter Oberin,*" Rahel said. She slowed her gait.

On the top landing before opening the door, she halted. She pinched one hand in the other and sized Finn up. She crossed herself and lowered her voice. "I want to speak before." She led him left to the front of the building. She isolated a key from a wad of them fastened to her waistband, unlocked the door to the porch, and locked it behind them. They were above the trees in front of the house. Her fingers fidgeted. The view of mountains and sky seemed upsetting to her.

"You love your wife?" A tear dropped from her eye. She turned away.

"Yes, of course."

"I like her, Herr Waters. Clarissa is a good person."

"Is she all right? What's happened?"

"I'm not like her." She faced him with a look of someone about to confess.

He wasn't equipped for this. "You seem like a nice—" he almost said *woman*—"a nice nun."

"I hate this here."

"Then can't you—"

"I stay because . . . because of my past."

Fate had delivered Rahel to him. He needed her. But any time now, Fortie would notice Clarissa's car was missing. "I'd like to see my wife."

"You sure you love her? Sure?"

"Yes." This time the intensity of his whisper affirmed that he felt it.

"She wants her baby," Rahel said. "So why do you do this thing?" She slid the back of her hand across her eyes.

Finn reached to seize her habit, then stopped. "What is this about? What *thing* does she have to do?"

"Our number four vow says, *I bind myself to labor for the conversion of fallen women and girls needing refuge from temptation of the world.* I was like that. Fallen. And before you come, I thought Clarissa was also."

"She's not going to be converted, Rahel."

Rahel's eyes got bigger. "You don't know, do you?"

"I know Clarissa's not supposed to be here. I'm here to free her."

Rahel drew in her breath. "You must do it today, then. *Abtreibung* is a bad thing." She searched for a word. "Abortion?"

Rahel backed away a full step from the face Finn made. She let him process her words, then leaning toward him, she whispered, "The doctor comes this afternoon."

"To give her an abortion? In a convent?"

Rahel seemed relieved. "It's not a good thing, you agree?"

"Good? It's all wrong *here*," he said, struggling with his whisper. "And it's *always* wrong if against the woman's wish." Finn felt himself moving into attack mode. "I'm her husband, and I'll take her with me right now."

Rahel's look turned dark. "*No. Mutter Oberin Aloysia* . . ." She looked at him.

"Mother Superior Aloysia?"

"Yes, that's right. Mother Superior and *Herr Fortier planen das*. She makes the rules."

"She's *my* wife. I'll walk her down the stairs and out the door."

"It is not easy, Herr Waters. Medication for nerves make it hard to walk." She mimed losing her balance.

"I'll carry her."

"Down four . . . stairs?"

"If I have to." He turned toward the door, ready to go.

Rahel stayed rooted. "All will see you and ring the alarm. Mother Superior will lock the doors . . . *automatishe*. She has *der Regler* in her pocket." She flustered and crossed herself again. "I hope I am doing the right thing."

"By doing what?"

"By speaking. Mother Superior is strict with the rules. She and Herr Fortier are very—like this." She crossed her first and second fingers. Her look shifted to irritation. "But she breaks the rules also. After communion she and Father Benedict drink." She inhaled and raised her hands as if surprised by someone wielding a gun. "I tell you what you must know. This abortion is this afternoon when we are praying."

Finn felt the ground dropping beneath him. "Clarissa needs your help, Rahel. Do you think we should let this happen?"

She shuddered. "No. I did abortion for my baby fours years before now. I come here to forgive myself, but I can't find it in nine months. But if I help you, I can be in trouble." Rahel was in the position that had hamstrung him for months: being a messenger others needed out of the way.

"And if you don't help Clarissa, won't you be in trouble, too, just in another way?"

The question froze her.

"You said you hate it here. But you can leave, can't you?"

She'd thought about her answer many times. "Too much *Versuchung* outside. I stay here to stay good."

"You are already good, Rahel. But what about the commandments? *Thou shalt not kill.*"

She winced.

"Please tell me how I can get Clarissa out."

Rahel blinked fast, nodding to herself. "Here's what you do. Come to the back of the Kloster at fifteen-thirty. The back gate. The washing truck goes out then. Come in before the gate closes and go up the loading stair. Hide in the . . . washing-kammer until you hear the bells. I bring her for you at fifteen-fifty."

"Where will the doctor be?"

"The Klinik office. After the sisters go up to pray at fifteen-fifty, he will do it. He is gone before we go to dinner."

"This has happened before, hasn't it?"

The door on the balcony below opened. Several nuns came out to catch the air. Finn showed her his clamped teeth and nodded one time to seal the pact with her. Her eyes went to the mountains and back to him. She signaled with her head, turned, and unlocked the door.

Forty-Two

MIDWAY DOWN THE corridor, Rahel let herself and Finn through the locked door that separated the residential quarters from the ward. She whispered to the sister on duty and led Finn to the last room on the left. Beyond that stood the door to the service elevator.

Finn had to scan the sheets to find his wife. She was that pale. Without hair, her head was small. Her hands were cold. He kneaded her left one in both of his.

"I'm here, Clarissa." She made sleep-filled sounds. Her eyes batted open. He expected her to light up the way he would have if she'd come to his cell in Hungary. She gave him a weak smile and turned to see who the other person was.

"It's me, honey," he said. "I'm finally here."

"Hi." She drifted off. When he worked her hand again, she freed it and rolled away from him.

Rahel bent down on the other side of the bed. *"Clarissa. Ich bins Rahel."*

Clarissa rubbed her face on the sheet. *"Ist es schon Nachmittag?"*

"Nein, ich habe einen Freund gebracht."

Clarissa rolled, surveyed the ceiling, and caught sight of Finn's shoulder. Slowly she focused on his face. "You're not a friend," she said. And to Rahel, *"Er ist nicht mein Freund."* She rolled on her back and covered her face with the pillow.

Rahel's lip curled as she addressed Finn. "Did you lie to me?"

Finn wondered if he'd arrived too late for everything.

Clarissa swung the pillow onto her abdomen like a child conceding a gag. "*Er ist mein Mann.* Where have you been?" She rolled to him and tried to gather him in.

He kissed her cracked lips. "Getting here, trying to find you."

"My father," she said, stopping, as if the words were a complete thought.

"I know."

"You know he brought me here?"

"Yes."

"He's a bad man." She nodded with exaggeration. "I have lots to tell you."

Rahel tipped her head to listen.

"We can do that later," Finn said.

"No, listen. I'm seeing the dream now. All of it."

"Which dream?"

"The one with the fire escape."

There it was again, the dream she remembered from that fire she'd seen or survived, the horror that seemed to have buried itself into her bones—the fire escape coming down from the basilica at BethAnn's funeral and nuns surrounding a man who was praying for his life. Maybe being around nuns had helped her after all. Was the man a symbol? Or was this prophecy? Was Finn the man in her dream?

"It's taken me so long to understand it," Clarissa said. "Now it won't go away."

"Her sleep is no good," Rahel whispered.

"They're giving me drugs. They make my mouth taste like copper."

He whispered in her ear. "I'm going to get you out of here." He glanced at Rahel to make sure she hadn't changed her mind. "I'm going to need you awake. So no more drugs, okay?"

"I'm here with her this afternoon," Rahel said. "I will stop the medications."

Clarissa grasped the intrigue. She looked hard at Rahel.

Rahel soothed her forehead. "Everything is good."

There was a knock on the door.

"*Danke,*" Rahel called out. "*Eine Minute, bitte.*"

A moment later when Rahel opened the door into the main floor hallway, Mother Superior Aloysia, a great wrinkled presence in white, with books in both arms, saw them from a distance. Her right eyebrow arched high. "*Und wer ist dieser Mann?*"

Rahel gave the slightest bow. "*Das ist Herr Waters. Er ist der Ehemann von Clarissa.*"

"*Sehr gut.*" But nothing about the Mother Superior's demeanor conveyed that *all was well.* "*Ich bin dank bar fur ihr kommen,*" she said.

Finn thanked her in German. Rahel led him to the stairwell. Before entering, he glanced back. Mother Superior was still watching them.

Four floors down in the front room, Rahel acted as if there was no drama at all. She said something simple to the nun at the desk. To Finn she said goodbye.

AT THE SALZBURG police station, Finn found the officer he'd spoken to earlier. Through a translator Finn told him about his visit to the convent. The officer pointed to a map. "The convent is out of my department's jurisdiction. Besides, there is nothing we can do until a crime has been committed."

"I understand," Finn said, but he didn't. "Still I'd like to enter this information in case you need it as testimony."

The officer looked at him askance and set him up with an administrator. At one o'clock, Finn headed back up the road to Hinterwinkl.

He drove as close to the convent as he dared—about a mile away—and turned into a road that was little more than a cart path. A clump of fir trees hid the car from the road. He set off up the ridge between him and the convent on a route he hoped would bring him to the back of the complex. The day was hotter than he expected. He drank his fill from a stream that ran through a cow meadow. He turned around often to see the landmarks he would need on the way back. And if Clarissa couldn't walk, he set his mind on carrying her.

He'd chosen his course well. At three fifteen, he slunk tree-to-tree, finally nestling himself by the convent's back gate. There he prepared to break civil and ecclesiastical law.

The laundry truck arrived late. As it left, Finn slipped in. He crouched behind a dumpster and surveyed the loading dock. Reflection made the windows above pure black. He would have to risk being seen. Bent low to the ground, he crossed the yard, mounted the loading dock stairs, and entered a small warehouse.

Hearing voices, he cracked a door. It was the laundry. Two nuns were stripping off their aprons and resetting their veils. He backed away and hid himself behind a canvas bin. A few minutes later, the nuns emerged and made their way into the main building through a pair of swinging doors. He sprinted on tiptoe to look through the crack in those doors just as a series of bells ran in the halls. Nuns appeared and entered the stairwell. When all was quiet, the service elevator whirred into motion, descending. Finn sought cover again.

The elevator car stopped on the loading dock level. The folding gate opened. A nun who was not Rahel pushed out a gurney with a patient on it. She lined it up to go through the doors where he'd been observing the corridor. If Clarissa was the woman on the gurney, this new nun was not an ally. But before he could run over and subdue her, she shoved the gurney through the doors. She turned right into a room. Above the transom hung the sign *Krankenstation*. Infirmary.

He stood by those double doors, trying to divine the moment when barging in would make the most fireworks. He wanted to confront the doctor just as he was bending close to begin the procedure. Would he beat the man? For the purpose, he palmed an eighteen-inch length of steel pipe.

He imagined the doctor tying Clarissa down. When he visualized him raising her knees, he pushed into the hall and leaned his ear against the door, listening. The door opened. The nun slipped out and collided with him. He grabbed her so as not to fall. It was Clarissa. With the white tunic and her face framed in buckram, she looked halfway to heaven.

In the briefest of hugs, her body told him she was present and determined.

"Where is Rahel?" he whispered.

She pointed to the door she'd just used. The doctor would know the deception within minutes. As he turned to flee out the loading dock, a commotion coming all the way from the front desk made them go stiff. Fortie's voice drowned out a woman's protest. Of course! Being loyal to Fortie, Mother Superior Aloysia would have alerted him that Finn had been there.

An alarm sounded. The loading dock's overhead door rolled down its track and thumped into place. "We can hide in the laundry," Clarissa said.

"It's the first place they'll look."

"What about the elevator?"

"They'd hear it."

Fortie yelled again. He was getting his way. Clarissa grabbed Finn's hand, pushed him through the door across from the infirmary, and closed it without a sound. They had entered a back hall leading toward the other wing.

Clarissa bent to remove her shoes. Her body was shaking. "We need a window," she said. He laid down the piece of pipe to remove his shoes. Carrying them, they ran down that hall. The only unlocked door in it was at the far end. It opened to a corridor, stretching to the right, a mirror image of the one they had just left. They found a supply room. A bedroom. A common bath complex. Another bedroom. But the windows in each were too high from the floor and too small to slip through.

"Come," she said, motioning him to a door she'd opened. And he went, expecting she'd found a way out.

The room was almost too small to be a chapel. The three pews were butted to the wall on the left, leaving a narrow aisle on the right. An altar in front. To the left, a life-size statue of a woman saint with arms raised to the heavens. To the right, a confessional. Simple half-arch windows of stained glass muted the sun. He and Clarissa were taking refuge in a place of God.

"I hope he's not the one to find us," she said, sliding into the middle pew.

He was shocked by the ease with which she knelt and put her hands to her chin. In the corridor someone was systematically opening and closing doors. Finn entered the priest's confessional, drew the curtain, and sat. The door to the chapel opened. He recognized Fortie's breathing. It lingered long enough to assess the scene. Then the door closed with a respectful click. Fortie's footfall moved away.

"One prayer answered," she whispered.

In the seconds that passed, Finn regretted his choice of hiding place. He was about to rise and take his chances behind the statue of the saint when the footsteps wheeled and returned. The door opened. Finn took a long breath and held it. And the door closed. Through holes in the lattice to his left Finn saw Fortie stride up the aisle as confident as a train conductor. He stopped at the end of Clarissa's pew. Doors were opening and closing upstairs, too. The floor overhead creaked. Clarissa didn't look up from her prayer pose.

"I know what happened to Uncle Jordan," she said. Her voice was calm. Its tone deadly.

"So it *is* you." Fortie let out a great sigh. "Come, darling."

Finn's chest burned for oxygen.

"And live in a world of lies? I'd rather die."

"You don't know what happened. You got it wrong from the beginning."

She said nothing.

"Mother Superior tells me your husband showed up. Where is he?"

"Come and gone. But you *will* have to deal with him sooner or later. He *is* persistent."

Fortie winced at the remark. Finn risked a light breath.

"I was wearing my favorite white blouse that day, Papa. The one Mother made me. And my Mary Janes."

"We don't have time for reminiscing. I'm taking you back to the doctor."

He moved to enter the pew, but her testimonial tone stopped him. "You and your driver left me in the car, the long black one, with the big headlights. The motor was running because it was cold outside, remember? You said you'd be right back."

"More tripe from the Kerlingger woman. Therapy can create any past you want. That's the sickness of it."

"You pushed down all the locks on the doors. I remember that."

There was a pause. "I've always treated you as precious cargo."

"After you disappeared down the street, I figured out how to open the lock."

"It's not believable, Clarissa. You're unstable. You always have been."

"What did Uncle Jordan ever do to you anyway?"

"Let's get the doctor to give you something to help you rest."

"Rest, my ass! You want to rip out my baby. It's your way of getting back at Finn, isn't it? Getting rid of all parts of him."

"I should never have let you marry that sonofabitch. He's so much his father's son."

"I can imagine he reminds you of it. Am I right?"

Fortie's hands rolled in irritation. "His mother's Jewish, you know. Her blood is part of that baby's."

"I didn't realize it at the time," Clarissa said, "but the missile blowing off the front of our house triggered the memory. I'd just come into the parlor. You and Finn weren't in your chairs, so I looked around and there you were, standing behind him. He was kneeling at the cabinet and looked just like Uncle Jordan . . . praying."

"This is nonsense. Now get up."

"What are you going to do with *that*? Shoot me? Your own daughter? In a convent? That will make the news. Too bad Finn's not here to report it."

Fortie held the gun in his right hand. He racked the clip with his left. The sound shattered the last of Finn's inhibitions. He regretted having dropped the piece of pipe and parted the curtain enough to scan the room. The only object with any mass was a large silver chalice on the shrine. He rehearsed flying across the distance, seizing it, and attacking.

"Don't make me do this," Fortie said. "I'm tired of chasing after your mind."

Clarissa exhaled something like amusement. "I was so proud of myself for being strong enough to pull up the door lock in the big black car. And more so for shoving the door open with my shoulder. I followed you around the corner into that alley. There you were, underneath a fire escape with a red towel hanging on it. You had Uncle Jordan on his knees. You remember, of course. Your driver was holding your coat. I thought you were playing a game and when I giggled and ran toward you, you and your driver and Uncle Jordan all turned to look at me. And there was a big bang."

"You never saw it, Clarissa."

"There was *blood* all over my blouse, Papa! All my life you've hidden that from me." She was raging now. "Remember what I cried? 'It's ruined. Ruined. You've ruined my favorite blouse.' "

"No one will believe this."

"Oh, yes. And you bought me a new blouse on the way home. Mother always wondered what happened to the one she made. She expressed her confusion in her diary. And her anger. I was confused, too, when I read it. It only made sense to me the other day. Sometimes when medication wears off, old memories appear."

Finn exploded out of the confessional. Within a second, he had the chalice in his hand. But Fortie was quick and closed on him, pointed the gun at his head. "You bastard. I should have known." And without looking at Clarissa, he said to her, "He's taught you how to lie so well. Turn around, Finn. Get down. Get on your sanctimonious knees."

Unable to advance and unwilling to die like his father with a bullet in the back of his head, Finn stayed put. Quiet as a specter, Clarissa rose from the pew, a prayer book in her hands. Not enough to knock

Fortie out, even if she could get there without him hearing her come. But maybe together they could take him. Distract him, Finn thought.

Behind them all, the door opened. So quietly. Without taking his eyes off Fortie, Finn recognized the person who entered as Rahel in a patient's robe. And—God bless her—she was holding the pipe. A blow to the head would deck most any man. But she would first need to get past Clarissa.

"So it's you, Albert," Finn said. "It's always been you." Slowly Finn dropped to his knees and spread his arms. The chalice was in his right hand. "But if you're going to kill me, prepare to be disappointed. I'll be damned if I turn around."

"No need to damage a sacred chalice in the process, Finn." Fortie was pouring sweat. "Put it on the shrine and we'll talk our way through this."

Rahel had gotten Clarissa's attention. She was showing her the pipe.

"The back of the head is the coward's way, Albert. This time you'll have to kill a man while he watches you. I hope you see my eyes with every breath you take until you die."

To conceal the sound of the women changing positions in the aisle, Finn lowered the chalice with a clang onto the floor. Then he did himself one better and skittered it toward the statue of the saint. Rahel squeezed by Clarissa. The rattling sound captured Fortie the way Finn had hoped, but by turning to watch it, Fortie picked up on the motion behind him.

He wheeled and before Finn could rise, he fired twice, fast as a stick on a snare drum. The women became one white mass with two crying voices, Rahel on top of Clarissa. The pipe clattered on the floor.

Finn leapt forward and chopped his right hand at the gun arm. He drove his shoulder into Fortie's lower back. The old man's knees buckled. The weapon came free. When Fortie reached for it, Finn slammed his elbow onto Fortie's hand. The crack of bones. Snatching the gun, he laid the barrel against Fortie's jawbone. Then he thought better of it. "Not here, Albert. Up."

One-handed, he dragged Fortie by the collar into the penitent's compartment of the confessional and yanked him onto his knees. He wormed the tip of the gun barrel into Fortie's neck until it locked in the soft depression at the base of his skull. Hearing only Rahel's voice now, he glanced, expecting to see her fighting for her life. But Rahel was cradling Clarissa. She had her hand flattened above Clarissa's breast. Blood ran through her fingers, the deepest red, blooming on the white of Clarissa's tunic. Clarissa's face was slack.

For Finn, the world of consequences again tipped on its axis. "Old man, are you praying to your god?"

Footsteps trotting in the hall. Rahel's cries stopped. Finn turned to see two figures in the doorway: Mother Superior Aloysia and a bald man clutching a stethoscope.

Fortie's head, too, turned, and he grasped salvation was at hand. "He shot my daughter. Save me."

To shut him up, Finn speared his neck with the tip of the barrel. "Doctor," he bellowed in English, "get your car to the front door and call an ambulance to meet us on the road." When the doctor hesitated, Rahel screamed a blister of German, and the doctor fled.

But Mother Superior Aloysia stepped fully into the chapel and folded her arms.

"If you want to watch," Finn said, "fine. You have your own crimes to pay for." He looked at Clarissa. Her eyes were rolled back. The corners of her mouth twitched. Finn shook Fortie's collar. "Your own daughter, by your own hand."

"It was accidental," Fortie barked.

"Bullshit! Your history's repeating itself."

When Fortie said nothing, Finn yelled, "Tell me, did my father beg for his life?"

"Not once, dammit. Nothing could get him to stop."

"Stop?"

"I'm sorry, so sorry for all of it."

"For killing my father? Killing your friend?"

"Every day."

"For lying to my mother? For crushing Clarissa's memory?"

As if in answer to her name, Clarissa groaned.

"I'm haunted."

"Why did you do it, Albert?" Finn screamed. "Why?"

"He was getting too close. He was going to ruin me, going to take the whole system down."

Finn took a guess. "Trèana Furasta? Did he know about the guns? The Walthers?"

"Yes, dammit. And damn you, too."

Without thinking, he drove the gun forward, bowing Fortie's head down. But at the last instant, he tipped the barrel up. The shot hit the wall. Filled with power at Fortie's terror, he fired again. In his peripheral vision Mother Superior Aloysia's white robes dervished from the chapel.

He saw his father nodding his permission to kill Fortie. He saw crowds of strangers urging him on.

But something made him defy them. Looking down, he laid a bullet square into Fortie's right calf and used the kick of the gun to swipe him across the back of the head. As Fortie howled, Finn stood before the altar. He placed the pistol on it as an offering. Then he and Rahel scooped up Clarissa and ran with her to the front of the convent.

Forty-Three

APRIL 13, 1990

As Clarissa leaned to kiss him, Finn raised his wrists from the arms of the chair to the length of their chains. For now, her perfume and her lips were his only taste of freedom.

"No Jordy today?"

"They wouldn't let me bring him," she said. "Don't worry, he's fine. Rahel is turning out to be a natural mother."

She sat. She assessed the ornate chair they had given her across from his. She looked around the room. Finn had done the same in the minutes he had waited for her. On the walls, Austria's leaders down through history were hanging larger-than-life in gold leaf frames.

"It's not exactly the intimate space I was thinking of," she said, "but if we're lucky, this will be the last time I see you restrained."

He barked amusement. "What do you expect? It's Austria."

"Yes, but talk about feeling watched! And not one woman among them."

Hearing her voice echo, he looked at the ceiling. Rococo. Fourteen feet overhead.

"But," she said, "things could be worse. If we were in America, they'd be reporting on what you had for breakfast."

"I'd be happy to tell them." He paused. "Outrage goulash with a side of disbelief."

"Bad for your heart," she said. "Promise me, if Waldheim frees you, you'll change diets."

"You forget," he said, "I grew up having to eat what was served."

She became quiet, and he worried he'd already poisoned their meeting. In those many months since carrying her to the front of the convent and laying her in the doctor's station wagon, these were their first minutes totally alone. He'd seen her, of course, the morning she gave her testimony at the hearing, which had been delayed through the autumn to allow her to recover—emergency surgery on her lung, a long battle with blood infection with her liver teetering on the edge of shutting down, and reconstruction of her shoulder, all while creating a new life inside her.

Since then, they'd had two supervised visits in which they were forbidden to discuss the case. Even Waldheim didn't know about the second one, which had been Finn's chance to hold little Jordan at two weeks old. In between times, her letters—and presumably his—had been redacted, forcing him to use his FOIA document skills to suss out what he could. What he did know was that while he was stuck waiting for all the international players to agree on how to definitively bury the Katyn story, Clarissa's world was changing dramatically.

As for this morning, his lawyer had explained, none other than Waldheim himself would decide Finn's fate. His odds for freedom stood at fifty-fifty. And if he were freed, America wouldn't extradite him *only if* he abided by the gag order *and* never returned home.

Given the breadth of the story's incriminating threads, it was never a surprise that the proceedings were extrajudicial. At all costs the players wanted to keep it out of the hands of the press. And the battalion of lawyers the government employed signaled the government's determination to cover its ass if details about Stalin's orders and Albert Fortier's extracurricular actions ever appeared. Finn could only guess how much of this Clarissa knew. But if Waldheim chose to make Finn disappear into the West's unnamed gulag, Finn had best make use of the time he had with Clarissa.

"No matter what they presented or have told you," he said, "I want you to know I didn't kill him."

Using photos of Finn's footprints and patterns of blood smears, the government's forensic experts created a scenario proving Finn had dragged a wounded Fortie to the shrine, and as the state's closing argument went " . . . *dispatched him there, in the same manner as Claris-*

sa Waters has testified to seeing her father-in-law murdered. Having just learned of his own father's death, Your Graces, Finn Waters replicated that scene. Regardless of the guilt of the victim—which cannot be proven—this is a clear case of revenge."

Clarissa scratched the armrest with her finger. "You heard my account, Finn. I lost consciousness. And Rahel was tending *me*. She wasn't sure how many times you fired."

"I shot him in the leg so he couldn't follow us out, never thinking he'd crawl to the goddamn shrine."

"He's gone, Finn. And as much as I'm messed up about every part of this, most every argument says he deserved it. My gut feeling is that when you didn't free his guilt by making him die like your father, he did it himself."

"I doubt he was that romantic. I think he knew there was no way out and didn't want to face the courts and the shame."

She blurted a cynical laugh. "Well, the governments and corporations seem to have *found* one, haven't they?"

"Yes," he said. "Money and power rewrite any narratives they need to."

"Forensics could go either way, I guess," she said, "but in a Catholic country, even if a Mother Superior is lying, she makes for a powerful witness. It drove me mad that I wasn't allowed to testify to how far back she and my father go. He knew her when she worked with the SS during the war."

"I wondered about that. Just so you know, your father was *alive* when she left the chapel." Glancing at the portrait of Emperor-King Francis Joseph I, Finn noticed the artist had managed to capture a scowl underneath all that facial hair.

"Your prints were on the gun and he had powder burns on his head consistent with an assassination. The rest is what they want to make it."

"I thought about killing him just like he did my father. But I heard the voice of Janis Semyonovich."

"Who's that?"

"The guard at Katyn, the man whose eagerness to confess started all this."

It was only recently, after reading through his father's articles from the *Christian Science Monitor* that Finn had learned how close his father had come to exposing Fortie's role in Katyn. Finn guessed he'd discovered Trèana Furasta shipping the guns and confronted Fortie about where they had been bound. If he'd lived, how different the world might have been. Katyn would have been hung around the Soviets' neck back in '56. Eisenhower might have sent troops into Budapest. No Cold War. Good legislation keeping corporations in check. Fortie's murderous act might have been small, but it gave incalculable benefit to the wealthy.

Clarissa was resting her chin in her hand and staring into the distance. "To live with that, my father's stomach must have been lined with titanium."

"Ditto for his whole generation," Finn said. "If Mother Superior is any indication, the Vatican catacombs hold more secrets than bodies."

Clarissa pointed like a schoolmarm. "Consider making that one of your next stories."

"You're assuming if I agree to their terms, I'll be free to write."

"Yes, I am. Have you heard from Sam?"

"Only indirectly."

"Any chance of him taking you back?"

"He's at loggerheads with his board right now; a whispering campaign about a corporate takeover. Which just points to the bigger problem: How to report the news when the system is rigged. If you ask me, *that's* the story that needs to be told."

"Orwell did it without making a fuss. 'All animals are equal,' remember?"

"Allegory is powerful, but publishers nowadays are becoming complicit in the deception."

"You haven't read Marty Cisneros's interview with a Pole named Dabrowski, have you?" she asked. "Dabrowski said there was an unnamed American journalist in his cell, tortured along with him. Marty wrote that it's filed as a missing person's case, which got me thinking that it should be world news." Her lips pressed into a white line. "Yes or no. Was that you?"

"We'll talk about that later," he said.

"That's a yes, Finn, which means we both have a lot of healing to do."

Healing would mean revisiting a host of wounds, some self-inflicted. He said nothing.

"So," she asked, "how come they're not circling like vultures?"

"The press? I wish they would. Right now there's a crack in the cover of the new world oligarchy."

"That's a catchy phrase. Does it mean what I think?"

He nodded. "Business, governments, courts, and the military having each other's backs and the People be damned! When all the press gets bought, they'll cover that crack, and we'll be doomed to being too desperate to care how bad things are."

Absentmindedly, her hand stroked where the bullet had entered her, and just like that, the old shape of depression returned to her shoulders.

"If we're to be together, let's agree on my being to blame for him shooting you."

"If?" She made a sound like the whine of a screen door spring. Her hands flexed on the arms of her chair. She seemed about to lay into him, then looked around. "Don't they provide tissues?" She rose, squatted by his chair, and stroked his wrist. "Caring for Jordan the Second is our way out of this hole."

He offered his palm. She laced her fingers into his. "I regret dragging you into this, Clarissa. I didn't see things getting out of hand."

She shushed him. "Things were out of hand before we were born. You were just following what life gave you, what the story gave you. Doing your job."

"You've been doing a lot of work on all this, haven't you?"

Clarissa's lips trembled, preparing for and abandoning several responses. "No one will ever replace BethAnn," she said, "but my new therapist is good. She's helping."

"Have you been able to tell her what happened?"

Clarissa bent to kiss his palm. "She knows everything I do."

His mind leapt to things he never wanted to tell anyone. And his sternum lit up with the memory of Vladimir hammering the pipe into it.

She got up, poured water into glasses at a side table, and placed one in his hand. "I hate the position they've put you in," she said, "put *us* in." And once sitting again, she nodded a long time, like rocking herself to come to terms with something. "They're very good at manipulation, Finn. Making you choose between freedom and your principles."

"No, they know that for me freedom without principles isn't freedom. They're making me choose *between* principles. Exposing the Katyn massacre and the corporate-government meld on one side, and being with you on the other."

For just a split second, it seemed she might smile. "Can you live with the massacre being secret?" She raised her hand, palm out, to hold off his answer. "Can you live with *me* with that as the price?"

"If Waldheim and those he's protecting were going to suffer as much as we are . . ." he bent to sip his water. "Maybe I could. I've been struggling with that."

She stared. He looked away. He brought his eyes back. "I never expected knowing how my father died would bring peace. And it hasn't. But I feel fresh air coming in. You gave me that."

She put her elbows on her knees and rubbed her palms together. "Can't you tell his story by burying the clues enough to comply with their gag order? Can't you do it in a way that sharp minds will pick up the trail you and your father found?" She touched a knuckle to the corner of her eye. "If only he'd exposed my father back then." That hand made a fist and she examined it. "To save his business, he ruined the life of a little girl, to say nothing of leaving a boy in Rockport without a father." She started pawing through her purse. "Our love, yours and mine, was built upon that murder."

"If I hadn't pushed him into a corner," Finn said, "he never would have come after us."

"No, you've got it backwards. I'm the one he had to silence. I've been his albatross. And I'm to blame for dragging you into this family." She shook the contents of her purse. "But the thing that troubles me is I could have *saved* your father."

He rattled his chains to get her attention. "You were a five-year-old."

"Don't you get it? If I'd come around the corner fifteen seconds earlier . . ." Her pawing in her purse became more desperate.

"There's nothing you could have done. They were going to kill him."

"Dammit," she said. "What's taking them so long?" She found a balled tissue and dabbed her eyes. They sat silent as the grandfather clock by the shrine to Saint Michael struck eleven.

The clock in the bar where his father had sat with the hooker had also read eleven. Budapest's Chief of Police Danko had gone far out of his way to help solve the mystery of the hooker pictures Fortie had laid down. He'd discovered they were taken to accompany what was to be Jordan Waters's last article, an exposé about how the sex trade operated after the Revolution.

When no paper in the West would touch it, his father had given it to the local one. Along with a scratchy microfilm print of the article Danko sent Finn, he had included an English translation. The women spoke of offering themselves for free, which was what all Hungarians were doing with their skills in the short, liberated time the country had. Pure socialism. That was the joy those women were feeling in the pictures. And his father's words had captured it perfectly.

But Danko's gift had thrown Finn a curve. Perhaps to excuse his own failings, Finn had jumped to judge his father's behavior. And he'd done it as easily as people formed opinions about war crimes using the lens that suited them. That mistake would always embarrass him.

"I grieve for the Poles," he said. "If Waldheim offers freedom and if I sign, Katyn will disappear, and their hearts will never have relief."

"What do you mean, *if* you sign? That's the second time you've said that."

The longer he didn't answer, the more hurt he was loading into their future. "If they saddle me with these stipulations, how will I ever live with myself?"

"You'll come home," she said firmly.

"And the price I'll pay is joining the corruption."

"No more than anyone else."

"That's just it. I'll be the poster boy for everything I hate. Even if people on the street don't know it, it'll confirm what they fear and can't give voice to."

"You're all the family I have left, Finn."

He looked away from her. "If I stay in prison, I'll at least have some integrity."

She slapped her hand on the arm of her chair. "And what will you do with it? Your priorities are screwed up. All you have to do is apologize for these little things that—"

"Things that are absolute bullshit." His voice rang in the room. "Theft of documents and using a false passport, neither of which happened in this country."

"You're missing the point. Their stipulation that you shot my father in self-defense is a godsend."

"No, it's their way out."

Her breathing was short. Her chest heaved. "It's the way out for all of us."

"The one thing they can honestly accuse me of is breaking and entering the convent. And they won't do *that*, because the Vatican doesn't want light shined on Mother Superior's escapades."

"Can't you live with that?"

"Your father killed himself. And if Waldheim grants me absolution for silence about my *innocence*, for god's sake, the crack closes. It's not even a pardon. They'll concede I haven't committed a crime. Privately, in governments and corporations, Waldheim gets seen as wise for preventing a stir between allies and enemies both. And I go off and choke on the silence. They're probably counting on that."

"Haven't you learned anything?" she asked. "If you disappear into prison thinking you can speak, *none* of the story will ever be told. They're not going to let you say what you want. Even someone with Orwell's talent wouldn't be able to help you. And if you ever succeed in getting it out, they'll leak that you shot him in a convent, shot him in a chapel. The ordinary people you'll need will run for the exits. Get used to it. Their heads will never roll."

A knock at the door resonated in the room. Finn's Austrian lawyer with the long sideburns, dressed in a suit Americans would wear to their fanciest dinners, crossed islands of Oriental rugs.

"Thank God," she said.

"I'm sorry to interrupt," the lawyer said.

Finn's chained hand waved forgiveness.

"What's the decision?" Clarissa asked.

"It's taken this long because of . . . You probably haven't heard the news."

Finn prepared himself for a cruel twist of fate—Waldheim dropping dead or some revelation that threatened to overshadow him in the eyes of the Austrian government.

"This month marks fifty years since the Katyn Massacre," the lawyer said.

Finn had been so buried in wrestling deception he'd missed that simple fact.

"And to mark it, Mikhail Gorbachev has just done something huge . . . for a Russian leader. He's admitted Stalin ordered the massacre. This morning he issued a formal apology to Poland. He said his researchers have finally unearthed 'evidence enough' to prove it."

The blow was like lightning, rending Finn into three. On the one hand, the Poles finally had the truth he had been fighting to get for them. The misery of not knowing what had happened would now give way to the misery of knowing. This was good. He heard their tears and cathedral bells tolling.

But for him, the chance to break the story was lost. He had paid all the costs it could deliver, and still it had gotten away. Over the years to come, his bringing it to light might have eased all that had befallen him and Clarissa. Which highlighted the third aspect, the Soviets, the descendants of the killers were going to get credit for doing something noble. He modeled an actor's stage spit. "Unearthed? Unearthed the evidence? You mean they opened the damn file."

Clarissa sat up tense. "Is this good for us or bad?"

"That's what the holdup has been," the lawyer said. "Waldheim's been weighing whether he needed to deal with you now."

"Oh, my God." She leapt out of her chair and grabbed Finn's hand.

"No, Frau Waters. It's been a good test. Waldheim realizes it doesn't change a thing."

"Of course not," Finn said. "My silence protects them all."

The lawyer nodded. "The good news is he signed the agreement. The chief magistrate's office is getting the papers ready, and they should be here to present them to you in about thirty minutes."

"And all Finn has to do is sign them?" Clarissa asked.

"That's right. All he has to do is sign and he can go free."

Finn looked at Clarissa looking at him. Her eyes were moist. Her jaw was set. He saw her desperation and her strength. He felt the kisses she had given him in good times and bad. In just this last hour, the Soviets had proven once again the powerful always succeeded on stacking the odds against the Everyman.

But Clarissa was right. There would be other stories. The war of decency was not lost. It was never lost. It could be fought on other fronts. And Finn could be free to do that. If he signed, or if he *didn't* sign, Clarissa would go home to her apartment and hold a little boy. And regardless of his choice today, that boy would grow into a man. He had no doubt, though, that it would be best if that boy had a father.

Finn turned to his lawyer. "I have only one request."

"Yes?"

"Bring me a pen that has bright red ink."

The End

If you have enjoyed this story, please encourage others to read it. First edition hardcovers and paperbacks are available through Shires Press, your local bookstore, Bookshop.org, barnesandnoble.com, IndieBound, amazon.com and my website. Ebooks and second edition paperbacks are available at Amazon.com. I cannot stress enough how sales and visibility are boosted by you taking a few minutes to write a review on Amazon. For this, go to Amazon.com and enter Thomas Henry Pope or Imperfect Burials to find the page.

For signed copies, reading group materials, essays, and links,
please visit:
https://thomashenrypope.com

To reach out directly:
tom@thomashenrypope.com

Thomas Henry Pope is a journalist, actor, songwriter, builder, and EMT. His boyhood travels behind the Iron Curtain exposed him to the failings of Materialism and laid the groundwork for this story. After dropping out of Stanford, he became a Buddhist, living off the grid and growing his own food. Since then he has worked in Hollywood, written for HuffPost, and taught English to foreigners. He lives in Vermont.

Thank you for reading. One book at a time saves civilization.

CPSIA information can be obtained
at www.ICGtesting.com
Printed in the USA
FSHW012036250521
81812FS